THE RECORDINGS

KYLE ZONA

This is a work of fiction. Names, characters, organizations, places, events, and incidents are either products of the author's imagination or are used fictitiously.

Copyright © 2023 Kyle Zona
All rights reserved.

No part of this book may be reproduced, or stored in a retrieval system, or transmitted in any form or by any means, electronic, mechanical, photocopying, recording, or otherwise, without express written permission of the author.

Edited by Avalon Radys
Cover Design by Dissect Designs
Interior illustrations by Mary Purdie

eBook: 979-8-9882211-0-4
Paperback: 979-8-9882211-1-1
Hardback: 979-8-9882211-3-5

First edition

To my mother

This novel contains themes of explicit violence,
suicide, murder, and molestation.

Mature Readers Welcome.

PROLOGUE

An Excerpt From

He awoke with a shake, not from someone else but from himself, a muscle spasm in his lower calf that pinched so hard his toes curled. His abdominal muscles strained, attempting to lift the weight of his thin frame, shaking, until he was finally sitting upright, hunched over. His long fingers clawed down to the pain and massaged the spot until all that remained was a dull ache. A sour expression settled on his face. The room was so cold, his covered limbs shivered beneath his duvet cover and blankets. He blinked, looking around the room, waiting for his vision to adjust, which at his age took a bit longer. His eyes drifted to the silvery moonlight that crept in through the window beside his bed. Above him, the tips of the stucco ceiling glimmered like stars as if he were still somewhere between reality and his dream.

His eyes trailed the thin line between moonlight and darkness, down to the other side of the room. The moonlight highlighted the polished silver frames that hung on display around his bed, filled with photos and newspaper clippings. The older man had surrounded himself with reminders of happier times. He'd been featured in newspapers and magazines for his community efforts. All of these memories were glorious to think back on, for the older man had been young then. Now his features just looked ghoulish and hollowed out. He could see his reflection in the framed photos, yet his eyes still twinkled with life.

For now, at least.

He ran his dry tongue against the back of his teeth where he felt a spongy layer of grime built up, like moss on a rock. He mustered the energy to yawn. His lips parted lazily, and his jaw opened like a bear trap rusted shut. A slight whine escaped from his chapped lips. He settled back, hunched over again and still sour. The older man stared down at the ruffled duvet cover, wondering if the power had gone out; the fabric was so cold against his frail hands. He looked back to the window and noticed, with clearer vision, that they were wide open.

He continued to stare curiously as a breath of wispy fog crept between the older man and the open window. He realized that more than just a few night critters had gotten inside tonight. His eyes followed the foggy breath until they locked with a bright-eyed pair that gleamed in the darkness across the room.

Someone was sitting there. Their eyes drifted up, the floorboards beneath their weight croaking loud like frogs on along a dark riverbank. Whoever was there took a step forward. The older man tried to make out their features but could only decipher a muscular silhouette, standing there calmly. The figure took another step forward, and the older man spoke wistfully.

"Ah, my little Rabbit has returned, come to say goodbye." The old man gasped between sharp inhales as he spoke. Too much activity for one night already. He made a loose fist and covered his mouth as a coughing fit came and went. The older man hated these, his throat already ragged and raw. He looked up with desperate eyes, trying his best to regain the ability to speak.

"Have a drink," Rabbit offered, his tone soft and polite.

A glass of water appeared from the darkness, and the older man could see Rabbit's forearm. His skin ruined with a tattoo of his nickname. The older man had given him that nickname because he was small and made a great agent. The older man gulped the water, looking away from the tattoo with a look of disgust. The water tasted too salty—no, too *something*. The older man looked back at the glass under the moonlight, which showed murky water that hadn't settled. The pipes were old, so the grayish tint of the water wasn't uncommon. This taste was, though, and the older man paused.

Licked his lips and swallowed.

To the right of Rabbit's dark silhouette was a long dresser. A few items included a home device speaker for the books he could no longer read, a stack of medication that the nurse came to deliver daily, and, lastly, a pile of white powder. The powder went from fine to coarse, with some half pills strewn about. He recognized them as the OxyContin pills he was prescribed to help with the pain of cancer. He looked at the water and then back to Rabbit.

The older man felt like a horse stuck in the mud, its limbs slowly numbing as the organs fail from oxygen deprivation. Death was imminent. All he could hope for was that his body wouldn't revolt and cause him to throw it all back up. His throat was sore enough.

"My own medicine. So, this'll be quick," the old man replied. His thin lips curled into a devilish smile, revealing long-stained yellow teeth.

"No." Rabbit's voice was flat.

"So, we have some time?" That same devilish yellow smile cracked across his paper-thin face. The older man looked down to the water and took the remaining gulp, where the undiluted powder collected like large sea flakes disappearing in his mouth. He set the glass down with a triumphant *ah*.

"Thank you. All that medicine has been out of my reach for so long." The older man wheezed. The taste in his mouth was so bitter, he might vomit. He pressed his fist over his mouth once again. His cheeks puffed out, his skin was indeed cracking like cheap porcelain. His face was too tight for such motion.

"I was worried they'd have come around again asking questions. I hadn't even thought of you," the older man muttered.

"No, you don't get that luxury, old man. I know what you did. I have no questions," Rabbit said.

"I'm surprised you aren't angry I replaced you," the old man said. "Maybe you aren't as immature anymore." As he spoke, his eyes wavered, his body slowly inching closer to lying down again, but he couldn't pull his eyes away from Rabbit's. "Yet, you're arrogant for trying to murder me, thinking you'll get away with it. Oh, Rabbit."

Rabbit's eyes moved up and down with steady, heavy breathing.

The older man erupted in a raspy chuckle as he watched Rabbit's face come into view. He could tell rage was taking over, with Rabbit's clenched fists, huffing like a bull about to charge. The older man was robbing him of this moment, this revenge. It was petty, but in his final moments, he had little to relish in.

He felt like he could let his body fall back, just one last time—but no.

His eyes burst open from a searing pain that poured across his chest. His ribs crushed under the weight of Rabbit's heavy body. His fists walloped on the older man as his vision grew blurry once more. The older man was trapped, pinned down between thighs that were now crushing his frame. He heard two loud, defining cracks and felt his skin rip, the bone coming out from beneath. His ribs, broken.

The older man felt himself hurl as his organs pushed their way out of him. His eyes blurred from the tears pouring out. He felt like a champagne bottle about to pop, the pain so immense.

Everything went black as if he'd blinked. He heard another crack, and this time was blinded by the sound filling his head. Rabbit recoiled a fist back under the silvery moonlight. Warm blood swarmed the older man's senses, not just from his nose but also from his tongue, now caught between his teeth. He felt a piece of him, no longer attached, floating in his mouth. He spat it out, then gulped for air, but the blood poured into his lungs now. Rabbit's arms swung through the moonlight. The gloved fist came into focus. Then everything fell a dark shade of red, blotting to black from the relentless beating. The punches came down, and slowly he felt his skin tear, his jaw no longer attached. No longer would he have to worry about choking on his liquids. His blood burst out, running down the back of his neck.

The older man's body cringed in agony like the fossil remains found at Pompeii.

Rabbit clutched the older man's arm so tight he vibrated, forcing him to stay alive on the brink of death. The older man couldn't see. He could feel only the screaming pain and the soft, cool exhale of a born killer leaning down into his face. The older man waited to hear Rabbit get the final word in, right before dropping into the dark abyss of death. He heard Rabbit inhale, and—

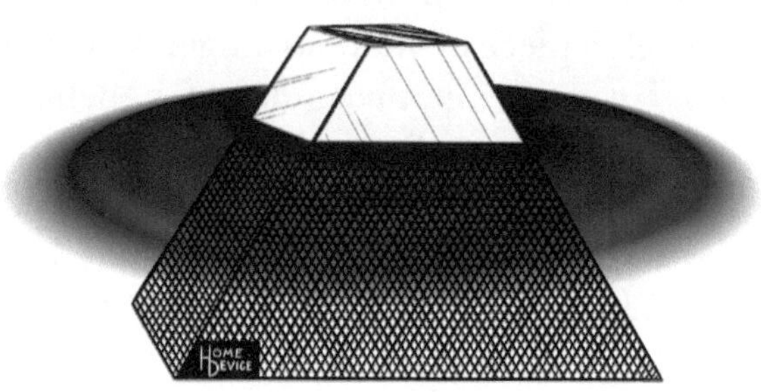

"Holy mother of—" Joseph Bailey sucked in a pained breath as he stood before the crowd.

He raised his finger, examining where the acute wound pulsed. A paper cut—he could see the thin red line forming over the tiny grooves of his fingerprint. A small flap of skin raised further as more blood jumped ship. He winced just seeing how deep the edge of the freshly printed book had cut him. A few drops of blood collected along the border, running down his palm to drip down on the pages he'd just been reading aloud.

The crowd released a collective gasp watching this unfold, yet they remained seated, eyeing him. Joseph looked up, feeling the edges of his lips pull down. He imagined the frown made him look like a sad catfish instead of an author doing his part in the charity event tonight.

"Ah, just a paper cut," Joseph said, feigning nonchalance.

Joseph looked away from the crowd, but their watchful eyes kept trained on him. His eyes moved to the bottle of water sitting on the podium. A damp napkin clutched the base of the bottle. He shook it off, reading the printed logo "Baxtor's Books Charity Event for Victims, Funeral Costs." He crumpled it and cleaned up his finger before pressing the napkin down against the podium with the pressure of his wounded index finger.

Joseph looked back down to the book. His eyes swirled, his chest growing tight with pressure. He was on the spot, literally. He couldn't remember where he'd left off, the page now polka-dotted with some of his blood. He shook his head, feeling flustered. Joseph had read to larger crowds than this before without ever getting a paper cut or losing his cool any other way. This was the last thing he would've expected tonight.

A colorless Keith Haring print slid across the page on what appeared at first to be a skateboard but then became apparent: a Band-Aid. Joseph met Emily's eyes. Her lips could barely contain her teeth. Her smile was radiant as she mouthed the words, "It's okay." Joseph held the bandage up for the small crowd before him, as if displaying his reward for the battle that had left him bloodied up. A soft murmur of well-meaning laughter flitted about the bookstore. Most of the chairs laid out were filled; a few people paused in the rows of books farther in the back.

"Thank you, Emily," Joseph said, setting the napkin down beside the book. He stretched the elastic fabric tight across his finger until the adhesive secured the bandage. The tip of his finger glowed red. He used the napkin to soak up whatever blood remained and slipped the waste into his pocket.

"What would we do without Emily Jay, everyone?" Joseph said, gesturing to Emily as she retreated to the side of the platform.

Emily looked back to the crowd, who offered a laugh, nothing major but enough to make Joseph feel a bit more comfortable. Although rhetorical, he knew the answer to the question: without Emily Jay throwing this community charity event tonight at her bookstore, everyone would be at home, mourning someone they'd lost in the explosive massacre that had taken place only four months ago. Baxtor Springs hadn't found the rhythm it once had, but Emily had done her best to champion that effort tonight.

"For those of you who don't know . . . when she invited me to do this reading tonight, she explicitly told me this would be *painless*," Joseph spoke to the crowd once more. This time, they chuckled with more ease. Joseph knew he wasn't some comedian invited to make the group feel comfortable, though; he was here to read a passage from his recently published novel. He wasn't the only author invited tonight, but he was the one to close out the event, which felt nice. The energy humming through the room electrified him.

Joseph looked back to Emily, who rolled her eyes and waved her hand, shooing him to continue reading. Joseph peered back over the crowd and spotted him for the first time: a man with bright blue eyes, pale skin, and ginger hair, who didn't so much as watch but stare at Joseph curiously. His eyes were piercing, and Joseph held his gaze for a few breaths before returning to the page. Tiny droplets of blood absorbed into the paper. He took a deep breath and continued.

"He heard Rabbit inhale, and"—Joseph turned the page carefully with his bandaged finger—"the old man waited, but there was only silence and an unexpected disappointment that followed him to death."

Joseph closed the book and let out a sigh as the audience applauded.

"Now, if you'll excuse me, I need to go wash my hands." Joseph smiled, stepping off the stage. There was a bathroom in the back of the store near Emily's office that he'd used earlier. Joseph's route through the bookstore took him past the ginger-haired man, who sat barely fitting in the chair with his rugby build. He wore a suit that rose at his ankles to show simple black socks. His face betrayed a tired expression. Joseph wondered about the man as he slipped into the bathroom not bothering to close the door as he washed his hands. He heard Emily address the crowd.

"Another round of applause to thank all our guests this evening," she said, and polite applause sounded from the crowd again. "And thank you all for coming tonight. The authors have already signed each book tonight. Each purchase also includes a drink ticket for wine and appetizers out on the patio. Fifty percent of tonight's proceeds will go to the funeral costs of those who lost their lives. Anyone looking to make an additional donation can use the QR code on the bookmarks included with purchase tonight."

Joseph exited the bathroom just as Emily smiled through a round of applause herself. Her hands humbly came together at her chest, her arms bare from the velvet green jumpsuit she wore, a collection of gold jewelry on her wrists matched the gold earrings resting against her obsidian hair. The crowd held a moment of silence, of solidarity. The evening's donations would help pay for the burial costs of people who had lost their lives so violently and abruptly. The entire crowd held their breaths at this moment, meditating on the tragedy of it all. Finally, Emily raised her head and looked to the authors lined up on stage. She waved for them to stand. "Thank you, again, for coming out tonight to Baxtor's Books."

Emily moved the podium to the side as people lined up. Friendly banter filled the small bookstore, and Joseph felt thrilled to see people buying his book.

Baxtor's Books was filled with stacks of books heaped to the ceiling and fake candles lit throughout, giving the store a relaxing, intimate ambiance. A tall waiter passed by with a tray of small bites prepared by Dana, Emily's girlfriend, the head chef and owner of a popular joint named after herself.

Dana's was simple and delicious, and her bites paired well with the wine and the ambiance Emily curated at Baxtor's Books.

Joseph spoke with a few of the other authors, wishing them well with their book releases, and each time he turned, he scanned the room for that rugged, ginger-haired man. But alas, he was nowhere in sight. Someone tugged on his arm, and as Joseph turned around, he half hoped to see that ginger-haired man's face. Instead, Emily stood there with two glasses of wine in her hands.

"Here you go," she said. Her expression grew soft as Joseph took the glass from her. "I wanted to say thank you for doing this tonight. If you see"—she pointed over to the cash register—"we're almost sold out of all those copies you supplied tonight. That discount you gave is going to help make our donation even bigger."

"Oh, it's nothing," Joseph said.

"Oh, yes, I'm sure from where you sit. *Rabbit's Revenge* has been climbing the charts since its release," Emily said, a glint in her eye that Joseph recognized as an opportunity.

"It just got published. Let's talk about where it sits in a few weeks instead." Joseph smiled.

"What about in a few days? I was hoping we could grab lunch at Dana's." Emily smirked.

"I'd love to get lunch with you," Joseph said. "What's the hook?"

Emily laughed, letting her head fall back slightly, revealing the sparkling earrings once more under the light. "Am I that obvious?"

"Yes." Joseph laughed with her.

"Well, I wanted to discuss whether I could purchase the rest of those copies off you, and I had an idea, too. But that can wait for lunch."

Joseph smiled. "I should have the other half of that misplaced order by next week. Would that work?"

"That should work perfectly." Emily gestured around the room, everyone with a bag in one hand, a glass of wine in the other. "I'll be in touch about lunch soon." Her shoulders dropped back before a wide smile spread. "Cheers."

They toasted, and soon Emily got pulled off by one of her staff asking if they had any extra drink tickets. Joseph found himself alone: the room crowded, yes, but he didn't know anyone besides Emily and Dana. And, hopefully, he might come to know the ginger-haired man who'd just come back into view.

He was heading right toward Joseph, his shoulders slinking back and forth through the crowd as he made his way. Joseph couldn't understand how he hadn't spotted the man again until now. He was a few inches taller than nearly everyone in the room, including Joseph, who took a deep breath and smiled at him. He let his face gently tilt to one side like some flirtatious lead in a romantic comedy. They locked eyes, if only for a moment, a piercing stare from those cold blue eyes. But the man turned and headed out of the store. Joseph would've felt rejected, but the ginger-haired man did have a copy of *Rabbit's Revenge* tucked underneath his arm.

Joseph hadn't lost all hope.

Joseph took a step back, making space for some guests to pass by, when he stepped on something. He looked down to a pair of all-white Chuck Taylor shoes, except when he lifted his foot, they were tagged with the zigzag design of Joseph's shoe print. His eyes darted up, taking in the owner of the shoes' tan legs with thin black hair underneath rolled-up jeans.

"I'm so sorry," Joseph said, rushed.

"It's okay," the man said, taking a step back. "Just some old Chucks."

Joseph's eyes flicked up to meet a pair of kind honey-colored eyes that popped over the mustard yellow sweater the man wore. Joseph smiled and couldn't think of a single thing to say for a split second. Looking in those eyes, it felt as though there wasn't a worry in the world. Before he could lose himself any further, he held out his hand.

"I'm Joseph—"

"Bailey," the man finished, pointing to a copy of Joseph's novel he held in his left hand.

"Oh, yes," Joseph bobbed his head, feeling foolish.

The man extended his hand. "I'm Arturo."

"No last name?" Joseph asked as they shook. Arturo's handshake was firm and lingered long enough for Joseph to feel how soft his hands were, delicate even. Joseph wasn't quick to let go.

"Arturo de Leon," he smoothly replied, taking his hand back.

"And what do you do, Arturo de Leon?" Joseph asked, shuffling on his feet.

"I manage that whiskey bar just down the street."

"Down the . . . ?" Joseph trailed off and watched Arturo nod his head to the left side of the room, as if the bar was on the other side of the wall. Joseph took note. Arturo's eyes seemed to wait patiently for Joseph to say something. The only thing that came to mind made Joseph frown as if he'd been caught.

"I have to confess, I'm not really from here . . ."

"Where are you from, Joseph?"

"West Coast, and you?"

"Here," Arturo said, glancing outside the window. "Born and raised. Are you just here for the weekend, then?"

"Please take some," a broad-shouldered woman said with a huff as she approached the two men with a sizable serving tray filled with various small bites and stemless plastic wine cups.

"Hey, Dana," Arturo said as he reached for a cake pop.

"Evening, hun," she said and looked to Joseph, who soon grabbed a cake pop, too.

"How's your finger doing, Joseph?" she asked.

"Not too bad, Dana, thanks for asking." Joseph placed his empty cup on her serving tray to take another.

"You two know each other?" Arturo asked. His eyes drifted from Dana to Joseph and back again.

"Somewhat," Joseph said between chews. "Only met about a week ago."

"Oh?" Arturo nodded.

Dana shifted the tray to her other hand. "He came in telling us this long story about how the printers had accidentally printed double the number of books, and he needed to get some off his hands. Emily and I were finalizing food, drinks, seating, and time slots for the local authors, but Emily already knew who he was. So, she set her sights on getting him to close the night out. It was so convenient." Dana poked her thumb over. "Emily was raving to him about how she'd seen his book come out and start climbing the charts. Not number one yet, but ninth, eighth on those lists she loves to keep track of."

"You mean bestseller lists?" Arturo chuckled.

"Mmhmm," Dana hummed with sass. "And, at first, poor Joseph was all, 'no, I can't, I shouldn't,' but when I explained the charity aspects of the event, he had no choice."

"I think you were guilt-tripped into doing this tonight." Arturo nudged Joseph.

"No, that's called peer pressure," Dana corrected him.

"I just don't want to make sales off a town tragedy," Joseph said. But his only real fear was being perceived as an asshole for turning down a charity event. The social media consequences for that could be devastating.

"The community needed a night like this. We'll need many more, too." Arturo paused, looking around them. "It's nice to see everyone wearing clothes that aren't funeral attire, at least." Arturo peeked back over to Joseph, who nodded along. "I think you made the right choice participating tonight."

Arturo then reached into his pocket and grabbed his phone. "I should get back to the bar. Violet's having an emergency, I think." He looked at Dana.

Dana reached her arms out and embraced Arturo with a peck on the cheek. "Always good to see you, hon." She turned to Joseph. "I'll bring you another glass in a bit," she said before sliding back into the crowd, taking the cups and napkins from various guests as she moved along.

Joseph glanced at Arturo, unsure of what to say. They were strangers, but the way Arturo looked up at Joseph only made him more eager to keep the conversation going.

"Do you like whiskey?"

"Yes!" Joseph exclaimed.

"Well," Arturo began, taking a step back and looking Joseph up and down, "perhaps you'll stop by for a drink when you're done soaking in the night."

"Perhaps," Joseph said, noticing how the lighting articulated the deep dimples in Arturo's cheeks. Joseph's knees almost melted. *Small town boys*, he thought devilishly.

"Perhaps," Arturo repeated, already turning and adjusting his copy of *Rabbit's Revenge* underneath his arm as he pushed his way outside. Arturo was polite, even holding the door open for a few guests who entered Baxtor's Books. Joseph didn't look away.

He had read the entire book that night.

The vivid details the author had included within those thin, eggshell-colored pages transfixed him. The details weren't limited to the prologue either; other little Easter eggs were hidden throughout the dialogue in the book. At first, he thought this was just the effect some books have on a reader, but then each paragraph—everything spoken—corresponded with his memory not only of that night, but of many others that had come before. Reading about how he'd murdered the older man, his body shuddered with fear since he'd thought no one had seen him that night. Not like the older man had any neighbors, either. So then, why hadn't he been arrested?

His mouth grew sour with thoughts of having to return to prison, not for something petty this time, either. Murder meant real time. He wasn't good in prison; he had a reputation of being a problem. He looked down to the tiny rabbit tattoo on his forearm, so minimalistic and yet it held the most curious blank stare. He'd gotten the tattoo nearly a decade ago, shortly after getting a cell and cellmate.

"Noah, this is only going to add more time to your sentence. Don't you think you have enough?" his old cellmate, Timothy, had asked him before permanently altering his skin. He held a thin needle in one hand. The tip of it turned white-hot above the lighter he held in the other. He set the lighter down and dipped the tip in an ink mixture of soot and lotion.

"The more time, the better," Noah had replied.

"Don't go snitchin', either. And stay quiet. I know how loud you fags can be," Timothy had said, peering back at the space where he was about to work. "Got it?"

"Okay."

"Good," Timothy said, getting to work. "Why you want a rabbit, anyway?"

"It's a nick—" Noah winced from the hot stinging sensation. "A nickname."

"I said this wasn't going to be painless, didn't I?" Timothy looked up at him with a stern face. "You're gonna bleed some."

Timothy continued to prick Noah's forearm, one dot at a time. The cell they shared grew quiet enough that all they could hear was their breathing. The inside was small, painted white brick walls and cement floors and ceilings. No metal bars, but a metal door with a small glass window scratched with graffiti from men who had come before Noah—but not Timothy. That guy had been there a long time, and he would never be leaving. Noah stared into the protected tube lighting that never turned off, only dimmed at that hour.

The book slipped from Noah's numb hands and slapped shut with a resounding *clap* that demanded his attention back to the present. Noah bit the inside of his lip. Since carrying out his revenge, he'd been able to survive outside on his own, which he'd never thought possible. He hadn't even graduated high school. His eyes trailed the book as it slid to a stop under the small square dining table with two plastic chairs that came standard with any suite at the Extended Stay in Baxtor Springs. The suite was nearly three times the size of his prison cell. With the money he'd stolen from the older man that night, he'd been able to pay six months upfront, which meant they wouldn't even run a background check on him.

Noah had also stolen the older man's phone, and he enjoyed browsing the internet using the free Wi-Fi offered at the Extended Stay. It wasn't lightning fast by any means, but in just the four months since he'd been there, Noah had been able to find a few online jobs that didn't require a background check, either.

He'd spent a few hours as a 1099 digital assistant, booking reservations for people via a new email address he'd set up for himself. Then he stumbled upon a business that helped online companies get much-needed reviews for new products. Noah applied and was accepted immediately. Deliveries were routine for him at the Extended Stay after that. He made a small amount per review, and it was enough to get by with the digital assistant work. He cashed his checks down the street beside a large department store for discounted clothing. Soon, he found life outside of prison wasn't so hard—after he'd successfully scratched his vengeful itch.

Tonight, the review company, delivered his next product. A book recently published titled, *Rabbit's Revenge*. Noah hadn't spent much time reading in prison. Mainly he'd watched television when he could. Though, tonight, he thought he'd give it a shot.

Noah stood up and felt the used carpet scrub the bottom of his bare feet with each step as he walked over to pick the book up. He preferred this carpet over the cold concrete floors that had penetrated his thin prison socks. On top of the table was the yellow packaging the book had come in, with the return label for him to ship it back poking out. Noah picked the book up, feeling how weightless his truth was. With his hand on the cover, he noticed that his tattoo was similar to the fluffy black rabbit on the book's cover design. As both versions looked at each other, the tattoo'd rabbit's eyes gleamed wide with fear, as if about to be slaughtered by the other.

He rubbed his thumb over the glossy eyes, petting the furry depiction politely, and his tattoo seemed to nudge him to turn the book over. Noah turned to see an author photo printed in black and white. The author's beady black eyes seemed to mirror the eyes of the rabbit in his tattoo. He was trying for a somber look, caught deep in thought. Noah traced his finger over the author's arms, shoulders, and head as he read his name out loud.

"Joseph Bailey."

He stared down, still rubbing the small image of the author, but he paused. He raised the book just an inch from his eye. He couldn't believe what he was seeing. A familiar wooden gazebo stood tall in the background behind Joseph. One that was very familiar—Noah was positive it was the same one in Baxtor Springs. Where he was now. He remembered getting off the Greyhound bus just four months ago in the park at the end of Main Street across from Benny's. The prison had provided the bus ticket. That gazebo had been around for ages, even sagged a little, but no one seemed to mind.

Noah smiled and opened the book once more to read the beginning, where his most violent details of revenge were printed. Vividly. Each time he read and reread the words, his memory of that night only became crisper. He knew finding the author would only be a matter of time.

Arturo de Leon politely nodded to the group of older
women who thanked him as they entered Baxtor's Books. He
held the door open for them, just a few seconds longer than
need be. Arturo's politeness may have come with an ulterior
motive, albeit harmless. He glanced back toward the author,
but Joseph had already disappeared into the crowd. Arturo
pursed his lips together. He wished he could've caught just
one more glance of Joseph's sharp jawline beneath his dimpled chin. Arturo sighed and let the door go, giving up. As
it completely shut, the cheery banter inside became nothing
louder than a muffled car radio.

Outside, Main Street was dark, but the air was still warm
with the remaining days of summer. Only four months
ago, this entire town square—on an average Saturday
night—would've been crowded with people at the bars
on either end of the road. The park in the center of it all
would've been showing one of its last cult classic films of the
summer. A few art galleries would have stayed open for any

couples out and about after Dana's closed on the opposite end of the police station.

Now there were too many shadows lurking in the corners. Arturo passed by the coffee shop, the bistro-style furniture not even chained up, the napkin dispensers gleaming under the lamp posts that lined the park's perimeter. A sign in the window advertised they were currently accepting applicants for all job positions.

Arturo's thigh twitched as he felt two vibrations from inside his pocket. His phone. He reached for it, feeling the book slip from underneath his arm. He picked it up and then checked his phone. The device automatically scanned his face and unlocked, revealing a list of expanding notifications. Among the long list of missed phone calls from his *tía* and social media notifications, there was now a fresh one from CNN. Followed by different news outlets within seconds, all reporting the same thing: "Twelve More Confirmed Dead in Baxtor Springs Massacre."

Arturo's chest sank, processing the notification. These updates had become routine, but they still felt like a gut punch. Every night for the past three and a half months, Chief Edmonds had confirmed as many identities as he could. By now, most people were just waiting for him to confirm what they already knew. The list had grown very, very long. Each name added was another person missing here tonight, never to enjoy Main Street again.

Banter erupted from behind Arturo. He spun around to see a young group of friends leaving Baxtor's Books. He hoped they'd make their way down to his bar, but instead, they turned, heading the opposite direction. Drunken laughter echoed down the street. Arturo rolled his eyes—they must be going to Benny's, a dive bar that had been around since before Arturo was even born. They'd maintained a reputation of cheap beer and access to live football games. If you heard a siren across the square, you knew another fight had broken out at Benny's. Arturo rubbed his hand over his face, pushing his raised eyebrows and judgmental thoughts down.

The patio outside his bar, across from the gazebo in the park, looked dull with empty stools around square tables, seasonal flowers still sitting on top. This area was typically packed full until two in the morning—sometimes even three—but tonight Arturo wondered if there was even a single customer inside. He looked down at his scuffed chucks turning bright yellow under the glow of the neon sign. He looked up and read: A Whiskey Bar.

He took another glance at his phone—nearly eleven now—before passing through the hand-carved doors with a whiskey glass etched on both at eye level.

Unlike Benny's, where the stench of stale beer built up day after day, Arturo's bar smelled of oak and leather. Edison bulb chandeliers dimmed overhead, creating an environment that felt intimate. Leather tufted booths lined the walls with polished wood tables spaced out in the center of the room. Artificial candles filled in the rest of the space, their faux glow dancing while jazz hummed from the corners.

Arturo's bar had been deemed one of the best date-night spots by the *Baxtor Springs Post*. A local award that hadn't done much for his business after the massacre.

Arturo's gaze traced the edge of the solid industrial-styled bar before spotting Violet standing behind it. The bar itself towered over her short frame. Arturo stopped in his tracks when he caught her fiery stare. She threw her hand towel over her shoulder with an annoyed *whack* and pointed to the far back of the bar, where he could see an officer standing. Arturo walked around to the bar, his heels scuffing lightly against the hardwood floors, heavy from his wine buzz.

"Yeah, everything is good here. I was going to get him home," Officer Steven Goldstein spoke to the receiver on his shoulder. He looked back and caught Arturo sneaking by. "Evening, Arturo."

"What's going on?" Arturo asked, already catching the vibe. It wasn't the first time they'd had to throw someone out. It still felt so uncommon whenever it happened.

Violet *shhh'd* him.

Arturo peeked around Goldstein's frame to see who was seated at the table. An unkempt man with his head extended fully back shaking the last drops from a shot glass into his open mouth. He slammed the shooter down with a loud *crack* against the polished wood in between a collection of empty crystal glasses. The man looked at Officer Goldstein with a nasty sneer. Dark circles under his eyes made the man look somewhat deranged, but nobody in the room would've blamed him for looking that way.

"Just here to give Mr. Rodriguez a ride home, that's all." Goldstein looked down and caught the sneer. "No trouble tonight. Come on, Rafael, I'm just here to take you home safely now. Let's get moving."

"I ordered another drink, not a"—Rafael paused to burp a foul smell that made Arturo recoil—"fucking rideshare."

Rafael's attention fell on one of the crystal glasses closest to the candle. He picked it up and tilted it around to see nothing inside. He slammed the glass down with a resounding *crack* that made Arturo want to yell at Rafael to leave. Instead, he looked to Officer Goldstein, who took another step toward the table. His hands slipped away from his hips.

"Artie, c'mon, we were Boy Scouts together," Rafael shouted, barely able to hold eye contact. "You're going to cut *me* off? This is my time of need, and I need another drink. Artie."

Arturo cleared his throat, "Officer Goldstein is offering to take you home. If you won't go with him, I encourage ordering a rideshare. Johnson should still be active on the app for at least another hour or so with the book event tonight. We even have a discount code if you need one." Arturo pointed to the damp collection of napkins between the glasses on

Rafael's table. The same QR code Emily had been talking about earlier printed on each one.

"Don't bother," Rafael said, staring at the napkins with a trembling lip. "You all act like I fucking pulled the trigger."

Arturo caught glances from both Violet and Officer Goldstein as they exchanged a worried look. Rafael didn't notice. He was already standing up so quickly that the chair tipped over. It slammed into the ground with a *thud* that slithered up Arturo's shins. Rafael looked to everyone and must've realized he had no option but to leave. Without a word, he barreled out the front door. Officer Goldstein loudly exhaled, annoyed.

"I should go make sure he gets home safe. The last thing we need is for him to end up dead in a ditch tonight at the hands of some angry survivor." Officer Goldstein looked at Arturo, then Violet, with a dark expression. "Thanks for calling me, Violet. Have a better night, you two."

Goldstein turned on his heel, his rubber boots squeaking against the hardwood floors. Without another word, he too left, and the door shut quietly, allowing a late summer breeze to wash over the room. Violet reached for the rag on her shoulder and then a spray bottle under the sink. She headed over to wipe down the table where Rafael had been sitting, Arturo trailing behind her, ready to collect the glassware left behind. Since opening the bar, Arturo had found this dance of theirs to come naturally.

"I'm sorry," Arturo sulked, his voice low. "I didn't see your texts till late."

"No apology needed. I had this place under control. I was trying to let you know." Violet sprayed the bottle, her voice soft. "We had a few customers, but they left around eight, and then he came in shortly after that. I entertained him to be nice. He'd been drinking before though." Violet rolled her eyes, hands on her hips.

"Benny's?" Arturo asked, placing the glassware in the sink.

"Mmhm," Violet said, unamused. "First thing he said when he stepped in was how happy he was it was just me in here. Said someone had complained about him being at Benny's, and they asked him to leave." Violet gave herself a beat. "I feel sorry for Rafael, I do. I can't even imagine being in his shoes. As I said, I was playing nice."

Arturo nodded, catching Violet's disheveled stare. The same look that many people had after the massacre. It wasn't Rafael who had pulled the trigger. His son, Joshua Rodriguez, had. Since that day, everyone had alienated the grief-ridden father. Arturo knew that everybody had gossiped about him, offering their pieces of advice or theories as to why his son had done it. Eventually, the gossip evolved into how Rafael had been fired from his job for *reasons not relating to the massacre*. Arturo believed that everybody celebrated that day, a form of justice in their eyes.

"He told me his wife left him a week ago and that she filed for divorce today. Said she doesn't ever want to see him again after what Joshua did. I can't wait for the gossip queens to find out about this. He would've drunk the entire bottle tonight if I'd have set it before him." Violet huffed. "When I told him he was cut off, he just lost it. Going on about how everyone in this town despises him. Do I *look* like a therapist?"

Violet paused, taking a step back and turning her body from side to side, showing off her retro band tee with a flannel wrapped around her waist.

"I mean, I could." She shrugged, her short brunette hair bounding above her shoulders. "But I'm not. So, I called Officer Goldstein when he refused to leave."

"Sorry you were dealing with that."

"Well, thanks, but I wasn't worried. I *had* everything under control." Violet held his gaze for a second.

"Of course," Arturo said with a half-smile. Everything had changed overnight. No longer was the bar semi-busy during the weekdays or packed every weekend. The jubilant atmosphere the people brought to the bar was desperately missed. That meant there wasn't much to do. Arturo found he hovered a lot more, and Violet was tired of it. "What else needs to be done so you can get out of here?"

"Nothing," Violet said, shaking her head. "Everything is fully cleaned and ready for tomorrow. I was just waiting for Goldstein to get Rafael out of here." Violet pursed her lips. "I was trying to catch the tail end of the charity event. Is it over? Or you think we can pop back for a little?" Violet grabbed her purse as the background jazz simmered from one track to the next.

"No, it's not over," Arturo said, knowing full well that he wanted to go back to see Joseph Bailey—but he also didn't want to come off desperate. "I'm feeling tired, though, so I'll just make myself a nightcap. You go ahead." Arturo set the clean glasses down to dry.

Violet walked past him. She stopped, looking down to admire the book Arturo had come in with.

"Is this one of the books from tonight?" Violet asked, looking at the small, fluffy black rabbit on the cover of *Rabbit's Revenge*.

"Yes. In fact, I met the author tonight."

"Was he cute? Oh." Violet paused, turning over the book to further examine for herself. "He *is* cute . . . Well, better to read a book than spend any more time on your phone being antisocial."

"You can't call me antisocial when I'm literally using my phone for *social* media and news updates. I even interact with my food delivery drivers," Arturo clapped back.

Violet was hardly listening to Arturo, though. She was nearly halfway out the door.

She turned to give one coy look. "Enjoy your book."

Arturo shooed her along with his hands. "Enjoy your night."

Warm air washed over the room once again, and Arturo dried his hands and looked back at the book. A new jazz song hummed from the corners, too. He stared down at the photo of Joseph Bailey on the back. Beneath a five o'clock shadow, there was a sharp jawline. His thin nose rested between a fiery gaze. The man was handsome, no doubt. Arturo replayed their conversation.

Perhaps, Joseph had replied.

Arturo looked at himself in the mirror behind the various whiskey bottles. He pushed two aside, allowing the amber glow from the bar to give him that golden-hour shot. He smoothed over his hair, pushing it back. He traced over his eyebrows. Perked his lips.

He felt fresh enough for a *perhaps*.

Arturo reached for a gated supply of expensive whiskey. Whether or not Joseph Bailey showed up, it wouldn't be wasted. He grabbed one of the twenty-four-karat-gold-rimmed crystal glasses along with an eighteen-year-old bottle of Elijah Craig. He set them down on the bar and reached for an orange. Peeling off a thin slice, Arturo twisted until a puff of sweet citrus filled the air. He inhaled deep, hoping the sweetness might dilute the bitter worries now creeping in. Violet had been only poking fun about him being antisocial, but she was right. He had hung out with her a lot over the past few months, and nobody else besides Dana and Emily. Arturo had matched with some guys, sure, but they were always grieving, and he could only listen for so long.

Arturo gulped his Old Fashioned, feeling it course down through his chest, melting away the tension that had remained after Rafael Rodriguez's exit. He looked around the empty bar, taking in the beautiful light fixtures and candlelight among the tufted leather seating. All the empty seats. He felt a pang of guilt sear in his side. Such a lovely environment to not share with someone. A reminder that while he might have been successful in business, he was still single. He should've gone back to the event with Violet.

Emily and Dana made better company than sitting around, waiting for a man who probably wouldn't even show, getting drunk as the night went on (and bitter, Arturo supposed, too). He plopped down at one of the center tables, sinking into a deep velvet chair.

Arturo took another gulp of his Old Fashioned, feeling a warm breeze brush against his neck. He looked back to see the soft faux candles glow around that chiseled jaw and dimpled chin from earlier. There stood Joseph, smiling.

Arturo smiled back. "Perhaps, huh?"

"Perhaps." Joseph laughed. He looked far better in person than he did in his picture. Arturo felt his shoulders sink away from his ears, his tongue coiling tight behind his teeth. A smile grew as if he'd just tasted sweet honey. Joseph looked back with an eyebrow raised, a half-smile on his face. He looked cockier than sexy, but Arturo didn't mind.

"Busy night?" Joseph grinned, standing in the center of the bar now.

"Busy enough to pay the bills," Arturo replied with a raised eyebrow. "Take a seat. I'm just about to make another Old Fashioned." Arturo could smell the pepper in Joseph's cologne—not a clean smell, but a musky, intoxicating scent. Joseph took a stool at the bar, while Arturo slipped around. The author rested his elbows on the edge of the bar, showing off a nice watch in the golden candlelit glow. No wedding ring, either, Arturo noted.

"How was the rest of the event?" Arturo asked, tossing the ice from his glass and grabbing one more for his guest.

"Great. Sold out of my copies tonight, so I'm feeling good," Joseph replied.

Arturo gestured to the bottles of whiskey behind the gated storage still open.

"Sounds like we're drinking the good stuff then to celebrate."

"This isn't the good stuff?" Joseph asked, reaching for the bottle of Elijah Craig beside him.

"It is, obviously, since I'm drinking it," Arturo said, pulling the bottle away, "but there are more lavish options." He revealed a bottle of Old Rip Van Winkle from the gated section. Arturo handed it to Joseph, who studied its black-and-white label, gold fringe, and small handwritten numbers in red.

"A classic, reliable bourbon that you should only enjoy straight up," Arturo said. Joseph handed the bottle back, Arturo's pinky rubbing against his warm index finger. Arturo let their hands touch, looking up to see a glint in Joseph's eye. Arturo tipped the bottle and poured for them.

"Two fingers deep, huh?" Joseph asked. He cocked his head down a little to see the pour. He looked up at Arturo, grinning devilishly.

"Mmhmm," Arturo said, setting the bottle between them. "Now, congratulations."

They clinked their glasses.

Arturo watched Joseph take a sip, letting his tastebuds play before swallowing the expensive crafted liquor. Joseph looked down at the glass of amber liquid and nodded his head. He was impressed.

"All right, now," he said, holding the glass up to examine.

"You're welcome." Arturo leaned back.

"How did you like tonight?" Joseph asked, turning the attention on Arturo.

"I haven't been to a book reading before, but I knew it'd be enjoyable with Emily at the helm. Dana started as a catering chef before opening her restaurant, so I knew the food would be incredible. Even if you all sucked up there, it still wouldn't have been a loss for me."

Joseph laughed and clutched his chest, feigning hurt, while Arturo came around to the front of the bar. He slid onto the stool right beside Joseph, only a few inches separating them now. Arturo indulged more in the scent of that peppery cologne.

"Have you always been an author?" Arturo asked. He turned away, not wanting to stare, even though he'd noticed how the bar's lighting twinkled in Joseph's soft eyes. Arturo poured them a finger more of the expensive bourbon.

Joseph nodded *thanks*, turning in his stool to face Arturo. One side of his face lit with that heavenly glow while the other side slunk into the dim lighting of the bar.

"I was an English teacher, at first. I found time to write textbooks between semesters."

"When you lived on the West Coast?" Arturo asked, turning in his stool to face Joseph, too.

"Yeah, back then," Joseph stared down at his whiskey. Arturo could see the muscles in Joseph's arms flex and relax as he rotated the glass on the bar. The whiskey inside swirled.

"What happened?" Arturo asked, his legs woven with Joseph's now, their feet resting on each other's footrests.

Joseph gulped what remained in his glass. "When I originally took the position, I hadn't intended on being there long. I was almost tenure, and that terrified me. I wanted to publish fiction, do more than push students to purchase my overpriced textbooks every year to keep me afloat." Joseph waved his fingers in the air. As if these thoughts smelled foul just speaking about them.

"You're quite young for tenure, aren't you?"

"Not when you're smart," Joseph said with a wink. "Did you go to college, er, university?"

"No, couldn't afford it. I worked in hospitality all my life until I was able to open this place." Arturo looked around, admiring the polished style again—and the fact that Joseph was there.

"Impressive," Joseph smirked. His hand hovered over, then slid a few inches past Arturo's knee.

"How long are you in Baxtor Springs for?" Arturo asked, an electric current running up his thigh from Joseph's touch. "I imagine you'll hop back to the West Coast soon?"

"I'm not going back," Joseph said, leaning forward.

"Oh?" Arturo didn't shy away.

"Yeah," Joseph continued, holding ground. "I've been living out here the past few months since inheriting property."

"I thought you said you didn't live here," Arturo questioned.

"My mother had a property out here to escape the West Coast when she wanted to unwind. After she passed, my father took it over and, well, now that he's passed, I'm the owner. I've been taking time to reset since I'm not teaching anymore." Joseph tapped his fingers along the polished bar. Speaking about his mother's death seemed to come easy for Joseph, Arturo thought as he took another sip. He wasn't so open about the subject himself.

"Oh, and to write another novel," Joseph said, a cocky air to his words, as he leaned in farther, nearly brushing up against Arturo. But Arturo felt a little jolted by the sudden shift in tone. He pressed a hand against the author's chest, and Joseph didn't push at all. He leaned back with a guilty expression that was still only half-lit by the polished glow of the bar.

"Woah, buddy, I'm running a bar, not a brothel here," Arturo laughed, trying to keep the momentum going. A change of scenery would help.

"Am I supposed to take you on a date first? Cause I'd be okay with that." Joseph flashed his smile again, recovering.

"So, if you're bad, I get a free meal out of this?"

"You'll be the one owing me a meal, now, okay," Joseph said, his mouth slightly ajar, his tongue running against the back of his bottom lip.

"All right, well." Arturo slid off his stool, walking away.

"Ah c'mon, I was just being cocky," Joseph said. Arturo looked back to see him giving the saddest puppy dog eyes. Arturo kept the silence going a bit longer, until Joseph added, "Please don't tell me I just fucked this up."

"I live upstairs. Stop being dramatic." Arturo shrugged and waved for Joseph to follow.

Arturo led him to a sturdy wooden door with a panel of glass that read, "Employees Only," in old typographic gold lettering. Arturo tapped his phone against the deadbolt, and a light turned on as the door automatically unlocked. They headed up the stairs and through another door that Arturo tapped his phone against to unlock once more. He opened the door for Joseph to enter, but he paused and licked his lips. Joseph was taller than him. He hadn't realized that while they sat at the bar. It was a little intimidating, but Arturo kissed him without much thought at all.

They stepped inside with eyes still closed as they kissed, doing a waltz that was as clumsy as they were intoxicated from the all the whiskey. Their bodies bumped into the dining room table, where a couple of vases clinked together, past the door frame to the bedroom and into the leaning mirror that vibrated with their frantic movement. Arturo pulled Joseph to the bed and rolled on top of him. He pulled away from the wet kisses and wandered down, unbuckling Joseph's pants. Right as Arturo was about to take him in his mouth, Joseph's gentle moan stirred up a light in the corner of the apartment.

"I'm sorry, I didn't catch that," a computerized voice filled the room.

Joseph yelped, and Arturo felt him slip out of his grip. He scurried to the other side of the bed. Glancing at his exposed lower half, Arturo could see that Joseph had gone completely soft. The build-up and the moment broken.

Arturo cleared his throat as he crawled up to Joseph's chest.

"Don't worry. That's just my home device," he said.

Joseph looked down to realize the soft situation himself. "Whiskey dick, it happens."

"It's totally fine. I've been drinking too much tonight, too," Arturo replied comfortingly.

"Nice place you've got," Joseph remarked.

"Thank you. I had some designers style it for me."

"Why not just say you designed it yourself?" Joseph chuckled.

"Cause that wouldn't be fair," Arturo laughed.

"Yeah, yeah," Joseph said with a drunken slur. He wrapped his arms around Arturo and pulled him in closer. Arturo looked back.

"Didn't realize you'd be staying the night," Arturo said flatly.

"I owe you breakfast tomorrow. Did you forget?"

Joseph slipped his briefs back on but kicked off his jeans and removed his shirt. Arturo removed his jeans but kept his shirt on. He never enjoyed sleeping in anything else. Joseph lay his head against the pillows, and all Arturo could think about was the last time he'd washed these sheets.

Arturo laughed. "Fine, but it's my pick."

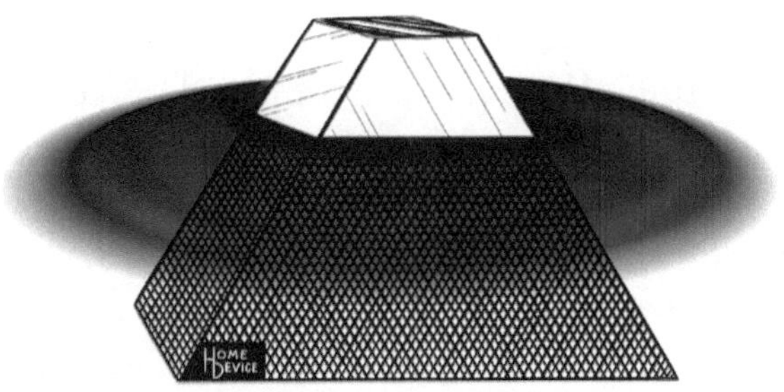

Joseph stirred awake from a repetitive *thump-thump, thump-thump* coming from outside. For a moment, he thought he was back among the busy streets of Los Angeles. His eyes crept open, softly blinking a few times getting his bearings. This bed was softer than his own, and usually, the sun couldn't break through his blackout curtains. Arturo lay on his back. One of his hairy legs rested on top of the sheets, glowing in the sunlight. Joseph smiled as he remembered last night.

The thumping noise continued outside, interrupting Joseph's musing. He pursed his lips, slipped out of bed, and strolled over to the window in nothing more than his black briefs. Behind him, he heard Arturo yawn, beginning to stir awake. Peeking through the wooden blinds, Joseph saw seven long black hearses creeping down Main Street. Each one passed over a large crack along the street where the *thump-thump* rhythm played.

More cars followed behind, but not a single car drove in the opposing direction, Joseph noticed. Family sedans and full-sized vans crept behind the hearses now. Joseph spread the wood blinds a little farther apart to peek down at the passing drivers, each one of them dressed in black.

A tingling vibration played through the wood floors against the bottom of Joseph's feet as Arturo slunk over like a puppy still learning to see.

"I don't think I've ever seen a funeral procession with so many hearses," Joseph admitted.

"It's so sad," Arturo said, sliding between Joseph's arms. His hair brushed against the author's chest as he looked back to catch his gaze. Arturo's kind eyes were glossy. "Today, they are burying Tammy Miller with her two children, along with the other four children who were lost in the massacre. They were at the gas station. The other four children were from the Taylor family. Tammy was watching them during their mother's chemo treatment. Tammy liked taking all the kids up to the lake on those days."

"Jesus, that's heavy." Joseph looked back to the cars still *thump-thumping* by. He let go of the blinds and slipped away from Arturo. Unsure what else to say, he scanned the apartment. The daylight wandered over the brick wall behind him, the ruffled bed on the other side, and the couch with a television and two chairs flanking each side of the coffee table. A small kitchen sat behind the living area. Joseph plopped down on the firm couch, facing the window. He could still feel last night's whiskey and wine weighing him down.

"Do you know much about the massacre?" Arturo asked.

"Not so much about the victims, but I know the gist of what happened that day. I had come to Baxtor Springs a few weeks before to get the keys to the house. I tried to avoid it. I didn't want the massacre to influence my writing. I hadn't fully formed the novel then." Joseph poked his head up to see Arturo turn around. "I didn't see the video released from the gas station cameras, but I read about it. Sounded horrifying. Some kid grabbed an officer's gun. They wrestled. The gun went off. The bullets fired set off an explosion at the gas station that burned a lot of people alive."

"Wasn't just the gas station. The entire shopping center went up in flames. Glass windows over four miles away shattered because of how big that explosion was. The gunshots blew up a tanker there to refill the gasoline reserve on the other side. It was a domino effect. The gas station exploded, causing all the cars in the parking lot to do the same, including a propane shipment being delivered just a few yards away. Liquor and beer were being delivered just on the other side of that. I mean, fucking Murphy's Law," Arturo said, shaking his head. He plopped down on the bed and wrapped his arms around one of the decorative pillows.

"How many victims?" Joseph asked.

"One hundred and thirty-five people burned alive in an instant, and twenty more passed from smoke inhalation and severe wounds. Seventy-five others are stable enough that they are either recovered or recovering. Police Chief Edmonds meets with the press every night to tell them which remains have been identified and how to claim them. They fear having to pay for any unclaimed bodies, too. They ask him question after question, but he always says the same thing. It's a federal case now, out of his hands. He's doing the press briefings as a courtesy to the victims, which they are still working through. The bodies—and body parts—are being kept in the morgue, which wasn't ever meant to handle a high number of victims. They have trucks out there to help preserve the remains as the feds work through identifying them. They change the ice every twelve hours, for Christ's sake. You can't release a body without identifying it first, and you can't release a body without funeral arrangements. The mother and kids being buried today were only identified a few days ago. The families, though, they knew." Arturo sank, looking tired from what felt like a classic case of word vomiting. "Sorry, it's all the news has been reporting on for the past few months."

"It's okay." Joseph paused with genuine interest as Arturo sighed with what sounded like relief. "What about the shooter?"

"Joshua Rodriguez. A minor, not even twelve. His father, Rafael, was downstairs at the bar piss drunk last night. Right before you got here."

"That must've been the guy getting into the police car," Joseph said.

"Yeah. Rafael is not a bad guy, but he's on a slippery slope. Police are already afraid someone might kill him in retaliation for his son's actions. It's all pretty fucked right now. The business included," Arturo admitted with a sober frown, his hands still wrapped around the comforting pillow.

"Are you normally stressed out with the bar?"

"Running a business isn't easy. But the massacre set us back. Not many people are coming out to drink when they have to pay for funeral fees and caskets. We've done our best to help donate to the families impacted. Everything's tough right now. That's why Emily put that charity event together last night."

Joseph nodded, feeling the weight of his head getting harder to hold up with each nod.

"Some food would do you good. You look a little . . ." Arturo groaned like a zombie, extended one arm out, reaching Joseph's arm. Joseph couldn't help but flex right before Arturo's hand made contact.

"Says the guy who kept topping us off last night." Joseph tilted his head, his lips pressed thin in a devilish smirk. "But you are right. I do owe you a meal . . . Is anything even open?" *Thump-thump* continued to play outside. "The Main Street Square seems occupied still."

"I know a place, but we'll need to wait out the procession before we can order a rideshare."

"Why?"

"Cause this line of traffic is going to go on for a long time," Arturo said.

"I have a car," Joseph said, poking his head up all the way. "It's parked behind the bookstore. Couldn't we take some backroads? I just need to freshen up, I think."

"Well, look at that. I have an extra toothbrush here, unopened, and you can borrow a shirt. Do you think you'll want to shower?" Arturo asked, standing up and walking to the edge of the bathroom. A large wardrobe stood against the wall.

"Just a shirt, really, I didn't break a sweat last night." Joseph crossed the room to rummage through the rather plain tees.

"Yeah, me neither…" Arturo was being coy.

Joseph laughed while grabbing a white shirt that would pair well with his dark pants, along with his gray and white sneakers. Arturo came out of the bathroom after brushing his teeth to flick through the hung-up clothes himself. Joseph brushed his teeth and shook off the hangover as best he could. When he came out of the bathroom, Arturo opened a vape cartridge with a flower logo etched on the side beneath the word "Indica."

"Weed?" Joseph asked.

"Yeah, do you mind?" Arturo asked, watching Joseph shake his head *no*. "Always helps after a night of drinking. Would you like a little puff before we go? It's nothing crazy strong."

"After I'm done driving us around for the day," Joseph said. "You can bring that if you want to smoke; I won't care. I have a convertible."

Arturo recoiled in surprise. "Well, then, let's take the long route to brunch. The backroads will be beautiful today."

They walked down Main Street alongside the funeral procession that crept at a snail's pace. Past the large crack in the road, the coffee shop was the only thing semi-busy, with older people dressed in their funeral attire, seated outside, newspapers in hand. A large photo collage printed on the front page displayed the latest confirmed victims. Past the coffee shops and empty storefronts for sale, Joseph noticed a sandwich shop across the street with a big sign that read, "Under New Management." Joseph wondered if that was because the previous owners had burned alive in the massacre. Arturo had described everything so bluntly earlier, but everywhere he looked, he could see the ripple effects of what he'd spoken about.

Behind the bookstore, Joseph saw his vintage oak green Porsche 911 with the top already off, revealing the light tan leather interior. They both slipped inside, and as Joseph fired up the motor, wiggling the stick shift back and forth to put the car into first gear, Arturo leaned over and kissed him.

Arturo stared down, slightly giddy.

"A stick shift? Just how old is this car?" he asked.

"She may be old, but she still knows how to have a good time." Joseph's eyes glanced around. "Now, where to?"

Arturo pointed straight onward. "Head out of here and make a right."

Joseph eased off the clutch as the car shifted gears. Arturo took a few hits. The smoke smelled herbal with hints of citrus. Once on the street, Arturo directed him to turn up a side road to avoid processional traffic. Within a minute, Joseph felt transported away from the Main Street Square. The trees above grew thick overhead, weaving together where only droplets of sunlight poked down around them. Joseph still hadn't gotten used to the forest nature of Baxtor Springs. On the West Coast, he'd been spoiled with planted palm trees and endless summer skies.

"Slow down a little here. There's a stop sign that comes up quick," Arturo said between taking another hit and pointing. "The chur—"

Joseph cut around a tight corner where he could only make out half the stop sign Arturo had warned him about. He dropped the gears down to first as quickly as he could, given the stick shift, and came to an abrupt halt. As the tires screeched, the smell of burnt rubber wafted in the air. Through the thinned trees ahead of them, Joseph saw groups of people walking, then stopping and turning to stare.

"The church is right here," Arturo said, pointing to the traffic approaching from the other side. "Make a left here, though. We can get on the other side of the procession traffic."

Joseph accelerated the Porsche forward and turned left. All the while, he couldn't stop staring at the dull white church that lingered in the middle of the vast manufactured clearing through the thin row of trees alongside the road. In the distance behind the church, Joseph could see headstones—some crumbling and some new—lined neatly in rows. The seven black hearses loomed just a few feet away from the front doors to the church. The people had now turned back, continuing their way inside for the funerals. As the Porsche glided forward, slipping into third gear, the opposite side of the church came into view. It looked as if it had survived a bombing, with so many new holes dug out, mounds of dirt beside them. Seven of them were outlined with a casket lowering system behind large bouquets framing giant portraits of those lost. Joseph knew the portraits would be of the families Arturo had mentioned earlier, but actually seeing their smiling faces hit differently.

Tammy Miller's portrait was the closest, and she smiled radiantly, holding her twin boys. All to be buried together today with a spot for Dad when his time came.

"That is so sad," Joseph said, forcing himself to look away.

Arturo nodded, taking a few more hits, then puffing them up in the air. Arturo stretched his long neck, and

Joseph turned to see his soft neckline above a collarbone that peeked out from his shirt. The trees grew thick again along the back roads, too wide to see anything but the fading green leaves that hadn't yet fallen. Joseph shifted into fifth gear, listening as the motor revved in response. Behind them, the littered remains of fast-food Styrofoam cups stirred in the air beneath a faded speed limit sign. The tips of a shopping center poked through the nestled trees, and Arturo pointed for Joseph to pull inside as they approached the parking lot.

Small window fronts lined each side of the parking lot, while farther back, a brick community center stood tall. The emblem of the Boy Scouts—a star on each side of an eagle's head to symbolize truth and knowledge—had been mounted on a sizeable wood-carved plaque next to the chained entrance. Beneath the plaque, a banner read, "Troop Meets Every Thursday. New Boys Welcome!" In an amateur attempt, someone had spray painted the drooping words, "HE WASN'T ONE OF US," over both the emblem and banner in a color Joseph would only call street-divider yellow. He parked the car and studied the wall.

"Who is *he*?" Joseph asked.

Arturo looked at the wall for only a split second. "Joshua Rodriguez."

"Oh," Joseph muttered. He should've been able to guess that one.

"The video showed him in his uniform that day."

"Why tag those words, though? I mean, hello, property damage."

"The building will be fine. The Boy Scouts just don't want to be associated with Joshua. He skipped Boy Scouts that day, doing what he did. Because there were so many victims from different counties, even some visiting from out of state—the FBI took over the case. They were hell-bent on a theory that someone in the troop had done something to Joshua. They interviewed the kids and their families countless times, for weeks on end. Even the troop leaders. Nothing panned out, though. Quite frankly, the entire troop and Boy Scout Association is tired of being looped together and blamed for what Joshua did." Arturo shook his head, staring at the graffiti while he unclipped his seat belt. "If someone vandalized a building when I was in the Boy Scouts growing up, they'd have made us all get out there and clean it up. They wouldn't have cared who did it."

"You were a Boy Scout?" Joseph asked as they both got out of the car.

"For a little while, yeah," Arturo said, a little short.

Joseph followed Arturo inside a thin restaurant located between a dry cleaner and a barbershop. Inside, there was an empty table by the front; behind it, a bench read, "Pick Up Waiting Area." Across from the bench, a few people were huddled inside the kitchen, wearing stark-white chef hats listening to music from someone's phone speakers. Farther past them, Joseph could see a shaded area down the hall, outside.

"Hey, Arturo," a small-figured woman greeted, coming out from the kitchen.

"That table you like is open in the back. I'll be there in a second. You want a round of coffee to start?" she asked, as if Joseph had frequented the restaurant as much as Arturo had.

"Yes, thank you, Mimi," Arturo responded, gliding past her, leading Joseph past the smell of fresh tortillas and roasted spices in the air.

"Well, you've been here before," Joseph said, ducking underneath the doorway and stepping out to a dining patio that overlooked a slight dip in the forest behind the village of shops. They both sat down, and Joseph slid his leg alongside Arturo's.

"Wow, that's a gorgeous view."

"One of the best in Baxtor Springs," Arturo marveled.

Before long, they heard mugs clinking down the hallway, announcing Mimi's arrival. In her other hand, she held a metal coffee decanter with steam rising from the top. She set both mugs on the table and filled the one closest to Joseph first.

"Sorry." She glanced at Joseph before turning to face Arturo. "I just wanted to say, I passed by your mom's grave yesterday, took some of our flowers and put them on her gravestone as a thank you," Mimi said, lifting the decanter to fill Arturo's mug.

"That's sweet of you, Mimi," Arturo said without looking up at her. "I'm glad the bar could donate something for your *tía*'s husband. How was the funeral service?"

"As good as it could've been," Mimi replied, holding the decanter up by her side as she turned to Joseph. "You know what you wanna order?"

"He probably has no clue," Arturo joked, nodding at Joseph.

Mimi pulled out a laminated menu from her apron and handed it to the author.

Joseph looked over the menu. Various brightly colored boxes separated appetizers from entrees and drinks. On the back of the menu, an entire page was dedicated to breakfast, served all day. The menu had been heavily used, fogged-up with scratches. Joseph didn't care what he ate. Anything would help him hold on to what little energy his hangover had left him.

"What do you normally get here?"

"Depends on what you want. They have healthy or greasy, meats or plant-based options. If you want me to suggest, you should try their huevos-less rancheros," Arturo said, pointing to the very bottom of the menu, where the dish was pictured and pixelated.

"We use a chickpea mixture to replace the eggs," Mimi filled in Joseph's curious eyebrows. "You'll barely be able to tell the difference, trust me."

"Okay, I'll try it," Joseph replied.

"Usual for you?" Mimi asked, and Arturo nodded. "I'll be back in a few."

Joseph reached for Arturo's hand, turning it over and gently tracing the ridgelines in his palms.

"I'm sorry about your mom. I didn't know she passed."

"She committed suicide when I was young. That's why I wasn't involved with the Boy Scouts for very long growing up. I would spend a few hours here after school until my *tía* could pick me up from her morning shift." Arturo spoke nonchalantly, more to the forest than to Joseph. When Arturo did turn to look at him, Joseph caught Arturo's soft eyes roll back into his head with dramatic flair.

"See—that look, that's why I don't like telling people. It's not a big deal. I wasn't even close with her." Arturo spoke fast, waving his hands as if for Joseph to wipe the expression of pity off his face.

"What about your dad?" Joseph asked, licking his lips, letting his jaw hang a little.

Arturo shrugged. "What is there to say? He was always trying to become something or do something, but nothing ever came of it. He couldn't provide for me, let alone himself, and eventually, I went to live with my *tía*, and life moved on. I've figured things out this far." Arturo shrugged his shoulders again.

Joseph worried he was striking out.

Mimi came by and set down their plates and topped their glasses off with more coffee. She kept the banter small; they didn't need much else. When she disappeared, they dug into the food, and the next few moments were silent. Joseph had to remind himself to eat slower.

Joseph felt a vibration in his pocket and grabbed it, noticing Arturo mirrored him, checking his own smart phone.

"A news alert?" Arturo asked, catching Joseph's gaze.

"Yeah." Joseph laughed.

"Jesus. I get so many of these news notifications a day, it's frustrating." Arturo's eyes had already returned to the screen, scanning wildly. They grew large, and Joseph smirked between bites of refried beans.

"Everything all right?" Joseph asked.

"This news story."

"Do tell." Joseph puckered his lips.

"You won't understand, you're . . . er." Arturo looked up. "You're not from here."

"Tell me anyway," Joseph said, shrugging.

Arturo looked between the phone and Joseph. "Okay, after the massacre, there were some suicides in town. People had lost their wives, their children, I mean . . ." He blinked, at a loss for words, and Joseph nodded. "One of them was Benjamin Fisher. The Boy Scout leader. He'd helped Joshua earn his gun badge a few months before everything happened, and we all assumed he blamed himself for it."

"How did he commit suicide?" Joseph asked, leaning over the coffee.

"Shotgun. Pretty straightforward, except . . ." Arturo looked back down to his screen. "They found a large amount of OxyContin in his system. Along with fractured bones that weren't relative to the gunshot blast." Arturo paused and chuckled to himself as if he'd just realized a truth. "Honestly, it sounds straight out of your novel that you read aloud last night. An old man getting poisoned to death with too much OxyContin and the killer losing his temper."

Joseph's head twitched to the side, a spasm pinching his neck.

"Ha!" he barked in wild laughter. "That's a funny similarity, but I assure you, I've written nothing more than fiction." Joseph continued chuckling as if recovering from the funniest joke. He sighed. At least Arturo hadn't read *Rabbit's Revenge* yet.

"Did the article say anything else?"

Arturo scanned it, swiping his finger up on the screen a few more times before speaking. His face scrunched, and he looked disappointed.

"Says they aren't hopeful. Police found no evidence or other leads after the autopsy. His house has been on the market for four months, so it's been completely cleaned, and various people have walked through. Police are asking for anyone with information to contact them."

"Split checks?" Mimi said, coming around, topping off their mugs once more.

"Just one, thanks," Joseph said, his nostrils flaring.

"About thirty," she said.

Joseph produced two twenty-dollar bills from his wallet and waved her hand away when she went to give him change.

"Thanks for your business," Mimi said, reaching into her other apron pocket and pulling out a few mints that she set on the table. She disappeared back down the hallway, and Joseph looked back to Arturo.

"Let's go to my place." Joseph smiled, biting just the very edge of his lower lip back.

He watched Arturo lock his phone and set it on the table. The dimples in his cheeks were back, and soon Joseph offered him his hand to walk out together.

The dry pancakes and stale coffee from the lobby of the Extended Stay Suites were good enough for Noah that morning. He hadn't slept much between devouring the novel and using the free Wi-Fi to do a web search on Joseph Bailey. There were a few social media profiles, but most held the same images and posts. Noah discovered little about Joseph's life, though. Noah saw posts of him vacationing in Palm Springs with men in Speedos, eating at fancy restaurants, and a picture-perfect post of him laughing beside a vintage Porsche that looked freshly polished.

He took a sip of sour black coffee and couldn't decide if he felt envious. Joseph was doing so many things that Noah never even had the chance to try. He eyed the remaining half of a pancake on the kitchen table and pushed it away. Noah needed to sleep, he knew that, but the coffee left him jittery. He wanted to see the author, meet him in person, and pick his brain. Had Joseph been there that night? Hiding in the closet? It didn't make sense, yet the details in the book were too accurate. Too spot on.

Noah looked back at the older man's stolen phone in his hands, where he'd pulled up a photo of Joseph on a beach by himself, flexing beneath a palm tree cabana. His eyes trailed Joseph's bare chest and arms, muscular shoulders, and rather hairy, thick thighs. It didn't help that he was handsome, too.

Noah locked the old man's phone and set it down beside the yellow Manila envelope the book had come in. A piece of paper stuck out with the words, "Love it? Keep it. Don't? Return it. Either way, leave a 5-Star Review to earn your income! Link your social media account to earn even more for posting! Email us for further details — Publishing X."

Noah had already left a five-star review for the book, which didn't feel as narcissistic as reading the reviews left by other people. Each review praised Joseph Bailey for his original, thrilling novel; Rabbit was framed as a wonderful antihero who'd reclaimed his life from some tragic government program. That was all fictional, but the murders and some dialogue were straight out of Noah's life. He frowned. The author had gotten some details correct—snippets, really—but not the whole truth. Noah hadn't told anyone the truth in so long, it no longer seemed relevant.

Reading the book last night had awakened an insatiable desire.

His eyes came back into focus on a friendly slogan printed beside the shipping label poking out just enough for Noah to read the letters: B-A-X-T. He pulled the tag out farther and realized the book was being shipped to just the other side of town, here in Baxtor Springs. He expected to read Joseph Bailey's name above the address, but instead, he read "Publishing X Returns." An idea bloomed like spring wildflowers. He didn't want to assume anything would be easy. Noah swiped to another social media post from Joseph.

He was now looking at a photo of a woman and young boy in front of a large castle. They were both smiling. Below the photo, Joseph had comment, "Gone but not forgotten. Love you, Mom."

Noah opened a new web browser and searched for the last name "Bailey" in the public property records for Baxtor Springs County.

"Bingo."

His eyes trailed back to the return shipping label. The addresses matched. His head tilted curiously. *Did Joseph own this company?* Noah wondered. A few more taps to search "Publishing X," but he found nothing more than the simple sign-up form he'd filled out months ago. The company was very private. Noah closed his search and routed to see how far Joseph's house was from him. The route said it'd take a few hours by bus. Noah didn't have cell service on the phone, so he downloaded the trip. He was confident he could get there without any problems. He only needed to worry about how he was going to confront Joseph.

On the way to the bus stop, Noah felt too jittery and stopped by a gas station to pick up a smoke. He saw a plastic display promoting CBD for its stress-relieving properties and bought two of the disposable vapes. Noah smoked while waiting for the bus, hoping it would calm his nerves.

A good few hours later, he walked up a long driveway freckled with small white pebbles. Each step, the crunch underfoot reverberated among the trees. He stuck out like a sore thumb and expected Joseph Bailey to come outside and demand to know who was coming up his driveway. Noah took another hit of the CBD pen, his chest holding the puff of smoke tight, just as a new thought occurred. What if Joseph was paranoid and attacked him? Noah exhaled the smoke. He could defend himself. He'd already killed one person.

Noah stood on the doorstep, his feet sinking in the bristled tan welcome mat. He raised a fist to knock, smelling thick lavender in the air. But he hesitated. A circle above the door handle blinked bright green. Without a sound, the door swept open, showcasing the entryway filled with various flowers before a living room in the distance that continued out of sight, to the left. Everything seemed delicately encased in a silence that Noah felt afraid to disturb.

Behind him, a rumbling motor grew louder, coming up the driveway. Noah flipped around, recognizing the Porsche from Joseph's social media. He could see that the author wasn't alone. There was someone else in the car. Noah stepped back, unsure what to do. Though now he was standing inside the foyer and worried they'd see him. He glanced to his right, where he saw an office, and without hesitating, he slipped inside. He left the door ajar because that's how he'd seen it. The room was a mess, with numerous yellow packages filling up nearly half the space. The other side was a large desk that offered no hiding place. Noah's throat was beginning to dry up.

He was running out of time as the car stopped outside, and the sound of the motor was cut.

Behind the various packages was a thin sliver of space that he could slip behind if he was cautious enough not to knock the stacks over. As he laid his body on the floor behind the books, slithering his legs down like a snake, he saw a bright yellow Post-It note on the desk with the Wi-Fi password neatly printed.

Arturo's linen shirt crept up the nape of his sweaty neck, causing an eruption of goosebumps to ripple down his back. He shivered, despite the hot setting sun. His back slowly slid down the tan leather passenger seat as Joseph pulled the Porsche around to the front of the single-story modern building. Arturo felt, well, small. Joseph cut the motor, and Arturo clutched the thin black metal vape in his hand. Eyeing it, he wondered if he'd smoked too much on the way back. *Impossible,* he thought, considering how much he typically smoked.

"This place is gorgeous," Arturo said, pawing at the seat, regaining his posture, as he took in the details of the home. Black steel beams with sharp edges framed wide panes of glass that reflected Joseph stepping out. Joseph tossed the keys into the cup holder and strolled around the sleek oak-green convertible to open the door for Arturo. He was quite the gentleman, it seemed, and though Arturo could complain about outdated heteronormative expectations, he couldn't deny how nice it felt to be spoiled, even just a little.

"Just wait till you see what it looks like at night." Joseph cocked an eyebrow while extending his hand for Arturo to take. Arturo reached for it and allowed Joseph to pull him out of the car. The white stone pebbles lining the driveway crunched beneath their feet as Joseph led them away from the closed garage and toward a covered patio with fresh lavender growing in neat rows. The large windows reflected them both under a beautiful sunset. Arturo wrapped his arm around Joseph's, and they interlocked hands. Arturo felt as if their reflection was a billboard promoting the American dream.

When they turned the corner, they walked into an overpowering smell of lavender. Arturo could see inside the house, past the foyer and into the living room, and he wondered why he could see beyond the entrance.

"Is someone here?" Arturo asked.

"We're here," Joseph said casually, walking through the front door as if it wasn't odd that it sat wide open. Joseph turned and waved for Arturo to catch up.

"Oh my gosh!" Arturo thundered, dumbfounded. He tried to lower his voice then, but it only came out like a hiss. "You just *left* your door open?"

"These are the old Estates of Baxtor Springs." Joseph smiled with his bottom lip pouting out. "I haven't even met my neighbors, and I know why; we all pay for the pure privacy."

"Pure privacy would be working against you if someone decided to stroll in and rob you. They wouldn't even have to break in, Joseph," Arturo said sternly, and Joseph laughed hard and loud, with one of his hands pressing into his chest.

"Should we check the entire house, you think?" Joseph said, dramatically clutching his collar bones now.

Arturo wiggled his jaw back and forth, caught between saying something sassy back or letting the entire idea go. He chose the latter. "No, I'm sure it's fine."

Joseph smoothed his shirt down as he straightened up, smirking. "We can go room to room. Some people also call that a tour."

"Ha ha." Arturo marched forward into the foyer. Joseph paused and gestured to the front door. Arturo watched the thick slab of metal drift shut on its own, silently. The door made a mechanical noise as it locked. A red lock symbol flashed three times, waving away any arguments Arturo had about the home's safety.

"My house is automated, nothing to worry about." Joseph waved his hand around the foyer, which, Arturo noticed, held exquisite displays of flowers in various vases. A steel and crystal chandelier floated above their heads as if by magic. The smell of clean laundry wafted from somewhere deeper in the house as the scent of lavender thinned out. Arturo crossed his arms, afraid to touch anything. To his left was an office filled with dark oak furniture glimmering in the soft sunlight that peeked through the window. Too many books and unopened yellow packages to count surrounded the matching desk in the center of the room, a giant computer sitting atop it. Various colored sticky notes had been posted to the wall as if creating a timeline. Arturo shuddered with excitement, recalling how Joseph had read the opening pages of his novel at Baxtor's Books. Was this the room where Joseph had created *Rabbit's Revenge*?

"Is this where you write?" Arturo asked.

"Yes, but I wouldn't want you to see any spoilers now," Joseph reached for the handle and closed the office door. "That offer for some weed still available? Now that we're home."

"We're?" Arturo said, although he didn't mind the sound of it. This place was huge compared to his small apartment above the bar. He had space to breathe here. There wasn't a single flyer promoting the Victim's Fund. No slow bar to hover around, annoying Violet. Arturo happily handed the vape over to Joseph, who took a few hits, blowing the smoke up toward the high ceilings.

"We're here, aren't we? You're going to stay the night, anyway," Joseph shrugged, saying the words so casually while the smell of lemon terpenes trickled down around them from the weed. He turned, strutting down the hall a few feet before he stopped to open a door. "Bathroom at all?"

"Just how long is this tour?" Arturo jabbed, catching up to Joseph to see a narrow bathroom with a toilet at the end.

"Long enough," Joseph mocked, handing him back the vape. Arturo took a few puffs as Joseph gestured forward into a large living room, where the furniture sat in the center of the space. Arturo followed, noticing a soft green rug beneath an oversized L-shaped tan couch lined with pillows in muted fall colors. Resting over the frame of the couch was a large faux fur blanket. The couch had two views: besides a large television mounted on the wall, the floor-to-ceiling windows offered a view directly out to the untamed forest that surrounded the perimeter of the estates. Arturo noticed how the house must change with the seasons with views like these. The ghost coffee table at the center of the room held nothing but a few dried rings from drinks that had perspired there before—the only sign of any mess outside of the office in Joseph's house.

Joseph continued a few feet to the left, where there was a large dining room table made from natural wood. The grain looked as if it had been a large tree cut in half and sanded down. The chairs around it were threaded with thick leather bands that complemented the wood. Small glass sculptures sat on top of the table. Behind it, gold-framed photos lined the wall. The chandelier above the dining room table consisted of three large Edison bulbs like the ones Arturo had in his bar. Only these were much larger. Another long hallway passed the dining room, but before that, to the left, was the kitchen.

Joseph walked to the wall and touched a screen, turning the kitchen lights on. Arturo laughed as he scanned the kitchen counters to the island.

"You have a boogeyman here, too?" Arturo asked, pointing to the home device that sat in the center of a large island topped with cookbooks, fresh herbs, and glass jars with labels: Flour, Sugar, Pasta.

"What?" Joseph asked, caught off guard.

"H.D.," Arturo said, tilting his head just past Joseph's shoulder.

"Yes?" The home device responded, its swirling red lights flashing.

"Oh." Joseph eyed the device from the corner of his eye. "Never mind, H.D."

"No problem," it replied cheerfully.

"You were so freaked out last night when you saw mine, and here you have one, too."

"It scared me, that's all, but that was last night. Tonight, I'll make up for it," Joseph said, extending his reach to Arturo's arm with a smolder.

"Should I schedule make up for it at seven, tonight?" the home device chimed.

"Never mind, H.D.," Arturo laughed, watching the home device fall silent between them.

"How about a drink?" Joseph offered, waltzing deeper into the kitchen, where an extensive collection of alcohol waited behind cabinet doors.

"What do you have?" Arturo asked.

Joseph withdrew a bottle and two glasses and set them in front of Arturo. The bottle was an aged Hibiki, a Japanese whiskey that Arturo was already very fond of. Joseph came back with two slightly cloudy ice spheres and set them in the glass. Arturo poured, just as heavy as last night, and took the first bitter sip that would get better as the night went on.

"Good stuff." Arturo raised his glass.

"Thought you might enjoy." Joseph winked.

"So, what's back there?" Arturo asked, pointing down the small hallway.

Joseph led the way once more and took a left when the hallway came to a dead end with doors on each side. They meandered through a laundry room, which smelled of fresh linen, then through one more entry. Joseph flicked, tapped his switch again, and bright iridescent light filled the room. Arturo shielded his eyes for a moment.

"Well, this is the garage." Joseph pointed to some metal racks that held various boxes. "I store decorations there, frozen foods there," he said, pointing to a large white freezer that must've been around since the nineties. "This way now," Joseph said, leading Arturo back through the hallway and toward another door. Arturo took another sip of whiskey as Joseph opened it.

Arturo followed Joseph past a bookcase built into the backend of his bed, which sat in the center of the room. The bookcase itself was overflowing with books, but on top sat only two golden lamps. Arturo imaged Joseph reading under them late at night, cozy beneath the various faux fur throws bunched at the bottom. To his left sat an en suite bathroom filled with skincare products, which lined a built-in, open-style cabinet.

Joseph continued past this, however, toward two large French doors that opened to a balcony. To Arturo, the room felt like its own private little world. A hidden getaway from Baxtor Springs that he never realized existed. The balcony was built into the trees, some of the boards even cut so the trees could come through. A smokeless fire pit sat around a simple love seat and two retro-style cable chairs over a weathered rug. Arturo walked to the end of the balcony and looked around, feeling as if he one with the forest.

"I can see why your mom would come here to get away," Arturo said, his shoulder rubbing against Joseph's as they stood looking out over the forest.

"Yeah, some rare birds live in this area, too. It's immaculate." Joseph smiled. "My mother would point them out to me all the time."

"When did she pass away?"

Joseph winced for a split second and Arturo could see that the question had pressed a wound. Joseph turned away from the forest, leaning his back against the railing, his forearm hair mingling with Arturo's.

"I was in my teens, and we were moving out to the West Coast. I stayed in the hotel room one night while she went out with friends to celebrate. That night, two guys got into a fight and threw some punches. One guy missed the other and knocked my mom out cold. Police called it a one-hit homicide," Joseph said with a gulp of whiskey.

"What was the fight about?" Arturo asked, not bothering with the *I'm sorry for your loss* pleasantries.

"Sports." Joseph shrugged his shoulders up high enough that they almost touched his ears. They fell with a sigh. "The cops arrested the guys, and the following day, my mother's lawyer and life insurance policy representative flew out here with my father. They explained that my father would oversee the trust my mother had left, along with her investments. This house is one of them."

"What was your father like?" Arturo asked, reaching his hand over to gently massage the back of Joseph's neck. Joseph closed his eyes, relaxing under Arturo's touch.

"He wasn't a father, and if only a few more days had passed, he wouldn't have been her legal husband, either. My mother was only moving to the West Coast to divorce him. She died before he signed the papers. In short, he got very rich in her death and shipped me off to boarding school the following day. I was furious, thinking that I'd missed my own mother's funeral only to learn later that he didn't even have one for her. To save money, he said. For a good time, he was even forging bills from the boarding school to get more money out of my trust for himself. He was a rat. I only recently found that out, though, after taking everything over."

Arturo's eyes grew large. "This was all about four months ago then?"

"Yeah, it's still a lot to process. It's why diving into the novel was so easy. I needed the escape." Joseph leaned against Arturo's touch.

"How was boarding school?"

"Not fun. I didn't want to be there to begin with. Won't lie about that. I wasn't the easiest teenager, being outraged all the time. They couldn't physically beat me—laws had changed—but they had this course that they'd make me run. Walls, ropes, mud . . . I mean rain or shine, even snow. You fucked up, you did the course, and I was always fucking up, so I was always doing the course. Eventually, I calmed down. I also, you know . . ." Joseph flexed his arm, his bicep bulb expanding beneath his textured polo shirt. Arturo playfully slapped his arm down, and Joseph noticed his glass was running low. "Want another?"

Arturo nodded.

"Wait right here," Joseph said and headed back inside.

Arturo stood, watching Joseph's figure walk through the house, grab the bottle, and come back out. He sat down on the loveseat, and Arturo joined. Joseph tapped his phone screen, turning on the smokeless fire pit. The heat licked their bodies. In the distance, a bird cawed. The sun was barely holding on now, the sky above cast in shades of pink and purple above the trees.

"My mother, though," Joseph continued, pouring them more whiskey, "she was a businesswoman who ran a tight ship. Her investments were from the department store boom back in the day. She owned many, across many states. Even when those crashed, she was able to flip her lots to larger chain stores, continuing to be profitable. She also enjoyed playing the stocks, as she'd call it. My father was always so jealous of her."

"That she was the breadwinner?"

"Yeah, he wasn't smart like my mother and me." The sun had now disappeared, the orange flicker from the flame washed over Joseph's face as he talked. "Life would be so different if she were alive. I miss her."

"You liked your mother then?" Arturo asked, curious.

"No, I *loved* my mother," Joseph embellished humbly.

Arturo sighed. "I wish I felt the same about mine."

"I could tell you got a little quiet when Mimi talked about visiting her grave." Joseph took a sip. "You don't visit?"

"No, to be honest, I haven't visited her grave since the funeral. Which, because of her suicide, wasn't even supposed to happen, so there was only my dad and *tía* there," Arturo said, recalling the only thing he remembered from that day. His dad swayed as he stood, his *tía* a mess of tears, and Arturo had just stood there silently. The weeping willow his mother was buried under was tall. It loomed over Arturo, hissing with each sway as if the tree were simply a collection of poisonous snakes.

"Why wasn't it supposed to happen?"

"Suicide isn't okay in God's eyes. It's cowardly. She'd already paid for the space, though. My great-grandparents are buried there, too. The church didn't want to refund the money, so they allowed a very private and small funeral with very little even said or read from the Bible." Arturo took a sip of the whiskey to distract himself.

They sat in the silence of the trees and sipped their drinks. The sky began turning indigo above them as Arturo cleared his throat.

"Do you think that makes me a bad son?" Arturo asked, breaking the silence that had become as thick as the forestry around them.

"For not visiting her grave?" Joseph asked. "No, it doesn't. We all do what we must to survive. The world is crazy enough. Maybe you will in time."

"I doubt it." Arturo tossed his drink back, much like Rafael had done last night. "All this talk is not getting me in the mood, though," Arturo said.

"It doesn't always have to be about the sex," Joseph replied, sitting taller, his chest puffed. "I'm glad that we can be open with each other."

"Me too," Arturo said, a little unsure at first. He hadn't allowed himself to think about his mother, how her death felt thrown in his face week after week with every new funeral. Arturo felt he could talk in this space, that he could truly be heard, without the distractions of his phone or the bar, only the silence of the trees and Joseph sitting beside him. He felt no judgment, either. He leaned over and kissed the author, and was kissed back. Arturo pulled away, laughing innocently. Joseph pulled his phone out and swiped through for an app.

"Oh my god, Joseph, c'mon, you don't even have a passcode on your phone?"

"You must think I'm just arrogant now," Joseph said, glaring at him devilishly with a wicked smile on his face.

"A little," Arturo scoffed.

"Press this button," he said, holding his phone out for Arturo.

Arturo looked down and then cautiously backed up, unsure of what he might find. He extended his index finger and pressed the button. The lights all changed to a soft, dim glow. Arturo nodded, impressed. They were tipsy and soon laughing, exchanging stories. No more did they talk about loss; they talked about travel, food, culture, and drag queens. Joseph had wild stories from attending and teaching at the university, and Arturo shared bar stories and talked about how many times his *tía* had been married. Four times, to be exact.

Joseph ordered some Thai food, and while they waited for the food to be delivered, Joseph suggested they watch some B-rated horror film and dimmed the fireplace. Arturo hadn't seen the movie before, and they watched it on the couch while eating their food and switching to light beers. They compared themselves to the protagonist in the horror film who was making *all* the wrong decisions, yet still surviving. When the credits rolled, Joseph pulled Arturo close and kissed him. He asked him if he liked the film and if they were ready for bed.

Arturo smiled; somehow, this felt like balance.

Noah hadn't moved at all.

He could hear the clinking of glasses and laughter trailing from somewhere deep inside the house. Not loud or close enough for him to make out what they were talking about. He was safe in this room. The first thing the author did when the couple had come inside was close the office door. *Spoilers*, the author had said. Noah nearly barked out loud with laughter when he'd heard it. Hidden behind the mound of mail, he realized the packages were returns from the reviewers. The ones who hadn't decided to keep the book. *What a pity*, Noah thought. His pride was a little damaged. He wanted to confirm but decided against opening any of the packages. He couldn't risk Joseph hearing anything from the office.

Noah peeked over the edge of the books to make sure the door was still fully closed when he heard footsteps approaching. Then, light banter and some crinkling plastic bags. Noah didn't even allow himself to breathe. He was so nervous about being found. He parted his lips to exhale slowly. As the footsteps disappeared, a vibration erupted from his pocket. He jumped but thankfully didn't disturb the stacks. The footsteps had gone, anyway, and the television was playing something loudly.

He stood up and stretched, pulling Benjamin Fisher's phone out to see a battery notification. He only had ten percent charge left. He stepped over to the desk and used the dying phone to see in the dark. Underneath the desktop was a wired keyboard, and seeing it, Noah paused. He had never seen a wireless keyboard in person before, but he'd seen commercials play between the shows they watched in the recreation area at the prison. He pulled on the cord that was charging it, and it popped out. The wire was a match for the older man's phone, too. Noah quickly plugged the device in, unsure if he would have enough time for a full charge. He looked around the office; even this room was bigger than his cell back in prison.

The large desktop screen lit up with a notification. Brightness washed over Noah, and he ducked, panicking that Joseph or his guest would see the light trail from under the door down the hall. Hurried footsteps would soon approach. Did the author have a gun in the house? He looked back at the keyboard, pressing the top row of keys until the brightness turned down. The volume, too, but that wasn't a bad idea now that Noah heard nothing from the computer, the house, or the people inside. He took a breath, studying the screen. Joseph hadn't locked his desktop with a password or anything. Noah wasn't too familiar with computers—when he was a kid, they were loud and clunky, but this one was silent, as thin as a stack of papers. Noah read the notification that popped up on the screen:

**Restore to your last cloud backup
performed *Today* at 2:23 pm?**

Yes, Noah thought, clicking the corresponding button. Fisher's stolen phone went blank with the manufacturer's logo and a small bar that showed its loading progress. Noah smiled, excited to have a snapshot of Joseph's digital world. He'd snoop through everything he could read; perhaps he could find some answers before confronting Joseph.

Noah waited on the edge of the desk chair while the phone booted up. He used the passwords already saved in Joseph's computer to help him set up the phone. It was all done in less than five minutes. He steadied his breath, thinking about how he needed to leave the property. Spend time studying his new favorite subject: Joseph Bailey.

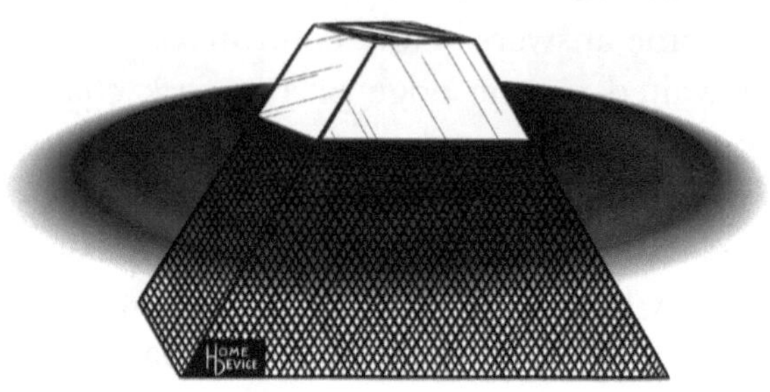

Joseph's eyes gently fluttered open to a familiar rhythmic vibration that pulled him from sleep. His phone was ringing. But he heard sad blues music blaring from his speakers, and he wondered how long he'd been asleep. In the darkness, his eyes scanned to the far left, where he could make out the edges of his phone turned upside down in the corner of his tan sectional couch. Joseph curled his fingers, pawing at the device. The sour taste of alcohol lingered beneath his tongue. He'd only been combing his fingers through Arturo's thick, silky dark hair a few moments ago as they laid in bed.

That seemed so far away now.

Turning the phone over, Joseph's throat pinched tight. Sophie Meyers's name was on the bright screen. She had been a fellow professor with a master's in economics and accounting, who Joseph became close with during his time teaching at the university. She was shocked when he hadn't returned the following semester, when there was plenty to gossip about. A new person had taken over as president, she had told him while making small talk. When he explained his father's passing and how stressed he was over his financial situation (especially since Joseph was almost guaranteed tenure), she didn't ask any questions, only offered to help him get a better handle on his portfolio.

In the reflection of the glass windows, Joseph saw his bare chest beneath an open robe and gym shorts. His untamed beard brushed against his collar bones as he craned, trying to put himself together and answer the call. Chip crumbs fell to the sides of his bloated, soft belly. His hand began to go limp as the realization sunk in: he was not awake. This was a memory, one that was both inspiring and haunting all at once.

Joseph turned to look behind him, then noticed he held an open bottle of whiskey in his hand. How had it gotten there? On the kitchen island, his home device sat underneath the blaring music overhead.

"H.D., turn the volume down," Joseph commanded, and the lights in the house came on full blast. He raised his hand, blinded by the light. "No, H.D., set my lights to nighttime." Still, the music persisted. "H.D., turn the volume down!"

"Okie dokie!" the home device replied cheerfully.

While he answered his phone, he took a swig of whiskey, hoping it would wake him.

"Joseph?" Sophie asked, a soft concern in her voice.

"Hey So—phie," Joseph said, the whiskey igniting his raw throat.

"I know it's late. I'm sorry if I woke you . . ." Sophie said, and Joseph could hear the worried tone in her voice now, his stomach twisting, though not from the whiskey.

"Is everything okay?" Joseph asked, as if he were worried about her.

"Oh—I'm fine—" she said, like an old computer booting up, "It's just—" she took another pause that made Joseph's hand tremor against the neck of the bottle. He raised it and took another glug as she let out a heavy sigh. Joseph imagined her shaking her head.

"I've finished going through the banker's boxes you gave me, and from what we discussed, I don't think you're aware of what your father did. I'm afraid there's . . ." Sophia's voice became so thin and lost in the sounds of papers ruffling around her that Joseph pressed the phone harder to his ear just to hear above it all. "There's far less coming than you expected."

"What do you mean? What about the investments? The properties she owned? Interest from investments? The last of her trust?" Joseph tripped over his words. He'd felt as if he'd just been punched in the face.

"Your father was living off the—your mother's—investments. He'd sold some large ones to invest in smaller things, but those investments weren't successful. He charged your trust a lot in ways that, well, I wouldn't call legal. He's dead, though, so you can't do anything about that . . ."

"How much is left?

"Before your mother's death, her net worth was close to a yard. Now there's . . ." Sophia sighed before she continued. "A little over two hundred thousand left in total."

He opened his mouth only to sound like a frog croaking, his mind spinning. A tightness grew in his throat before he snapped his jaw shut, his teeth grinding against each other.

"You're going to need to find the money somewhere, though. The cost of that house alone is going to sink you by the end of next year. Unless you sell, which—" She stopped herself, drawing in a deep breath as if waiting to see a firework explode in the midnight sky. "I'm sorry. I know you don't want to sell the estate because of your mother, but . . ." She took another beat. "The property taxes are expensive, not to mention the cost just to maintain everything properly. Right now, it looks like your only income is the severance pay and the royalties on your textbooks. Those textbooks don't make what they used to. What if you updated them?"

"I can't do that," Joseph said, rolling his eyes.

"Okay, no textbooks—you're an English professor, though." Joseph winced at Sophie's words; a professor isn't what Joseph would call himself anymore, not after last year. She continued: "And that publishing company that Dean reached out to for you, what's going on with that?" Sophie seemed to be shooting from the hip, trying to fix his situation because she was a good person like that. She had always been on Joseph's side, even when he was under scrutiny for being the youngest professor ever hired at the university. Joseph didn't know how to respond. He felt the weight of all his secrets and mistakes heavy against his chest, making it hard to speak up.

"That company wants fresh new material, and I haven't been able to drum up anything lately."

"Okay—I know this is a lot to take in," Sophie said. When she paused again, Joseph could only hear the beating of his heart. "From what I can tell, if you keep your expenses low, you can live off the money coming to you for about four years. Luckily, the severance gives you more time, but—" More silence. "You're gonna need to do something eventually."

"Okay." Joseph sounded empty.

"I'm sorry I'm not calling with better news."

"It's okay. Thanks for looking everything over. Talk later."

Joseph tapped the screen to hang up before tossing the phone back into the corner of the couch. Leaning his head back, he tilted the bottle upside down as if inspiration could be found at the bottom. Tears welled in his eyes. Both from the whiskey burning his throat and the very thought of being poor for the first time in his entire life. His hands curled into tight fists, shaking with a vengeful desire to have gotten them around his father's neck. He'd murder him for how careless and downright cruel he'd been. Joseph felt betrayed, and yet, he wasn't surprised in the least.

"H.D., play a different fucking record," Joseph demanded, his words slurred. He stood up, wavering under his own weight, before heading to the kitchen to grab a fresh bottle. In that moment, he wanted nothing more than to drown his earthly woes with all the alcohol he could drink while dancing the night away to loud music, waiting for the alcohol poisoning to take him out. The home device's red lights swirled around and around, and by the time he had a fresh bottle of bourbon in his hands, he'd lost his patience. Technology was always advertised for being smart enough to help simplify any daily task. Like streaming any album instantaneously. With the bottle open, he flicked the top across the room carelessly. His stomach twisted into tight knots as it prepared for more alcohol.

A loud bang thundered through the house. Even the pictures behind the dining table shook. Joseph, mid swig, was startled. He swallowed down the wrong pipe, and his throat seized. He coughed so hard he lost his grip on the bottle. The base of it slammed down on his right foot, and a sharp pain followed. He hollered, choking on the liquor at the same time. With watery eyes, he could make out the bottle rolling away to the base of the couch, leaving a trail of wasted liquor behind.

Thunderous banging came again, and Joseph snapped his attention toward the front hallway. Gearing himself up, he hobbled over to the edge of the wall and slowly peeked around the corner. He leaned out on the foot that wasn't throbbing in pain and could spot the steel front door rattling against the frame with a relentless, steady rhythm, as if a rabid beast were trying to break in. Joseph approached his front door. With each step, he could feel the ground vibrating beneath his feet, as if a nest of spider's eggs had burst open, crawling up his toes and past his calves. The pain in his foot subsided as adrenaline overtook him. He realized it wasn't just the ground shaking. A tremor ran through his entire body he was so terrified, like a child believing the haunted house maze was all real.

Joseph slammed his finger against the touch screen and turned on the patio light. The pounding stopped, and the house settled into a thick silence.

He peeked around the glass side of the door. Nobody was there. Not a single soul. Only the rows of tall lavender with the silhouette of trees in the distance. An explosion of noise burst around him, as if the front door had just been broken down. Joseph tapped the icon on the door. It lit up red, displaying the locked symbol. But Joseph couldn't sigh with relief. His heart was still racing.

"Ah, my little Rabbit has returned, come to say goodbye," an elderly voice slithered from behind Joseph. He flipped around so fast, he almost lost his balance. But he couldn't see anyone. The elderly voice erupted in a heavy cough, and Joseph charged down the hall into his living room. His eyes trailed through the dimly lit house, checking all the shadowy corners.

And yet, again, in the reflection of the large glass panels, all he could see was himself.

Joseph heard heavy breathing crawl down from the ceiling. He looked up to see the outlined edges of the built-in speakers, and realization dawned on him like sunlight after a heavy storm. The home device. Joseph couldn't bring himself to tell the device to stop playing whatever it was playing, though. Suddenly, he was thrilled; he hadn't felt so alive since his last days at the university. Joseph could feel that euphoria rush over him, as if he were a teenager again, drinking the rest of his mother's champagne from the bottle.

"Have a drink," a different voice said, younger but cold.

Joseph hung on to every word that dripped around him.

"My own medicine. So, this'll be quick then," the elderly voice said before grunting in discomfort. The kitchen island came into view, and Joseph stared at the home device. What was he hearing? Was it a podcast? Or maybe the device was playing a television show—thriller? Damn, technology never worked as advertised.

"No," the younger voice said.

"So, we have some time?" Another coughing fit. Joseph thought of the news story that Arturo had told him over brunch. What was the older man's name again? Joseph couldn't remember.

"Thank you. It's been out of my reach for so long." The older man gasped in a different tune this time. Joseph imagined him laughing. "I was worried they'd have come around again asking questions. I hadn't even thought of you."

Joseph stood there, frozen. Everything sounded so real. He felt like a fly on the wall, witnessing the moments before a great crime took place. He had two characters already, and that was enough to go off. Even some dialogue that could only breed more inspiration—which now simmered hot under Joseph's skin.

"No, you don't get that luxury, old man. I know what you did. I have no questions," the other voice said.

"I'm surprised you aren't angry that I replaced you," the older voice said. "Maybe you aren't as arrogant anymore. Doesn't mean you aren't an idiot for killing me. You won't get away with this, Rabbit."

A furious scream filled the space, and the pounding bass once again vibrated the walls. Joseph could hear the distinct *crack* of bones breaking, then a gurgled whimper. Someone was throwing punches at what sounded like a thick watermelon about to explode. Only then did Joseph want to tell the device to stop playing whatever this was. Before he could, silence as thick as mud dropped down on him.

Through the speakers, Joseph heard someone shuffling about. He took a few steps toward the home device, staring it down curiously. A loud blast erupted from the speakers, and Joseph squealed, dropping his body to the ground and covering his head. This was just a nightmare, Joseph knew this, and yet he couldn't help reacting as if an active shooter was in the neighborhood. He knew how the rest of this night would go anyway. He would be up all night, turning over in his mind what he'd just heard. He would pick up the bottle of bourbon and drink what was left as great inspiration brewed inside him like a wild thunderstorm.

Except, the nightmare evolved somehow. The sounds of that recording abruptly stopped playing with the sound of Joseph's front door unlocking. He stared curiously down the hall, hearing light footsteps paired with thin, steady breathing. A nervous feeling festered within his chest, and he felt even more on edge than he had the entire nightmare. He wanted to wake up but feared whatever he was hearing would be waiting for him. Like the old man's murderer that night.

Noah had just unlocked the front door. The sound of the mechanical lock felt like nails on a chalkboard. The hair on his arms stood up as he prepared for the worst. He crouched there, waiting for the author. Waiting to be found after being here for so long, unnoticed. Nothing happened, though, and he saw the freshly updated clone phone light up in his hand. A notification from the security app let him know that the front door had just been unexpectedly unlocked, with a time stamp on the message.

Noah bit his lip back as he processed this.

If he was getting the notification, then so was the author. Noah couldn't leave the notification unread. He took a deep breath. He knew what he needed to do. Still, he paused, checking to see if there was any activity in the house. He heard only the sound of himself breathing. He looked down at his shoes and slipped them off. The thin prison socks were all he had, but they dampened his footsteps as he made his way down the hall.

Noah's heartbeat was like a bass drum in his chest as he slipped through the dark shadows of the hallway and out to the living room. Outside he could see the trees under a white glow from the moon above. Where would that author's phone even be? Light snoring came from the other side of the house, past the dining table. He followed the soft sounds of sleep, turning to his left to see a bookshelf, and before it, a bed. With the windows as the backdrop, he spotted the tips of someone's feet in the bed at the end.

A bright light erupted in the room, and Noah froze, caught in the glow. It was a phone with the same app logo and notification that Noah had just seen in the foyer. The phone was reminding the author of the missed notification.

He was right to have worried.

With no choice, Noah drew in a steady, deep breath and reached over the bookshelf for the author's phone. He reached his fingers past the back of Joseph's head. The other person was lying on their stomach, facing away. He felt the smooth edges of the device and gripped them tightly as he pulled the phone up. It tugged back, and Noah felt the muscles in his neck strain. He used his other hand to unplug the device from its charging cable. He let it fall to the bed with a barely noticeable *pat*.

Joseph turned over, his breathing washing over Noah's forearm in short bursts as if he was having a terrible nightmare. Noah brought the phone to his chest, pressing it firmly against him as the screen illuminated once more. He backed up one step at a time until he was out in the hall. Then he sidestepped till he was back in the dining room.

Noah hunched over the phone like a savage animal guarding their food. The phone didn't have a passcode, much like the computer. Once unlocked, a notification popped up on the screen: Backup Restored. He dismissed it, and then another one immediately popped up, alerting him that another phone had been activated.

Noah smiled, satisfied that he'd taken the risk to check Joseph's phone.

Dismissing the notification, Noah then clicked into the security app, and a password screen popped up. For a moment, Noah felt stumped. Then, he pulled out the cloned phone with Joseph's latest backup and searched through the settings for passwords. *Voila.* It took less than a minute for Noah to be inside the author's security settings, where he quickly deactivated all notifications from the app. Next, he checked the history and deleted what he'd just added to it. He made sure to use the clone phone outside, after he'd locked the front door, making sure to leave no digital trace of himself.

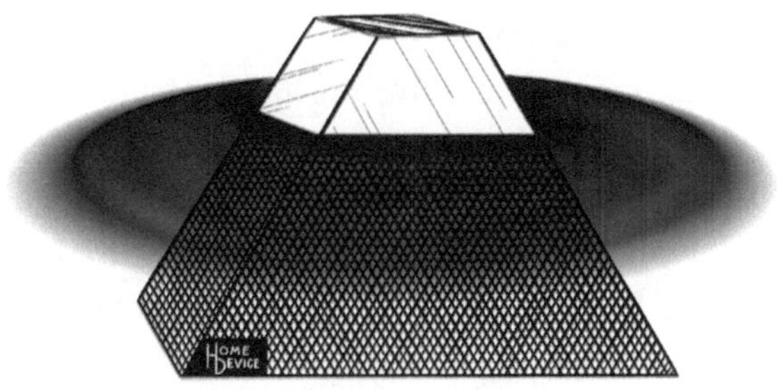

Joseph woke, feeling as if he'd been inside a sauna for too long, panting heavily, desperate for cool air. He licked his chapped lips and slipped a leg from beneath the comforter, allowing the built-up heat to escape. His body drenched in sweat from the nightmare. A soft snore purred from beside him, and he looked to see Arturo lying there. No more than a foot away and entirely oblivious to Joseph's panicked breathing. Joseph couldn't recall the old man's name in the nightmare, but it came to him now.

Benjamin Fisher.

He would have to search the name, find out whatever he could. What other choice did he have? What if he slipped right back into the nightmare? He couldn't bear being trapped inside of himself again. He already knew what the older man sounded like. He'd just never thought he'd ever identify the voices in the recording, as he'd always hoped it hadn't been *real*.

Joseph looked away from Arturo and toward his night-stand, where he saw his charging cord lying, lonely. Where was his phone? He rubbed the sweat from his brow and tried to recall the day, starting with brunch, and then things weren't as hazy. He'd gotten way too drunk with Arturo and maybe paired with the weed—

That same noise from the nightmare sliced through his thoughts: the noise of his front door. The smart device locked with a slight hum, a faint whiff of lavender in the air. He felt dizzy. He'd awoken from the nightmare. Right? Joseph questioned himself before quietly pushing the heavy duvet away. Choosing not to disturb Arturo, he silently moved into the hallway, writing a mental checklist. Find his phone, check the security app's log, and then panic if Arturo's security anxiety had been necessary after all.

In the dark hallway, Joseph picked up a natural pace, only to feel little relief standing in the silvery moonlight slanting through the windows. Joseph saw—just like in his night-mare, just like that night—that he was alone. He stepped forward, and a light cast over his eyes. His phone lay on the dining room table, bouncing the moonlight off his screen and onto the frames that hung on the walls. Joseph paused. He saw his reflection in the framed photos, much like how he'd described the older man seeing his own reflection in his novel, moments before his death. Joseph felt an itch grow in the back of his throat. He grabbed his phone and checked the security log. He smirked. No activity from the house and no missed notifications.

All of that talk from Arturo earlier was only stirring up Joseph's paranoia.

He shook his shoulders and tried to relax, taking a few deep breaths to clear his mind and assure himself that nobody had been inside his home. As he turned, the outline of the home device sat on his kitchen island. Joseph's stomach squirmed with doubt. For safe measure, he walked down the hall to check the front door, where nothing seemed out of the ordinary. He couldn't smell the lavender anymore, but he could smell *something*. He'd smelled it when he'd given Arturo the tour—a strawberry banana smell that didn't fit with his house. At first, Joseph had supposed that it was merely Arturo's vape, but that had tasted somewhat lemony.

Joseph looked to his office. The door was ajar enough that he could peek around. Following the scent inside, he paused; perhaps it was the nightmare, maybe it was just suspicion, but Joseph felt as if someone had been inside there. He shook his head, dismissing these thoughts as nothing more when his eyes landed on the keyboard. The wire was unplugged from the back of the board. He tried to remember, had he unplugged that? He hadn't been inside the office much lately. He wasn't writing. He only came in to store the packages that were still stacked haphazardly around the room.

His phone pinged in his hand, and he snapped, looking at the screen. An email from Emily: "re: Lunch tomorrow?"

Search his name, Joseph's thought demanded. He didn't want to, but he had no choice.

He left the office and strolled back toward the living room. Joseph clicked the browser on his smartphone and searched the web for Benjamin Fisher. Within milliseconds, over a million search results populated, and because he shared his location, the search engine narrowed his results locally.

The first few links were ads for new books on fishing, new cosmetic must-haves, and whatever else the search algorithms provided. Beneath those suggestions were news articles. Joseph scrolled through the headlines, all dated a few years back, but he didn't feel deterred. He found many articles quoting Fisher on Boy Scouts and a few news stories. Joseph didn't want to read about him, though. He needed to find a video of Benjamin Fisher speaking. He narrowed his search results to videos, and not too far down was a local Baxtor Springs news station YouTube account. Joseph clicked on the title, "Boy Scout Leader Benjamin Fisher Helps Reunite Rodriguez Family" and waited for it to load.

Joseph checked the volume to ensure it wasn't too loud and faced away from the bedroom and the hallway. He cupped the sides of his phone as the video automatically played. He squinted down, seeing a woman beneath a ball cap, holding a microphone with crowds of emergency services before her. She lightly jogged past an ambulance with the back doors open. A young, pale, dark-haired girl sat on a gurney with an oxygen mask around her face. The paramedic checking her took one look at the news reporter and aggressively crossed her arms, shouting at her to go away. The news reporter didn't stop, instead motioning for her camera person to keep up.

In the distance, Joseph saw another ambulance that looked exactly like the one they'd just passed. Except there was a young Boy Scout beside another very frail and pale girl on a gurney. The reporter saw someone standing in the distance, a tall man with a wide-brimmed sun hat over thick, black-rimmed sunglasses. He, too, wore a Boy Scout uniform. He turned to see the reporter getting closer and smiled.

"Troop Leader Fisher, please, what happened today?" She paused, holding the microphone out for him.

"I helped our sweet, sweet Joshua Rodriguez locate his missing sisters today. The media knows them as those 'missing hikers,' but locals know 'em as the Rodriguez Sisters. They went missing about ten days ago, and every day I've been out here with Joshua helping him locate them. We never gave up hope. Thank you, Lord, oh thank you. Oh, Joshua! Come here!" He called over to the young man in the Boy Scout uniform. He glanced at the news reporter, who smiled. This was her story. No other news outlet had arrived yet.

Joseph swallowed dryly, seeing Joshua for the first time. He was so young, and he looked so innocent. Joseph couldn't imagine him being the reason Tammy Miller and her twin boys had been buried yesterday.

"Joshua, how does it feel to have found your sisters?" she asked, lowering the microphone to him.

He sniffled, trying to collect himself. "I couldn't be more thankful for my troop leader, who hasn't stopped looking with me since the day they went missing."

"I'm going to nominate this fine young Boy Scout to receive his heroism badge," Benjamin said, beaming from ear to ear, and Joshua erupted with a smile that read pure joy. An officer came in between the reporter and threw his hands up, stopping the interview. Without missing a beat, the news reporter turned to her camera person, her microphone at the ready.

"I'm Debbie, and this is Channel 11 Local News. We'll have more updates for you on the condition of the sisters as the day goes on, but, it looks like things are taking a turn for the best." She smiled wide. Behind her Joshua hugged Benjamin Fisher tight around his waist, and Fisher ran his hands through the kid's hair. The police officer blocked them from the camera's view to start asking questions.

The clip dulled as a new video autogenerated, titled "Town Heroes Fisher and Rodriguez Awarded Heroism Medals." A countdown had started, and Joseph exited the video. He swiped the video back, just a few seconds, and played it again.

"Thank you, Lord, oh thank you," Fisher said in awe once more.

Joseph double-tapped the video back a few seconds and turned the volume up, his face inching closer to the device.

"Thank you," Fisher said, in awe, on-demand, again.

Joseph paused the video. Deep in his mind, he could hear the old man's voice from the nightmare, sounding so terrified. *Ah, thank you, it's been out of my reach for so long.* It was Fisher's voice in both digital recordings. One audio, the other visual, however both sent a shudder down Joseph's spine, reverberating through his limbs and fingers as if frostbite was setting in.

"Can't sleep?" Arturo asked as the lights in the house turned on, a blinding stark white that made Joseph jump, unintentionally throwing his phone in the process. The device fell with a hard clatter before landing at Arturo's feet. Arturo profusely apologized for startling him, while figuring out the touchpad to dim the lights overhead. Joseph took this small moment to collect himself, wiping the moist sweat off his forehead, forcing air to expand his lungs.

"H.D., dim the lights, please," Joseph said, looking over at the device. He turned around to see Arturo holding his phone out. The screen hadn't cracked, but the left edge was dented. From where Joseph stood, he could see both smart home and phone devices. He shuddered, knowing they were both listening right now. Had there been one in Fisher's bedroom that night? Joseph figured he'd never know. Arturo told him the place had been on the market for quite some time already. The police were already asking the public for help. Their investigation was dead. Joseph told himself these technical facts as if it meant the police would be shelving the homicide in the cold case files section.

"Scared of this device, too, now?" Arturo asked jokingly.

"No, no," Joseph said, taking the phone into his hand. He let his arm dangle at his side. A silence filled the room, and Joseph felt the need to apologize, as if he'd been caught sneaking around. "Sorry for jumping. Guess I'm not used to having people over here."

"Well, that sounds like a personal problem." Arturo pulled him in and kissed his lips softly. Joseph couldn't close his eyes, though. Instead, he stared at Arturo's eyelids; delicate lines flowed like contrails in the sky. When Arturo pulled away, he looked at Joseph curiously.

"I couldn't sleep, was thinking I'd make myself a night-cap," Joseph lied, holding up his phone. "Was looking up a recipe, but since you're up, maybe you can take over?"

Arturo smiled and looked about the kitchen. "You have oranges over there," he pointed. "I can make us some old fashions if you have some bitters and perhaps a sugar cube or two."

Joseph opened a cabinet, revealing a large pantry of soft drinks and snacks, baking supplies, and other staples. "I have all those here."

"Good," Arturo slipped around the kitchen with elegance, shooing Joseph to take a seat.

He gladly did because it offered him another moment to collect himself. He looked down at his phone and scrolled through apps mindlessly, focusing on his breath. His heartbeat faded from earshot—nothing to pulse loudly over the words of Benjamin Fisher that still quaked through his body.

"You doing okay?" Arturo asked, approaching him with the drinks.

Joseph put on his best smile and took a gulp.

"Yeah, Emily emailed me about having lunch tomorrow at Dana's," Joseph said, winded, staring at his emails.

"You look like you could use a vacation, to be honest." Arturo took a sip of his drink, and from behind the rim of his glass, Joseph made eye contact with him. Arturo's kind eyes made Joseph feel he wasn't being picked on. Joseph knew he was easy to read, so he played into this.

Joseph cooed at the idea. "I'd love to get away for a few days. I know of a lake house only a couple hours away that we can stay at, too. After lunch with Emily, let's shoot for it."

"I need to chat with Violet, but I think that could work . . . Perhaps." Arturo smirked.

"Perhaps."

They clinked glasses, and Joseph couldn't fight himself from downing the entire drink in one big gulp. The cool liquor bubbled down over the wildfire of anxiety howling in his chest.

Noah walked under the black awning that read "Dana's" in a white cursive font and checked the clone phone again. He had arrived exactly fifteen minutes early to the author's lunch date. The air was cooler inside than outside, where the sky was cloudy with a steady heat that danced dirty in the humidity. The ambiance wasn't quiet at Dana's, which was comforting to Noah after yesterday. Being stuck in that office, he'd felt like a contortionist waiting for the artist to tell him to change his pose.

The hostess smiled and led Noah to a nice table with a lovely view of Main Street Square's leaning brown gazebo, next to a table of older women playing a card game. A bottle of chardonnay sat next to the table in an ice bucket. Noah objected, instead pointing to a table in the far back near the kitchen.

The hostess gave him a funny look.

"Oh, please, save this table for other guests. I'm just eating alone today," Noah appealed politely.

His hands came together at his chest as if praying for a miracle. The pale-blue oxford button-down he wore had the sleeves rolled up, revealing his rabbit tattoo. The hostess saw it, smiled, and gestured for him to follow her. As he walked behind her, Noah couldn't help but feel out of place. This was by far the nicest restaurant he'd been to in the last—what? Fifteen years? Thankfully, across from the Extended Stay, the discount clothing store had a good selection. He'd purchased the oxford shirt, along with a pair of light jeans and cheap sneakers this morning. He'd also sprung for a pair of real socks that weren't prison-paper-thin. Noah at least looked the part. He was sure of that, even if he didn't understand what the hostess meant when she excitedly talked about the *plant-based culinary experience.*

"Waiter will be right with you," the hostess said as she made her way back to the front, where Noah could hear a group of people laughing, waiting to be seated.

No sign of Joseph yet.

Noah sat in a teal-colored chair that was, honestly, comfy. He looked around the restaurant with a bird's-eye view from the back of the room. His gaze drawn to the various gold-framed art pieces that hung on the cream-colored walls around the establishment. Many of the pieces reminded Noah of the artwork he'd spotted behind the dining room table inside Joseph's home. Oddly enough, this restaurant felt precisely like Joseph's taste. There was a sense of perfectionism in this restaurant, as if the owners were waiting for a Michelin Star to be awarded at any moment. The same level of obsession was reflected in Joseph's home. Even though the early hours had been dark, Noah had still been able to make out enough details from the décor to know that the author was wealthy. The pop culture references and small sculptures around the house seemed strategically placed to direct a visitor away from the austere, surgically pristine quality of the house. Was Joseph expecting some magazine to come take photos of the house? Noah chuckled to himself.

"…I switched shifts with you last weekend. You can switch sections with me." A voice close to Noah broke his playful reverie. He looked to his left, where just over a short wall was the waiters' station and the kitchen chase doors. Two waiters were crammed into the small space, still getting ready for the lunch rush, and their banter poured over the privacy glass that cast their shadows.

"I thought you liked Emily," a flat, husky voice replied.

"I do like Emily. I think she's great"—a feverish pause—"I don't wanna see who she is dining with today, okay?"

"Why is that?" The husky voice dropped to a low whisper. "Cause you fucked them?"

"Hush!" There was a beat before they spoke again, this time in a low whisper that made Noah arch his body closer to the blurred window listening.

"Y'all did fuck," the huskier voice gasped.

"He was my professor. It didn't even last long."

"Sounds hot," the husky voice said, more of an average volume.

"Colton, please. I'm being serious here. I don't want him to see me."

"Yeah, yeah, okay. I'll cover your sections so you can stay hidden away in the back like some peasant. But . . ." Colton stretched out that *but* with a tone that went an octave higher before finishing his sentence: "We're square for you covering me last week."

A broad woman bustled through the chase doors and interrupted the two waiters.

"Am I running an episode of *The View* here, or have either of you checked any of the newly seated lunch rush?" She had her hands on her hips and a stern look on her face as she stood before the waiters' area. She reminded Noah of the prison warden. Before leaning back in his seat, Noah peered forward to catch the name on her tag: Dana.

"I'm just putting some of these in for Sergio, but you're right. I'll go check on *my* section," Colton said dryly, walking out of the waiters' station. Noah watched Colton walk away, the ties of his apron tucked neatly below his love handles. Noah admired them. What must it be like to eat freely without prison portions.

Noah could see that Dana was right: Many more people were now seated inside, and the hostess was already making her way back to the entrance, where a couple stood waiting. The group of older women now left (leaving cash on the table), while another group of younger people took selfies as Colton approached them with water glasses. Another man was settled next to them, glancing condescendingly at the group. He leaned back, stretching, his face flushed red. Noah squinted to read the spine of a book closed on his table: *Rabbit's Revenge* sat atop a folder holding many papers. Perhaps the older man was a blogger. Noah imagined asking him, sarcastically, if he would like a direct quote from the author's muse.

Joseph Bailey hadn't arrived yet, but that didn't stop Noah from riding the euphoric wave of being a fly on the wall. Had the author felt the same when *Rabbit* had gotten his revenge?

"Afternoon, my name is Sergio. I'll be taking care of you today." Sergio stood opposite Noah with an unimposing build, short dark hair faded up high and buzzed low, a black dress shirt tucked beneath the apron fastened around his waist. He looked down as if he was caught off guard, and a warm smile spread across his face. Noah knew what Sergio's energetic eyes were saying—Noah was fresh meat—and quite frankly, so was Sergio.

"Thanks, *Sergio*," Noah's thin lips curled into a smile while he took note of the name tag—for good this time.

"Of course." Sergio smiled and held Noah's gaze. "Water for the table?"

"Yes, please. Is there Wi-Fi here?" Noah smiled back.

"Of course, the network is Dana's, password is Food—capital F." Sergio smirked like a child coming down Christmas morning to see the presents have doubled beneath the glittering tree. His gaze lingered just a second longer, his dark brown eyes seemingly ready to stir up trouble. "Be right out with that water."

Noah flicked the clone phone upright in his palm and unlocked it. Without wasting a second, he swiped the screen up and *tap-tapped*, connecting to the Wi-Fi, then *tap-tapped* Sergio's name into the search bar. If what he'd heard was true, he wanted to confirm it. A few contact cards came up—Sergio BarCute, Sergio Hernandez, Sergio Teacher's Aid—but no identifying pictures were attached to any of the contacts. Noah clicked on the first one and then clicked on the message icon. The messaging app popped over the search results, and Noah could see a simple exchange of small conversations that never led anywhere.

He went back to the search results and tapped on the next name on the list. He clicked over to messages once more, and this time, long exchanges of messages appeared. Some of the most recent messages from Sergio Hernandez were so long that they had ellipses at the end to expand the message. However, the messages were months old. He tapped the top of the screen over and over, where many messages continued to load.

"Here's your water. Anything to order?" Sergio said, setting the water down. He stood upright, grabbing a pad and pen from a pocket on the apron.

Noah glanced up. "Not just yet. I still need to look over the menu. I'm not too familiar with . . ." Noah paused, letting his finger swirl over the top of the menu. "Anything here."

"May I recommend . . ." Sergio leaned over the table. Noah caught a hint of Sergio's salty aroma. Dried sweat mixed with aftershave?

"Please," Noah said, pushing the menu over to him while his thumb continued to tap the top of the clone phone screen, obscuring Sergio's view.

Sergio went over the menu items using his index finger to point out what was best, the tip just lightly caressed the edge of Noah's thumb. Neither of them retreated from the touch.

"I'll try that, but please, don't be quick," Noah responded, the smile still projected on his face. "I have some work to piece together. It can be so . . ." Noah rolled his eyes and waved the clone phone before Sergio lazily. "Tedious is the word, I suppose."

"Of course, no rush then," Sergio said, taking the menu. He disappeared again. The only thing that lingered this time was Sergio's touch.

The messages wouldn't go back any further, and Noah realized he was at the start of the conversation. It started simple enough, a few "heys," the "how are yous," and eventually, "wanna meet up?" Noah scrolled farther down to see that Joseph had sent Sergio a video, only a few hours after they had agreed to meet. Beneath the video, he'd messaged:

"I love how eager you are when I fuck you."

Noah's eyebrows rose. His curiosity was piqued. He clicked on the image, and it took over the entire screen, with a play button hovering in the center. Sitting in the back of the restaurant had its privileges, and even though Noah hadn't suspected this being one of them, he double-checked that the volume was down before pressing play. As he watched, he could feel an erection growing against the inseam of his briefs.

The recording was shaky at first, but eventually, it focused undeniably on the waiter's face. Sergio Hernandez licked his lips as the camera panned down over his neck, showing his knees spread wide beneath his shoulders. His chest was bare, not built but not soft, either. Sergio wore a jockstrap with a thick band. Noah could see Sergio's fingers grasping the backs of his thighs. The camera panned down farther—whoever was filming was fully erect with enough girth to make Noah sit up straighter in his chair.

The camera panned back up to Sergio's face. He bit his lip, looking down hungrily at the cameraman's erect self. Sergio's biceps flexed as he pulled his legs farther back, his eyes glossy, and Noah thought of what Joseph had messaged after sending the video—*how eager you are*—when the camera panned over a messy room that came to the edge of a mirror. Joseph Bailey stood tall at the edge of the bed, where the curve of Sergio's butt hung just slightly over the edge.

The camera panned back down, and Noah had to adjust his bulge underneath the table. Joseph began to push his thick head inside Sergio, slow at first, but as every inch of Joseph plunged deeper, he picked up a steady pace. Sergio's mouth opened wide, and his head fell back. Noah imagined Sergio's elongated, honeyed moaning while watching his longer hair bounce in rhythm with the author's movement. Soon the recording shook too much, and Noah couldn't make out anything else.

"Here you are, Mr. Bailey," the hostess's voice trailed over.

"Please, call me Joseph," the author said, taking a seat only a few tables away with his back turned toward Noah. The author looked so different being wide awake as opposed to the sweaty sleeping mess he'd been last night.

Noah glanced over as carefree as possible, not wanting to look too eager in case Joseph spotted him. He didn't want to spook the author, but he couldn't help but grin as Joseph scrolled away on his phone waiting for this *Emily*. Noah couldn't help but wonder, did the author suspect the lack of home security notifications on his phone yet? Noah had gotten two already when the author was on his way.

No, it didn't seem so. Noah leaned back and sighed—all he had to do was sit back and watch his prey.

Sergio came back, blocking his view of the author. Noah didn't mind. He was delighted to see Sergio again—*eager*, even.

"Here's a dry martini that should pair well with your *tedious* work. I like your tattoo, by the way," Sergio said. He set down a thin martini glass where a single twist of lemon lay skewered on a silver cocktail stirrer, a small rabbit sat polished and pretty on the tip. "On the house." Sergio smiled innocently.

Noah gazed back up, happy he wasn't worried about money. He knew they shared a spark—even if only charged by lust. Sergio seemed like the kind of guy who would tell you whatever you wanted to know after a few drinks. There was plenty that Sergio could tell Noah about Joseph—more than the basic cropped, filtered, and polished social media lifestyle Joseph promoted. Even more than the text messages and videos altogether.

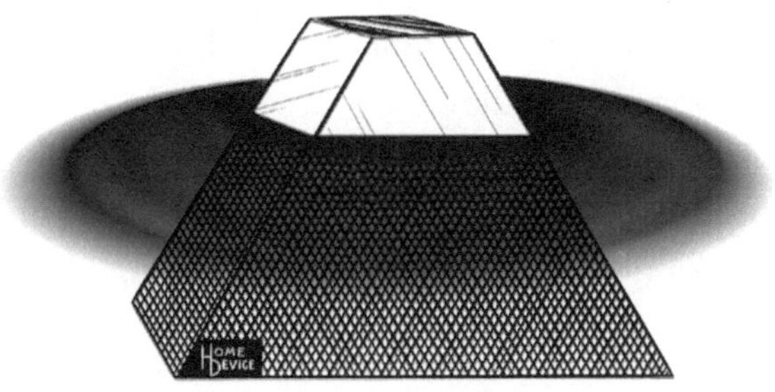

Joseph Bailey sat at a small table, the seat before him empty, but he'd expected that. Emily called right before he'd entered Dana's, letting him know she was running ten minutes late. Joseph didn't mind. He intended to order a drink, steady his nerves—but a waiter hadn't come yet. He stared down at his phone, hesitant to rely on the device to pass the time but too afraid to sit alone with his thoughts. Just like last night, when he'd been too scared to sleep in case he slipped back into the same nightmare. Too scared to check his phone with the image of Benjamin Fisher standing beside Joshua Rodriguez still on his browser. Both alive in the photo—both now dead, and under ludicrous circumstances.

Joseph looked away from his table and stretched his neck, casually looking around the room. The overall style and artwork were a great distraction from his thoughts. He made a note to eat here every chance he could. Money wasn't an issue anymore. His publishing investment was paying off now. Even though Joseph assumed Emily would cover the bill, if he had to pay for anything, he wouldn't mind. On the night of the reading, Saturday, *Rabbit's Revenge* had already climbed a few spots on the notable charts. As comforting as that was, even thinking about the book made his mind wander back to his nightmares, where Benjamin Fisher's final moments with the real-life killer echoed.

"Afternoon, Mr. Bailey."

Joseph turned to see a stout guy with a slight smile and a well-groomed beard. For the moment, Joseph couldn't tell if he seemed friendly or if the man was looking at him oddly.

"Yes, do I . . ." Joseph began, feeling uneasy. "Do I know you?"

The waiter looked down at him just long enough to spike Joseph's anxiety: *What if this is the killer?*

The waiter smirked as if he knew a secret. "I don't think we know each other. I'm Colton. Emily let us know you were coming through. This is her favorite table."

"Oh." Joseph leaned back in the plush turquoise chair.

"Anything to get you, Mr. Bailey?" Colton asked.

"Please, just call me Joseph," he replied in a thin voice, hating that the title reminded him of his teaching days. "Just a whiskey, neat."

"Be right up." Colton turned around and walked away. His figure was built but not intimidating enough that Joseph got a murderer vibe from him. Joseph sulked. Was it even possible to look at someone and just *know?*

Joseph blinked, his eyes glossed over with his thoughts, and when his focus came back, he realized he'd been staring directly at the ginger-haired man from the other night. He sat on the other side of the room, the overcast glow from the adjacent window bestowing him with a mysterious, even ominous, air.

Oh, stop being dramatic, you idiot, Joseph told himself. He'd locked eyes with plenty of men in his time—some he'd fucked, others he merely walked by—most of them had meant nothing at all.

But then Joseph spotted a copy of *Rabbit's Revenge* on the table. The man was writing something down in a folder. Joseph was transfixed by the pen, now wondering if this man was the killer. The pen stopped moving. Joseph looked up to see the man's eyes lock with his, staring directly back. Joseph couldn't break the eye contact, and a cold madness rocked his body.

"Here you go." Colton stepped between them, breaking the line of sight as he set down a thick crystal glass with tan liquor. "I'll swing back when Emily gets here."

"Do you know when she'll be?" Joseph asked, buying himself more coverage.

"She shouldn't be much longer."

When Colton turned around, Joseph took a large gulp. No matter how much whiskey he drank—which was a lot in the past couple of days—he'd never get used to that first sip. The way that smooth liquid burned over his tongue and down his throat, telling his nerves to calm down. For fuck's sake! Out of his peripheral vision, he thought the ginger-haired man was staring at him still. Joseph refused to look back, refused to let his anxiety run any further. He downed the glass and set it down softly.

"Ah, Emily. The usual?" Colton said, slipping by the table.

"Yes, please." Hearing Emily's calm voice gave Joseph relief.

"Me too, please," Joseph asked. *Just one more to help steady the nerves*, he thought to himself.

Colton flashed his smile, eyeing the empty glass in Joseph's hand and nodding before walking away. Joseph let out a steady breath as the liquor simmered. Emily took her seat, breaking his line of sight with the ginger-haired man once more.

She wore another jumpsuit today, but this time all black. Emily's arms were exposed with flittering rose gold jewelry that looked lovely under the lighting. Her obsidian hair tucked behind her ears revealed matching diamond earrings. She set her clutch down on the edge of the table. Joseph felt underdressed, but then again, who wouldn't in front of Emily? He smoothed the horizontally striped blue sweater down over his chinos and gave his best warm smile.

"I guess I wasn't running as late as I thought I was," she said, waving her phone in front of him and then tucking it inside her clutch. "Couldn't find this damn thing."

Joseph snickered, feeling mocked by their devices.

"Can't live without them," Joseph said, playing off his intrusive thoughts.

Colton approached the table to set a fizzy champagne glass down and another whiskey neat for Joseph. Commanding their attention, he informed them that Dana already had some plates coming out for them.

Emily took a sip, closing her eyes, allowing Joseph the opportunity to lean his weight left, just slightly, to see if the ginger-haired man was writing anything else down. He was, and then he raised his hand and waved. Joseph's eyes bulged. He did not want to wave back. That would be admitting too much, he feared. The man continued to wave, however. After a pause, Joseph realized the man was trying to wave down Colton.

Emily set her glass down, not far from Joseph's hands, which were wrapped tightly around his own crystal glass.

"What is that?" Joseph asked, eager to speak about anything that didn't have to do with him.

"A French 75. It's one of my favorite drinks," she said with a smirk. "Plus, we're celebrating." She raised her glass.

"Celebrating?" Joseph said, taken aback. "Why is that?"

She smirked and eyed his whiskey. He raised his glass and clinked his rim to hers.

"Don't you know? You *have* to know." Emily took a sip and set the glass down. Her attention was on her phone as her fingers swiped and tapped.

Joseph took another gulp without her seeing. She turned her phone around, revealing a few lists. Joseph spotted his novel on the *New York Times*, slotted at number three, the Amazon lists, slotted at number two, and then a few others. Joseph licked his lips, fighting down a single thought: *How many people had truly read the book so far? Was the killer one of them?*

"What's this one?" he blurted out and pointed, escaping his thoughts.

"It's from BookScan; they show the raw data of book sales."

"They just send this information out?"

"Well, to bookstore owners and publishers so we can know the trends—of authors, our market, you know. Even Hollywood looks at these lists for acquiring the rights to their next big inspiring picture. Just being on these lists gets your name in front of a lot of people."

"No one has come knocking on my door," Joseph leaned back and took a sip of his drink with Emily looking at him. *Tick. Tock.* Probably only a matter of time, though, the alcohol reminded him dreadfully.

Colton returned, setting down a few plates, the food delicately arranged over vividly designed dishware by the likes of Jonathan Adler. In the shuffle, Joseph saw the ginger-haired man avert his eyes. Joseph felt his emotions teetering dangerously close to paranoia. Impact imminent. He vowed right then not to look at that man for the rest of lunch.

Joseph took another gulp of his drink, and again Emily didn't notice. She was busy putting a little of everything on her plate as Colton explained the fall-themed dishes from Dana's upcoming menu. Joseph looked around the table, taking in the smells of the spices wafting up from the hot, steaming food. His mouth watered, and he followed Emily's suit. Mirroring her actions gave Joseph comfort.

"Thank you, Colton," she said after he'd delivered a fresh round of drinks. Focusing her energy back on Joseph, diving right back into business.

"I imagine by next week you'll have moved up. The number one book this week already has a dagger next to it. They won't last long."

"Dagger? Doesn't that mean foul play was involved? Bulk purchases or something, right?"

Emily paused with her hand over her mouth, enjoying her first few bites. "Indeed, I mean, if you look here"—she held up her phone, scrolling back to the top—"this conservative author took the top spot this week, but that'll fade by next week." She paused, thinking to herself before laughing. "If they make it that long. It's not uncommon for the *Times* to remove someone from their lists, or flat out refuse to put someone on, if they suspect something. They do a lot of investigating. After all, publishing can be a shady industry."

"Well, no dagger near my name," Joseph marveled, sitting up taller if only to help himself relax. He rolled his shoulders back, easing the tightly wound stress in his body.

"Of course." She swirled her fresh French 75 a little, making more bubbles fizz from the candied ginger at the bottom. "Now, I was hoping we could score another night for *Rabbit's Revenge.* Just you this time, though. You could read again or sign books?" Her voice went very thin as she raised her glass.

"*Or boooooth,*" she finished, stretching her words.

Joseph felt his smile; thoughts of more exposure under the recent revelations made him want to become a recluse. Emily was drinking to celebrate, while Joseph found himself drinking to make it through the conversation. His stomach pinched. After another sip, he cleared his throat.

"I appreciate the idea. I don't think right now is the best, though, you know?" Joseph watched Emily take a long sip. He could tell that she was stalling for time, building her argument. Last time he tried to talk his way out of an event with her, Joseph ended up being the closing guest.

"It's not happening tonight," Emily reassured, setting her drink down. "And trust me, there is a huge demand for your book. I called the publishing house to order more, and they said they're backordered. Can you believe it? Your book is already getting the numbers. This is the time to ride the wave and get it to number one." Emily's eyes glowed with excitement.

"Well, I'll be able to deliver the other half of that misplaced order by Thursday, I think," Joseph said, trying to veer the subject toward something he could deliver on.

"Oh, that'd be *great*. I was thinking of having the event this Friday, anyway."

"Perfect," Joseph said too quickly, the jaws of her bear trap business talk got him.

"If you drop them off by midday, that'll give you enough time to grab a bite before the reading." Emily winked. She wasn't about to back down.

"You are persistent," Joseph sneered, trying to reach for an excuse—anything but the truth—to get Emily to back down. Unable to find the words, he searched the room. The ginger-haired man rose behind Emily's head. His high stature—even from afar—was intimidating.

Joseph watched the man toss cash on the receipt booklet. The ginger-haired man marched toward Joseph now, fishing for something in his coat pocket. Joseph froze, the man only pulled out sunglasses and continued right on by. Joseph averted his eyes, catching a whiff of that same familiar strawberry-banana scent.

Joseph froze. That was the scent he'd smelled in the foyer last night. Unmistakably so. But how could that be? Joseph worried. He slinked down in his chair.

"Don't tell me you're going to become some J.D. Salinger type," Emily said, her head dramatically falling to one side.

"Would that be so bad?" Joseph asked, perfectly happy with the idea.

"Nobody has been killed for your work; don't become reclusive just because you're not used to the exposure. It's good—trust me." Emily extended her hand over to Joseph's, which offered little consolation.

Joseph bit the tip of his wet tongue back. Emily's sarcasm was as sharp as the unspoken truth.

"Plus, it'll help raise money for the victim's fund, like last time, which was so helpful to the families dealing with this tragedy and all those funeral costs that came with it." Emily leaned back, staring at the bottom of her champagne glass, looking smug. Joseph couldn't avoid this card when she played it last time, and this time he feared the same.

"I'll think about it," Joseph said, nodding along to play the part. "We're going to get away for a few days so I can recharge a bit."

"We?" Emily pounced.

"I met this guy at the reading the other night. Arturo de Leon," Joseph answered.

"Oh my gosh, we love Arturo. We should all get dinner." Emily's shoulders shook back and forth as if she were a cheetah stalking her prey. Joseph knew that Emily would use a dinner—with Dana and Arturo there for encouragement—to push him to do the event at the bookstore, since he wasn't saying yes this afternoon.

"Dessert, anyone?" Dana said as she sauntered up beside the table, holding a circular plate with something chocolate in the center.

"Hey, baby," Emily said, and they kissed.

"That looks delicious." Joseph marveled at the dessert.

Dana sat down at the table. "Why, thank you. These have all been contenders for the fall menu coming up, but I don't know—next week, I might decide on something completely different. Did I hear Arturo's name? He good?"

"Yes, he's fine, hun. They're just dating," Emily reassured her.

"It's still very new," Joseph said.

"Well, isn't that sweet?" Dana said. After a beat, she added, "Don't fuck that up now. I know how you gay boys like to jump from one to the next real quick."

Joseph laughed. "Oh, but I just reserved the U-Haul."

Dana slapped Joseph's forearm playfully. "Don't you be playing now; the library isn't open for reading today."

They laughed, and Dana provided enough distraction that Emily didn't even bring back up the book reading. When they got up to leave, Dana covered the bill, chopping it up to the dishes not even being on the menu. Joseph said goodbye to Emily as she reminded him to call her when he was back and confirm the delivery of the books later this week.

Joseph slipped outside under the gray clouds, slightly intoxicated but not enough for him to worry about driving. He'd stick to the back roads, thanks to Arturo's tour yesterday.

Emily talks a big game, Joseph thought, *just like my Mom did.*

His mother lived on in his memory, as radiant and confident as she'd always been. She'd thrived off making business deals, especially when they had financial rewards, much like Emily had been trying to secure today. Joseph wanted to believe in his mother back then—just as he tried to believe in Emily now—but life never worked out as planned. Even as a much older man, he couldn't help but feel like that kid beside his mother.

Joseph scoffed as he came to a stop at the posted sign. A heavy-duty truck that looked like it was used for construction passed through the intersection. The back of the truck was filled with various types of headstones covered in the fresh dust from the newly carved names.

The first name he could read was Elena.

He continued past the stop sign, distracted. His mind was occupied, busy deep diving into the old hard drives of his memory. His mother's name had been Elena—Elena Bailey. He could so easily recall the last time he'd seen her. His memory was good like that. The sun had loomed high over the downtown buildings, baking them in the dry heat while the people passed by . . .

Above A Whiskey Bar, Arturo paced back and forth around his bed, which was covered in freshly washed clothes and a small, neutral-colored weekender bag he would bring with him tonight. That was, if Violet looked confident enough running the place herself, with one or two extra people around to help. He didn't want her running the bar alone anymore, regardless of what she said. The bar no longer felt safe—what if Rafael had done something the other night? What if he got kicked out of Benny's and wandered down here again? Arturo paced, worrying about both the bar and what to pack. Were they going to eat somewhere fancy up there? Would they just be fucking the whole time? Or would they be out on the lake canoeing or sunbathing?

Beneath his feet, the door to the bar thumped open with a rowdy crowd entering. Arturo checked his watch—they were busier than normal. Regardless of how good this news was, it was just another thing to worry about. He looked at the clothes and decided to check things out downstairs. Maybe he'd cancel on Joseph if push came to shove.

Downstairs, Arturo slipped between a few tables filled with off-duty local law enforcement officers and other emergency services. Violet set drinks on a serving platter that Sergio Hernandez picked up, waltzing past Arturo with easy effort.

"*Jesus* it's so busy," Arturo said, approaching Violet.

She looked over at him and smiled. "You forgot, didn't you?"

"Forgot . . . what?" Arturo asked.

He glanced around for a sign but found nothing.

"Appreciation night for first responders to the massa—"

"That's right now?" Arturo asked, feeling caught off guard.

"Afternoon to evening event, it's been on the books for over a month now," Violet shook her head with pity.

"Need any help?" Arturo offered, still sounding lost.

Violet looked as if he'd offended her. "No, Arturo. I even hired an extra hand for the night. Sergio, from Dana's. He's already helping take orders and clear tables. Trust me, everything is good," she reassured him with a firm glare.

Arturo pouted; he'd have to worry about what to pack, after all.

"I'll just hover for a little bit then," he said, making his way behind the bar, where Violet's glare didn't leave him. To appease her, he didn't hover beside her, instead opting for the middle of the bar, where a chocolate malted rye stood among the other bottles. His *tia* always told him chocolate helped when tequila couldn't.

Arturo reached for a glass, pouring himself a little rye, noticing Police Chief Edmonds sitting at the very end of the bar by himself.

In front of Edmonds were two glasses filled with only melting ice cubes. The police chief stared at them, as if waiting for them to reveal some great truth. He frequented Arturo's bar, nightly, and Arturo had grown to know him very little besides some stories and drink preferences. The chief's wife, Sara, he knew better. She sometimes came in only to order a Shirley Temple and chat his ear off until her husband got off work. The police station was just across the town square, and the couple had met here after work every day since the bar had opened. If the chief were having a bad day, they would stay for a few drinks, but on a good day, they'd stay only for one, and Mrs. Edmonds would glow on those days, a prisoner to her husband's inconsistent sunshine.

Today, Edmonds was having a bad day—a bad couple of months, really. Arturo grabbed another glass for Edmonds and filled it with the chief's preferred whiskey, a neat Johnnie Walker Blue Label—when the drink was free. Arturo slid the glass down to him, and the chief's face lit up.

"Well, thank you, good man," he said, lifting the glass in acknowledgment.

Arturo sulked, hearing the slur in the chief's voice. He regretted handing him the glass and could only watch dreadfully as the chief tossed back the entire pour of whiskey in one gulp. As he set the glass down, Arturo noticed tears in the man's eyes, but he couldn't tell whether they were from the alcohol or something else. Arturo felt a glare behind him and turned, just briefly, to see Violet giving him a stern look.

"Where's the wife?" Arturo asked, calculating an estimated time of departure for the chief.

"She's coming"—he hiccupped again— "to get me. I'm just here letting them catch up alone." He paused and then realized Arturo didn't know who he meant. "Her sister is here for the week starting tonight, so they're out to get dinner and then pick me up here after."

"Well, that's nice." Arturo smiled, clearing the empty glasses and setting them off to the side. Sergio quickly removed them to the other end of the bar.

Arturo turned back to see the police chief wiping his eyes. Arturo gave the room a quick look. Most of the officers were occupied in their conversations, tossing back drinks themselves, laughing and joking as if the massacre had never happened.

"I wouldn't be good company anyway," the chief blurted, his weight sliding to the left where he extended an elbow. His cheek bunched together in rolls as he rested his head on his palm.

Arturo leaned into the chief, providing them some privacy.

"Looks like it's been a bad day, and it's not even late yet. What happened, Chief?

"I confirmed sixteen victims today. That's the most I've ever read aloud during all of this." He pointed around the room to everybody with their backs turned to him. "The survivors have come together with some petition to have me replaced. They think I'm not doing enough. Do they not understand this isn't my department? The FBI is investigating this shit; I'm just doing a courtesy. With the Boy Scouts' troop leader's death being investigated as a murder, the parents are worried about their own children being interviewed again by police for weeks on end. They think I'm losing my grip on things."

Arturo fell silent. What could he say that would possibly make a difference?

The chief continued: "Don't they remember the people who committed suicide just days after everything blew to holy high hell?" His eyes rolled up to the ceiling before he let out a rancid burp.

Arturo turned away to grab the chief a bottle of water, but he only eyed it with little interest and continued. "We were quick to assume Fisher had done the same, god forbid I make a mistake ever."

"What about the drugs found in his system, any leads there?" Arturo asked, thinking back on the news story.

"Oh, please—the OxyContin? That's too common of a drug nowadays." The chief took a swig. "I'm just waiting out my time now. They'll replace me with some young hotshot who can worry about everything and go home to his wife and argue with her about the stress of this mother fucking job." Edmond's eyes darted up, and he let out a growl that halted for another hiccup. "I've always done a thorough"—another hiccup—"job."

The door to the bar opened, and a small woman entered; as the door closed behind her, the smell of pine trees swept over the room before marrying with the cedar and black pepper aroma of the few real candles lit on various tables. Arturo hadn't noticed that Violet had changed all of them from the leather and oak smell earlier. Arturo could no longer deny how committed Violet was to this place, maintaining the atmosphere that Arturo strived for.

"Hon—ey," Edmonds said, very drunk now, and she gave a smile.

"How much do I owe ya, Artie?" Sara asked.

Arturo cringed slightly at hearing the nickname. He couldn't place why he hated it, but he couldn't bring himself to correct her. Sara Edmonds had enough to deal with.

"Don't worry about tonight. Have a good week with your sister and the old man here," Arturo said, waving his hand. Sara smiled, slapped a twenty down for tip, and got Edmonds to wrap his arm around her as they walked out, laughing about something Arturo couldn't hear, but he smiled anyway. He looked back down to see the twenty already swiped. Violet now hovered behind Arturo.

"Before you decided to cover his entire tab tonight, I was serving him." Violet put a hand on her hip. "Also, who runs a business giving away free drinks? You let the chief get drunk here—for free, I might add—way too often."

Arturo couldn't even respond. He was so stunned by her tone. Her eyes focused on him like a hawk, every point she made correct.

"You're right, you're right," he said, hands up defensively.

Violet turned back to Sergio, who came with more drink orders, and they got to work. Arturo sighed. It felt nice seeing them perform that familiar dance.

Arturo put the chief's bottle back in its cage and diverted to his phone, where he had no messages. Was Joseph thinking about him at all? Arturo wondered. He decided to take the initiative and text him.

**I should be getting out of the bar soon.
I think I can catch a car over.**

He watched the text send, blue bubble and all, and then looked up to catch Violet's gaze. He'd need to go pack. Arturo found himself looking over the crowded bar at the door to his upstairs apartment. Violet set some freshly made drinks on a serving platter that Sergio picked up and whisked away, dropping the drinks off at not just one table but various.

"You do have everything under control tonight." Arturo said.

"I know," Violet said, her teeth gleaming as her lips spread into a wide smile.

"I'm going to take the next couple of days off. Would that be good?"

"Uh, yeah—you're the boss," Violet cackled, making it painfully obvious.

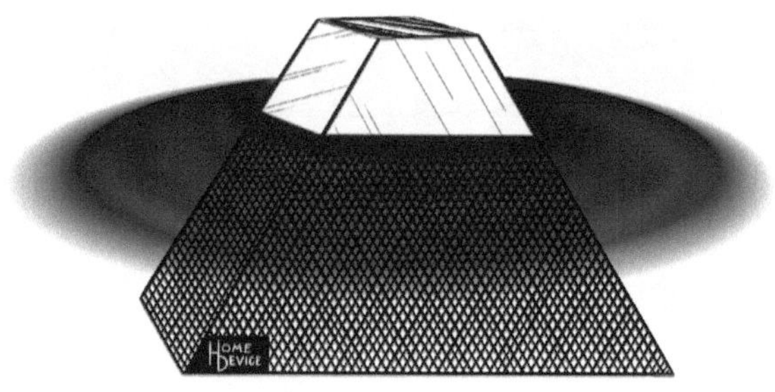

Just past his teenage reflection in the window, Joseph had watched people pass by on the busy downtown streets. They moved to a beat he couldn't decipher, though he longed to. The West Coast had been a complete mystery to him at that age. He'd been so intrigued by everything, even the colorful glimmering lights of the theatre just down the street. The windows at the hotel were framed in a gothic mullion walnut trim that seeped down into the checkered tiles along the floor. To his left was the lobby, where a group of people were checking in with their bags in hand, while behind him, he heard the light rap of his mother's fingernails.

He turned around, seeing the back of Elena Bailey, her delicately thin wrist resting on the shiny walnut counter at the lobby's bar. Her pinky coiled into her palm while her three fingers kept a rhythm of impatience. Before her, the bottles of liquor glimmered like the theatre marquee down the street. Every detail of the bar—including the lobby and the hotel itself—reminded Joseph of the wealthy university he'd toured earlier that day. His mother had had a meeting with the president who presided over all matters—including one dear to her. Joseph smiled. The tour had given him an appreciation for the design of this bar, where tips of spires trickled down to floret borders that framed the top of the bar. His mother sat beneath a stone rendering of the Green Man with leaves, his tongue dangled from his wide-open mouth, and bulging eyes stared down at Joseph.

"The green man means change is coming, good change. That's why we have so many of them on campus," the tour guide had explained earlier, enthusiastically.

"Joseph, *darling*, come take a seat," Elena instructed, tapping the barstool beside her twice. Her short brunette hair didn't move as she returned to her impatient woes. The bottom of her tan silk trousers swayed around the edges of her red-bottomed high heels. She straightened her posture as she unbuttoned her blouse just slightly to reveal a long, curved line of diamonds that hung between her cleavage. She turned back with piercing brown eyes to Joseph, who stood with hesitation before the stool.

"What are you waiting for?" Elena tucked her hair behind her ears, revealing slightly blushed cheeks and diamond earrings that matched the necklace.

"But it's a bar . . ."

Elevator doors blocking the view of the front desk opened, and a group of men came out. Each one taller than Joseph, and each of them dressed in business suits with bulky phones glued to their hands and faces. Joseph looked down at the suit and tie he'd worn for the campus tour. He felt as if he was playing dress-up.

His mother rolled her eyes, dramatically tilting her head.

"Yes, and I plan to order some things. Sit down already." Elena poked at him.

He sat, and already he could smell his mother's perfume, which was a calming lavender scent from some big designer Joseph couldn't recall. She looked back down at her clutch and pulled out a few credit cards as a swing traffic door opened off to the side of the elegant bar, thudding back and forth behind a bartender who stalked out. He was tall, towering over Joseph and his mother as he looked down at them. Joseph could smell a mix of peppery citrus wafting behind him.

"Miss, the bar is currently closed." His voice was as deep as his eyes were dark.

Elena peeked up from her open clutch, holding her room key card in her hands. "Damn," she said, looking hopeless. Something Elena never was. "I hope I can get a couple of bottles sent up to my room instead?" She leaned forward, extending her neck to let the diamond necklace rock just slightly ahead. "I'm staying in the penthouse. The last name on the room is Bailey. I'm Elena."

Joseph watched his mother extend her left hand with her thick diamond ring facing up, bouncing the sunlight behind them like a disco ball along the ceiling. His mother in action, her charm so straightforward, and Joseph was in awe of her.

"Adrian," he gently shook her hand with a courteous bow of the head. "What would you like sent up, Mrs. Bailey?"

"Please, Adrian, Elena is just fine." She leaned back on the stool and continued. "I just need champagne, something mid-priced will do." She didn't blink as she spoke, and Adrian nodded militantly. "And maybe, hm . . ." Her finger tapped her lower lip, indicating she was lost in thought.

"Perhaps some ginger ale for your son?" Adrian suggested.

"Perfect. Any food?" She turned to ask Joseph.

"Burger?" Joseph asked, unsure of the options.

"How'd you like it cooked?" Adrian didn't miss a beat.

"He'll have it medium rare and an extra side of fries, too. Lots of ketchup—Heinz, of course," Elena answered for Joseph.

"I'll have it sent up shortly, Elena." Adrian gave a smile before retracting to the back of the bar through the swing door. His mother closed her clutch and slipped off the seat, leaving only the scent of Adrian to linger. Joseph thought he smelled as good as he looked. Even at that young age, Joseph knew he wanted men to look at him like they did his mother. She was a modern-day enchantress back then.

"Joseph, *darling*," she called from behind him.

Joseph slipped off the stool and caught up to his mother, who stood holding her clutch out so the elevator doors wouldn't close. When Joseph got inside, his mother pressed the highest golden button, and the elevator closed, revealing a dim reflection of them both. Mother and son. Joseph noticed the diamond ring on her finger again. Just seeing it made his skin crawl.

"Today was thrilling, don't you think?" she asked, beaming down at him.

"Yes," Joseph crossed his arms.

"Oh, c'mon now—what is it?" She asked, dropping her weight to one hip.

"Why are you still wearing that?" Joseph asked accusingly.

"This?" she raised the diamond ring and marveled with a heavy sigh. "Because it feels nice. Because I feel naked without it. Because he didn't buy it for me—it's your grandmother's ring—so I don't even associate it with him."

"Well, I do—and I don't like it."

"Clearly," Elena chuckled back to her son.

The elevator doors opened to the penthouse, with a study in modern lines and minimalistic designs, pops of color. Fresh flowers met them in the foyer. The view was the sun, high in the sky with the ocean resting behind the downtown skyline. His mother set down her clutch on the entry table, then plopped down on the oversized couch in the living room.

"I get that all of this is new for you, but I need you to trust me. You might not understand it, but I'm not ready to take the ring off yet. That's my own thing. You don't need to worry about that. What you should worry about is what you're going to need for your upcoming summer courses. They start in two weeks!" his mother exclaimed, throwing her arms up with excitement.

Joseph had heard her words, rolled them over inside his head once or twice, but they still didn't compute. His mother was right. Only a week ago, she'd taken him away from the East Coast, away from his father—and Joseph didn't want to ever return. The ring, though, made him feel as if this was all one big joke.

"What?" he asked, taking a few steps forward.

"You heard me, and you heard me correct." Elena smiled, her shoulders relaxing away from the delicate tips of her hair. "Two weeks to find a condominium to live in, and then the summer to get you enrolled in a new high school for the upcoming fall. In the meantime, I think the summer classes will be incredible for you." Her face inched forward with each word. She was excited for Joseph. He could see that glint in his mother's eye.

"What classes did you enroll me in?" he asked, "Don't I need to take the SATs and apply?"

His mother's gaze dropped. "No, you don't need to do any of that."

"Is this because you're donating a building to the campus?" Joseph poked.

"Well,"—she paused—"no, these courses are open to the public, but I'm sure when you take your SATs and submit your application come senior year, you'll be at the top of their list. Did you like the tour? The semester is almost over, so don't think it's this dead around here all the time. I had my best years at that university, trust me."

"The campus was cool. It was big. They gave me a long tour. Showed me where the building is going to be built. Did you decide on the name?"

"The Bailey School of Business, of course."

"Sounds so official."

"That's because it is, *darling*," she said, extending her hands to grab Joseph's before pulling him to sit across from her. "I don't want you to worry about your father or me during this divorce. I'm making sure that he walks away with a nice chunk of money. He can go start a new life. " She laughed. "And it's for the best. Once that estate sells, everything will find balance, you'll make new friends out here, and you can always travel to see your dad on weekends. Even vacations, I assume. When he gets established, you know."

"I don't care to."

"Well, let's give it some time and space. Things are still very fresh. But trust me, when I say—" The elevator doors opened, and squeaky rubber shoes made their way across the granite floors, halting his mother mid-sentence. "Things are looking up for us."

She winked and then popped up to her feet and strode over to the dining room table, where Adrian had come in, setting down the bottles and mixers, a glass of limes, too. Silver tins over white plates, and Joseph was salivating. Adrian held the black checkbook, which his mother signed. She declined to have him open the bottle of champagne on his way out. She'd enjoy popping it open herself. Joseph couldn't believe his eyes when his mother filled both glasses with the bubbly champagne. Her shoulders shimmied as she made her way over to her son. She reached her hand out, and Joseph took the glass from her, watching the trails of bubbles appear like magic inside.

"I want to celebrate, just a little. Don't get used to this."

"Celebrate, what?"

"You, all of this is for you and your future. Once you get published with that wonderfully creative head of yours, you'll meet the love of your life, and I'll plan the best wedding ever for you both. I can already see it." She drew in a deep breath and paused. "You just gotta trust me."

"Okay, I trust you. But I don't want to get married. I'm a forever-bachelor."

"You're thirteen, *darling*," his mother said, laughing.

They talked about the summer courses, and where his mother wanted to live, and how great their life was going to be on the West Coast. Before they had poured their second glass, his mother got a phone call from some university friends who wanted to take her out to celebrate the building and her moving back out west—officially. Joseph felt bubbly and didn't mind being left alone for the rest of the evening. His mother let him finish the rest of the champagne, allowed him to order room service and even rent a movie if he was asleep by the time she got back. Which, she promised, wouldn't be *too* late.

Now, the older Joseph knew how the rest of her night would go and who would be flying in the next day to quickly ship him off to boarding school. He let his mind release the memories as he got closer to home. He longed for a Xanax and a nap. As he pulled up to his driveway, he received a text message from Arturo, saying he was excited to see Joseph later. Joseph let out a long groan. In the oceans of grief, he'd forgotten. While thinking about what to reply, he noticed a cruiser in his driveway, and as he scanned his property, he saw someone standing in his foyer.

Joseph's stomach twisted; he could recognize that ginger hair from a mile away.

Thoughts of running away for a few days ignited Arturo in a way he hadn't felt in a long time. Joseph was intoxicating, and Arturo enjoyed this newfound fix. Arturo tossed his phone on the bed while a rideshare app found him a driver to take him to Joseph's estate. Baxtor Springs only had one consistent driver named Johnson. He was deaf and took care of his parents, who were survivors of the massacre. People tipped him well, too.

Arturo packed a few outfits along with his copy of *Rabbit's Revenge* to read just in case there was any downtime. *To be cute,* Arturo playfully imagined he'd say to Joseph with a wink. At the very last second, he added a few jars of his favorite dried flower and some new rolling papers. *For the downtime,* Arturo assured himself.

His phone buzzed, letting him know that Johnson would be arriving in a few minutes. On his way out, Arturo waved to Violet and Sergio. On Main Street, Arturo felt a hint of summer still lingering in the air. Besides a few beat-up cars sitting outside of Benny's down the way and some squad cars parked opposite, the street was empty. Arturo heard footsteps to his left, and when he turned, he saw Officer Goldstein approaching, still in uniform.

"Looking for the chief?" Arturo asked relatively flat. Seeing Goldstein again only ignited how annoyed Arturo had been the other night with Rafael.

"Is he still there?" Goldstein asked, checking his watch with wide eyes.

"No, Edmonds left a bit ago." Arturo tossed a thumb behind him. "Is it true that they're petitioning to have him fired?"

Goldstein took a step back, his mouth a jar. "How—he knows?"

"We're a small town in a big county, Goldstein. Everyone talks." Arturo shook his head, crossing his arms around the weekender bag as a cold breeze—a reminder that fall was near—slipped by them. "Who are they even going to replace him with?"

"We don't know yet." Goldstein looked around, bemused. "The town is furious, though."

"And Chief Edmonds is to blame?"

"Someone has to be, I guess. Edmonds has been the chief of police for so long that people assume he's losing touch. People come together when they want change nowadays, and after seeing good little Sara carrying Edmonds out of your bar almost every night, I can't blame them. He shows up only to read those names and then slinks off to drink, then back home just to rinse and repeat." Goldstein let out a sigh, and the air grew thick between them with the weight of the truth. Even Violet had called him out for it just earlier tonight.

In the brief pause, Arturo watched as Goldstein's eyes drifted from his feet to his chest, his arms still wrapped around the bags.

"Who would replace him? With all the police who died in that massacre, I know the station is stretched thin."

"Detective Stuart Kline is the most senior, but he's never had any experience as a lieutenant, captain, or even a commander. I assume those positions will be temporarily filled by some officers wanting overtime in the surrounding counties, like Pittsburgh, maybe even Harrisburg, if they're desperate." Officer Goldstein paused, realizing he'd gotten a little lost in police politics. "Are you going somewhere?"

"Just away for a few days, with a-a friend." Arturo hesitated. "I didn't appreciate the other night."

"Who said I appreciated it? I did my duty, and I got him home safe," Goldstein said, his voice rising slightly.

Arturo felt heat rising in his chest. "Everyone is on edge here, and if he's unhinged, then we're all in danger. People are afraid there will be another massacre, only involving more bullets next time."

"Violet called me. I showed up and helped him leave," Goldstein said, as if to placate Arturo, but he stood tall, his neck lifted from his chest. "I'm trying my best here, Arturo."

"Unlike the chief?"

Arturo could see that his words wounded Goldstein, who was no small man by any means. The officer took a few steps back, blowing out a long breath to break up the stagnant air between them.

"I was coming to talk to you tonight." Arturo was listening. "I wanted to ask if you were attending Fisher's funeral. We could go together."

Surprised, Arturo paused. "What?"

"Since it's being investigated as a homicide, the church is moving forward with providing him a proper burial. A lot of people are going to be there on Thursday. I know how close Fisher was to you after your mother passed. He was there for me when my grandfather passed away. I figured you'd want to pay your respects, and you don't have to go alone."

Goldstein's words ripped through Arturo, and a memory floated to the forefront of his mind. A few hours after his mother had been lowered beneath the weeping willow. His *tía* had insisted they hold a wake with too many family members packed inside the house. Family members he'd both never heard of and never heard from, and they'd brought their friends. Except Arturo wasn't with any of them. He was with Fisher. They stood in the upstairs main bathroom, not worried about Arturo's father and *tía* coming up to check on him. They were occupied down there with music that only grew louder as the hours passed. Fisher told Arturo they'd be mourning, or whatever, till sunrise.

Fisher exhaled into a toilet paper roll filled with crumpled tissues.

They passed this back and forth, each time taking a hit and blowing it out of the window. The window, an odd design, could be raised or lowered. Fisher had it lowered so that the smoke wouldn't bunch up at the top.

Arturo's forehead relaxed while a slight hunger set in for the first time since discovering his mother two days before.

"I can't believe your mother would do such a thing to you, Artie. What a coward—a big ol' selfish coward," Fisher spoke low. Arturo listened to his every word, allowing Fisher to warp his thoughts like cancer spreading. "To abandon her child like that, *tsk-tsk-tsk-tsk-tsk-tsk-tsk-tsk*."

"I just wanted to make sure you knew," Goldstein said, ripping Arturo away from the memories.

"What?" Arturo blinked, letting the memories run down the gutter along Main Street.

"The funeral, Thursday?" Goldstein asked, a look of concern on his face.

Arturo shook his head. "No, I didn't know there was a funeral scheduled."

Arturo caught a flicker in Goldstein's eyes as headlights pulled up. Time was up, and Arturo couldn't have been happier. He turned to see a silver Camry pull up beside him, and Johnson waved at him. Arturo returned the gesture before turning back to Goldstein, whose eyes squinted now from the headlights beaming directly on him.

"Thanks for letting me know," Arturo said.

"If you get back in time, you're more than welcome to join me. I'll be there," Goldstein said as Arturo opened the car door.

"Yeah, I'll see about it. I haven't thought about how long I'll be gone for," Arturo replied and slipped into the car with a strong pull and a loud *thump* as he closed the door.

Johnson whisked him away from Main Street and back to Joseph's. Arturo tried to distract himself by concentrating on his driver's heavy-bass tunes, but these childhood memories were too powerful, too visceral. He had forgotten much of the time around his mother's suicide. Goldstein hadn't, though. All he could see was that door to the bathroom closed and his eyes staring at the window as Fisher passed him the joint. He leaned forward to blow the smoke through the toilet paper roll contraption. He dreamed of disappearing into the air like the smoke he exhaled from his lungs. He felt like an abandoned bastard child, and this feeling was fact.

According to Fisher.

Arturo couldn't wait to get away and back into Joseph's house. Away from the bar, the chief, and any more funeral talk for that matter.

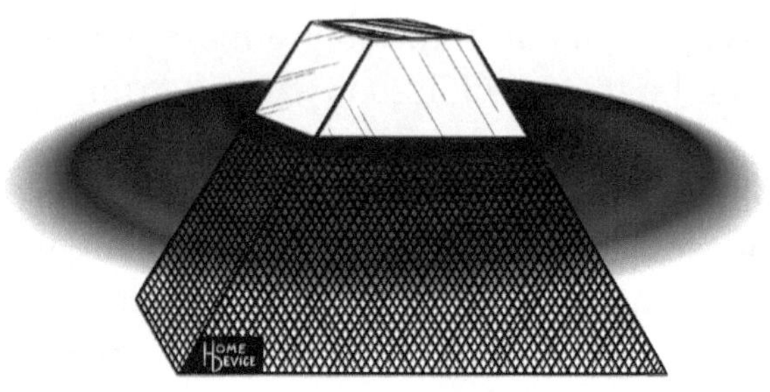

Joseph shifted the car up a gear and sped along the small pebbles that made up his driveway. They clattered against the sides and underbelly of the car like a violent hailstorm. Joseph didn't care if the paint got dinged. He'd had a feeling that the man with ginger hair had been following him, and now Joseph had caught him snooping around his house, only confirming his suspicions. Joseph watched as the man turned and lowered his black sunglasses. Joseph stared directly back at him. The ginger-haired man walked toward the driveway and out of the house. Joseph's gaze shot forward to see he was approaching the garage door too fast. He slammed on the breaks, downshifting as quick as possible, and the car drifted to the left, stirring up a storm of rocks and dust in its wake.

The car rumbled angrily when Joseph cut the engine off frantically. He looked around, tasting the whiskey on his breath from lunch, feeling the rush of adrenaline coursing through his system.

Before the dust had settled, Joseph threw his door open, nearly hitting the nondescript cruiser parked next to him. The car was parked as if positioned for a quick getaway. Joseph came around the back of the Porsche, and his foot tripped along a deep gash his tires had left in the driveway. He caught himself on the backend of the Porsche and found his footing just as the man with ginger hair approached.

"Who are you?" Joseph asked, jutting his ear out.

"Mr. Bailey?" He sniffed the air, pursed thin lips. "I sure hope you haven't been drinking and operating that fine vehicle."

Clouds drifted behind in shades of bright pink and dark blues as Joseph sized this unexpected visitor up.

"I'm a detective with the department; the name's Stuart Kline." He stuck his hand out, but Joseph only stared at his own reflection in those black sunglasses. The tail ends of Stuart's shirt hung out past his ample belly. He was a broad man, towering over Joseph, who stood tall himself. The buttons on his dress shirt gleamed with a slight pop of pearl, his tie stuck to the side from his enormous chest, loosely tied at the top. He held his hands behind his back.

"I don't mean to cause any alarm, Mr. Bailey, but—"

"But what? I saw you at the reading, then I saw you at lunch, and now you're at my residence completely uninvited. You even stepped inside my house."

"The door had—" Kline looked around a little dismayed. "Well, it just opened as I heard you driving up."

"So that's an invitation to let yourself in, Detective?" Joseph sneered. Anger rippled under his skin. He felt violated. "Why have you been stalking me?"

"I assure you; I wasn't following you the night of the book reading. But today, when I saw you, I—"

"You what?" Joseph demanded, taking a step forward.

"I just want to ask you a few questions, is all. Maybe we can chat inside?" He revealed his hands now, which held a copy of *Rabbit's Revenge*, the folder he'd had at Dana's earlier tucked inside. Joseph's throat tightened, and he took a step back.

Joseph knew the detective had already smelled the liquor and witnessed him driving. He drew in a sharp breath, though only one nostril was working.

"If I say fuck off, you gonna give me a DUI?"

"Please, Mr. Bailey." Stuart turned, motioning to the front door. "I didn't pull you over, and I'm not even on duty right now. It's just a few questions, putting things together."

Joseph's neck twitched. *Putting. Things. Together.* The words repeated in his mind like Benjamin Fisher's had in his nightmare. Joseph nodded his head jarringly as if he were going through withdrawals. He stared at Stuart, who politely smiled and gestured for them to go inside. Joseph didn't move, though. He'd seen enough true crime documentaries during his lonely time spent in this house. He knew he shouldn't be so trusting, so he continued to challenge.

"You have a badge?" Joseph asked.

Stuart willfully produced a leather-bound rectangle that had his image and other fine print. He flashed him the badge on his hip with a holstered weapon beside it. He looked like someone off any generic crime television show. Joseph was unsure what a real detective's badge in Baxtor Springs County would even look like. He let out a soft chuckle of defeat. Stuart turned and led the way into his house as if Joseph had no choice in the matter.

Joseph trailed behind, smelling Stuart puff a strawberry-banana flavored vape pen. Joseph gnawed on the inside of his cheek as he watched Stuart stroll inside, past the door frame, as if he'd been here before. Joseph choked—not *if*. He swallowed hard, and his fingers ran over his sweating palms.

It felt as if the rollercoaster ride had just begun, and he was still fidgeting with the seatbelt. *Tick. Tock.* The detective hadn't come with a partner, and in the emptiness of the surrounding area, Joseph had an idea why. No witnesses around to intervene.

"Smoke that often, Detective?" Joseph asked.

"Trying to cut back on cigarettes," he said, stepping inside and looking toward the office to his left.

"Oh, perfect, do you mind if I charge my phone?" Stuart asked, shaking his phone in the air. He didn't turn to look for Joseph's approval. Instead, Stuart strolled into the office and grabbed the cord off the desk generally used for the wireless keyboard. Stuart must've charged his phone that night he was here; how else would he know where to find it?

Joseph watched Stuart leave the office, peeking as he walked by to see that his phone was on the desk. A small, yellow charging-battery icon popped up on the phone. Joseph argued with his anxiety: Stuart was telling the truth, the phone's batter was low. But Joseph's mind retaliated with a million reasons why none of this felt right. Feeling overwhelmed and powerless, he slunk behind the detective in silence.

"Gorgeous house," Stuart said, continuing down the hall, past the guest bathroom and into the living room. Joseph was still in the hallway, where Stuart's footsteps echoed around him like a cave of wild bats disturbed. He felt his face become flushed, and his hands were trembling. In the nightmare, he'd heard the door open and the footsteps. But he wasn't dreaming now.

Waltzing to the large windows, Stuart paused with his hands behind his back, resting to admire the views of the forest that the house provided. Joseph walked to the kitchen, his hands fidgeting too much, but there was still some Hibiki left. He poured himself four—no, five—fingers and took a gulp. Stuart was aware of Joseph's activities but didn't seem to care.

The silence between them was dry enough for a wildfire to sweep through.

"Detective, what are you doing here?"

Stuart turned around, crossed to the kitchen, and pulled out a stool. Sitting down at the island, without a word, he set both a copy of *Rabbit's Revenge* and a thick Manila folder down. He adjusted the edges of both items, so they sat perfectly parallel to each other. The home device just inches away. The reflective top appeared to stare up at them—listening, recording.

A frigid shiver, like lighting, shot up Joseph's spine as he saw a name printed on the folder that read, "Benjamin C. Fisher."

Joseph pressed his back against the wall. Stuart's back slightly turned from him as he opened his copy of the novel. Stuart had highlighted paragraphs, a sentence here and there, in bright orange, perfectly parallel lines. Stuart was neat, maybe even obsessive. Joseph took another gulp. When he looked back, Stuart faced him, patiently waiting.

"I wanted to ask you a few questions about your book, a few details that I've highlighted here really caught my eye." Stuart paused as if waiting for Joseph to acknowledge his words.

"I didn't know Benjamin Fisher," Joseph stammered out.

"Ah," Stuart smiled. "Clearly, you know who my questions are about though." Stuart stared at Joseph for what felt like centuries. Joseph retreated into another gulp. The bitter taste crept down his throat, burning, as he tried to squabble together a defense.

"His death was breaking news. His name is also printed on your folder," Joseph croaked. He would have pointed but feared the detective would see how unsteadily he was holding the whiskey.

Stuart nodded, then opened the file. Joseph gasped, horrified, whiskey splashing over his fingers and dripping onto the floor. Inside the folder were photos. The mangled remains of a body with a shotgun erect between their legs, sitting in a chair. Beside this was a photo of Benjamin Fisher alive and well, as if these were his before and after shots.

"I don't mean to shock you, but there are some details that line up a little too well . . ." Stuart extended a finger to the page, scanning down until he paused with a triumphant *oh*. He read aloud an orange highlighted section.

> "Directly across from him in the pitch dark, the older man heard a steady exhale, causing him to pause. He peeked over to the open window he always kept shut to keep night critters from getting under the house. He could make out the eyes before him. He looked back to the window and noticed, with clearer vision, that they were wide open. Someone sitting there, in the darkness . . ."

Stuart looked back to Joseph, making sure he was following along.

"Now, in this photo here," Stuart said, but Joseph's eyes were closed; he could hear papers ruffling. "Oh please, Mr. Bailey, look at this photo. Pretend it's your book. Do you see the open window there?"

Joseph looked at the photo, which displayed a wide dresser beneath the sill of an open window. Vases filled with mossy green water, the stems of flowers that had wilted, the dried-up petals scattered over the dresser. In the corner of the photo, Joseph saw something that made him pause. He drew in a hollow breath as he stretched his neck to look closer at the edge of the home device in Fisher's house.

"It's just a window, Mr. Bailey. A simple yes would suffice," Stuart said, pulling the photo away. Next, he revealed a photo shot from behind where Fisher sat. The damage from the shotgun had split the older man's head in half, horizontally, and the bottom half, bone fragments and teeth, looked more like the rotten remains of thickly sliced turkey speckled with larvae. Above this, on the ceiling, was the other half of his head, strands dangled down like leftover balloons after a raging party.

"Do you see it?" Stuart said, turning his face up.

Joseph could see the dresser better in this photo, and he could make out the short home device sitting on the edge, with its little black wire running down to connect with the outlet on the wall. His eyes drifted up from the picture to his home device, which sat just inches away.

"He's sitting in a chair directly across from his bed, from the open window." Stuart pointed from the photo to the highlighted areas in the book. Back and forth, maddeningly seeking the truth. "Then you go on to say,

> . . . The moonlight highlighted the polished silver frames that hung on display around his bed, filled with photos and newspaper clippings. The older man had surrounded himself with reminders of happier times . . .

"Now, I know this one is gruesome, but please take a look, Mr. Bailey." Stuart asked with a hint of pleasure in his voice as he brought back the first photo, the one shot head-on. His fat finger pointed behind Fisher's corpse to the walls, where, coincidentally enough, silver framed items hung. Joseph could make out, in crisp newspaper font, the headlines about

Fisher having saved the hikers. Other headlines declared him a great member of the community with the Boy Scouts. It was all real. Overwhelmingly real.

Stuart raised his hand only to press the tip of his index finger harder down on the book, as if the great truth was right there, printed on the page before him for everyone to see. *Though*, Joseph pondered, *was it?*

"What is it you're trying to say?" Joseph placed his back against the kitchen counter, his shoulders against the cabinetry.

"I'm just following a hunch. Do you also see the pile of crushed OxyContin on the counter? Just like you wrote in your book, not all the pills had been fully ground up. You can see the other half of a tablet right there. The book is doing well for you, isn't it? Life must be good, if not at least better than it was on the West Coast." Stuart's smile made Joseph's skin crawl.

Joseph's body floated away from the wall, his mouth dry. "You've been checking up on me?"

"Of course. I'm a detective," Stuart said condescendingly, shaking his head, the same way his rat father would speak to him. Joseph's blood boiled.

"What is it you want?" Joseph looked down, away from Stuart's intense gaze.

"So, am I right?" Stuart said, honestly shocked. He laughed aloud and slapped his knee once, twice, three times. Each time a shudder ran through Joseph, and he wanted this man to disappear. "The book and the murder are connected. I just knew it, too many." He composed himself upright. "*Coincidences.*"

"What do you want?" Joseph spat through gritted teeth. He feared the worst. Thoughts of being blackmailed. An unbearable overweight murderer to control his life. He hadn't felt this powerless since boarding school. Stuart could kill him and then write up the police report, putting all the blame on Joseph. How innocent he'd make himself seem after answering a 9-1-1 from the gunshots fired.

Stuart is here to tie up a loose end, Joseph told himself. No one was supposed to know who murdered Benjamin Fisher. Only the killer would be able to put these things together. Joseph tried to breathe deeply, his chest puffing.

"Somehow, I don't think you killed him, though. You don't look . . . Well, *you know.*" Stuart paused, staring at Joseph with blatant judgment.

Joseph's chest heaved, his breath hot as fire. He felt as if he'd just run a few laps at the boarding school.

"Now, tell me what you—" Stuart started to speak, but Joseph didn't care what the detective was going to say. Joseph had already made up his mind. At lunch, he'd worried about teetering on the edge of paranoia. One that he might not have been able to recover from, but this was different—just like the detective had said, there were too many *coincidences.* Joseph didn't bother to recount them. He merely snapped.

With the quarter-full glass of whiskey in his hand, he lunged at the detective with the force of a locomotive. The adrenaline fueled him forward with a might Joseph hadn't felt in years, one he hadn't allowed himself to feel since his mother's one-hit homicide. Stuart shrieked as they both fell back. Whiskey splashed in Stuart's face, and he closed his eyes as the back of the stool slammed against the ground. Stuart threw his hands up defensively before Joseph slammed the base of the glass into Stuart's jaw. He howled in pain, struggling to see, wiping the whiskey from his eyes when he saw Joseph crack the glass against the ground. The base was still intact, but the top ring shattered into a mixture of juts and jagged edges.

Joseph clutched the shattered remains and slashed them back and forth against Stuart's face. Each time, the detective screamed louder in agony. Shards of the glass broke off and sparkled like diamonds, except the ones soaked in Stuart's fresh blood, which collected like tiny rubies. Blood splattered out along the kitchen island and floor as Joseph continued relentlessly.

Stuart threw his hands out. They pressed hard into Joseph's chest, but not hard enough to knock him off balance. Joseph saddled the detective's stomach and squeezed his legs, rendering him useless, much what how he'd written in *Rabbit's Revenge*. Stuart wheezed, his hands bloody and torn, and he shuddered in a state of true terror.

No one is here to hear the screams, Joseph thought. *Just like no one is going to know about what I published or how you murdered Benjamin Fisher.*

Stuart was still a bull, blindly thrashing his body angrily around as he tried to buck Joseph off him. Blood wept down Stuart's face in steady rivers, further splattering the ground around him, while Joseph raised the glass and slammed it down on Stuart's face, twisting his palms back and forth to work the glass deeper into Stuart.

Die! Die! Just fucking die already, you mother fucker, Joseph wailed to himself on repeat.

Stuart whacked Joseph's hand away, throwing the heavy bottom of the glass against the wall. Stuart's face was bleeding excessively. His eyelids—what remained of them—blinked rapidly, causing the glass shards to dig deeper. He hollered as his eyes filled with yellow pus. Then he simmered, gurgling his blood. His body cringed from the overwhelming pain he must've been feeling, twisting in ways that Joseph could never have even written about.

Let alone imagine.

Blood pooled around Stuart as Joseph was sure death would come any moment. Except Stuart continued to croak, lifting his hands in agony. He was still trying. Joseph grabbed the man's thick, bright ginger hair and slammed his head into the ground over and over and over and over and over. Joseph's head filled with the dreadful sounds of bones cracking and snapping. Too enraged to wonder what the difference was between this and the recording that inspired his book.

Stuart's skull cracked open like a giant egg, brain matter oozing like sludge. Joseph heaved, breathing like a wild animal. At this moment, he was no longer powerless, and he would no longer allow for plans to fall through. He was entitled to this life and lifestyle. Joseph had proved that to himself tonight; he'd never been in a situation so dire.

Air from Stuart's lungs still tried to escape, although Joseph was positive he was dead now. Choking noises still erupted as if he wasn't, though, so Joseph didn't move. Stuart's blood collected around their bodies and the knocked-over stool. As Joseph caught his breath, a wave of exhaustion came over him.

He looked at his hand, strands of ginger hair collected in the crevices between his fingers. He meticulously pulled each strand out, letting them fall on Stuart's mangled remains. He finally lay there as motionless as roadkill.

Through his jeans, Joseph felt his smartphone. He relaxed his legs around the motionless body, and the gurgling stopped. He checked his phone. A text from Arturo had come through, and Joseph could hardly focus, but he understood the message. Arturo was already on his way over, excited to see Joseph. He'd sent a second text with a link to track the ETA of the rideshare.

Arturo was only minutes away.away.

Joseph's eyes snapped up, looking desperately around him. He saw blood splattered along too many walls, trickling down like nails on a chalkboard. To his left, the home device stood on the kitchen island. Silent, but it had heard everything. Joseph shivered, taking in a deep breath to compose himself. *Nobody will ever know*, he told himself with a deep breath that swelled in his chest. When he exhaled, his fingers were already typing to Arturo. His life would continue as planned now. Joseph felt elated. All he needed to do was move that damn cruiser—and the body.

Joseph looked back down at his phone, the screen bright enough to blur the remains beneath.

Let me open the garage for you, Joseph replied.

Arturo was still fighting off the images that Goldstein had so easily conjured from his childhood, and he felt conflicted the entire ride to Joseph's. He didn't owe Benjamin Fisher anything, but he couldn't deny that smoking weed during the aftermath of his mother's suicide had helped him check out. He hadn't had to deal with her death at the time—or any other time, for that matter. Fisher had said it best: *big ol' selfish coward*.

The rideshare turned up Joseph's driveway, and Arturo forced this history aside. He smiled, checked his reflection in the rearview mirror to see he looked convincing.

Johnson made a U-turn in the driveway where Joseph's Porsche sat parked at an angle. After signing *thank you*, Arturo left Johnson's car with his bag in hand and checked his phone to rate and tip.

"Joseph?" Arturo called out as he walked up to the open garage.

The light was off inside. The forest felt eerie to Arturo, as if it huddled around, watching his every step, including the one past the safety sensor. The tree limbs that surrounded the house burst alive in a ghastly white glow as Arturo stepped inside the garage. He looked toward the door to the laundry room, noticing it was cracked open just a few inches.

He also noticed that the garage was different from the last time he'd seen it. Only what? Twenty-four hours ago? The storage racks created a ninety-degree angle that blocked off more than two-thirds of the garage. Arturo doubted the Porsche could even fit inside now, and that old car wasn't big by any means. Even the items on the racks looked messier, more haphazardly thrown than perfectly organized like the rest of Joseph's house. Large cloths hung on the backside of the storage racks, obscuring Arturo's view of—of what? A little makeshift room?

"Joseph?" Arturo's voice a long, thin whimper.

He pushed open the garage door, another lightweight black metal frame that matched the front door, only regular-sized. The smell of bleach was strong in the laundry room, which didn't make him feel any less wary. Arturo stepped farther inside, and he jumped when the washing machine sprang to life, whirling around with a minimal load of clothes inside. A light on the machine indicated that the spin cycle had just begun. Arturo turned away and continued forward, peeking inside the bedroom to see a glow from the bathroom. A shadow was moving about inside.

Arturo walked to the bedroom through the connecting hallway, when without warning, a smell so intense slapped—no, punched him. Square in the face. Arturo clutched at the doorways for support while his legs buckled, and the room swirled with the single most traumatic memory of Arturo's entire existence. Remembering it made him feel like he couldn't breathe enough air, no matter how deep of a gulp he took. He feared he was having a heart attack, but wasn't he too young to have one?

His vision became infected with swirls of pink and white tiles. Nearly three decades ago, he'd created a trench in his mind for this trauma he'd experienced. To protect himself. To survive. And to do so, he'd made sure to bury it so deep, not even light would touch it. There, he chained the memory to the floor and buried it alive. Flattened the space above as if there had never been a trench at all. He never returned, for he never wanted to deal with these memories.

Except tonight, the trench collapsed, and Arturo was pulled down in its wake.

Six vanity lightbulbs sat in a neat row above the bathroom mirror, and they'd been on long enough that when Arturo entered the room, he broke out in a sweat. He was just a child, barely ten years old.

It was strange that the vanity lights had been turned on. Normally, that bathroom had always been for guests, and his mother had enjoyed maintaining a clean space.

Just in case someone pops over, his mother would say.

There was a lot his mother used to say.

She hadn't moved since Arturo burst inside the guest bathroom having to pee really bad. She usually would've screamed for him to get out, to respect her privacy. Except now, she lay inside the white, glossy alcove bathtub with her arm resting along the wide edge. Her face leaned to the left, nestled in the corner of the wall. It was as if she were sleeping, but her eyes were wide open. The tub was filled with water colored dark maroon, and around her neck, a vibrant gold cross of good faith floated in the water between her breasts—beads the color of red paint dripped from her clean manicured fingernails.

Arturo could see his murky reflection in the glossy pink tiles that lined the walls like graph paper around him. As if a million tiny television screens were about to display what he'd do next.

"Mom?" Arturo felt the word come. He lifted his arm to extend his finger. He'd poked her, watching the tip of his fingernail indent his mother's skin. Her skin was warm, but she didn't react. Her arm lost balance on the porcelain edge of the bathtub and slipped down with a slap against the water. Her hand splashed a few drops of the murky bathtub water over Arturo's face, and he could smell the blood, his mother's, so strong. His body shook from the core, and he didn't want to believe any of it was real. He'd thought that maybe if he didn't move, eventually, he would wake from the nightmare.

Her arm no longer resting on the ledge to support her, his mother's body slid down into the bloody water. Her eyes stared not at Arturo but just past him. He couldn't stop staring at her, though, while the smell of blood grew stronger around him. Only then did Arturo spot her wrists, which she'd cut. Thin clouds wisped around her wrist in the tub before disappearing into the depths.

"Arturo, you here? I've been trying to call your mother all afternoon!" His *tía* had said, coming in through the front door like usual without knocking. He could hear her setting bags down behind him in the kitchen and marching over. Arturo wanted to slam the bathroom door shut to protect her. He knew things would never be the same after hearing her shriek that heart wrenching, guttural sound repeatedly as she discovered what Arturo's mother—the very sister she'd grown up with, spent her entire life with—had done. She would later ask how long Arturo had been standing there, but Arturo wouldn't know.

Every minute in that bathroom had felt like an eternity.

He saw the bathtub. His mother's necklace still floating on top of the water like a small boat in a vast ocean growing darker by the second.

"Arturo," he heard someone shout, but it wasn't his *tía*.

The memory faded away as bright white fluorescent lights flicked on, casting gray walls and black steel beams in sharp relief. *This is Joseph's garage,* Arturo understood, though his vision hadn't fully returned. Cool air collided with tiny beads of sweat trickling down the sides of his face. His body was jiggling, and he could feel his knees bend over something firm, and a sturdy beam supported his back. He realized he was in Joseph's arms. He understood now. He was being cradled, like a baby coming down from a tantrum.

"Arturo, I'm going to set you down." Joseph's voice came through the tunnel with a huff.

Arturo felt himself slip down to the cold ground, the tunnel vision retreating an inch more. He could see that Joseph was sweating, too, his face awash with concern. Joseph tugged at Arturo's feet, removing his shoes, then his socks. Joseph raised both palms to show Arturo, who still couldn't fully concentrate or understand what Joseph was doing. Joseph lowered his palms down on top of Arturo's feet. Immediate pain stabbed into the bottom of his feet with various little pricks, and Arturo's eyes widened as the darkness retreated from his vision entirely. He realized that Joseph was pressing his feet, somewhat hard, down on the pebbled driveway.

"Ouch!" Arturo recoiled back as an electric jolt burst him awake.

Joseph released his hands and gently pulled Arturo's arms out. Without asking, Joseph slid his fingernails up and down Arturo's forearms. He repeated this, and while soothing, Arturo also felt it demoralizing somehow. Joseph's face remained calm and soft, while Arturo felt tears welling in his eyes. He concentrated on keeping them from falling, his lips tightening beneath his scowl of anger.

"Hey, it's okay, you're okay, take a breath," Joseph said calmly. "You had a panic attack."

"I'm so sorry. I didn't mean to——" Arturo started, speaking a mile a minute, pushing past the ocean of wild emotions he felt.

"You're okay now. Keep pressing your feet into the rocks. Focus on the sensations in your arms. Be in the present with me," Joseph said.

Arturo tried, but his mind wouldn't let go of the memory, similar to how his mother's gold necklace had floated around her corpse that day; refusing to sink. He took a breath. "Yes, I mean . . ." He paused to breathe and then the words vomited from his mouth: "Everything just felt off when I came in. I had a flash of my mom when I smelled the—well . . ." Arturo didn't want to say it or even acknowledge the smell. He felt his fingers trembled for a smoke. His chest tight, he wondered if an inhaler would be better.

"What did you smell?" Joseph asked.

"I smelled blood, so much." He forced the word out again, "blood. I just feel like—I relived finding my mother's body." The tears that had built up now leapt over the edge, one after the other, creating perfect rivers down his face. Arturo hated having to acknowledge how his mother ruined his entire life. He hated her furiously in this moment as the emotions overcame him.

"I'm so sorry. That stupid paper cut opened, and I had a hard time finding Band-Aids." Joseph held up his finger, wrapped in a plain nude-colored bandage. "What do you smell now? Let's focus on what is right now," Joseph suggested, massaging Arturo's shoulder with his uncut hand.

"Lavender," Arturo said, looking over to the front door.

"Okay, keep focusing on that. I'm going to get your bag and mine, and we can hit the road." Joseph stood up.

"Should we even go? I've just ruined everything, I fear." Arturo felt the anxiety whispering to him, demanding him to worry.

Joseph leaned over and used his undamaged hand to raise Arturo's chin.

"Everything is fine. Panic attacks happen. Fear isn't always the truth. You are safe. That's the truth," Joseph said and then turned to walk back inside.

Arturo rubbed his feet back and forth against the pebbles. The pain was pleasant; he told himself more out of fear that the panic attack might strike again if he thought of his mother's suicide. He'd been able to speak about her so casually earlier, and he wanted to regain that control. He turned back to the front door and took in a deep inhale of lavender. Joseph was so caring and still wanted to get away together. Maybe, Arturo thought, Joseph was entirely correct. Arturo pulled out his vape and took a long hit of the indica strain to calm him down.

As he exhaled into the night sky, he saw the wisps of smoke mingling with the air. Much like his mother's hair floated in her bloody water—Arturo took another hit. And then another. And another. And then he began coughing so hard from all the hits that his vision blurred with more tears.

"Do you want a Xanax?" Joseph said, coming outside with both bags in his hands, the keys to the Porsche jingling.

"Nah, I'll smoke a bit more. I'm not a big fan of pills," Arturo admitted.

"That's okay. You can even catch a few Zs on the way up, too, if you like. I have to clear my head, anyway."

"Not about me, I hope," Arturo mumbled, and he could feel desperation in his voice. Just a twinge, the kind that implied what Arturo was thinking: please don't end things over this; I want you around.

Joseph paused, thinking, and then barked in laughter.

"No, *darling*," Joseph said, his thumb swiping trails of tears from Arturo's cheek.

"Emily is trying to get me to do another reading later this week. I just feel out of sorts with it." Joseph swished his hand toward the Porsche, dissolving the thoughts. "But enough about that, let's get on the road." Joseph pulled Arturo toward the passenger door and opened it for him.

Arturo vaped a bit more while Joseph got in on the other side. The motor roared to life, and they were driving away from the house. Arturo distracted himself with the old-school radio. He eventually landed on a song by Robyn, which had been named the song of the last decade by *Rolling Stone* magazine. Within a few moments of being on the highway, even without the help of a xanny, Arturo's body gave way to exhaustive, deep, empty sleep.

Noah watched everything from the balcony that night.

Large glass windows framed a stage, the set Joseph's manicured house. The dim lights turned on, and two men walked in as if Noah had just made it to his seat in time for the play. A very violent play. Noah couldn't help but wonder, had Joseph been watching through that window the night he murdered Fisher, just as he was watching now? He felt like he was having an out-of-body experience the more he watched.

The author looked nervous, downing a glass of liquor while the other man did a lot of pointing—aggressive pointing. He found something familiar in the expression on Joseph's face. As a child, Noah had debated a lot of what he should and shouldn't do, like when he'd tried to tell his mother at the Baxtor Spring Inn & Delicatessen, where she enjoyed stopping for sandwiches on their way home after a long day. She'd worked at the time, and maybe that's why her judgment had been so weak.

"Mom, I don't know if I want to do Boy Scouts anymore," he had told her while staring at his timid reflection in the display glass, where potato salad, macaroni salad, fruit salad, and various meats listened to him instead.

"Honey, sometimes we don't like things, but that doesn't mean we quit. Otherwise, we'd end up quitting everything. Push through. You're my strong little boy. Now tell the man what you want on your sandwich." She pointed to the man, who leaned over with a stained apron. Noah wasn't all that hungry to begin with, but the club sandwich with extra mayo was filling.

When he failed to convince his mother, he tried his father next, after a doctor appointment where Noah had bent over, spread his cheeks wide, and felt another older adult poking inside him—all the while being forced to hold still. They were at Leslie's Pharmacy to buy hemorrhoid cream for Noah, and his father was furious. He'd only imagined taking his son there to show him how to buy condoms when he was ready, but instead, his son wouldn't stop pushing his shit out too hard. His father hadn't just raised his voice—Noah remembered how he'd screamed at him. Howling on that the family was strapped for money already, and they couldn't be buying just *anything*. He had slammed his hand on the dashboard so hard that the fake leather mold had cracked. Noah cried out, fearful that his father's rage would turn on him next.

His father's rage then and Joseph's now were the same, and Noah was beside himself seeing it live-action before him. His chest filled with a charged static electricity that felt itchy. That rage existed in him, too. *Is this how I looked on top of Fisher?* Noah wondered. He was so calm and collected—at least in the beginning. He couldn't help smiling with pure joy as he watched someone else lose it *just* as he had; there was comfort in the representation he saw.

Noah watched Joseph drag the body behind the island as if moving it off stage. Then he was running outside, and then back inside, throwing clothes all-around, packing a bag. Then he was out the door, and the humming Porsche drifted away.

Noah waited on the outdoor patio furniture until it was safe.

He scrolled through his clone phone that automatically connected to the house's Wi-Fi. He checked on Joseph's location and could see that the author was already nearly an hour away and still moving. Noah set a location alert on his phone so that if Joseph came within a thirty-mile radius of the home, he'd be notified. He figured that would give him enough time to slip out unnoticed.

Noah looked around. The place would be all his till that notification came through. He smiled and felt at home. Not the size of a prison cell, not the size of the Extended Stay, but the size of an actual house that had space for him to be.

He stood over the mangled remains of—Noah checked his badge—Detective Stuart Kline. He even collected a few twenties from Kline's wallet. Noah told himself it was a tip for all the work he was about to do.

The detective's large body slid to the garage with little effort over the bloodied tile floors. The only hard part was getting him past the doorframe to the garage and back in his cruiser. As Noah heaved, exhausted from all the lifting, he noticed the matte black shine of Kline's pistol still attached to his hip.

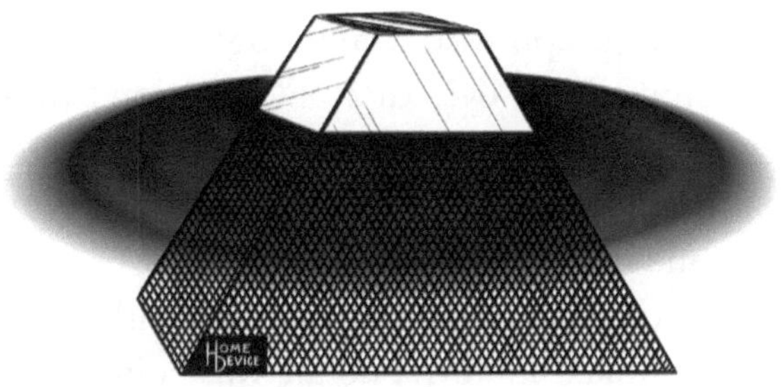

Joseph hadn't turned the car off just yet, even though he'd been parked outside of the lake house for a while now, watching the smoke from the tailpipes rise in the rearview mirror. Arturo's head lay to the side with his seat reclined; he looked so peaceful—unlike Joseph. Although now that they'd arrived, he felt a little relief being far away from home—now a crime scene. The mess would be waiting for Joseph when he got back. He reached for the keys and turned the ignition off; he'd have to make a move eventually. The car keys jingled and stirred Arturo.

"Here?" Arturo asked, struggling to raise his eyelids.

"Yeah," Joseph said, and he reached for Arturo's hand and kissed it.

Arturo smiled and pulled Joseph's hand back toward him, pulling his body closer, and kissed him. Arturo closed his eyes, lost in the excitement of this new relationship, and Joseph watched him, unable to close his own, afraid of what he might see. He worked his jaw as if gnawing on something hard, his lips on puppet strings. Arturo's face was smooth, unlike the sliced open remains of Detective Stuart Kline. Joseph wondered if he was entering rigor mortis now behind the kitchen island.

"Did you kiss me with your eyes open?" Arturo asked, more alert than Joseph would've thought.

Joseph blinked, his eyes dry. "Please, don't be silly. Let's get inside. I could use a drink."

"What time is it even?" Arturo asked.

"About one in the morning."

"Oh, the witching hour," Arturo said with a laugh.

The car cranked loudly. The air was cold on this side of the lake, and the guys moved quickly because of it. As they grabbed their bags and walked to the front door, the lake lay in the distance, unobstructed, licking the moonlight that fell from above before crashing, dully, against the shore. A dock ran into the water; beside it, a boat beat against weathered wood every few seconds. One side of the house—a cabin—gave way to trees, and the other met water that disappeared into the dark fog creeping along the lake's surface.

Joseph reached for the door, using his thumbs to punch in a four-digit code. The smart lock activated, the noise different than the one at Joseph's house. Yet the memory tickled like a soft breeze behind his ears. He went inside, expecting to smell dust and hints of fried fish that generally clung to the corners of the kitchen ceiling. A small lamp cast a glow in the entryway, and Joseph stopped dead in his tracks. The light shouldn't be on, he thought.

"Ooph—" Arturo blurted as he bumped into Joseph from behind; both lost grip of their weekender bags.

"Shit, I'm sorry," Arturo needlessly apologized, reaching to pick up the bags.

"Hello?" Joseph called out.

The floorboards creaked under their collective weight.

"You think someone is here? Aren't we alone?" Arturo asked, standing back up with both bags in his hands.

Joseph walked forward, afraid that Arturo would see the fear on his face, and flicked on a light switch that made the house whirl with life. The fireplace erupted with flames in a single row that danced on top of a large pile of broken glass. As stylish and modern as this décor choice was, Joseph could only picture the shards of glass scattered around Kline's frame as he struggled to survive.

Joseph looked back to the group of switches along the wall and flicked off the one that operated the fireplace. Inside the small cabin, they stood in the living room with a kitchen and bathroom behind it, the stairs that led up to the loft above, and beneath those stairs a door to the cellar. The lamps around the room were made from reclaimed wood that glistened as if freshly polished. Books were scattered everywhere, along with candles, their wicks burnt to hook ends. A blend of plants filled the space as well: snake plants, aloe, succulents, and ZZ plants, too. They each brought life into the room, and Joseph took a deep breath of cleaner oxygen.

"Joseph," Arturo said curiously, rustling a paper from the open secretary desk with a matching dark wood chair seated between the kitchen and living room. Arturo picked up a document from the printer that was facing up. He read out loud:

> Joseph—Always a pleasure to hear from you. Congrats on the new book. I'm so happy everything is working out for you. You have, and always will be, welcome here. I took the liberty to have housekeeping come and spruce up. Stocked the place up with the essentials. You know where the good wine is. Enjoy your stay here. Your mother loved this place.
> Best—
> Dean Scott

"Who is Dean?" Arturo asked, his eyes flicking up from the page.

"He was the president of the university where I worked out west," Joseph replied curtly, not wanting to admit the nepotism his mother's reputation provided him.

"You've must've had a close relationship," Arturo said, still looking at the paper. "Did people call you, like, professor?" Arturo set the letter down and took a step into Joseph's space. He let out a soft breath of warm air that prickled through Joseph's cotton shirt, caressing his chest.

"Mmhm," Joseph said, his hips twisting from side to side, gently, as Arturo's fingers hooked on to the belt loops. Arturo pulled Joseph's body closer, until their lips were mere inches from touching.

"Oh, did they?"

Joseph pushed back, looking down at the ground.

"It was kind of a long drive."

"Oh, yeah." Arturo let go, stepped back. "I wasn't terrific company on the way up, either."

"You're fine." Joseph walked to the entryway, turning off the lights. "Tomorrow, we can wake up and see the lake." He pointed outside the large A-frame windows of the cabin. The lake's waves had begun to appear, twirling like playful otters under silvery light as their eyes adjusted. "It'll be a new day."

"I am excited. I'm going to try to not think about the bar or donations and just relax. Recharge or whatever they call it nowadays," Arturo said with a wink. "Now, where are we sleeping?"

Joseph picked up their bags and led him straight upstairs, then hopped on the comfy bed with open arms. Arturo nestled within like an excited puppy. Joseph felt the warmth of another body against his chest, and Arturo's body soon melted in his arms with a gentle snore that filled the silence of the cabin and lake outside. Joseph lay motionless, hoping that sleep would overcome him soon as well, but nothing seemed right. Arturo's body was too warm, and his too hot. When Joseph could no longer take it, he opened his eyes and immediately noticed the light from the fireplace roaring from below. Though he thought he remembered putting it out.

Someone coughed, just downstairs.

"Arturo?" Joseph called out.

A horrific gagging noise responded from below that made the hair on Joseph's neck stand up on high alert. To his left, the bed was empty; Arturo was no longer there. Had he gotten up? Joseph slipped out of bed, toward the railing of the loft that overlooked the living room with wild eyes. He saw someone perched over the fire, the figure's back to him. Still, with the eeriest sensation rippling through his body, he knew it wasn't Arturo. The ginger hair stood still, the fire licking the edges of his figure. Joseph slunk around to the side, grasping the railing as he made his way down the stairs. Stuart Kline coughed again. A tiny spec of glimmer fell from his face, landing in the pile of glass collected beneath ferocious flames.

Joseph watched, his back pressed against the wall in horror. Stuart tilted his face away from the flickering fire toward Joseph. Two thin salmon-pink muscles stretched, barely holding his jaw in place, revealing clenched teeth, white and bloody. His eyes were foggy with yellow pus discharging from the corners, like tears dripping into the open layers of his face. He raised a hand, smacking the side of his face; his jaw rattled back and forth, tearing at the seams, and small pieces of glass wiggled out from inside of him, falling into the fire. Blood dripped, too, fresh, from his chin, and with each drop, the fire sparked, growing just a little bigger each time, excited.

Joseph watched as Stuart looked back at the fire, gagging loudly, like a cat with a nasty hairball. With trembling fingers, he reached into the back of his throat. The fire emitted just enough light that Joseph could see Stuart's pink tongue twisting around his fingers as he reached down his throat. He gagged again, and Joseph shuddered, staring as his eyes rolled back into his head. His knuckles ripped the edges of his mouth open, splintering the muscles until they cracked like an egg, slowly and delicately until he found what was in his throat. His fingers drew back, slowly, exquisitely, leaving his jaw to hang unevenly; even so, that twisted smile returned with clenched teeth.

At the tips of his fingers, he clutched a long, thin piece from the curved whiskey glass Joseph had used to murder the detective.

"So many of these. Hard to—" The man broke off to cough again, this time in a horrible fit, and he dropped the shard of glass into the fire. Joseph couldn't take his eyes off Kline, the fire so bright now that every detail was too vibrant. His coughing turned into a thick gurgle as bits of his own shredded esophagus flew from his mouth. Tiny bits of glass embedded along the bits like cancer showing up in a screening. Except this was no medical office, this was on the expensive rug in front of the fireplace.

"So hard to talk—with—these—in—my—throat." He dragged out the words, struggling to enunciate with the amount of blood dripping from his tender lips, dribbling down past his crooked chin , and into the fire. He laughed now, locking eyes with Joseph, who couldn't move. Joseph felt wholly immobilized, rooted into the ground of this terrible dream, his bones and surrounding muscles paralyzed.

"Hey now," Stuart said, laughing through blood-stained teeth. "Don't be so scared; it's just . . ." Stuart leaned forward, raising his eyebrows unnaturally high and wagging his face left and right. ". . . us here."

Joseph didn't doubt him; in nightmares, he was always alone. He couldn't look away from Stuart's face, even as he tried desperately to, and Stuart seemed to find pleasure in how hard Joseph's muscles strained, his jugular veins like exposed subway tunnels running beneath his tender flesh—still lucky enough to be intact. Stuart laughed wickedly, making his blood splatter around the walls, which then dripped down with the shrill sounds of a poor violinist playing. Joseph's body melted with the wall now, and Stuart approached, hobbling on his left foot while his right dragged behind him at a crooked, broken angle.

"I came to ask you a question," Stuart said, taunting Joseph, his face less than a foot away. The bloody, creamy pus dripped from Stuart's chin, catching on Joseph's sweater. "Did you think about who I was?"

"That doesn't matter," Joseph said, forcing his lips to curl into a triumphant smile, but Stuart held his same deadpan expression. "You're dead," Joseph's voice squeezed out, but even he could hear how unsure he sounded.

"Yet I'm living in your mind rent free," Stuart got so close that Joseph gagged on the smells. "Now answer my question, who was I?"

"Stuart Kline."

"*Detective,*" Stuart corrected him as the left side of his jaw sagged, causing his bottom teeth to jut out like a bulldog's bottom jaw.

"You're just one small-town detective—fuck off." Joseph spat, even as his voice shook.

"Small towns are different. People talk. People look out for each other."

Joseph scoffed. "I have my alibi. It's happening right now."

Stuart's head fell back, limp, and he stared up at the ceiling, drawing in a long, snotty-sounding breath. The blood from his chin, with the yellow pus, crept down his neck, producing an odor so foul, it tickled Joseph's nostrils. Joseph watched Stuart's head bouncing from the left, down, right, back, and around again, each time Stuart repeated Joseph's words.

"I *have* my alibi," Stuart said, mocking him. "I have my *alibi.*" Each time his voice amplified around the room, becoming a chorus of ear-splitting pain. "*I have my alibi.*"

Joseph snapped once more. His muscles cracked like concrete as he lunged at Stuart, wrapping both hands tight around his neck.

"Going to kill me again, are you?" Stuart's voice was steady, no matter how hard Joseph squeezed. "You still don't even know who killed that old man, the one in those recordings." Stuart's eyes flashed with excitement, even as his head shook like a bobblehead in Joseph's hands. Bloody pus splattered along Joseph's forearms and fried his skin like hot oil. Joseph screamed, loud and guttural, his feet giving out from the boiling pain on his skin. He could barely keep his hands around Stuart's neck as his knees crumbled, his body defenseless, pushed down to the ground. He looked up at Stuart, standing on his knees, horrified.

Stuart's head cocked, lazily, to one side, staring down at him. "Better hope they don't come to find you like this, because it looks like you're beginning to lose it, Joseph." He then leaned down to Joseph's face, so close that Joseph could see the tiny decaying nodules of Stuart's tongue twist and bend as his chin sagged, his pink muscle strands tearing at the seams and swaying back and forth in his peripheral vision. His words loud and guttural, but Joseph could still hear him loud and clear:

"You're beginning to lose it, Joseph."

Joseph screamed, flailing his arms about, trying to push Stuart off, away, but Stuart didn't move. His grasp on Joseph's shoulders grew painful. The bloody, creamy pus collecting on his chest burned like acid through his sweater. The fireplace spit out fresh flames that spread along the walls to the ceiling, consuming everything. Stuart shook him harder and harder and harder and—

"You're okay!" Arturo screamed while sitting over Joseph, shaking his shoulders so hard that Joseph could feel Arturo's fingernails digging into his skin. Joseph instinctually pushed Arturo off, who fell back on the bed amid the cloudy duvet, and Joseph gasped for air, trying to clean his airways from the smell of Stuart's bloody pus that lingered within his nostrils.

"Sorry, I was having a nightmare," Joseph said, his eyes peeking over to Arturo.

"Well, no shit." Arturo sympathetically slipped close again, his hand gently rubbed Joseph's tight shoulder. "What was happening? You were screaming so violently."

"I can't remember, honestly," Joseph lied.

Noah woke to sounds of motorized blackout shades rising, allowing speckled sunlight to creep past the tree branches and along Noah's exposed flesh. The trees that stood thick around Joseph Bailey's house were magical to wake up to, like something on the National Geographic channel he'd occasionally watch in prison. A falcon sat in one of the trees. Its head turned all the way around to rest on its back while balancing on one leg, asleep. Noah, using the free Wi-Fi, had been able to discover it was a peregrine falcon. *What a miraculous sight,* he thought in awe. How nice to enjoy a view without needing to look past barb wired fences and guard towers.

He turned, stretching his naked body in the silk sheets of Joseph's bed. The pillows smelled of a musky vanilla scent that he labeled, mentally, as Joseph's smell. He stretched his arms out, spreading his legs as he rolled over on his stomach. He lay there like a dog splooting. He checked to see Joseph's location, still at Lake Wilburton, and decided he was safe to stay longer.

He checked Joseph's email and saw a reply from Dean Scott saying that Joseph could stay at the lake house for as long as he liked. Noah enjoyed the sound of that and felt even more unrestrained in this glass palace.

Nature called, and Noah could feel himself clench a little. Throwing off the covers, he walked past where the peregrine falcon sat peacefully, the thick glass of the window leaving him undisturbed by Noah's movements. He continued, noticing how warm the tile floors were in the bathroom. When he sat down to relieve himself, he also admired the heated toilet seat. Toilet paper so thick and soft, he didn't hold back on using as much as he desired. The toilet paper in prison scratched. If Noah used too much, his inner cheeks became dry and caused so much friction, his skin would sizzle with irritation.

Not at Joseph's, though.

He stood up. The toilet didn't have a button or handle. Before he could worry, it automatically flushed everything down until he could only see gleaming porcelain beneath a thin puddle of clean water.

Noah reached inside the shower, flipping up a stainless-steel shower handle. Cool water rained down from the broad shower head. While he waited, he turned to see his reflection in the mirror, where the water was steaming hot already. Noah rolled his eyes with delight. He hadn't known a bathroom could be this nice. Even the mirror before him had refused to fog while displaying a little digital calendar and clock in the bottom corner. Noah could see his tattoo, which looked fresh with crisp black lines under the bathroom lighting. The rabbit's ears were slightly tilted back, its eyes peering around as if hiding from the falcon just outside.

In the book, Joseph's tattoo description wasn't accurate, which brought back Noah's memory of the violent play he'd witnessed last night. Had Joseph seen Noah commit murder?

Noah stepped under the hot water, not bothering to adjust it; he'd always enjoyed a hot shower. Through the steam, he spotted a line of skincare products he'd never heard of. Nearly three different body washes, and Noah tried each one. When he stepped out of the shower, his skin was red, and steam rose off him. He grabbed a towel and wrapped himself, water dripping around his feet as he stepped to the mirror once more.

He spotted a toothbrush sitting on a pedestal charger. He ran his tongue over the thin layer of grime on his teeth, the reached for the toothbrush and found the paste in a stack of drawers to his left-hand side. In prison, he hadn't had an electronic toothbrush but with Joseph's, he brushed his teeth twice before rinsing his mouth. He returned the toothbrush to its original position. He smiled, his teeth a wall of white bone that sparkled.

He toweled off his muscular, lean build and walked with a relaxed sway in his hips to the bedroom closet. He dressed in Joseph's clothes, which consisted of name-brand briefs, jeans so soft they felt like sweatpants, and a sweater that made Noah feel he'd just stepped out of a catalog. He grabbed his phone and noticed a few missed text messages from Sergio through a private messaging app on the clone phone.

Sorry about missing you. I picked up some shifts at this bar. Want to stop by for a drink?

He read Sergio's message as he waltzed to the kitchen. He rummaged through the fridge and the cabinets until he landed on dry cereal and freshly squeezed orange juice. He didn't bother with a bowl or a cup. He indulged drinking from the bottle and eating handfuls of cereal while replying with his free hand:

Can you come over tonight instead?

Noah sat at the island, looking around the house. Joseph's style was something out of a magazine he would read to pass the time in prison. Everything was so meticulous and well placed, including a weathered copy of *Rabbit's Revenge* on the island, along with a folder that read "Benjamin C. Fisher" on the tab. He eyed it but decided he didn't need anything in that folder. Fisher was already dead. What more was there to tell?

Noah looked to the top of his phone, realizing that Sergio had only messaged him about three hours ago. He wouldn't hold his breath for a response.

His eyes couldn't wander anymore from where he sat, nearly a few feet from where he'd watched that detective get murdered. The air in the room was stale with disinfectant and an eerie sense of unresolved energy. Noah drank the rest of the orange juice and set it down beside a small pyramid device that read "Home Device" thinly in the corner. The H and D intertwined.

Noah slid the box of cereal away from him, and he eyed the home device curiously. He picked it up and rotated it. There weren't any buttons on the device. When he set it back down, he looked up and noticed the ceiling had speakers that blended in. He looked back to the home device, thinking surely they had to be connected.

"Home Device. Hello. Turn on. H.D.?" he said, growing defeated when it lit up, red lights whirling around as if thinking.

"Something I can help you with?" the home device spoke, its voice calm and flowing.

"Yes, just play some music."

"Any genre?" The voice was enthusiastic.

"My top played," Noah said, and the home device swirled around before music slipped through the speakers. Jazz, and not smooth or relaxing, but thunderous applause and loud trumpets. "H.D., turn it down," he instructed, then added, "please."

The device listened, and then it was just Noah with a live jazz performance playing around him. The band slipped into a beat he could snoop around to. His eyes roved over the walls of the living room that lead back to the office.

Inside, Noah grabbed one of the bright yellow bubble-wrapped parcels still untouched, stacked against the wall, and ripped it open. He didn't care how loud the plastic sounded tearing or how a few of the bubbles popped loudly. He turned the package upside down, and a copy of *Rabbit's Revenge* fell out, plopping along the floor until it landed face down, and he was staring, again, at the photograph of Joseph Bailey before the gazebo in Main Street's square.

Noah tilted his head to the side, much like his own tattoo, filled with curiosity.

He grabbed the next small package and ripped this open. And the next. And the next, until all the books were unwrapped and exposed. The packages he'd crumpled to the side after removing the shipping labels. He was familiar with the return label that consistently showed that the book was being shipped from Publishing X to Joseph Bailey. Except underneath that shipping label was the original one showing that the book had been sent to someone else first: Marcelina Fry in Alabama, Dexter Moore in California, even one to Natasha Davies in Canada. Noah thought of the insert he'd received himself with the book that read, "Love it? Keep it. Don't? Return it. Either way, leave a 5-Star Review to earn your income!" These seemed old; they weren't advertising the social media part. It appeared that the people didn't love it enough to keep the book. Noah felt a twinge of pain, which he'd known was coming the moment he saw all the packages that day.

He sighed, also recalling how little he'd been able to find about this company on the web. The clone phone proved convenient, of course, but the screen was small. He turned and peered at Joseph's desktop computer. The afternoon sun glistened down over it from the skylight above.

The author had plugged the keyboard back in, and Noah paused. He was feeling a flush of worry. Had the author set a password? Noah panicked, quickly waking the mouse. The computer screen instantly lit up to the same desktop as before with the various icons and files. Noah let out a steady breath and got to work clicking, searching, consuming.

"More wine?" Arturo asked, sitting up. The lake was calm today; not even a breeze rippled against the water. The steel-shelled rowing boat hardly moved from where Joseph had stopped it. The middle of the lake was a gorgeous place to be, the trees stood on high-risers like a chorus ready to harmonize about the beautiful weather. Water still dripped from the wide paddle ends of the ores tucked to the side of the boat.

"Yes, please," Joseph said, sitting up himself. Both of them had laid towels over the main and forward thwarts of the boat. Both spots were large enough for them to lie there, wasting the afternoon away, soaking up the sun. Neither of them even bothered to bring a shirt or sandals, only sunglasses, swimwear, and sunblock were essential—well, so was the wine.

Arturo reached for the picnic bag Joseph had packed after waking from his nightmare. Arturo had been able to fall back asleep, but he felt sorry for Joseph, who hadn't. The grapes and cheeses had been devoured early on. All that remained were a few dry crackers bottles of wine Joseph had packed for them. Each bottle of rosé had a hand-drawn French chateau design.

As Arturo opened the bottle and poured the wine, his eyes wandered along Joseph's body, which sparkled with beads of sweat beneath the warm sun. His legs extended out and over the edge, allowing his feet to dangle in the water freely, the tan hair that covered his calves slowly thinning up to his thighs and the smooth skin around his speedo line. Arturo stared at the bulge. Joseph caught him, giving a playful smooch before taking a sip of wine and lying back. He brought his free hand to the arch in Arturo's foot and gently massaged.

"Looks like your finger is doing a lot better," Arturo noted, his own eyes behind the shield of rounded sunglasses. Joseph recoiled his hand as if he'd touched a hot burner, taking a momentary pause before he examined the tip. His cut had healed into a thin white line.

Joseph merely shrugged. "Look at that."

"Paper cuts heal quickly if the cut is just right. You're lucky," Arturo said, setting the wine bottle back in the bag, taking in the views once more. Joseph gave an *mmhm*. In the far distance, Arturo could see a large wooden post with a faded Boy Scout emblem on the front of it. A large lifeguard tower sat at the end of a dock, which Arturo recognized.

"I used to come to Lake Wilburton for Boy Scouts when I was younger, before my mother died." Arturo let the words trail out, afraid to finish the sentence in case a panic attack were to strike him on the lake. "I've never had a flashback like that," Arturo continued. "I felt like I was a kid again." Arturo took a few puffs of his indica, while Joseph sipped more of his wine.

"You had a panic attack," Joseph said. His voice was slow but calm, and Arturo found his reflection staring back at him through Joseph's glasses.

"You seem to have some experience with them," Arturo said, "taking my shoes off and the way you rubbed my arms."

"I've had a few myself, to be honest, a few months ago before I left the West Coast. It's why my house has all the lavender near the front door, little suggestions that are supposed to help us remember something good or bring us back to the present—but a panic attack will strike regardless of what you do. That's the sad part."

"Do they happen often?"

"No, not for me. I hope not for you, either. You want to talk about it?" Joseph paused and then added, "We don't have to if you don't feel like it."

Arturo looked away from the summer camp in the distance and back to his wine that was as motionless as the water around them.

"I mean, I feel like this is the type of environment people pay thousands of dollars for to get over their deeply buried traumas." Arturo looked around. Dead tree trunks that had fallen over crept into the water, rotting limbs disappearing into the dark depths below.

Joseph chuckled but didn't say anything more.

"Right before I came over, I ran into Officer Goldstein. We used to know each other in the Boy Scouts, but we've never been close. He was talking to me about Benjamin Fisher. Because his death was ruled a homicide, the church is green lighting his funeral later this week since he was such a town hero. Goldstein wanted me to know."

"Why's that?" Joseph asked, his interest piqued.

"Well, he talked about how Fisher was there for me after my mother died, and it made me remember my first joint. Fisher gave it to me at my mother's wake. People were allowed to come to this, unlike the church's funeral, which forced us to keep things very small. I hardly remember most of that day." Arturo took a sip. The rosé light and sweet. "The entire car ride up to your house, that was on my mind. I was trying to remember just . . . anything from that time in my life. Then I came inside your place and smelled all that . . . blood, and it just hit me all at once."

"It brought you back to when your mother died?" Joseph asked.

"When she committed suicide, I was the one to find her. I went into shock. That's what my *tía* said. She and my father tried to keep things normal for me and insisted that I continue to go to Boy Scouts weekly, do normal things." Arturo sniffled dry tears, waving his hand in the air as if trying to coax the very memory. "My mother was very active in the troop, however, and her absence was felt. My father already had a drinking issue, but her death sent him over the edge. He blamed himself for not seeing the signs of how depressed she must've been. He'd often drink, always picking me up late from Boy Scouts, and Fisher spent the time waiting with me. We'd smoke a joint. He'd talk to me. He was caring." Arturo sighed. Each of these words felt like lifting a heavy dumbbell. "My *tía* surprised us one time and caught us smoking. She was livid but angrier at my father, who'd been arrested for a DUI that night. That's when she pulled me from Boy Scouts."

"Is that when you moved in with your *tía*?" Joseph asked.

"Yup," Arturo huffed. "She became my legal guardian; my father never even tried to fight it—always too lost in his sorrows." Sweat trickled down his spine, and he laid back on his towel, feeling it bunch up along the hot blanket. "After that, my *tía* kept me on a tight leash. She thinks she saved me, or whatever. We didn't see eye-to-eye about my mother's suicide."

"How so?" Joseph asked.

"She sees my mother as a fallen angel, and I see her as a coward. She abandoned me, us, everyone. Without her, everything fell apart. I was angry, but unlike you, I didn't have a boarding school to set me on course. My *tía* always grounded me. She feared I'd be an addict like my father or end up depressed and suicidal like my mother. She constantly brought up these two things as if they were the only options I'd ever have in life. She would always say, *These things are our bloodline.*"

"Well, I don't think you're an addict. Although we do drink quite a lot."

"We're gay. What do you expect?" Arturo laughed. "Plus, I've never stopped enjoying weed." He smiled.

"Did you ever see Fisher again?" Joseph asked.

Arturo shook his head. "No, which sucked 'cause I felt like he was the only one to—" Arturo huffed. "God, this sounds so fucking lame."

"No, it doesn't," Joseph said matter-of-factly.

"He was the only one to understand me at that time. He was close with my mother, too. She donated a lot of her time to the troop. He was there for me without judgment, like—well . . ." Arturo almost paused, his mind telling him how stupid he must sound, but he persisted. "Like you, Joseph."

"Me?"

"Yeah, I feel calm around you, and you're caring. I believed I was dying last night, and you were my savior."

"Many people describe their panic attacks as feeling like that. Or like a heart attack. You're not alone in that feeling, even though that feeling isn't true. You weren't dying. And you have nothing to feel ashamed about. There's enough of bullshit in the world. We can be there for each other. Can't we?"

Arturo paused. Isn't this what he wanted? All that time spent scrolling through profiles and searching for a date.

Reading books that promised easy ways to navigate grief, but they never helped at all. And yet, here was Joseph. Confident and secure, nurturing.

"Yes, we can," Arturo said, his voice low as if he were afraid someone would hear him be so vulnerable around a new lover.

"Would you like to attend the funeral together? I'd go with you," Joseph offered. "Sounds like Goldstein could've been right. Regardless of the relationship you had with him in the past, he is trying to make sure you get to say your peace. Fisher was there for you. Even if his methods were hazy. I wonder what life would've been like if your *tía* hadn't caught you two that day," Joseph pondered, sipping his wine.

Arturo had never thought of that before, and suddenly his mind was overwhelmed with thoughts of *what if*. He imagined he'd have been happier and more secure in himself. Fisher had a disdain for his mother after the suicide, though, which had left a solid impression on Arturo at a young age. All the *what ifs* his mind ran through only happened because of his mother's cowardly actions that day. He bit his tongue back and swallowed.

"I don't know, but things would be very different, I imagine," Arturo replied, monotone.

"Well, then pay your respects to Fisher. For what he could've been in your life and what he was in your life during that time. I think it'd be really good for you to go. We can't change the past. The only thing we can do is try to make peace with it. I think that's what Goldstein was trying to tell you," Joseph said.

"Okay, okay, okay," Arturo said, his mind now made up. "We'd have to leave tomorrow then, the funeral is . . . I guess I have to look that up," Arturo shrugged.

Joseph pulled his phone from the small picnic basket and tapped away on the screen until he paused and looked up. "The service is tomorrow around noon."

"We're going to have to leave so early," Arturo groaned.

"Leaving early wouldn't be a problem for me. I want to be there for you," Joseph replied reassuringly. "Plus, I need to clean up and put together a shipment of books together for Emily. We can do that after the funeral. It's good to have plans for after so your mind doesn't dwell."

From: Dean Scott
To: Joseph Bailey, Lauren Henry
Subject: Referral for Lauren
Date: March 3, 2016

Hi Lauren,

I hope all is well.

I wanted to introduce you to Joseph Bailey, an English professor at our university for nearly ten years. He is currently
stepping away from his position to explore publishing his
own set of novels. Joseph is the son of Elena Bailey—if you
recall, one of our most prestigious donors. On top of that, I
know how skilled you are in getting things to print, even to
film. Let me know if you have any questions, but I'm sure
you two will work out an incredible deal.

Best,
Dean Scott

From: Lauren Henry
To: Joseph Bailey
Subject: Re: Referral for Lauren
Date: March 4, 2016

Hello Joseph,

Delighted to meet you, and I'm very excited to see what the future holds.

Before we can discuss all the details and options for you, I will need you to sign the NDA attached. After that, we can get to work.

Looking forward to it,
Lauren Henry
CEO
Publishing X

From: Lauren Henry
To: Joseph Bailey
Subject: Re: Referral for Lauren
Date: March 6, 2016

Joseph—

Thank you so much for signing the NDA. I've added it to your file.

Now, let's talk business. Publishing X can handle all of your publishing needs, whether it be editors, proofreaders, readers, and reviewers—or even ghostwriters. We've had very successful campaigns for various novels that have now been made into limited series and award-winning films. Depending on how much you're able to invest and where you are with your draft, we could have the book ready to print by next week. Media deals in the next three to six months usually follow.

Do you know how much you'll be able to invest upfront?

Thank you,
Lauren Henry
CEO
Publishing X

From: Lauren Henry
To: Joseph Bailey
Subject: Re: Referral for Lauren
Date: March 9, 2016

Joseph—

An upfront investment of $200,000 can cover many things. We can divide your investment down the middle into two separate ones. Your first project is fully funded, with your next one at the ready. With each project fully funded, if you don't need the ghostwriter services, we'll be able to spend more on advertising and reviews.

Let's discuss our options and the path forward as we invest in your future.

First, we need to know if you have a project or idea already in the works. If you don't, we have an incredible creative team of ghostwriters. They need a little from you (genre, authors you like, etc.). These teams start at $50,000.

If you do not require the creative team's services, we can gladly accept your completed manuscript.

Once we have your manuscript, we will begin editing and getting it to print. During that time, we will also be focusing on a campaign to raise awareness of the book—small ads here and there, nothing too much. We will off-set print the first twenty-five thousand copies of your book, which will go to Publishing X's influence team. This will help you attain many five-star reviews on all platforms. These reviews will drive up your sales in the general public and position on the bestseller lists. We will also begin targeting several metrics (such as age/buyer habits, etc.) to ensure your book continues to sell.

Please Note: Our influencers are not required to keep your print. If they don't want the product, they'll return ship them directly back to you. Regardless of the influencer's personal opinion, your five-star review will be honored, or they will not be paid.

The extra copies you obtain can be sold to a local bookstore at a cheaper discount or even sold online via retailers like eBay.

To have a successful campaign, we need to show your book is not at number one right off the bat. We want to maintain that your book climbs the charts, and within three months be at number one (or very close to it). After a month of holding at the top, we will begin to work with our production contacts to sell into either film, television, or streaming series.

During this time, we can begin looking into your second project, building off the success of the first.

Between selling copies, reprints in paperback, the media aspect, even merchandising, your investment of $200,000 can quickly flip a return of a few million within our network.

All we'll need is that manuscript from you.

Lauren Henry
CEO
Publishing X

Noah paused.

He read the date at the top of that last email once again. March 9th, three days after the massacre in Baxtor Springs. Two days after he'd murdered Benjamin Fisher. Lauren Henry wouldn't understand the type of goosebumps Joseph must've had. But this still didn't answer the question—how did Joseph know about Benjamin Fisher being murdered?

He scrolled to the following email, dated June 5, and found the manuscript for *Rabbit's Revenge* attached. He opened this file and scanned through it. Most of the words hadn't changed from this draft to what was printed through this publishing scheme. One that benefited people with money to play with. Learning this stung a little, although Noah had known some of this already—he was an associate of their "Review Team." He had been for the past few months.

He clicked over to Publishing X's website. Nothing had changed on that front, even when Noah had signed up. The website layout was simple. They advertised themselves as a full-bodied company set in creating various forms of content. They had a contact button but no public address—only a "Join Our Team" button. Lauren Henry had said that twenty-five thousand reviews was just the start. Just how large was their network, and how extensive was it? She was making some pretty hefty claims and yet, she was delivering on them. After she and Joseph had gotten in contact, she had the manuscript no more than two months later. A week after that, *Rabbit's Revenge* was published (digitally at first, and then paperback copies followed), and the reviews racked up, helping the novel climb to the top of the bestseller lists.

Noah shook his head, afraid he'd seen too much. Or wasted time.

He wasn't here for Publishing X. He was here for Joseph. The two were linked, yes, but Noah didn't even know how he would approach meeting the author. A part of him was fearful, and for a good reason. The author was more deadly than his polished look conveyed. A territorial beast.

He looked around the office and tried to focus his thoughts. *One step at a time,* he reminded himself, the big question was how Joseph knew.

The afternoon sun beamed down through the two skylights in the office, and Noah could see dust gently floating around the room. The desk had coffee rings stains in the wood, and various papers made up an untidy pile off to the left. Noah's eyes trailed to the copies of Joseph's novel that he'd stacked so neatly just a few hours ago. He swiveled the chair over to the opposite side of the room, unsure if perhaps he'd finally hit a dead end.

Noah frowned, feeling his ears drop back.

Index cards hung flat, pinned to the wall, between two large bookshelves that hosted thick textbooks with Joseph Bailey's name on them. English subject matter. But Noah was more interested in the index cards. They were pinned to the walls in neat rows, much like the book and folder out on the kitchen island. He read the titles on the top row: Act I, Act II, Act III, Epilogue. Beneath the epilogue, in smaller handwriting, Noah read, *to tie into the next book*. He stood up and walked around the desk, peering closer at these notecards. He could see his nickname scribbled on some of the cards.

Act I: Rabbit—Dialogue from Recording 067

Noah recognized this as the start of the book, the part that had described his revenge so well. He tilted his head, scanning over each of the cards. Some didn't have anything scribbled on them, but a good majority did. Each one referenced a different numbered recording. Joseph hadn't been at the house or on the property peeping through the window. He'd heard a recording of it. How preposterous. The older man hadn't been recording anything when he died—Noah would've known—and yet, how would Joseph be in possession of these recordings? None of these index cards sat right with him. He returned to the computer and searched, not just the email but the entire system for one word.

Recording.

A folder called "The Recordings" popped up inside another folder titled "Inspiration." Noah clicked, opening the folder, and found a collection of nearly forty numbered recordings, none of them in sequential order.

Noah opened the first one, "Recording 067," and began listening.

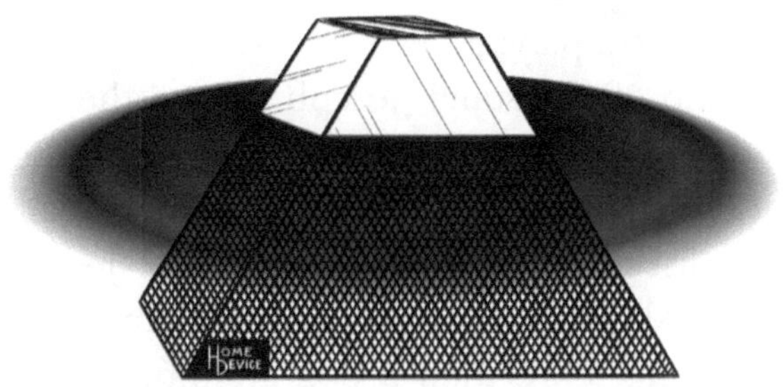

Joseph stood beneath bright white lighting that exposed everything in the cellar, from the wood beams above to the dark mahogany stained wine racks filled with bottles. Joseph did know where to find good bottles, yes, but tonight he was feeling reckless and grabbed an *incredible* bottle instead. With an invitation to Fisher's funeral, he might find the killer there—if Stuart Kline had been correct. *What are you thinking?* Joseph reprimanded himself; *Stuart Kline is dead.*

He grabbed a dusty bottle of wine and huffed out a big breath of air. He read the green banister in gold foil: Gran Reserva 904, bottled in Rioja, Spain, in 1964. Joseph pressed a hand against his face, cheeks, and forehead, still warm from the hot sun they'd bathed beneath all day, and decided to grab a second bottle. He would drink until he was drunk enough to pass out and sleep without any recollection of his choices, past or present.

Arturo's footsteps crossed above where Joseph stood in the cellar. Dust trickled down from the cracks, collecting on Joseph's shoulder. He brushed it off and headed back up. When Joseph was halfway up the stairs, he heard the crackling sounds of a record player. The needle, always so sensitive, touched down on a live recording of a classical symphony performance. Light applause rose and faded, and then the orchestra played.

At the top of the stairs, Joseph turned the corner. The fireplace danced with life, and for a split second, Stuart was sitting on the edge, staring down at it. The tickling smell of that yellow discharge dripped in the back of Joseph's throat, who shook his head so hard his lips blubbered noisily about. He was nothing more than a dog attempting to shake off stress.

"You doing good?" Arturo asked.

Joseph focused once more. Arturo came into view, sitting on the edge, turning his face to look back at him. The look stopped him dead in his tracks. Arturo wore nothing more than a pair of black hip-huggers. The dancing fire only accentuated his bulge in the background as he stood, turned, and walked to Joseph.

"God damn," Joseph said, his eyes glued to Arturo as he approached.

Arturo's arms swayed confidently with his walk, and the firelight seeped around his arms, accentuating the curves of his body. Joseph could feel his tongue begin to salivate, yet it was bittersweet. The taste of the yellow pus still dripped in the back of his throat.

"Good, 'cause if it's our last night here . . ." Arturo's voice faded out, like a great song.

Joseph bit his bottom lip hard, hoping that the pain would dull his anxiety.

"I grabbed two incredible bottles of wine." Joseph forced a smile, a fake playful laugh. "Let me grab some glasses." He slipped into the kitchen, leaving the lights off to try to collect himself. He could feel his forehead furrow. He felt so conflicted.

Arturo had a body that would turn anyone on, yet Joseph couldn't even feel a stir. In between grabbing the wine opener and glasses, Joseph felt an anger simmer beneath his skin. He never assumed he'd have erectile dysfunction in his midthirties, but then again, Joseph never thought he could have murdered someone, either. He hadn't thought of the side effects.

Joseph uncorked the first bottle and didn't bother to decanter it. He filled both glasses quickly, and as he took a swig, sticky sounds of bare feet on hardwood floor approached from behind. Arturo's hands gripped Joseph's hips and swayed them from side to side gently. He could feel Arturo's hands slithering up to the lower dimples in Joseph's back. For a moment, Joseph thought, *I could try to take instead—*

"I want you to fuck me," Arturo said, his warm breath washing over Joseph's ear, running goosebumps down his back and legs, and yet nothing stirred. "Or I can fuck you, too, but I did shower while you got the boat in and got the wine." His hands slipped away from Joseph, taking a wine glass from Joseph's hand. Arturo turned and walked back to the living room.

Joseph grew even more desperate as he watched Arturo slip off his hip huggers and fling them back. They landed at Joseph's bare feet. His eyes shot up to see Arturo's round behind, still teasing him with shadows from the fire that licked and caressed his sides. Arturo sat down on the couch and tilted his wine glass slightly up, taking a long yet thin sip. Joseph looked down at his wine glass and took a gulp. Buying himself some more time, even seconds, were worth it. He topped his wine glass off.

"Cheers," Arturo said, licking his bottom lip.

"Cheers." Joseph walked over and clinked his glass to Arturo's before taking another large gulp. The wine was old and truly needed more time to breathe, much like Joseph.

"Let's set these down." Arturo leaned forward, setting his glass down on the framed glass coffee table that reflected the clouds passing by outside.

Joseph nervously took another gulp before putting his glass down. The wine was making his throat dry. A sinking suspicion that the wine was working against him grew. Arturo wrapped his arms around Joseph's lower back, rising on his toes to kiss down Joseph's neck, his fingers tickling the center of his chest as Arturo unbuttoned his shirt. Arturo worked each button, his hands moving farther down, as Joseph tried his best to send the mental signals to become hard, to impress. Arturo's hands started to unbutton his shorts, his fingers cold against Joseph's skin as they began to pull back his Speedo's band. Joseph stepped back, though. Parting from Arturo's soft lips, he lifted him off his feet instead.

Arturo licked his lips, smiling. Joseph looked away from the firelight that glinted in Arturo's eyes and set him down on the couch. He turned Arturo's frame. His back was arched with his head resting against the backend of the sofa. Joseph was in a personal hell. Joseph licked his lips and kissed down Arturo's neck and shoulders. His tongue ran down along the valley that crept down his back. Arturo moaned under his breath as he spread himself open. Joseph continued to let his tongue wander down alongside his hands as he stroked himself, trying to arrive. Arturo's skin was soft and wet in those areas that Joseph desired to be inside. He smacked Arturo's right cheek, causing him to yelp.

Surprised, Arturo's knee lost its spot on the couch, and his foot shot back, clashing with the table. The sound of glass shattering along the ground behind Joseph made his skin crawl even more. Wine splashed across his face in tiny dots, much like Stuart's blood had as he turned to see the damage. *Oh god,* Joseph thought. The wine bottle had been knocked over, pouring out into a growing puddle—exactly where Detective Kline had vomited the bloodied bits of his esophagus in the nightmare. Joseph looked away and saw that some of the wine had splattered along the wall, running down like Stuart's brain matter had done along the kitchen walls in his real life.

It was all too much for Joseph.

Arturo had disappeared into the kitchen and returned with a small bucket, roll of paper towels, and a cleaning spray, too. Arturo picked up the bottle of wine, carefully cleaned it, and then started on the puddle. Joseph wanted to move, to help, but he felt paralyzed, caught in the liminal space between reality and his nightmares.

"I'm sorry," Joseph replied to the silence between them. Arturo was now soft, and soon he slipped back on the hip huggers.

"I gotta ask, you know," Arturo said calmly. Joseph's stomach dropped. "What's going on?"

"Going on?" Joseph replied. His eyes snapped to Arturo's, and they stared at each other for a while.

"If we're not sexually compatible, that's okay." Arturo paused, and Joseph felt pressure to speak, but he couldn't exactly find the words. Watching Arturo clean up the blood-red wine only reminded Joseph of what was waiting for him when they returned.

"You just seem a little different." Arturo broke the silence.

"Nothing has changed—please don't think I'm not into you, Arturo. You are understanding and attractive."

"Well, what is it then? I can be there for you like you were there for me last night." Arturo tucked the rags into a bucket and walked to the kitchen. He returned to wipe the floor down, collecting any wine that might have remained. Joseph felt like his head was filled with thick mud. If he wasn't honest in this moment, he feared he would lose Arturo and soon be found and convicted for his crimes. Nobody could run forever, but even those who do always have a solid alibi—*and that's what I have, goddamn it,* Joseph thought. Trudging through the mud, he let the words flow. He knew where to begin.

"I met Dean Scott a few days before being shipped off to boarding school. My mother had left my father and took me to the West Coast. She always said she had a lot of contacts and some giving back to do out there. So, when we landed, we headed straight to the university. I got a tour and met Dean Scott, who had just been elected as president for the entire university. When my tour was over, I joined the last few minutes of their meeting. She was donating a building to the school that day, one that would help the business wing take more applicants." Joseph paused while Arturo collected the shards of glass with damp towels and put them in the bucket.

"We talked about how I'd always wanted to be a writer. He said they had a great program there. When my mother passed, he sent me a personal letter with his phone number, telling me to give him a call when I was ready to apply. He told me it was what my mother would've wanted, which was true. He was still the president nearly five years later when I applied. I was immediately accepted. Dean always looked out for me. He was like a father."

"He spoke fondly of you in the letter," Arturo noted.

"Yes, and we did grow very close. After I graduated, a professor who normally taught 101 English had retired. He gave me the position. I was the youngest professor at the school. I felt very accomplished. Being a teacher, I was able to publish some textbooks that earned me royalties. Things were nice. I almost made tenure, too. But then . . ." Joseph's voice faded. He didn't want to admit what he'd been doing. He feared Arturo would see him as a big red flag once he knew. Arturo broke Joseph's inner turmoil.

"Then what? You got the idea for *Rabbit's Revenge?*" Arturo asked humbly.

"No," Joseph said flat, tears welling in his eyes. "I got bored. I was on a few dating apps that mainly led to hook-ups. I wanted something a bit more substantial, and I talked with this handsome guy. I didn't realize he was a student on a waitlist for my class."

"How did you not know?" Arturo asked, shocked.

"It's not like many students are trying to sleep with an entry-level professor." Joseph downplayed his position now. "But when I found out, we'd already kinda been fucking on and off for a year. He was in my class, all smiling and innocent looking. We were both consenting adults, but no one else in the room knew our connection. It was thrilling until it wasn't."

"So, did Dean find out?" Arturo asked.

"He found out all right, but he wasn't alone." Joseph could recall that day and allowed himself to be vulnerable enough to explain it. "It was the last day of the semester; it was the last class, too. Most students didn't show up 'cause everything had been posted and graded. But this one did."

"What was the student's name?" Arturo asked.

"I'd rather not say," Joseph replied, and Arturo nodded, understanding. "He came at the very end of class, and nobody was there. We didn't expect that Dean would've been giving a tour to a few financial donors that day. He walked in with a few other colleagues, and everything blew up. And there was no denying it. I was deep inside the guy at the time."

"Holy shit," Arturo's jaw dropped in shock. "So, then you got fired?"

"Yeah, for not respecting the relationship between teacher and student. Especially when some of these students looked up to us as mentors. Dean retired a few weeks after. He was able to secure me a severance package for the first year after the incident. Then my father passed, and I inherited my mother's entire estate, or what was left of it—which was very, very, very little." Joseph paused. "I moved back to take over the house and focus on publishing the book. Dean helped me find a wonderful content publishing company. The rest has been easy."

"Why is he always looking out for you?" Arturo asked.

"My mother had known Dean for years before I'd ever met him. Before I was even born. He's always looked to me as his son. Not like my birth father was ever a real father to me, anyways, just one who laundered money through my trust and my mother's estate. I respected Dean, too, and he didn't have any kids. I think it was a mutual respect rather than bloodline."

Arturo nodded. "So, what brought all of this up tonight?"

Joseph's lips grew tight, his teeth gnawing at the soft skin inside.

"Just being here, I guess," Joseph stammered a bit. "He was a father figure, the wine spilled. I feel like a disappointment in all regards. Especially in pleasing you."

Arturo rolled his eyes. "It's okay that we haven't. I just wanted to make sure. Also, I'm the one who should be sorry. I spilled the wine."

"It's okay," Joseph said. He wiped the drying stream of tears from his face. "We should probably head to bed if we're going to make it to the funeral tomorrow. We can take the other bottle with us when we leave."

Arturo nodded. "Yeah, that'd be smart. I'll need us to swing by my place for my suit. You have one, yeah?"

"Mmhm," Joseph said, nodding. "Probably easier if you change at your place, and I'll hop inside and change, too. You can wait in the car. I've learned to be very quick about these things."

Arturo nodded, confirming, and Joseph felt—well, not better, but not as heavy, either. He bit off some more of that delicate skin that lined the inside of his mouth. Misplaced anger was dangerous to hold on to for too long. He wanted Arturo to say something, but he stood up instead.

Arturo emptied the bucket of glass into a trash can, and a shudder ran through Joseph as he heard the sounds fill the house for a brief second. Joseph clicked off the fire and crawled in bed. Soon Arturo did the same. Arturo rested upon Joseph's chest, and they lay in silence as if nothing had happened, just an easy early night. Joseph stared at the ceiling to avoid sleep and the nightmares that waited.

"But you've been teaching me all day," A pipsqueak voice came through the desktop speakers from an early numbered recording. Noah remembered details from the memory as it played with crisp, clear audio. "I already built a fire tonight. That's manly, isn't it, Mr. Fisher?"

Noah recognized the voice he heard. It was his own. He couldn't stop himself from listening to more after he heard Fisher's murder. Each recording was a scab that itched, demanding to be picked at. The seat inside the office seemed to implode as if he was being pulled from behind and thrown into his memories. His shoes were suddenly too big to fit. His clothes melted off him like running water, leaving tiny beads on his body. He had his arms wrapped around his stomach for warmth in front of the fire. He was nothing more than a boy on a camping trip. On the other side of him sat Boy Scout Master Benjamin Fisher.

The fire grew between them, and Noah could see the details of the surrounding forest come into better view. The frogs croaked near the lakeside, not too far from where they'd set up camp. He remembered how Fisher had helped him obtain his hiking badge before coming on this trip, and in the lake today, he'd achieved his fishing badge, and tomorrow before Fisher dropped Noah off at home, he'd have earned his camping badge. The cherry on top. Noah had always been eager to earn badges with Fisher, and his parents were always happy to get him out of the house, but they never really cared to ask what he'd done, earned, or did over the weekend trips.

Fisher sat in his chair on the opposite side of the fire. Behind him, the logo of the tent Noah had pitched all by himself reflected in the campfire glow. The warm fire cascaded over his exposed skin. The underwear around his waist gripped him sloppily, still wet from the lake. Fisher was in his wet boxers, too. The light from his smartphone went dark as he set it down on a log. Noah, as a child, hadn't noticed anything odd, but now as an adult listening, he realized Fisher had been recording them then. Had Fisher planned this out, hoping to get a bonus digital memento?

Fisher laughed hard. "You won't need to do anything else now—just lie back and enjoy. Come over here." He patted the seat between them where the phone lay—its metal edges glimmered with moonlight. Noah did as he said, feeling the sand stick to the bottom of his pruney feet and then to the blanket Fisher was sitting on. He sat next to his leader, his scout master. Fisher smiled, producing from his shirt pocket a small neatly wrapped joint. "I felt like you could use this," he said.

"What is it?" Noah asked.

"I don't mean any harm, but you are so innocent. It's magnificent. It's a joint. Smoke some. You'll relax. All the other boys in the troop enjoy it. It can be our secret."

Noah eyed the joint cautiously. "Our secret? What if my parents find out?"

"Oh, I don't think your parents would care too much. They barely said goodbye when they dropped you off. Are they always like that?"

"They're just busy with work, you know?"

"You think their work is more important than you?" Fisher asked, leaning his face into a lighter that flickered with flame. The smell reminded Noah of a skunk's spray. "Don't be quiet now. Do you think that?

He hadn't ever thought of this before. "It's just working. I can keep myself entertained while they are busy. I play video games, and now I'm getting all these badges."

"Sounds lonely," Fisher said. "Here, smoke some. I'll take care of you. And don't worry, I won't tell if you don't."

Noah smiled, fulfilled with something he'd never received from his parents. They always made taking care of him seem like a burden. The joint sizzled bright orange as his throat grew hot. He felt tears begin to ride up into his eyes and his throat closing up. He worried that if he dropped the joint, the whole forest would blaze. Fisher quickly took it from Noah's dainty fingers.

"You gotta breathe, boy." He laughed hard again as Noah exhaled and coughed loudly. His eyes watered. Everything seemed to slow down. Noah's head swayed from side to side with the trees, bobbling back and forth.

"It's nice, isn't it?" Fisher said.

Noah felt a slow wave pour over him, like a warm blanket leaving little to worry about. He smiled at Fisher, nodding his head.

"Yeah, it's good like that," Fisher said. "You're so cute right now. Your beady little eyes remind me of a rabbit. That's what I'll call you, my little Rabbit." Fisher continued, "Don't close your eyes. I want you to watch everything."

When the fire eventually died out, Fisher wasn't finished, but at least Noah didn't have to watch anymore. The fire logs crumbled over themselves, and they cackled loudly, sending sparks into the sky that looked like fireflies.

Noah felt sick to his stomach, blinking many times until the office came back into focus. He felt tears in his eyes and a hollowness in his chest.

He continued to play the next few audio recordings, which consisted of grunts and some chatter but mostly from Fisher's side. He must not have realized that phones back then weren't top-notch recording devices. A lot of coughing ensued during these recordings, too, which led Noah to believe he wasn't the only boy breaking rules smoking pot with the Scout Leader. How many boys had he groomed using this technique, Noah didn't want to wonder.

And then—

"Oh, my sweet, sweet boy," Fisher spoke in a low growl at the start of another recording.

Noah's eyes stung with tears as he listened to the rest, and he couldn't help but slam his fist into the desk. He was furious. How could he have been so stupid? He thought getting himself arrested would've ended things. Instead, Fisher had merely replaced *his Little Rabbit* with a *sweet, sweet boy*—another victim. The recording continued to play—Noah disgusted—as he heard the small voice of the new boy speak, and the conversation that ensued only fueled Noah's rage. He erupted to his feet, like a wildfire consuming a tall dried-out tree trunk.

Fisher had been a predator. No one had ever listened to him, but they would now. There was no other choice.

He looked down at the keyboard so he could type faster.

Noah searched the web for Rafael Rodriguez and found him. He'd set up a free social media account with no name or photo. Rafael's page was public, which showed a recent post that read:

> Benjamin Fisher helped save my daughters when they were lost. He is a hero to our family. Please feel welcome to come and pay your respects today. The service will begin around 11:00 a.m. at our local church on . . .

Noah shook his head in utter disgust. His nostrils flared with hot breath. He sent the recording off to Rafael.

The clone phone pinged, letting Noah know Joseph was within thirty miles of the house. He quickly exited out of everything on the desktop. Noah looked around; everything was clean. His eyes landed on the police folder with Fisher's name on it. He stashed that away in the office among the books before going to the garage.

Noah smiled as he got another notification.

A text from Sergio Hernandez: *Do you want to come over for lunch at my place? I have the afternoon off.*

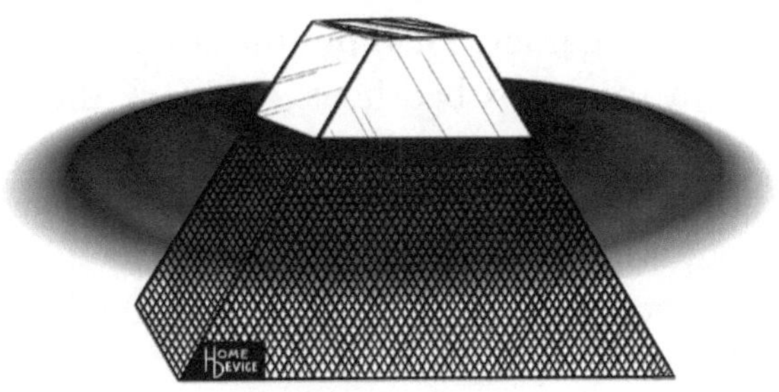

Joseph was able to get coffee on the way back into Baxtor Springs, and once more when he stopped at the bar so Arturo could change into his suit. When they met back at the car, Joseph was impressed with how good Arturo looked in a sharp black suit and thin tie. His dark hair gleaming in the sunlight, he looked ready for a photoshoot. Joseph handed Arturo a double espresso as he got inside the Porsche, and soon they left Main Street square behind. He'd already halfway finished his extra-large iced coffee.

"Okay, so I'll just run in quickly and change next. How are we doing on time?"

"Doing well. Even if we take twenty minutes at your house, we'll still be good on time. So, no rush, really," Arturo said, looking over at Joseph. His eyes were always so kind, and underneath what he said was a simple nudge: he wasn't going to wait in the car while Joseph got ready.

Joseph turned up his driveway, his lips pursed, prepared to repeat himself, or say this was what they had *planned* last night. There was no way Arturo could enter that house. Otherwise, what might Joseph be forced to do?

Joseph eased his foot off the gas pedal as he saw the cruiser parked in his driveway. Precisely the same way Stuart had that night. Joseph knew without a doubt that he'd hidden the cruiser in his garage. He'd put the storage racks around it, along with some old bedsheets, to block the view from outside. Yet, there it was, parked in the driveway. He down-shifted as he got closer, and the cruiser's door opened. Stuart Kline got out of the car, his face still bashed in. Thick strands of blood dripped from his chin, swaying in the light breeze.

You're losing it, Joseph.

Joseph braked. His throat itched. He wiped his forehead and then looked back to Stuart—no, standing alongside the cruiser was a man in his late forties with chestnut brown hair, stray salty strands sprinkled throughout. A crooked nose and a puffy right ear. He could tell he'd been in some fights, but Joseph wouldn't have suspected that if he hadn't looked closer. The man was thin, his cheap suit baggy on his frame.

"Afternoon," the man said, and Joseph's heart hammered in his chest. "I'm Detective Vaughn." He flashed his badge. It matched Stuart's from that night, except the name read, Detective Lewis Vaughn, Baxtor Springs.

"Afternoon, Detective," Joseph said, getting out of the car. He rested against the side for support. He felt like his knees were going to buckle.

"I'm Arturo de Leon. This is Joseph Bailey," Arturo said, coming out of the car.

The gash in the driveway drew a dividing line between them.

"Nice to meet you both." Vaughn eyed Arturo dressed in his black suit. "Are you going to one of the funeral services this afternoon? I apologize if I'm interrupting. I just have a few questions."

"Questions?" Joseph asked, his stomach squirming.

"Yes, a fellow detective—my partner, actually—has gone missing. When I checked his location, it said he was here. Any chance you've seen this man?"

Detective Vaughn held up a color-printed photo on glossy paper. It was Stuart Kline, his smile not twisted, jaw intact, eyes kind and straightforward. The photo dangled between the detective's two fingers and thumb, waving in the wind. Joseph couldn't look away from Stuart's piercing stare, his photo now taunting him with the same remarks from the nightmare.

Smaller towns are different. People talk. People look out for each other.

Joseph's stomach churned painfully, like a blender turned on high, about to explode. He felt a brush of cold prickle the hairs on his neck. Stuart's body was still behind the kitchen island along with his phone. What stench was locked inside, waiting for a door to crack open? Once they'd smelled that, they'd find a perfect crime scene.

"Detective Kline?" Arturo asked, shocked.

"You know him?" Vaughn asked.

"Not personally, but I've served him at the bar a few times." Arturo shook his head, looking away as if trying to think. Vaughn's eyes turned to Joseph.

"No, I haven't seen him, either," Joseph spoke in a tuneless voice. A simple lie that should suffice, he hoped.

"Gotcha," Vaughn said, eyeing them both.

Joseph looked away and stared down at the gash between them.

"What happened to your driveway?" Vaughn asked.

"Oh, the tire marks, I—" Joseph hesitated.

"He was in a rush to pack the bags for our getaway trip. That's what I don't understand. We've been away the past couple nights." Arturo casually shrugged. "When did the detective go missing?"

"His wife reported him missing within the past twenty-four hours. She's tried calling him but no answer. I checked his location and saw he was here and headed over. Then you both showed up, good timing."

"We've been out of town," Joseph mustered.

"Yeah, we were up at Lake Wilburton."

"Camping outdoors?" Vaughn asked with a smile.

"Stayed at a house. It was a nice little escape." Arturo cleared his throat. "Although, yes, detective, we are on our way to attend Benjamin Fisher's funeral, to answer your earlier question. We cut our getaway short because of it. Joseph needs to get changed, and neither one of us has seen Detective Kline. Are you sure the location is right?"

Arturo began walking to the front door, Detective Vaughn following suit. Joseph knew the smart door would be open already, based on his preferences. The technology he'd painstakingly integrated into the house was now going to give him up.

Joseph fell in line behind them. Each step forward felt closer to his obscene truth being discovered. This time, he wouldn't be able to reinvent himself by going to boarding school or moving to the West Coast to live comfortably as a professor under Dean's care. Or become an author in his mother's luxury estate, where he'd hope to live out the rest of his days. Instead, he would be in prison rotting away for murder. Arturo and Detective Vaughn would testify as witnesses at the trial, allowing the jury to swiftly convict Joseph in the name of justice.

A trickle of ice-cold sweat trailed down the nape of Joseph's neck. His stomach churned again. The coffee still wasn't settling right. He felt his throat pulse and his back muscles seize. He gripped his stomach, momentarily debilitated. The pain was so immense, Joseph threw a hand out, pushing Detective Vaughn a few feet ahead as he tumbled forward and vomited dark black coffee all over the lavender flowers.

"What the—you okay?" Detective Vaughn staggered back.

"Joseph!" Arturo whipped around with concern.

Joseph felt Arturo rub his shoulder as he attempted to stand up straight, pressing his palms against his thighs. The knots in his stomach snapped him back down.

"Are you okay, Mr. Bailey?" Detective Vaughn asked.

Joseph waved a hand. "Yes, just had too much coffee this morning—I think you both should go."

Another round of vomit was coming. Joseph could feel it. He looked back to Arturo with the front door already open behind them. The mangled remains of Stuart Kline were just around the corner, in the kitchen. Arturo turned and jogged inside, past the foyer and down the hallway. Joseph vomited loudly now, expecting to hear Arturo shriek as he discovered the crime scene around the corner.

Instead, Arturo returned with a hand towel from the guest bathroom. Joseph wiped his mouth and collected himself enough to stand. Arturo and Vaughn helped him stagger to the L-shaped couch. They laid him down on the side that overlooked the views of sunlit forestry. Joseph couldn't see behind him. Could they see the blood? It would only be a matter of time until they did.

Arturo and Vaughn stared down at him, worried.

"I don't think you're gonna be able to make it to the funeral," Arturo said.

"Yes, you should go now then. Take my car if you need to," Joseph said.

"There is no way I know how to drive that old thing," Arturo said, chuckling lightly. "Can you double-check that location, Detective?" Arturo asked.

Vaughn nodded and pulled out his phone, and then scratched his head.

"Looks like he's at the church right now," Vaughn said, turning his phone to show a tiny blue dot on a map. "I'm very sorry for the mix-up."

"Okay, well—" Arturo paused, looking down to Joseph. "You can't attend in your state, obviously, and I don't drive . . . Would you mind giving me a lift, Detective?"

Vaughn smiled. "I can give you a ride if you need one. Just don't give me a low rating."

Arturo chuckled politely.

"I have to go. I'm very sorry," Joseph said, making his way down the hallway to the bathroom just in time for another round of vomit to land in the toilet. The shit-colored liquids spewing from his mouth had a layer of yellow foam mixed in—his stomach acids. All Joseph could picture was Stuart's pus dripping down from his tear ducts beside his ripped irises. Joseph vomited again from just the image alone. He hugged the toilet bowl. Guilt leached into his conscience like a parasite, draining him of his energy.

"I'll text you to see if you need anything later tonight. I'll take care of this lavender, too, when I get back, okay?" Arturo offered, leaving.

"Okay, thank you," Joseph muttered, hearing their footsteps walk out on to the driveway.

In the silence that followed, Joseph slinked to the kitchen, behind the island. The crime scene had been cleaned up. The body moved, but what about the cruiser? Joseph clutched both sides of his head, his brain feeling as if it might split in two.

He had killed the wrong person.

He also couldn't go to the funeral, where Joseph assumed *Rabbit* would most likely be. *Rabbit* had to have been the one to clean up the crime scene, Joseph thought, pawing at his neck, fanning the collar of his shirt. What was *Rabbit's* end-game. Money? He felt uncomfortable in his own home. It no longer felt private; the amenities and features now seemed tainted. Joseph looked at his phone, the wallpaper lit up, and the facial recognition passcode showed a little unlocking icon at the top. Not a single notification, though, and yet all around him was proof that someone had been inside.

Joseph clicked through to the settings of the security app and saw that every notification had been turned off. He felt nauseous, almost enough to vomit again. *Rabbit* must have used Joseph's phone, and yet, there was no history in the security log. Joseph scoured the app for any proof but found none, and then he had an idea.

He deleted the last time the door had been opened when they arrived and talked with Detective Vaughn. Joseph closed the app. He swiped down, trying to find what he knew must have happened, and yet there was no further trace. *Rabbit* was covering up his tracks, while making his presence so evident.

Joseph trudged past the living room, then the kitchen, and down the hallway. He smelled that same strawberry-banana vape smell lingering in the corners. He took in a deep breath—he smelled body odor, too. A faint enough scent that a dog could track it. He continued to the garage and opened the door. The darkness inside was thick. He flicked on the light and saw that the storage racks hadn't changed, and he couldn't see past the dark bedsheets, still perfectly in place. He stepped down the small flight of stairs and walked past the freezer. He pushed the storage rack aside, making enough room to peek past.

The cruiser was gone, the space empty.

No—not empty.

Joseph vomited once more, clawing at the storage rack for balance. His mind raced with a montage of crime scene investigators discovering evidence of Joseph all over Stuart Kline's body. His prints found on the the steering wheel in the cruiser. Soon, he feared, Detective Vaughn wouldn't just stop by to question him—he'd be arresting Joseph for murder.

Arturo cracked the window in the cruiser, letting in some fresh air. The interior of the car smelled very old. Even the passenger seat had cracks in the leather, revealing a fluffy synthetic material underneath. Between them sat the black radio with various knobs. Each one's label had been rubbed off over time, but the sea-green colored lights displayed that they had nearly ten minutes to make it to the funeral on time. Arturo noticed his jacket was still buttoned, ruffled up around his chest. He undid it, feeling the jacket relax on his frame while Vaughn continued a dull conversation about how his cauliflower ear was recovering. He paused, looking at Arturo, who didn't exactly know how to respond, other than a polite *oh*.

Vaughn cleared his throat. "What bar do you work at, again?"

"I don't think I've ever seen you there," Arturo said. "Being close to the police station, I see practically everyone. It's A Whiskey Bar."

"Oh, I know that one. I haven't been drinking. Lately, the massacre has been a free excuse for some, but not me. Before the feds took over the investigation, I was helping the morgue sort through bodies, collect DNA, interview family members, requesting their DNA to help us, them too. I've been going to therapy since I'm no longer working the case. I'm not saying I'm never going to drink again, but right now isn't the best time. Being away from that investigation is good for me. Now I can focus on the normal local shit again."

"Yeah," Arturo said, thinking about how nice it had been to escape with Joseph for two nights. "How many more bodies are left to be identified? Do you know?" Arturo asked.

"Not that many more. When we handed the case over, we'd already covered about forty percent of the acres affected."

"What did that include?" Arturo asked.

"Well, the gas station—which was pretty easy to work through. They had cameras uploading to a cloud, so even before Joshua reached for that officer's gun, we could start identifying people. We put together pictures, some grainy but still passable, and that list was passed around to the community, local news, and social media people. The cameras in the grocery store were still on an old VHS machine system that, well, was burned to a melted blob when we found it. So, it took a lot of time to identify who was inside the grocery store. Taking charred pieces to the morgue to discover what limb it was, or in some cases, only to discover it was melted plastic. It was so much death. I'd never seen anything like that. No one had, for Christ's sake."

"It was a busy Saturday," Arturo mused.

"Some of the remains were of people who had been caught mid-shopping, still pushing carts. Just black roasted carcasses frozen in place through the grocery aisles."

"How was Stuart handling the massacre?" Arturo asked.

"Not well, he took the first opportunity to jump off working the massacre when he could. That ended up being Fisher's suicide-ruled-homicide case. Which seemed like a complete dead end to me."

"Because his place had already been cleaned?"

"Exactly." Vaughn tossed a hand up. "There's nothing to go on with that case."

"Do the feds think any of this is connected?"

"Why would you think that?" Vaughn asked, cocking an eye over to him.

"Joshua Rodriguez caused the massacre. He was a Boy Scout. Someone murdered Fisher. Boy Scout Troop Leader. Your partner is missing, who was investigating it. I mean, connect the dots."

"I'm sure Kline is going to pop up, and we'll all laugh about how we thought he was missing. No point in looping everything together when we have only just begun looking into the possibility of him missing. His location says he's on the move. He's fine."

They both grew quiet as Vaughn pulled into the church's parking lot, past a printed sign tightly strung between two thick wood posts that read, "Grieving? Please don't do it alone. We are here to help! Snacks and refreshments are offered every Tuesday and Thursday. Plenty of seating and plenty of people here to listen. Baxtor Springs will never forget the victims." The church sat in the center of the lot, its tall white steeple rose high above the tree line, yet the church itself was a small wooden building that had just been repainted the previous year and could only house about fifty people inside. On the other side was the cemetery that buttressed the woods. The holes in the ground reminded Arturo of something from a war film.

The parking lot, since the massacre, had increased in size to accommodate more visiting families and the subsequent funerals that followed. The forest beside the church had been cut back, the ground cleared out and covered in mixed pebbles to accommodate the masses. While donations weren't mandatory, the church expected a full hat of contributions before any funeral would begin.

"Well, thank you for the ride, Detective Vaughn," Arturo said. "If you could let me out here, that'd be great."

Vaughn stopped the cruiser, and the glossy black lock popped up from inside the door. Arturo got out while people walked around the car toward the church. Arturo turned back and leaned in. "Good luck finding your partner."

"Yeah, yeah." Vaughn smiled, and then something must've caught his eye to the far left of the parking lot. Arturo looked over to the parking lot filled with cars. Another police cruiser was parked in the far back. Police Chief Edmonds was walking by with other officers toward the church.

He closed the door, and Vaughn slowly pulled forward through the crowd of incoming people. Arturo stood for a moment, taking in the humid air filled with the scent of fresh-cut grass and flowers wafting from the cemetery just a few yards away. A large weeping willow swept the surrounding grass with its long, green limbs in the far back. It had grown so large in the years that passed since Arturo stood beneath it, watching his mother's coffin lower.

"If that's your boyfriend, and he's trying to find parking, tell him he's gonna have to try the lot across the street," a sharp voice came up behind him. Arturo turned to see his *tía* approaching. Her dark brunette hair was short and puffy around her aging face. She wore a black dress with a shawl over her shoulders. Arturo noticed that she was wearing a gold necklace, but she closed her shawl, reaching for his arm. She wrapped her arms around his and pointed forward. "We should try to get seats fast though; we'll hold a spot for him."

Arturo smiled and slipped into her stride. "*He* is not my boyfriend."

"Oh, but there is a *he*," she mimicked. "Huh?"

Arturo laughed as his *tía* pushed them through the crowd and past the church's thick double wooden doors. He was hit with the familiar stale smell that seemed to linger only in old buildings that stood too long. He coughed, the thick air catching in his throat, and everyone sitting in the pews whipped their heads back to look at them. The light conversation of the room only stopped momentarily. The service itself hadn't started, but already he could see many familiar faces. Even Goldstein was standing off in the corner across the room.

"Just here, I don't need to be too close," she said, pointing to the third to last bench in the row. When they sat down, Arturo could smell *Tía*'s perfume of florals brush past him. "After this, let's get some lunch. I'm starved." Without waiting, she turned to say hello to someone who greeted her as Maria.

Arturo looked away from his *tía* and back toward Goldstein, who he caught looking at him. He waved, and Arturo politely returned the gesture and then turned away. He spotted the Rodriguez sisters sitting in the front row. When they had gotten lost in the hiking trails, they'd been small and fragile, but now they were fully grown with kids and husbands by their sides. Both sisters wore a slim-fitting black look that was elegant but not attention-drawing. Arturo noticed that their father, Rafael, was not sitting among them.

The priest stepped up and politely asked everyone to be mindful of their devices and to take the opportunity while they passed the basket around to double-check. Arturo felt his phone slipping from the dress pants and caught it. He made sure his phone was on silent, and instead of returning it to his pocket, he lay the thin device on his lap.

The priest paused, collecting the basket, and then he took a breath. He opened the good book to a bookmarked spot. When he spoke, his grainy voice echoed through the church. When he finished, he invited Chief Edmonds to the podium to say a few words and then asked the Rodriguez sisters to close out the ceremony.

"Thank you, Father," Chief Edmonds said, standing behind the podium, grasping both sides. He was a hunched figure, though he used to stand tall. The police chief gestured to the priest before facing forward. He wiped his mouth, the stubble on his cheeks scratching through to the microphone. Arturo's skin crawled hearing the friction, and his ears prickled.

"I'd like to thank everyone for coming this morning." He paused, looking over the crowd, even making eye contact with Arturo. "Benjamin Fisher had served this community for years as the leader for Boy Scout Troop #4059, here in Baxtor Springs. Many of us knew him as the guy who taught us our knots, showed us community, and how to be respectful members inside of that community. On top of that, he rescued the Rodriguez sisters who almost died after getting lost inside our most challenging hiking trails." Edmonds took a pause, his eyes scanning over the room once more. "I'd like to ask the public to please come forward if you know anything regarding his murder; please do not hesitate to get in touch with us. We want to hold the person—or persons—accountable for what they did to one of the town's greatest."

The church doors burst open then, and everyone's head shot to the back where the warm heat and bright sunlight erupted inside with a man. When everyone's eyes adjusted, they saw Rafael Rodriguez standing there. He was panting, sweating, and his eyes locked in on the chief at the podium. The audience glanced at the few officers around the room. Without hesitation, each of them placed their hands on their holstered weapon. From where Arturo sat, he could smell pure alcohol wafting off Rafael.

"Rafael, now, no trouble, you hear?" The chief said across the room from behind the podium.

"Oh, of course, *chief*," Rafael said as he lifted a small black box. The room gasped, collectively recoiling from him as if it were a bomb. It was not, however, only a portable speaker with Bluetooth capabilities. In his other hand, Rafael tapped on his phone screen until the room filled with a muffled noise and heavy bass. Rafael increased the volume, and in turn, the fear in everyone's eyes.

Maria squeezed Arturo's arm. He looked at her. She returned a severe gaze. A voice boomed from the speaker, and the entire room shifted uncomfortably.

"Please stop, I don't want to—" a soft voice pleaded.

"Is that what you say to the man who saved your sisters? If it wasn't for me . . ." a deeper voice trailed off.

"I don't want to do this anymore."

"Or what?" The deeper voice boomed.

"I'll tell."

"Is that Joshua?" one of the Rodriguez sisters asked from the first row. She raised a hand over her mouth, horrified.

"And just who do you think would you tell? Your family won't believe you. Do you know who I am to them?"

"Then I'll go to the police," the smaller voice piped up.

"Oh my god, that's Fisher's voice," someone from the crowd said with a gasp.

"Nobody will believe you. Try the chief, why don't you? The last one that ratted on me went to jail. You're better off just killing yourself. Now shut up. I was close to finishing there, my *sweet, sweet boy*," Fisher's voice snarled. Then the recording stopped, and nobody said a single thing.

"Someone anonymously sent me this audio file," Rafael's voice boomed, all eyes on him. "It was taken only one hour before my boy tried to kill himself, setting off the massacre. Police Chief Edmonds, why were you covering for this fucking pedophile?" Rafael roared. "Did you molest my son, too, Chief?"

Rafael screamed with such anger that the room shifted away from him. He threw the black box like a brick at the chief. Edmonds dodged to the right, and the speaker crashed right through the stained-glass wall behind the podium. High-pitched screams erupted over the sound of glass breaking as Rafael charged down the aisle with a ferocious growl, heading for the chief. Edmonds threw himself behind Fisher's casket, dodging with a look of utter terror on his face. Rafael missed the chief and instead collided with the side of the casket. The wood splintered with a loud *crack* before it thudded against the thinly carpeted floor, banging loudly.

Arturo, along with the rest of the crowd, hopped to his feet. He felt something slide down his legs and bang against his foot. Arturo knelt and grabbed his phone. Through the shuffle of slacks, polished shoes, high heels, and dresses, he saw Benjamin Fisher's remains half sprawled out in the open casket. The skin had been drained of its color. Shards of bones protruded out of what remained of his face, his jaw dangling with jagged teeth still set within. Arturo gasped, horrified—he shouldn't have come. What he remembered of Fisher was nothing like the current state—seeing his carcass felt like looking down at some alien being with sharp teeth. Arturo felt the tug of his *tía*'s pull. They joined the herd of people leaving the church. The officers tackled Rafael, who was attempting to get to his feet and charge the chief once more.

Outside, even in the open air, Arturo's chest was tight with fear that bullets would begin flying inside. His *tía* wrapped both of her arms around his frame, and they walked with haste toward the parking lot. For a second, Arturo realized the many cars parked could be the death of them all, just like some of the victims in the massacre. They jogged faster. Passing through a few rows of cars, the commotion of people still getting out of the church simmered behind them.

"I'm guessing you don't have a ride back?" His *tía* asked in a judgmental tone, her puffy hair bouncing with her stride. Arturo shook his head. "You have to get a car at some point, Arturo."

"I don't need a car, *Tía*," he replied. She gave him a look, but he continued. "But I'll humbly accept a ride from you, since I don't want to wait for a ride share to pick me up in this mess."

His *tía* let out a sigh, and her stride slowed a little as Arturo glanced back at the church, where the stream of people exiting had ceased. Those who remained inside were surrounding Rafael and his family, and things looked tense. Arturo was relieved to be far from it. His core still trembling, he turned back to see his *tía*'s car. Vaughn was standing right beside it, shaking his head.

The smell of blood washed over Arturo, and he panicked, trying to hold back the sheer anxiety of having those memories flood over him again. Fisher's body was back inside the church, and even then, he hadn't smelled the blood. His *tía* let out a shrill scream that sent pins and needles down Arturo's back.

Parked beside Maria's sedan was the cruiser Arturo had noticed earlier. Vaughn was looking inside the opened trunk. Vaughn turned his head away from the sight, bringing a fist over his mouth as he tried to compose himself. The stench of blood morphed into something baked and rotten. Inside the trunk was a corpse that lay in the fetal position, the head turned up to the sky. The skin a shade of pink coral with bits of thick yellow crust hardened between deep, open gashes. The eyes, the ears, the mouth—the person's entire face was unrecognizable. Yet, Arturo knew it was Detective Stuart Kline. He could spot the shiny badge still attached to Kline's hip.

"Jesus Christ, I need a drink," his *tía* said, covering her nose and mouth.

"Me, too."

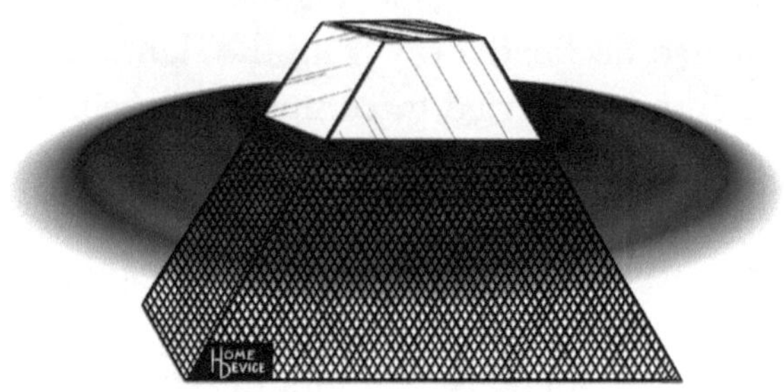

Joseph's phone vibrated in his pocket, making him jump. He hadn't left the garage yet. He was still too stunned. He grabbed his phone and checked the screen. Emily's name glimmered, and he answered the call as naturally as possible.

"Hey, hey," Emily said, radiating a smile through the phone.

"Hey, what's up?" Joseph asked. His voice was hollow, as if someone had removed a long sword from his throat.

"You okay?" She asked with immediate concern.

"I'm not feeling so hot . . ." Joseph mumbled, rubbing the cold sweat off his neck with his free hand.

"Oh, no," Emily said, saddened. "You think you'll still be able to drop the books off tomorrow?"

Joseph smirked. "This feeling will pass by then. Friday night will still work for the reading."

"Oh, wonderful! You said yes," she exclaimed.

"That I did," Joseph replied.

"Yay!" Emily cheered. "Okay, well, rest up, and tomorrow you'll feel much better."

Joseph nodded and said goodbye. When he hung up, he remembered how he'd wanted a Xanax after having lunch with Emily. Now, though, he *needed* one. He made his way to the office, where he kept them inside his desk drawer. He passed by bare footmarks along the floor and stopped. Were these from his *little rabbit*? Joseph feared the worst. His eyes scanned the usually unused couch in the room and saw that the fabric was dimpled, indicating that someone had sat there. Joseph's mind raced, feeling again the claustrophobic sensation that the walls were closing in, his throat closing up as he tried to inhale. There wasn't enough oxygen in the room he feared, and he charged toward the office.

Joseph slid open the door and barreled toward his desk, ripping open the right-hand drawer, where the orange prescription pill bottle rattled inside. He broke the safety tab, and the top flew off toward the other side of the room. Joseph froze in place when he saw where the white lid landed. His hands trembled so much that some of the Xanax popped out from inside the bottle like popcorn *pop-popping*. Sweat dripped down the sides of his face with fresh fear. Every copy of his book had been removed from the packaging he'd received from Publishing X. Each one delicately stacked in perfect towers around the room. He stared at the bunny depicted on the book's cover. He felt mocked and trembled in fear.

"How long did this take you?" Joseph spoke aloud to his *rabbit*, wondering if he could hear Joseph. Had his *rabbit* even left the house? He popped one of the few pills that remained in the bottle. He swallowed it with some leftover water in a bottle on his desk near the dirty coffee mugs. Had he poured this glass? he wondered. He turned and felt his feet shuffle along the office floor, past the books, into his hallway, and toward the couch. He plopped down face-first on the sofa, letting the Xanax wash away his fears and drown him in deep sleep.

Noah knocked on the door, his knuckles rapping beside the oxidized brass apartment number. He waited, nervously smoothing out his shirt and, essentially, first date jitters. He wore a fresh outfit from Joseph's closet. They almost had the same build, even wore the same size shoes. Noah wore basic chinos and a silky oversized button-up, both in black, with a pair of white trainers. He'd never worn an outfit like this; he relished how the silk shirt caressed his chest with every bit of movement.

He'd thrown out the clothes he'd worn inside Stuart Kline's cruiser, just in case anyone had seen him. He didn't think anyone had, though. The parking lot was empty when he'd done the deed. He hadn't bothered to stick around for what would ensue.

Footsteps thumped on the opposite side of the door and then paused. Noah stood tall, inhaling a breath of confidence. The door opened with a sultry aroma of peppers and lemon. His stomach felt hollow, and he realized how hungry he was.

Sergio Hernandez stood before him in a basic short-sleeve white tee with a black apron cinched around his waist. He had on blue jeans and tan socks.

"Sergio," Noah said with a smile.

Sergio paused, looking at him. A delayed smile came across his face. "Good to see you, stud. Come on in."

"Smells delicious." Noah slipped through the doorway. He followed Sergio into a single living room space in a color spectrum of nudes and tans, with a few generic framed pieces around the room, providing some pops of green. In the kitchen, a pan simmered a sauce, another pan held boiling water, and the oven light displayed a tray with little mounds of dinner rolls baking. A bedroom door was cracked open just past the kitchen. From the distance, Noah could make out only a tidy bedroom with the bed made up. The place was put together enough, but nothing like Joseph's.

Noah shut the front door, where a set of car keys hung along with some reusable shopping bags.

"Thanks. It's a pasta dish my mom made all the time," Sergio said, stepping into the kitchen and handing Noah a thin wine glass already filled.

"Does she live around here? Your parents, I mean?" Noah asked, taking the wine glass and sniffing it.

"They both passed away in the massacre." Sergio looked away as he said this. His tone flat, an attempt to keep his emotions down.

"I'm so sor—"

"It's okay," Sergio interjected and then raised his wine glass, giving it a swirl. "Set your bag down."

A silence fell between them before Sergio spoke again.

"This is a dry Riesling. Have you had something like it before?"

Noah turned around and looked back at his wine glass. "I have not."

"It'll pair well with the *cacio e pepe* I'm making."

"Is that Mexican?" Noah asked.

Sergio laughed at him and shook his head. "No, stud, that's Italian. My mother and father were third generation here. You thought I was Hispanic?"

"Sorry," Noah apologized. "To be honest, I was released from prison a good few months ago. Was sent as a kid, so I don't have the best perception of things." Noah surprised himself with his candor. Perhaps the clothes gave him self-confidence.

"Prison? For what?" Sergio asked. He stepped into the kitchen to stir the pot and then turned around. "Also, you haven't tried the wine. If it's too dry, I can open something else. I have liquor, too." He chuckled, a hand on his hip while he waited with a smile on his face. Noah rolled his shoulders back to relax.

He tried the wine, which was dry but enjoyable. He finished the rest and handed the glass back to Sergio. "That's delicious."

"Perfect," Sergio poured him another full-sized glass and gave the sauce a shake.

"I went to prison for petty theft. I did some property damage at a local gas station and was arrested. No one was hurt. I got sentenced for a few weeks, but I acted up a lot to stay in."

"Why stay in?" Sergio asked, squinting a little. As if the answer was tattooed on Noah's skin—which, in a way, wasn't it?

"I felt safer in there, but then they released me 'cause they needed the cell for harsher sentences and—what is that word? Voilà?" Noah said, looking away from Sergio, who chuckled. He noticed a home device deep in the kitchen, the lights blinking.

"Your pasta timer is done," the home device notified the room.

"H.D., thank you," Sergio said.

Noah stared at the device curiously while Sergio added the noodles to the saucepan, giving it a shake and a stir. Noah took a seat at the kitchen table, where colorful candles were mixed between small succulents.

"How's it being out? You're still adjusting, I imagine."

Noah shrugged, taking another sip of the wine. "It's an adjustment, sure. But I'd take it over being back any day."

Sergio nodded while he cut the burners off on the stove.

"That's good you feel safe," Sergio said, and Noah nodded.

"I have one of those, too. That H.D.? How do you like the thing?" he asked, gesturing to the home device when Sergio looked back at him.

"Yes?" H.D. asked.

"Oh, nothing—thank you, H.D.," Sergio responded politely.

"Eh, I don't know. The Home Device company had some data breach a few months ago. I'm not too happy with their security settings, either. I've meant to replace it with one from Google, Apple, or Amazon," Sergio said. "But they all have their own collection of lawsuits for this and that. None of them are as cheap as the Home Device, though."

"A data breach?" Noah's ears perked.

"Yeah, a few months ago. They sent an email out saying there was a data breach and to change login information, be vigilant about checking your bank records for any fraud. Things like that. Except maybe a day or two later, a story dropped from the people who had hacked. They said they discovered the home device was always recording and storing everything in the cloud. Most people didn't even know it was doing this. Not like they had a choice; there was no option to turn this feature off. And the security was very shitty. They found a lot of bugs in the coding, too."

"What does that mean?" Noah took another sip of wine.

Sergio grabbed plates and used tongs to twist the pasta before plating it.

"Well, for example, one of the bugs affected this guy on the other side of the world. I think in Germany? Anyways, he asked his home device for all of his data to be sent to him, which included many hours of his recordings. Except, when he reviewed them, he realized they weren't of him; the recordings were of someone else. The company ended up claiming it was an anomaly, but . . ." Sergio took a sip of wine.

"It was an anomaly that they'd been recording everyone through their devices?" Noah laughed. "That makes no sense."

"Welcome to 'Merica."

"So, that's kind of random—even lucky—if you got someone else's recordings?"

"I guess? But what would you even do if you got, let's say, someone's entire life recorded? You'd spend your whole life, what? Listening and hoping they'd mention a password aloud? A bank account? Some hideous secret?" Sergio laughed, cracking fresh pepper over the pasta on the dishes, along with some grated Parmesan.

While Noah watched him, his imagination ran wild. Moments in time were connected now. The home device he'd seen at Fisher's house the night of the murder, the home device he'd become so accustomed to at Joseph's, and now another one here. Through pure coincidence, the home device had inspired Joseph. Noah had done all the actual work and still only scraped by at the Extended Stay. Did he want payment? He didn't know, but as Sergio set the food before him, Noah knew one thing. He was hungry.

"Another glass?" Sergio asked.

"Yes, please." Noah smiled back at Sergio before downing the small puddle that remained in his glass. "So, if you know all of this, why do you still use it? The home device?"

Sergio tilted the bottle of Riesling. His bicep flexed some while he poured it.

"Convenience, I guess." Sergio chuckled, setting the glass back down and grabbing the bread from the oven. He put it at the center of the table in a woven basket, and steam rose between them.

While taking his first few bites, Noah noticed a wall of photos just outside the bedroom door. These were more personal ones. A few pictures of him with family, friends at a concert. He paused mid-bite and peered over Sergio's shoulder, his face still trained to the food on his plate. He noticed a photo of Joseph and Sergio shirtless, embracing each other at some colorful, glittering place. Noah felt a sting of jealousy. His eyes scanned up, where he could also see a framed degree. He read the embossed green metallic penmanship: Baxtor Springs Community College. Sergio took a few bites himself, savoring the meal. He smiled like a kid.

"I thought your degree was earned on the West Coast," Noah thought out loud.

Sergio turned, seeing the wall behind him. He caught the glimmer of a small diamond earring that pierced Sergio's lobe. He turned back with a quizzical expression, and Noah sunk a little, biting back his lip.

"What gave you that impression?" Sergio asked, flat but curious.

"I overheard you at the restaurant that day I got your number." Noah smirked, watching Sergio's expression. He looked caught red-handed. Noah leaned over his plate of food and pointed down. "This is delicious, by the way."

Sergio nodded, accepting the compliment. "No wonder Dana is always yelling at us back there." Sergio rolled his eyes. "How much did you hear?"

Noah smiled with thin lips, sitting on a secret. Sergio's eyes were penetrating. *Eager*, even. Noah recalled not just what he'd heard but the video, too. He let his head bob from side to side as he thought of what to say. "Enough."

"Well, it doesn't matter anymore. I don't think I'm going back to university now that my parents are gone, and I . . ." Sergio took a sip of wine, trailing off, before finishing his thought. "I still need to figure things out. Grow up, too, I guess."

Noah took a sip of the wine before sitting back in his chair. The wood was hard against his back, but he didn't mind. The food was good, the wine was great, and the company was attractive. What if he'd never gone to prison? he wondered, just for a moment. Would he have had a boyfriend like Sergio? Would they have an apartment like this together? These daydreams became dispelled, for Noah realized it wasn't Sergio sitting across from him in this brief fantasy, but Joseph.

"Oh, I thought it had more to do with Professor Joseph Bailey," Noah said bitterly. His daydream melted back, and he could see Sergio come into view once more.

Sergio puckered his lips. "He's not a professor. Not anymore. To be honest, I don't think he ever was a legitimate one, either."

"What?" Noah asked, curious.

"He was hired as a professor at our school right out of college, when he was twenty-five, I believe. The university had done some profiles on him being the youngest professor, and he was, let's say, *hot shit.*" Sergio looked at Noah, and then his lips tugged to one side of his face. "Okay, maybe you don't understand, but to be a professor, you need about eight years more of school, programs, time spent teaching, et cetera, et cetera. But he didn't do any of that. He was almost tenured by thirty-five. Most people would kill for that job security, you know."

"How did Joseph do it? Was he that smart?"

"No." Sergio laughed. "The president of the university had a real thing for him. Had a real thing for other people, too. He thought these new-age teachers would bring in more students, more money—you get the picture. They were going to launch an investigation into his actions. Dean had been hiring illegitimate people for years, and he retired before anything could come out about it."

"Do you think Joseph and Dean were fucking?"

"No, no," Sergio said, his hand waving between them. "It wasn't like that, but it was something weird. A father-son complex is my guess, but who knows."

"Oh." Noah turned sour. "But now Joseph is an author."

"He can be whatever he wants. He has the money to do so," Sergio said, taking a sip of wine. He pushed his plate away from him, half-eaten.

"Sorry, I didn't mean to bring up a poor subject," Noah lied.

"It's weird—" Sergio paused, looking at Noah's clothes. "He wore an outfit just like the one you're wearing. When I first opened the door for you, it felt a little like déjà vu. Like old times."

"Old times?" Noah asked.

"Yeah. We met off a hook-up app and ended up dating for nearly two years."

"What happened?" Noah asked.

"We were caught by faculty." Sergio sighed, and Noah let the silence sit between them. "...caught fucking. When I think back on it now, I realize how stupid it was—*I was.* We kept our relationship private, never meeting on school grounds, always dating outside of the city, and we never told anyone we were with each other. I never thought we would be caught, but we got comfortable being together so long. Then he just cut me off, cold turkey."

"Sounds lonely," Noah said.

"It was," Sergio agreed. "One night, I was at a bar in Boys Town with friends after everything ended. I saw him at the bar ordering a drink—a beer. I approached him to tell him in person I was sorry. He hadn't responded to my text messages or phone calls. He blocked me on everything, too. It was . . . *tough*. I thought we had a future together. I thought even my parents would meet him and like him. Him being a professor, it was just a fact we glossed over back then. I sound so stereotypical."

Noah took a sip, knowing that Sergio would never get the opportunity to bring anyone home to meet his parents.

Sergio shuddered. "When he saw me, he got so angry, it was like he snapped. He broke the beer bottle in his hand against the bar, it splashed everywhere, and everyone was looking at us. He put it to my neck, told me he'd kill me if I ever came around again. Security pulled him off and kicked him out, and then me, too, shortly after."

"Ah," Noah said, marveling. "He does have a thing for glass now, doesn't he?"

"Mmhm," Sergio agreed casually and then paused. His neck twisted in confusion, like a curious puppy. "What?"

"Well . . . when he murdered that detective—when he snapped, as you put it—he crushed a glass against his face over and over and over. I mean, there was so much blood. Joseph violently beat that man to death. I saw the whole thing." Noah spoke the words delicately, savoring them as they slithered from his mouth. "You know, the one they've been searching for lately?"

"Detective Kline?" Sergio's wine tipped forward as his hand grew limp. "But I just saw him at Dana's a few days ago."

"If he hasn't been reported missing yet, he will soon. Trust me—and keep your glass up. Don't go spilling everywhere now," Noah scoffed, leaning forward to push the glass back upright.

"Did you tell the police?" Sergio sank away from Noah, bringing his wine glass to his chest.

Noah puckered his lips and let his eyebrows fall, conveying a look of pity. He shook his head back and forth, *no*. He dropped the little façade. Tonight had already been very informative, anyways.

"We need to call the police. You need to tell them."

Sergio slammed his glass down on the table, the wine sloshing up the sides, running down the stem. He marched past Noah to his phone on the countertop next to a cutting board and knife. He gripped the device with both hands.

Noah leaped from the dining table and charged Sergio, body-slamming him to the very back of the alleyway kitchen. His phone skyrocketed through the air and banged against the wall behind Noah. He staggered, looking at Sergio, who was scrambling to his feet. He charged once more and toppled over Sergio, and they wrestled. They slammed against the stove, causing the pot of steaming hot water to pitch right off the oven and over Sergio's frame. He screamed in agony as he lost control, and soon, Noah was shoving his face against the hot pot still steaming with the water that collected around them now. His face sizzled like hamburger meat.

Sergio kicked out, and Noah stumbled back a few feet. *Thump thump thump*, each footstep echoed around the apartment. Water splashed around as Noah charged once more. Soon Sergio was between Noah's legs, which were wound tightly around his rib cage. Noah crossed his forearms, knowing that momentarily, Sergio would be incapacitated.

"What do . . . you want . . ." Sergio spoke with all his strength. His voice came out in a thin whine, a burst of words. ". . . from . . . me?"

Noah didn't release his grip as he spoke. "To add to the recordings."

Just a matter of time, really, until Sergio's resistance melted away. Noah relaxed his own body afterward and caught his breath. Sergio was heavy against his frame. Noah sat up, pushing him off. Sergio's head thumped against the ground hard. He didn't wake, though, and Noah looked at the car keys by the door.

Arturo and his *tía* sat in silence on the ride over to her housing tract on the east side. The only sound between them was from the AC blowing cool air, and occasionally the worn suspension joints squeaking between stop signs. Arturo felt too jolted to say anything. He assumed the same for her. Violent images hung in his mind like an art gallery he couldn't escape. Benjamin Fisher's body on the church floor, his chipped bones stuck out of his face like mountain ridges. Detective Stuart Kline's entire face, too, shredded to pieces. The smell of blood and the heat from above only made it worse. He thought of being in the bathroom once more, his mother's body slipping under the water. He tried to distract himself by looking out the window, cracking it slightly to allow his vape smoke a clean exit.

His *tía* had never moved from the east side of Baxtor Springs. Initially, because she hadn't wanted Arturo to change schools and lose all his friends. He remembered how he'd argued with her that Fisher was his friend, and so were the other boys in the troop. She wouldn't have any of that, though, after she'd caught them. The farther east they drove, the more Arturo's mind seemed to melt into his childhood. Nothing in this neighborhood had changed, from the flower beds and matching trees planted in everyone's yards to the pastel homes. His *tía* pulled her car into her driveway alongside her small one-story house. They parked inside her garage; the aluminum door closed behind them before they got out and made their way inside.

"Take a seat," his *tía* said, pointing at a long sectional couch that slinked around two sides of her coffee table. She sat down to remove her black heels. The shawl fell open now, and Arturo could see the gold necklace with matching cross dangle around her neck. When she stood up, she smoothed her dress out over her tiny frame. She turned and walked to the bar, which had gold accents and various decanters sitting atop. Arturo took a seat on the couch, in the corner where a few gold fringe pillows lay in a pile. He grabbed one and set it in his lap, then wrapped his arms around it for comfort. *Too much gold*, he thought.

He stared out the window at the view of the surrounding apartment buildings. Balconies filled with trash or clutter, weather-worn paint aging the buildings.

"I'm doing a shot. Do you want one?" she asked, not turning to face him. "My nerves are fried."

"Yes, please." Arturo sighed, staring blankly at her vintage wooden coffee table, his eyes resting on a few memoirs and YA books lined up beneath. He felt empty. The day had been traumatic. A drink would steady his nerves.

His *tía* moved around the space effortlessly, returning to the living room with a bottle of Patrón in one hand and two shot glasses in another. She set them on the coffee table and headed to the thermostat to turn the temperature down. Again, the sound of an AC hummed between their silence.

"Oh, I forgot lime and salt," she said, storming back into the kitchen. A few things rattled, and she reappeared with her hands full. Arturo sat there, still dazed, wondering if she would *just* sit down. She was making him feel more paranoid. When she finally sat, Arturo noticed that her hands trembled as she held the knife against the round lime.

"Here, let me do that," Arturo said, taking the knife from her. Cutting limes at the bar was second nature to him. While he sliced them, his *tía* poured the shots. Lick, salt, shoot, and biting the lime happened fast.

"That was horrifying," his *tía* said. "I didn't think we'd make it out alive. All those cops around the room could've fired at him and shot one of us. And who was that in the trunk?"

"I assume Detective Stuart Kline . . . He's been missing for a day or so. The guy who dropped me off was his partner, Detective Vaughn. He was looking for Kline earlier."

"Why was he talking to you?" his *tía* asked. She shifted her weight, as her gaze bore down on him. He noticed her necklace again, and Arturo sunk back, afraid to be so close to it. He anxiously cracked his knuckles one at a time.

"Vaughn? Coincidence, I guess." Arturo shrugged. *Crack crack.* His *tía*'s gaze didn't let up. Arturo continued. "I was going to the church with the guy I've been dating, but—*crack, crack*—he got sick right when Detective Vaughn came knocking on the door, and he saw I needed a ride here."

"Who are you dating?"

"Joseph Bailey. He's an author." Arturo smiled, cracking his other hand now.

"That name sounds familiar," she mused, trying to place it.

"He did a book reading for that charity event at Baxtor's Books last week. Tomorrow he's doing another book reading—just him, though. You probably know him from that." *Crack, crack.*

"Last week? Yeah, that sounds familiar. You met him last week?"

"Mmhm," Arturo hummed.

"Sounds like you haven't been dating all *that* long," she said dryly, letting her hand wave up from her lap. "What'd he write?"

"A thriller."

"Did you read it?" *Tía* raised an eyebrow.

"No." Arturo slunk down, feeling guilty. "I mean, I plan to . . . We've just been spending all our time together."

"Oh," his *tía* said, sounding as if she'd had an epiphany. "That's right, new crazy love. *Anyways,* not to sound sour, but I wouldn't want to read a thriller now or maybe ever. Too much death lately. I've been sticking to young adult novels, keeping things light." She put her hand on Arturo and leaned in. "I hope Joseph didn't do anything now."

"What?" Arturo's eyebrows knitted together. "You haven't even met the guy. Why would you say that?"

"He got sick at the same time as—oh, what's his name?" She snapped her fingers. "Detective Vaughn came knocking around?"

"No, it wasn't anything like that, *Tía.*" Arturo shook his head like an annoyed teenager. "He had too much coffee, that's all."

"Okay," she said, leaning away from Arturo. His *tía* then dramatically raised her shoulders to her ears, and her tongue plopped out in disgust. "*Uck!* I can't stop thinking about the funeral—that *recording.* I never imagined Fisher would've told anyone to kill themselves, let alone one of the boys in the troop. Poor Rafael, learning this. He has lost so much already." She stretched out her hands and fingers in frustration. Arturo reached for the bottle and poured them both another shot. She took hers without salt or lime this time.

"I was chatting with the chief just the other day at the bar, *Tía,*" Arturo said. He took his, too. "He said people have been blaming him for things in this town, and that he hadn't done anything wrong. I felt bad for the chief, but now . . . Fisher had talked about him as if they were together in it. Rafael even—did he accuse the chief of molesting his son?"

"Yeah," his *tía* said flatly. "Fisher must have groomed him long enough to make him feel so alone, so helpless. I wonder how long that was going on for—the chief must have known something. It's all just horrible." His *tía* leaned forward and removed her shawl now. She used the edge of it to dab her cheeks and forehead. The necklace dangled, and Arturo couldn't help himself.

"Is that my mom's necklace?" Arturo blurted bitterly.

His *tía* looked down at her chest, the whites of her eyes growing large. She reached behind her neck and unclasped it. Arturo could see the gold sparkle under the natural light that came in through the windows. She was handing it to him, he realized, but he didn't move. His *tía* placed the necklace in his hand anyway. The cross and chain were weightless.

"It is. I got it for your mother when we were young. Cost a lot of money, too—well, at the time, anyway. I assumed we might visit her grave after the funeral. I saw some fresh flowers left there a few days ago. Did you visit?" She slowly raised an innocent gaze to meet Arturo's.

"No, I haven't visited. That was Mimi from the Mexican joint."

"Bless her," his *tía* said, touching her heart.

"I don't want to visit her grave, though, and you know that," Arturo said bluntly. "She wore this necklace the day she *offed* herself," he didn't mutter it this time. Instead, he spoke loud and clear about how he felt. The two shots weren't helping, either. He struggled, trying to keep his cool and not throw the chain across the room. He was afraid the memories attached to this piece of jewelry would conjure another panic attack. He tried to hand it back to his *tía*, but she turned away, leaning over the coffee table to pour another round of shots. Arturo felt wildly uncomfortable, unsure how to say he didn't want to hold this cross anymore. He cleared his throat, but his *tía* went on, passing him a shot. She took her own with little hesitation or reaction.

"You don't have to say it like that," his *tía* said, wiping her mouth. "You can just say she passed."

Arturo scoffed, took the shot, and slammed the glass down with a thud. "But she didn't just *pass*, did she? She abandoned me. Abandoned you, my dad, everybody. She's the entire reason our family fell apart." His words were sharp, and something about saying them felt good. "She did a lot more than just pass away."

Arturo looked at his *tía* now, who sat unflinching. Her cheeks were red and puffy. It was a look that Arturo had seen often growing up, whenever he'd done something wrong, which felt like all the time.

"You know, it's unfortunate. Your mother did so much for you, and you hate her for just *one* thing that she couldn't handle. I've done so much for you, and you can't even talk about her respectfully for my sake. In my own home. She was *my* sister. You were nothing more than a kid back then." Her words were piercing, her tone matching his. "For Christ's sake, you're still acting like a kid now. What do you even remember from that time?"

Arturo rolled his eyes and huffed, looking away. His *tía* poured more shots and took hers, exhibiting the same control as last time. Arturo bit the inner lining of his cheek, rolling it back and forth between his teeth. His *tía* wasn't wrong. The memories from his childhood were so foggy. This fact only bothered him more, though. He felt like he was being parented again, and his *tía* would never be his mother. Nobody would ever, not even his own mother. She clearly didn't want the job.

"I'm not a kid anymore. And I remember plenty," Arturo spat out, feeling that anger turn inward, caught between his pride and ego. He tossed back his shot and slammed the glass down again.

"Okay, well, let's talk about what I *know* you don't remember," his *tía* challenged him. "Do you remember how your mother was after our parents died from cancer two weeks apart from each other? She had to be checked into a hospital. She was so depressed. Or how about the night your dad got his first DUI? How frantic your mother was calling me at two in the morning to make sure I could come over and help you get to school that day, so she could handle everything?" Her soft tan eyes glared at him.

"He only had one DUI, *tía*," Arturo shot back. "That was the same night you pulled me out of Boy Scouts."

"No, that was his third—and last—DUI." For a split second, Arturo's eyes glossed over, and his *tía* found her opening. "Oh, come on, you're not a kid anymore. You're old enough to hear all of this. Your father got his next DUI six months later while your mother was already working to pay off his debts from the first. And then she died, and he got his third before going off the deep end."

"I don't remember her having a job," Arturo admitted.

"Well, *Arturo*, she had two. Both were part-time, and she scheduled her shifts while you were at school, and one of her shifts always got off later than she'd like on Thursdays—until she found out Thursday nights corresponded with the Boy Scouts. They, too, met every Thursday night. She enrolled you right away while your father continued to blow her money on booze and takeout. She was saving to leave his ass and get an apartment for the both of you. She knew he wasn't going to do anything to change. He, too, was a fucking kid."

Arturo looked away from her overbearing stare and crossed his arms. He couldn't remember living with his mother or what the house had even looked like besides that god-awful guest bathroom. In a quick flash, though, he could see piled pizza boxes next to the trash can, toppled with beer cans and a swarm of flies enjoying the mess. His father was asleep on the couch with a puddle of foaming brown drool building around his parted lips. Arturo was holding a Boy Scout manual in his hands, some loose string, and a dimming desire to learn knots with his dad that day.

"I had taken you to some of those meetings with the Boy Scouts. I knew Benjamin Fisher, too. I always had a weird feeling about him, but no one had ever complained about the guy. When your mother passed, I caught you both in the upstairs bathroom smoking a joint—for Christ's sake. I was so angry, and I told him he knew better and to *knock—it—off*. To think of you being alone in a room with that man makes me disgusted. How he talked about your mother is the same way you're talking about her now. It's disgusting. When I caught you two smoking weed again after your father's fucking third DUI, I was furious with all of you, and I became strict. I wasn't going to lose you to the addictions of your father or depression like your mother."

Arturo still didn't look at her, and she wouldn't stop talking. As if his parents' troubles were his curse. Each word felt like another brick slamming against his chest.

"Why were you even at Fisher's funeral then, *tía*?" Arturo barked.

"I knew he had helped your mother make some side money back then. I guess I went to pay my respects. But now, I wish I hadn't. I believe Fisher was grooming you, grooming all you Boy Scouts."

"*Ay dios mío, tía*," Arturo said. "Stop making this into some conspiracy."

"Where there is smoke, there is fire. If you can't see that he was trying to groom you, Arturo, then I don't know what to tell you."

"He wasn't like that," Arturo said. "Not with me, ever."

"Not *yet*," his *tía* growled. "Thank God for me always stepping in. You know, I won't be here forever to take care of you, to tell you these things." She extended her hand out to his forearm. "And that's tough to swallow, but it's the truth."

"*Tía*, I take care of myself already," Arturo shot back angrily.

"You know what I mean. I'm the only family you've got left in this world. We already don't see each other enough, and when we do, you always seem so upset and cut our time short. I'd like us to be able to talk about things. That concept you have of your mother abandoning you is so harsh and downright unfair." Her face morphed into a concerned frown. She corked the bottle of Patrón and breathed quietly. Arturo knew his *tía* was right—her memory was still intact, too. For someone her age, that wasn't always a given.

"So, tell me then, since you seem to know it all," he huffed, still annoyed. He looked back to the cross in his hand and handed it back to his *tía*.

She put the necklace back on, allowing it to glisten, catching the sunset through the windows. His *tía* pointed to a photo across the room on the window ledge. Behind it sat a vase of fake flowers; the dust had settled between the crevices of the faux rose petals. The framed photo was simple—a woman had her arms wrapped around him, and for a moment, Arturo didn't recognize her, and then it dawned on him—it was his mother embracing him. Her face was glowing with a smile and deep dimples. Her hair was so curly and large from the humidity. She wore a brown Boy Scouts uniform shirt that was open enough to see that same cross necklace. The tails tied at the top of her high-waisted jeans were perfectly rolled up above sandals that matched Arturo's. Beneath the standard American Flag that came with the shirt, on her shoulder was also a rainbow flag, the old school one before it was updated to better represent the community as a whole.

Had she known? Arturo wondered with disdain. He'd only ever have more questions about his mother, never answers.

"That was your mother. She was always beaming when she was around you. She always wanted to support you. She would have done anything in the world for you, Arturo, and she was always encouraging you to do everything. She loved you so much."

"Yeah, just not enough that she wouldn't kill herself." Arturo stood abruptly and made his way for the door. He opened it and didn't look back to see his *tía*, who he was sure sat there shocked and dismayed. The outside air felt cool around him, and he felt like he could breathe. Not enough to relax, his body still rigid with anger. Arturo walked to the street and realized, like salt on the wound, that his *tía* was right about one thing. Having a car right now would've been ideal for him.

Underneath a streetlight, he pulled out his phone and started tapping for a car service when the screen flashed. A call was coming in. At first, Arturo thought it was going to be Joseph. He would've been thrilled, excited to dive right back into the safety of his world that felt so disconnected from everything in Arturo's. When he checked his phone, however, he saw it was Dana Whitman calling. Arturo blinked hard, annoyed not to see Joseph's name on the screen. Ignoring the call, he looked up at the surrounding apartment buildings with the Extended Stay at the far end of the street.

A chill blew by as the sun crept beneath the tree line. Arturo wrapped his arms around his body, then glanced down at his phone when Dana's name popped up once more. He swiped it open and put the phone to his ear.

"Hey Dana." Arturo forced a smile on his face.

"Hey, sorry if I'm buggin', I just—have you seen Sergio Hernandez recently? I already called Violet, and she hasn't, but she told me to try you. I know he's worked some shifts at your bar, too," she said, then paused as if waiting for an answer. "I just . . . he didn't show up for his shift tonight, and he's not answering any of my calls, and I'm a little worried."

"No, I haven't seen him," Arturo said. His mind eager to leave behind whatever transpired with his *tia* and help out a friend. He could feel his mood shift, just enough.

"The restaurant is so busy tonight, and I know he's trying to save up for his folk's funeral costs and . . . I just don't think he'd miss work unless something was wrong. He's all alone on the east side . . ." Her voice slipped into a long sigh.

"I'm on the east side right now," Arturo said, looking down the street. "What's his address?"

"Oh, Arturo, thank you so much. Hopefully I'm worried for nothing. I'll text you his address right now. Please let me know when you get ahold of him."

"Of course," Arturo said.

Arturo's screen darkened as he waited for Dana to text him the address. Underneath the streetlight, his shadow was his only company. His *tía* hadn't run out to chase after him. She had grown used to Arturo storming out of the room as a kid. She never entertained these outbursts, which only made Arturo more upset.

The east side of Baxtor Springs was quiet. Between some of the apartment buildings, strings of tiny round light bulbs ran between balconies. Each of them seemed empty, the lights off, and Arturo knew it wasn't even that late. A chilling reminder how the massacre had affected this area, too.

Now, many of the buildings had "FOR RENT — MOVE IN ASAP" signs. Some were attached to the balconies, looking down at Arturo as he walked by, promoting, *"GREAT VIEWS — 3BR 2BA — VERY AFFORDABLE."*

His phone buzzed with the address, and he was relieved to stop staring at the empty apartment buildings, like the remains of an abandoned city. Checking the address, he saw it was only a five-minute walk. As he walked, he remembered how the night had always boomed with life when he was growing up here. Food trucks lined the streets, each one a different type of cuisine. The smells from each truck would battle on the roads, trying to draw in customers. Supporting local business, this is where Arturo fell in love with service and serving people good drinks.

He could only hear his own footsteps echoing around him now, trudging through memories of better days.

Once he found the apartment building, he walked upstairs into a large square, where each door faced a pool in the center courtyard. Arturo rechecked his phone. The apartment number was 405. He went up through a staircase alley tucked next to the mailboxes and started his climb. The lights in the stairwell were low, casting a greenish-blue hue that felt dirty. As he rounded the corners and continued up, he saw spiderwebs cling to the corners near the lights. These, too, were abandoned.

Arturo approached Sergio's apartment and knocked on the door forcefully. The door popped away from its frame with little effort. It squeaked as Arturo watched it open, and everything came into view. His stomach flipped at the scene before him.

A lamp had been knocked over near the door, the shade tilted at an angle that only lit the door. Opposite, the light from the oven cast an eerie orange glow around the other side of the apartment. Half-eaten food and two glasses of wine sat on the table. Arturo saw his reflection in the kitchen floor, which had at least a quarter inch of water collected about. The uneven floor dipped to a threshold that separated the dining room from the kitchen. It acted as a dam, retaining the water in the kitchen, which puddled around a large pot sitting upside-down with brown bits stuck on the end. A burning smell hung in the air.

"Sergio?" Arturo called out.

He tilted his head forward, just barely passing the frame of the front door. In the reflection along the water, he saw his forehead ripple, and behind the door, he saw someone else's forehead move about, too. Arturo peered behind the door and screamed as a dark figure charged at him, sending Arturo flying back and crashing into the wall. The back of his head erupted in pain. He kept his vision trained forward though, desperate to keep his attacker in sight. He watched the figure's fist slingshot back, a blur of a tattoo on a forearm, followed by a punch to his face. Arturo was blinded and crumbled to the ground as sounds of very heavy footsteps thudded out of the apartment, followed by a car burning rubber heading out toward the street, into the night.

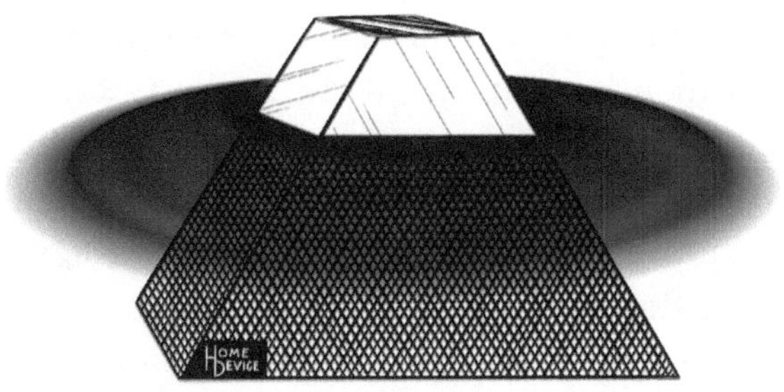

Joseph's favorite thing about Xanax was how everything felt so fine after waking up. He knew that if he didn't get a whole night's sleep, he'd be groggy, but even that would be fine, too, for now. The dark rest he fell into wasn't filled with any nightmares, none at all. Something had woken him up, though. He could almost fall right back into sleep when—

Boom boom boom.

Joseph pushed through that calming fog, like a weighted blanket he struggled to get off. He raised his eyebrows, and soon his eyelids followed. He looked around, and for the briefest second, he understood he wasn't waking up to the nightmare where Sophie had called or when Stuart Kline gagged fishing glass from his throat. This was, perhaps, real?

Joseph reached for his phone, no missed notifications from Arturo or anyone else. Except his security system had notified him of recent activity. He expanded the notifications to see that nearly an hour ago, the garage door had opened and closed shortly after.

Boom.

That sound again. Then he heard a clattering from the garage. The walls vibrated, the picture frames around him jostling from their perfect alignment. He slowly turned his body, allowing his feet to plop down to the ground.

He glided down the hallway, and soon his hand was on the door, which he opened slowly. As he stood at the edge of the pitch-black darkness of the garage, he felt a curious lack of fear. He could hear someone breathing, not slow and steady, but panicked. Joseph flicked on the garage light. The beams along the ceiling flashed a few times before fully lighting the room, which looked as if a bull had been trying to get out, bucking everything in its path. Joseph's eyes trailed down his metal racks, the plastic bins broken open and fully askew with old paperwork from the university.

Whoever was in the chair had fallen backwards, knocking a storage rack over. The other racks sat undisturbed, with the black sheets acting as a room divider. The storage rack that had fallen was the one Joseph had slid back to see that the car was missing. A manly figure lay on the ground, feet pointed up to the ceiling, shaking. Joseph stepped down into his garage and stalked over to whoever lay there. The man was still whimpering but hadn't tried to move a muscle to break free. Joseph leaned over, staring down at the person. Something about them seemed familiar—but their entire face was bright red with patches of charred skin. The wounds had a peppery fresh smell to them.

"Who are you?" Joseph asked in a near whisper.

"Joseph, please, help. I need help—please," the bound man pleaded, whimpering louder with each word. Joseph watched as their entire frame continue to shake. The pain they must've felt was immense, yet Joseph didn't have an urge to jump up and call for help. This person was in his house, and his house was already a crime scene waiting to be investigated.

"How do you know my name?" Joseph asked with steady hands.

Duct tape had been wrapped around the person's frame and chair backing. Joseph had to use all his strength to get them both upright. With the chair on all fours, the blood flushed down from their face making them resemble tender raw meat left out too long.

They looked around the garage, their eyelids like crispy butterfly wings flapping up and down. Their body shivered in pain, and they seemed too unfocused to reply. Still, Joseph felt calm. He knelt closer in front of whoever this was.

"I asked you a question," Joseph stated. The person—whoever they were—was still silent. Without warning, Joseph raised the back of his hand and struck their soggy cheeks. The person squealed and snot began to drip from their face.

"Joseph, please." They looked at him with only one eyelid fully open, their voice low enough to be a man, "It's me, Ser—gio, gio."

Joseph sank back. His bottom hit the ground with a thud as he understood. The last time he'd seen Sergio, he'd threatened his life. Said he would kill him. He even tried to, but the security bouncers had removed him. No one was here to protect Sergio, Joseph realized, but he hadn't come here on his own. He was placed here by the killer—*Rabbit*.

"Why did they put you here?" Joseph asked. He rested his forearm on his knee, his dangling fingers swirled around and around like his thoughts.

"Please, Joseph—Mr. Bailey . . . It's *me—ee*. Please untie . . ." he sniffled, "*me—ee*."

Joseph grunted, and with great force, kicked his leg out. The bottom of his heel slammed into Sergio's shin. He screamed out in pain. Thick strands of saliva shot from his mouth as he howled. Joseph couldn't tell if it was sweat or beads of his blood collecting on Sergio's forehead down to the sideburns of his face. Still, he looked flushed, a grayish pink that wasn't a good sign.

"Why did they put you in here?" Joseph asked again.

"He said—"

It's a he then, Joseph noted.

"—that he was going to add to—"

Joseph cocked an eyebrow and sat up straighter.

"—add to—" Sergio's voice quivered as if he were freezing, "the recordings."

Joseph felt a dryness catch in his throat, an emptiness that filled his chest. His body felt immobilized. *He was going to add to the recordings.* Joseph knew what that meant. There were many recordings already. Joseph eyed the garage. The black sheets and storage racks still stood behind Sergio's trembling body as if a theatrical backdrop had been placed. His feet now tapped against the ground frantically, as if he were having caffeine jitters. Joseph's eyes snapped to Sergio, the disgusting mess before him.

"Who is *he*?" Joseph asked, his voice low and hollow.

Sergio trembled, his only open eye slowly closed. He blinked, and his face sagged until his chin was resting on his chest. His breathing was shallow. He lifted his head—or at least attempted to. Joseph considered that Sergio was on the edge of passing out. *Not my problem,* Joseph thought, annoyed more than anything.

Sergio lifted his head, the muscles in his neck straining. Once Sergio's head was about halfway lifted, Joseph licked his lips and closed one eye. Joseph grabbed an old textbook from a stack nearby and whipped the book in the air.

The hard binding of the book collided with Sergio's good eye, across the nose. Blood burst out and gushed over Sergio's frame. His head whipped back in the process, causing the blood to splatter so high it even got the ceiling.

Joseph relaxed his body back over his knee.

Waiting and watching.

Sergio's head hung down again, swaying from side to side. Blood dripped from his nose into a single line that dribbled over the jeans he was wearing. He lifted his head and forced the eye to be open. A lump the size of a baseball grew underneath the other eye.

"Who is he?" Joseph asked, again, patiently. His voice was still calm. Still polite.

"No—ah," Sergio mumbled, and Joseph grabbed for another book.

"Rabbit tattoo," Sergio shrieked in fear.

"No, that's a character in my book," Joseph said plainly.

"No. He has a tattoo."

Joseph squinted. The lines between reality and fiction blurred together now. The old man—Fisher—had referred to a *rabbit* in that original recording. Something about the skin being ruined, Joseph recalled. He hadn't thought anything of it when he wrote the character, but now things *clicked*.

"On his forearm?"

Sergio nodded. Joseph could smell rotten meat waft with each nod.

"Not the man with ginger hair, correct?" Joseph said, returning his attention.

"No, that's Detective Kline. His name is Noah, No—ah." Sergio shook his head. Joseph let go of the book, intrigued. "You kill—*killed* Kline, though. You're going to do—the same to me, aren't y—you?"

"Tell me more about Noah," Joseph said, a smile twisting on his face.

"What do you—"

"*Everything*, Sergio." He spat, losing patience.

"He's just some white boy, a tattoo, buzz-cut hair." Sergio's body quivered, and his head sagged down again. "I don't know what else to say."

Joseph nodded his head. "Is that everything?"

Sergio shrugged. "Does it even matter?"

"I guess not. I will find him one way or another."

"You are, aren't you?"

"What?" Joseph asked, standing up.

"Going to—"

"Oh, kill you—yes, I am. But trust me, I'm doing you a favor on this one. Your poor face."

Joseph dusted off his thighs. He was the judge and the jury. No one was here to stop him. His mind was made up. He looked around the mess Sergio had made and found a plastic bag. Nothing too fancy, but it would do. Sergio didn't even resist as Joseph put it over his head, tugged it, making it very tight. The bag crinkled, inflating and then slowly deflating.

"It doesn't happen all that quick. It might take fifteen minutes or so—sometimes even thirty," Joseph said while lifting Sergio's covered face. It resembled a robber, with a stocking knit tightly masking his facial features enough not to recognize him. Joseph swiped his thumb over Sergio's forehead as if a priest blessing him. "I'm sorry it's not quicker. I just can't handle all the blood again."

Arturo breathed deep, preparing himself to stand. The thudding in his head had simmered to a low radio frequency humming in his ears. His left eye was swollen, not shut, but enough that both eyes created a blurry crossed vision. On his feet, he tilted the end table back upright and used it to balance his weight. He stopped, breathing heavy, his body sore in odd places, and the thumping wasn't from his heart. The footsteps were returning. Arturo stared at the triangle of light that made its way into the apartment. The front door still open.

A flashlight clicked on outside and shimmered through the doorway. The closer the light got, the more obvious Arturo was in the center of the room. He almost thought to hide until he heard them speak.

"I just got here," a voice said over the light. The familiar sound of a shoulder radio button clicked, and then the flashlight dropped. "Arturo? What happened? What are you doing here?"

Goldstein clicked off his flashlight and flicked on a light switch. His wide-framed body passed through the doorframe and over the worn carpet-lined floors. Arturo felt relieved, though his hands still trembled.

"Dana called, said Sergio hadn't shown up for a shift and asked if I could check on him. She was worried."

"You don't live on this side of town, though," Goldstein replied.

Arturo felt as if he was being interrogated.

"I visited with my *tía* after the funeral. When I was leaving, Dana called me."

Goldstein nodded, listening to Arturo while he inspected his face. His eyes filled with pity.

"When I entered, someone attacked me, but I didn't see them."

"Did you enter unannounced? Was it Sergio?"

"No," Arturo shook his head, the flurry of shadows replaying in his head. "He was taller than Sergio."

"You check the rooms?" Goldstein asked.

Arturo merely shook his head.

"Touch anything?" Goldstein followed up.

"No." Arturo shook his head again, his eye still singing with pain.

"Stay right here," the officer instructed.

Arturo watched Goldstein click the flashlight back on, shining it toward the back of the apartment, which was still dark. He pushed open the bathroom door and stepped inside. Goldstein stepped out without a single word and continued to canvas over the apartment.

"Place is empty. I'm going to give Detective Vaughn a call to come over. I'll need you to stay to file a report. Vaughn might have questions for you, too." Goldstein then added, "*Obviously*." His hands were on his hips, and still, he leveled Arturo with a look that wasn't fully trusting.

Arturo raised his hands to suggest innocence. "I can wait," he obliged. "What were you doing here?"

"Got a noise complaint from someone in the building. A neighbor thought domestic violence," Goldstein said. He turned around to call Detective Vaughn. While Arturo waited, his eyes trailed around the apartment. Goldstein had turned on every light, even the lamp knocked over to Arturo's left. The apartment was warm from the glow of the oven still on.

Outside the bedroom, he spotted a photo.

For a moment, he was bewildered, and his eyes couldn't believe what he was seeing: a single photo of Joseph and Sergio embracing each other. They were standing in some club, with their shirts off and glitter across their chests. It was a small photo in a small frame. Arturo leaned forward, Goldstein's back still turned to him. His mind raced as he pieced it all together—Sergio was the student from the university. The one that Joseph had been sleeping with. The entire reason why Joseph didn't make tenure and lost his life on the West Coast.

Arturo remembered Joseph telling him about Sergio beside the fire with no judgement whatsoever. Arturo had felt humiliated for spilling expensive wine and being sexually rejected, again. He hunched forward now, each thought another weight on his back.

Did Sergio know Joseph was in town? Or vice-versa? Arturo wondered as a shiver trickled down his shoulders, clung to his lats and seized around his rib cage. Arturo hadn't heard from Joseph all day. He was tall, too, like his attacker had been. Had Joseph been the one making the escape earlier—Arturo's attacker?

Arturo swallowed, reassuring himself—*no, Joseph wouldn't do that; they cared for each other.*

He looked around the room, unable to piece together a different story, though. Arturo didn't want to believe any of it. *Just thoughts, like the panic attack,* he reasoned with himself. Goldstein clicked off his phone and put it in his front bulletproof vest pocket. He motioned for Arturo to follow him outside.

"You're still in funeral clothes," Goldstein said. He didn't look at him when he spoke, just blankly stared across the courtyard alongside Arturo.

"I wasn't able to change after. My *tía* said she needed a drink after what happened."

Goldstein chuckled in a way that only made him sound more exhausted than ever.

"I could use a drink after today, too," Goldstein marveled.

"What happened after everyone got out?" Arturo asked.

"He tried for the chief again. We had to restrain him. Took a lot of us, too. The priest was up in arms about Fisher's body. The church is now refusing to allow the burial until an investigation into that recording can be made. A lot of people in town were traumatized by the funeral today. They are asking for the chief to publicly step down." Goldstein breathed heavily. "And they found Detective Stuart Kline's body in the parking lot. I'm sure you saw that."

Arturo nodded. "Is the chief going to step down?"

Goldstein shook his head. "He's agreed to recuse himself from the investigation, though. Since he was mentioned on that recording."

"What about the feds looking into the massacre? Are they aware of the recording with Joshua?" Arturo asked.

"We've sent it to them, but the investigation is in their hands now. And they refuse to tell us anything. They want all the credit." Goldstein rolled his eyes. "I think a lot of us just want closure."

Arturo nodded. *But closure doesn't come without truth,* he thought. He took in a deep, slow breath and opened his mouth to exhale. Goldstein raised an eyebrow watching

Arturo, perhaps smelling the tequila that lingered on his breath.

"If Fisher was molesting Joshua," Arturo said, "was there anyone else? He mentioned there being a *last* one. As if someone came before Joshua . . ."

"Not *if*—he *was*," Goldstein stated.

Arturo nodded. "Who else then? It sounded to me like whoever the last one was had reported it to the chief, but . . ." He didn't know where else to go with his line of thought. He didn't want to think the chief was roped into any of this, and yet, the mere fact that he was made Arturo's body heavy against the guardrail.

"Yeah, except the last person to check out Benjamin Fisher's folder was Stuart Kline."

"Was the folder there when they discovered the body?"

"Nope."

Arturo looked at Goldstein, shaking his head. They were both still as they leaned over the guardrail, staring out at the sky above them. The sun had now fully set, and Arturo could see the dark circles underneath Goldstein's eyes, illuminated in the glow of the moon.

"Fisher just . . ." Goldstein's voice faded.

"What?" Arturo asked firmly.

"He wasn't molesting me. I'll tell you that. I never would've suspected him of that."

"Me neither," Arturo said. "But my *tía* thinks differently."

"How?" Goldstein asked, rotating his frame to look at Arturo.

"She thinks he was grooming us, in some form. In this case, molestation. People that groom are normally smart and can blend into their surroundings while gaslighting their victims." Arturo paused, not wanting to sound too *by the book*—this was their childhood, after all. "I think for Fisher, specifically . . . he was the cool guy to us kids. He let us do whatever we wanted on those weekend camping trips with him. No one was there to supervise him, and he could've taken advantage of that."

"Not with me," Goldstein said. "He never took advantage of me."

"He didn't molest me, either, if that's what we're saying," Arturo said with a flat tone. "He did bring a lot of weed, though, and at the time, us kids didn't think anything of it."

"We only smoked with him, though," Goldstein stated matter-of-factly. "There wasn't any funny business in that. It was just our secret in the troop until it wasn't."

Arturo cocked an eyebrow and rotated his own frame to see Goldstein better.

"What?" Arturo asked.

"Well, after your mom passed away and you moved in with your *tía*, someone complained about the weed. Chief Edmonds talked to all of us." Goldstein paused, thinking hard. "But you weren't there for this. It was after you were pulled out."

"My *tía* did catch us smoking weed one night. She could've reported him."

"She pulled you out instead," Goldstein said. "And Fisher bad mouthed you and your aunt. Your father, too."

Arturo leaned back a little. "Do you remember what he said?"

"That you all refused to deal with the death of your mom, that she was selfish—and selfish people hurt others—and hurt people hurt people so… He told us to stay away from you all, that you weren't mentally stable."

Arturo scoffed, hearing it echo around the empty courtyard. The words stung, not because he felt misunderstood but because it was true. Arturo still hadn't visited his mother's grave. Hearing what Goldstein had said, that he'd refused to deal with her death, he wondered, *What was there to deal with?* She had killed herself.

"You all lied to Edmonds then? About smoking weed?" Arturo asked.

"He didn't smoke weed with everyone. That would've been too noticeable. I was the only one asked. It was only you, me, and that juvenile kid who smoked with Fisher. Eventually, Joshua must've, too. I never thought about that—till now." Goldstein sounded wounded. "Both of you were gone, and I didn't rat on Fisher. So, I denied it was ever happening." Goldstein nodded, then shrugged, seemingly convinced he'd done nothing wrong.

"What juvenile kid?"

"Come on. He went to prison for some petty crime. What was his name again? I remember hearing that they transferred him from juvie to adult prison when he came of age. He was always doing things to extend his sentence. He's probably still there now." Goldstein looked away from Arturo.

"What *things*?"

"Causing fights, even with officers, and those added up to a lot of extra time."

"Sounds like he wanted to stay in," Arturo said.

"Nobody wants to be in jail, Arturo. Do you even hear yourself?" Goldstein looked down to the courtyard where someone was walking up, and his posture changed quickly. No longer leaning over, he stood tall and smoothed out his uniform.

"Detective Vaughn," he greeted.

"Evening, gents," he said in a calming voice. "Arturo, nice to see you again."

"Likewise, I just wish . . ." Arturo's voice trailed off as his eyes trailed back to the open apartment door, and Vaughn nodded.

"Of course. Goldstein, I'm going to have you start taking photos of the place. Please be mindful of where you step. As of right now, we're just treating this as a missing person's case." Vaughn handed him a small camera from his bag before looking at Arturo. "Arturo, how'd you end up here?"

Arturo recounted the sequence of events as Goldstein disappeared into the apartment. Vaughn collected himself.

Between them, the only noise was the camera shutter going off inside with a *beep beep—click*. Vaughn asked him questions, simple ones. Arturo had filled him in on Dana's request, and he nodded along without any suspicion.

"Thank you." Vaughn stuck his hand up and smiled. "I think that's all I need from you. If I have any more questions, should I try you at Bailey's house or the bar?"

Arturo paused. He wanted to say Joseph's, and his eyes wandered to the corner edge of the picture frame in the apartment. Vaughn hadn't discovered it yet, neither had Goldstein. They would, though, Arturo told himself. They'd be coming to Joseph's regardless. Arturo wanted to see him first, though.

"I'm probably going to be at Joseph's place for the next few days, I imagine, but I'll have my phone on me." Arturo patted his pocket, but it was the wrong one. His phone was in the other.

"How's he doing, anyway?" Vaughn asked.

"What do you mean?" Arturo paused, concerned.

"He was sick earlier today. Have you checked in on him at all?"

Arturo shook his head.

"Well, I hope he feels better. I'll be in contact with you," Vaughn said. They shook hands, and then Vaughn entered the apartment. Arturo stood outside, leaning against the guardrail still, and sighed. Today had been a whirlwind of emotions, and quite frankly, he wanted to confront Joseph about Sergio and make sure that Joseph had absolutely nothing to do with any of this. While he walked outside the building, he called Dana to fill her in on what had happened. She was distraught.

Soon enough, Arturo hung up and requested a ride share back to Joseph's house.

Noah stared at the clone phone's tilted polished screen. He was hunched, squatting as he watched. The edge of the phone peeked out just enough to get a perfect view of everything that happened. It was still happening. Joseph stood over Sergio's body, still duct-taped to the chair. The bag around his face no longer crinkled with his faint breath or any sign of life. Then, without warning, the body spasmed. Joseph jumped back. Noah did, too.

Joseph's eyes looked toward the camera, and Noah held his breath, afraid he'd been seen. On the clone phone's screen, he could see a soft white glow becoming stronger against Joseph's face. Noah looked up to see a light coming from the other side of the garage windows. The pebbles along the driveway crunched underneath the weight of a car. Noah knew that sound, he'd become familiar with it after leaving with Stuart's car. When he'd returned with an unconscious Sergio, he hadn't parked in the driveway but instead off to the side, where the driveway curved behind the house.

From behind the storage racks, Noah watched Joseph inch closer to the garage door, trying to look out the window. Noah still hadn't let his breath out. If Joseph were to look to his left, he'd see Noah standing there, dead center.

"Fuck, someone's here," Joseph said and checked his phone.

Noah knew that no one had messaged Joseph saying they were coming over. Noah would've seen it come through.

Sergio's body spasmed, once again distracting Joseph. He turned around, and Noah watched from the clone phone. Joseph kicked Sergio square in the chest. He flew back a few inches and thudded hard against the ground. Lifeless, like a sack of potatoes. Joseph then turned and rushed inside, leaving the garage light on.

The door slammed shut.

The car coming up the driveway slowed to a stop. He heard one of the car doors open and waited for it to close before making his next move.

Arturo slipped outside of the silver Camry, going through the motions with Johnson as if on auto pilot. His mind still spinning with the framed photo he'd seen on the wall at Sergio's like a record on repeat. Sergio and Joseph smiling and laughing as their bodies touched. Their arms locked around each other. Arturo couldn't help but feel bitter.

Had Joseph called Sergio *darling*, too? Arturo was envious, disgusted, jealous. Somewhere in the center of it all, he felt a little stupid, too; he'd only just met Joseph. Standing in the driveway even now, he felt Joseph's house was tainted with Baxtor Springs, though it hadn't been before.

Dink. Clank.

Arturo attempted to look but winced. His eye still swollen and sizzling from being attacked. A faint white glow came from the garage windows. They were a little too high for him to see into, but even then, they were foggy with privacy film. The noise had come from inside. Arturo thought of the storage racks in Joseph's garage and how they'd formed a private area that he couldn't see into earlier.

How long ago that felt now.

Arturo made his way to the front door, feeling as if he was balancing a giant bowl of water on top of his head. He was exhausted, but when he smelled Joseph's leftover vomit and lavender flowers competing for the air around him, he walked hastily. At the large steel door, he could already hear footsteps fast approaching. The door swung open, its enormous frame looked ominous, the soft glow of light from inside cast a shadow from Joseph's tall frame over Arturo's face.

"Arturo?" Joseph said, looking shocked. "Why didn't you tell me you were coming over?" He stood there with just a towel around his waist, steam wafting off his shoulders and a layer of sweat glistening over his body. Arturo wrapped his arms around his chest, nervous about bringing up the photo, but it was all he could think about. Joseph looked gorgeous, and it served only as a reminder that they hadn't had sex, hadn't done anything. What was worse, Joseph breathed heavily, as if Arturo was interrupting something.

"Should I have given you a heads up? Was I interrupting something?" Arturo asked.

Joseph scoffed and shook his head as if he was waiting for the punchline of a joke. Arturo didn't say anything, though. He'd asked a question.

"No—you weren't interrupting anything. I was just . . ." Joseph waved his hands around again. "*Yuck*, it smells like barf out here. Come in, come in."

Arturo didn't move, though, as if his feet were glued to the ground. He hadn't stepped into the light yet, and once he did, Joseph would see his face. He'd have questions, but Arturo didn't want to answer anything. He wanted Joseph to answer instead.

"*Honey*, come inside—my god, what happened to your eye?" Joseph stepped forward, and Arturo could smell a strong scent come off Joseph's exposed body. It overpowered Arturo's senses like a pungent cologne. Arturo wrinkled his nose. His eye stung from being bruised both above and below. Joseph peered down, and his hand rose. In the shadows that surrounded them, it only made Arturo feel like he was back in Sergio's apartment with the attacker once more. Arturo swatted Joseph's hand away and walked past him into the house. He didn't look behind him. He heard the door lock, though. Joseph's footsteps caught up with him before they even passed the guest bathroom.

"What happened today?" Joseph asked, concerned, stopping in front of the living room. Arturo stopped, too. In the light, he felt more at ease. Joseph cautiously stepped forward and slipped a fist underneath Arturo's chin, tilting his head up. "Please talk to me," Joseph pleaded. "You can talk to me about anything, you know that." When Arturo didn't speak, Joseph added, "*Babe—Artie*—please."

Arturo felt a shiver run down his spine hearing that nickname: *Artie*. Joseph had said it the same way Fisher used to, which was the same way he had called Joshua his *sweet, sweet boy* in the recording at the funeral.

"Don't call me Artie. Don't call me babe, either. I don't like pet names," Arturo said, his voice shaking. He'd owned a bar, which included hiring and firing people. Neither of those situations made him as nervous as he was now.

"Did you know Sergio Hernandez was in Baxtor Springs?" Arturo asked, and he could see Joseph's skin turn a shade paler.

"No, why was he here? Stalking me?" Joseph answered relatively flatly.

"No, his parents died in the massacre. He's been in town for a few months now. So have you. You never saw him?"

Arturo asked, turning so his better eye could stare Joseph down.

"*Ba*—Arturo, no, I didn't. I barely left my house. I got everything delivered, and the day I stepped out was when I met Emily and now all of this. I had no idea that he was in town." Joseph took a beat. His eyes shifted away from Arturo's gaze. "What does your eye have to do with him?"

Arturo had to pause to think about how Sergio had gotten mixed into his long—never-ending—day. He raised his hand to his forehead and rubbed it, feeling the suit jacket bunch up, pinching his elbow space.

"Sergio's missing. I went to check on his place tonight 'cause Dana asked me to. When I got there, somebody attacked me, fled. I had to give a statement, and now I'm . . ." Arturo's voice faded in exhaustion.

"Here," Joseph finished for him, calmly. "Let's get you out of those clothes."

He grabbed Arturo's other hand, but his arms still hung there like dead weight as Joseph tried to pull him.

"You had nothing to do with it? I saw a photo in his apartment of you two together. Detective Vaughn is going to come asking questions, and I—I need to know, right now."

"You think I kidnapped him and attacked you in the process?" Joseph asked, taking a step back now.

"I heard a noise in the garage when I got here. Was that him?" Arturo asked. His anxiety swirled, like a tornado that could destroy everything in its path.

Joseph gestured to the floor around them, and Arturo could see water droplets along the hardwood floor. The rug polka dotted with water around Joseph's feet. Arturo felt the overwhelming feeling of being at a loss for words.

"Arturo," Joseph said, looking at him more sternly now. "I've been sick all day. I just started to feel good enough to take a shower. Now you are here."

"Why is your garage light on then?" Arturo asked.

"I went in there to find some Zofran, made quite the mess trying to find it."

"What's that?"

"It's an anti-nausea medication. With that out of the way, I could get on my feet, which didn't involve me kidnapping Sergio or attacking you. Trust me."

"Then I'll go turn the light off," Arturo said.

"I already did that," Joseph replied without missing a beat.

"No, you said you were showering when I knocked, you must have left it on. It'll just take two seconds, anyway." He started for the garage, and Joseph was suddenly in toe behind his every step. Arturo felt like a child for a moment, racing his *tía* for something she knew he shouldn't be doing. A funny feeling that he had interrupted something piped up again, and Arturo slowed down, losing the race. He stopped along-side the washer and dryer and gave Joseph a curious look as he turned around and stood in front of the garage door. As if guarding it like a statue.

"It's a real mess in there. Let's get you out of those clothes, and you can shower."

Arturo didn't budge, though. "Joseph, stop being silly. If a light is on, turn it off. And if it is off, then good to know we double-checked. You're acting weird."

Arturo stepped around Joseph and opened the garage door, where the light was indeed still on. Inside, the stor-age racks were still standing tall and creating a barrier. Any sinking suspicion Arturo had left soon evaporated. One of the black sheets on the storage rack closest to him had fallen to the side, so he could now see past it to the other side of the makeshift room, where a pile of papers and books and cracked bins sat in a heap. As Joseph had said, it was *a real mess in there.*

Sergio Hernandez was nowhere to be seen. Arturo turned and felt tears start to well up until he couldn't hold them back. He cried, and Joseph came up and wrapped his arms around him.

"You've had an insane day. Please, let's get you out of those clothes. You can shower, and we can ice that eye of yours," Joseph said, comfortingly so.

They left the garage after turning off the light, and Arturo soon tossed all his clothes on the bathroom floor while Joseph went to the closet to change. The hot water washed over his back and shoulders, which ached less the longer he stood. Arturo knew everything would be worse tomorrow. He stepped out to find a fresh towel and a pair of shorts on the closed toilet seat. Arturo dried off and slipped them on. He felt too bare still, his skin too exposed. He wandered into Joseph's closet and grabbed an oversized sweater. He swam in the amount of fabric and found it comforting.

Arturo walked out to the living room, where Joseph handed him some pain killers and a bag of ice. He tapped his lap with a pillow already propped up, and soon Arturo lay down and let Joseph take care of the ice. Joseph ran his fingers through Arturo's hair mindlessly as if he, too, had had a long night. They sat in silence together. Arturo sighed, reminding his still anxious thoughts that Joseph had a long day, too—he'd been sick.

Before the pain killers could kick in, Joseph got them both into bed.

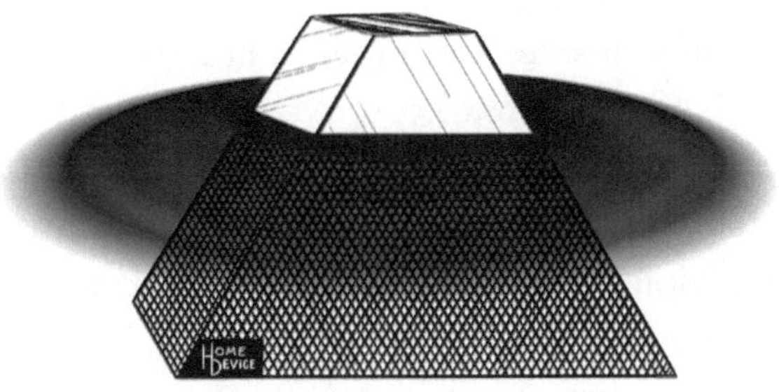

The black-out motorized shades lifted, and Joseph looked up from his phone to watch. The trees were covered in the golden hour morning light, revealing that some were already transitioning to fall, while others still held on to that forest green foliage. He sighed and looked back to his phone.

He was going to add to the recordings. That was what Sergio had said. Joseph had turned this phrase over in his mind in every which way he could think. In the time spent awake, he'd already searched his phone for any new recording added. He checked the HomeDevice app. All the recordings from Benjamin Fisher had been stored here, even those that didn't have any dialogue, per se. Most of the recordings had been grunts and thumps—Joseph skipped over those scouring for any other dialogue that could be used in *Rabbit's Revenge*. He scrolled to the bottom of the recordings, but he didn't see a new one. He searched through the other apps on his phone—Notes, Voice Memos, even his photos and videos. His last resort was the search bar, and even that yielded nothing.

Joseph's head hurt. He was focusing so hard.

The only new thing he could find was that the side entrance to the garage had been opened and closed before Arturo stormed inside. Joseph felt a little relief knowing his name was Noah and that he, too, had a rabbit tattoo on his forearm. Joseph had to remind himself. This wasn't a character from his book. This was the person who'd inspired it all, and he was violent. Joseph could hold his ground, though, if it came to that.

Thankfully, before giving Arturo the painkillers last night, he'd taken some himself. They'd worked like a charm. He didn't dream and therefore didn't have any nightmares. He felt rejuvenated, enough, at least.

Arturo stretched beside him, caught between two pillows. He reached his hand over to Joseph's chest. Joseph looked over, watching Arturo nestle over. His eye wasn't swollen shut anymore, but it was bruised with hues of black and purple. A small scab had formed at the corner of his eye, where the skin must've split.

"Your poor eye," Joseph said, giving that same sad catfish frown again.

"Does it look any better?"

"A little," Joseph replied. "It'll still take time, though." Arturo lay back and closed his eyes with a sigh. "Did you get a look at the attacker at all?"

"No, it was dark. I thought I saw a tattoo on their forearm, but——"

"Was it of a rabbit?" Joseph asked, too eager——too curious.

Arturo opened his eyes and gave him a funny look. "Like the character from your book?"

Joseph felt as if Arturo had just jabbed his thumb deep into a pressure point. Joseph winced and forced a loud *ha*, refusing to answer.

"No, I didn't get a good look at it, but it was small," Arturo said.

"Shame," Joseph replied. "Are you going to get up? I have a few errands before the reading I need to take care of."

"I might not go to the reading tonight, if that's okay?" Arturo gestured to his face.

"That's fine. Do you want a ride back to your place?" Joseph offered.

"I'd like to stay here. If you don't mind."

"Not at all." Joseph wrapped Arturo in his arms and kissed him softly on the shoulder.

"Maybe I'll read your book to pass the time."

"Oh, please, plenty of other great books in my house that you can read that don't have to do with murder or violent beatings in the middle of the night," Joseph said and then bit his sarcastic tongue.

"Yeah." Arturo paused once more. "Any self-help?"

"Plenty of those, in the office. I wouldn't mind your help with something."

Arturo perked up.

"I have some copies I need to deliver to Emily before the reading," Joseph explained. After he showered and got dressed in a pair of chinos with a sweater that could transition into the night, Joseph and Arturo packed the little Porsche with all the copies of the books that could fit. A few would need to sit on Joseph's lap as he drove, but he didn't mind. All he could think about was sticking to the plan set in motion by his investment with Publishing X. This brought him comfort, unlike wondering where Sergio's body had been, or even Detective Stuart Kline's.

Joseph drove away, watching Arturo find the hose and pull it toward the front walkway. Behind him, books shifted from one side to the next, each turn taking him closer to Main Street. By the time he arrived, it was in the late afternoon. For a Friday, the street was surprisingly busier than Joseph had ever seen it. More people were walking about, the coffee shop filled with people reading and tapping away on laptops. The small park in the center of it all had some people enjoying the last rays of summer while a dog excitedly jumped for a frisbee, catching it midair near the gazebo Joseph had taken headshots near. The brown wooden structure with its peeling paint leaned a tad to the left. *Had Noah recognized the gazebo behind Joseph in his author's photo?*

Joseph's left eye twitched.

A truck alongside a light pole was adding banners to each one on Main Street that read, "We Remember the Miller Family," printed above a photo of the happy-looking family, and below it, "Need Help? Please come to our weekly meetings now hosted at Baxtor's Books every Thursday, 5 to 7 p.m." Beneath that, "You're not alone. Speak with someone today: Suicide Prevention Lifeline 1-800-273-8255." The next banner was of a different family, and the next a young kid, and the next a freshly newlywed couple.

Joseph was able to find parking in front of a nondescript cruiser and knew it was Detective Vaughn's. It still reminded him too much of Stuart Kline's recently recovered one. He grabbed a large stack of his novels and headed into Baxtor's Books. He pushed through the swinging doors, and inside he could hear a bustle of people moving about. Setting the books down near the cash register, Joseph turned, seeing Detective Vaughn facing him with a group of three people. A woman with long black hair turned, and he saw it was Emily. Her eyes were puffy and red, matching the flower print blouse she wore tucked into her flowing pants. Joseph wiped away at the knot growing inside his stomach, as if some leftover crumbs remained on his shirt from breakfast.

"Well, I last saw him Monday and Tuesday before he went to help Violet at The Whiskey Bar—the owner, Arturo, went out of town for a few days with—" Dana turned to see Joseph. She tossed her thumb over in his direction as he approached slowly, trying to hear as much of the conversation as he could. He'd been spotted, though. Joseph gave a slight wave as he joined the group.

"And you?" Vaughn pointed to the waiter from the other day, Colton. He was average-looking in a button-up that looked used.

"I worked that shift with Sergio on Monday and Tuesday at Dana's." Colton took a step forward, his chest puffed out. "I do need to be upfront with you, though, Detective."

Joseph's eyes snapped to Colton's, who was already staring at him. He looked like a dog on alert, hearing something funky in the distance.

"Yes?" Vaughn asked.

"Earlier this week, Emily had a meeting with Joseph at Dana's," he said, gesturing to each person as if connecting the dots for the detective. Emily nodded with an *mmhm* attached. Joseph followed suit, his mask still in place. Colton continued. "Originally, that was Sergio's section, but when he saw Joseph, he asked to switch sections with me. Nothing uncommon, but he did say that they'd fucked or something—*I guess*." Colton shook his head and shrugged. "I'm just telling you what he told me."

"I was aware they knew each other," Vaughn said, pulling out his phone. He turned to Joseph. "We found this photo of you two in his apartment last night. Care to elaborate?"

Everyone looked at the photo and then at Joseph. A radiating spotlight warmed his skin while he prepared himself for an Academy Award-winning performance.

"I had a relationship with Sergio on the West Coast for about two years," Joseph said, looking at Vaughn. "We broke up over seven months ago. It was mutual, nothing bad. He had that photo up in his apartment?" Joseph asked, peering at the photo with sad eyes before closing them and shaking his head. "How bittersweet."

"Yes, did you know that he was here in Baxtor Springs?" Vaughn asked.

"No, I didn't," Joseph said, but he couldn't escape Vaughn's hard stare. "Listen, I know how this might look—but I promise you. I hadn't seen him once on this side of the coast. I didn't even know this is where he was from."

"Never asked him?" Vaughn asked.

"No—he only said—and I apologize . . ." He gestured to the four pairs of eyes watching his every move. "He said he grew up in a shit town out east that he didn't even want to return to for the holidays; he stayed with me instead."

"How'd you end up in Baxtor Springs?" Vaughn asked.

"My father lived out here and passed away. I took over the estate, and now I'm doing a book reading tonight to help raise money for the victim's fund." Joseph looked to Emily.

"Yes, a good amount is needed to rebuild the stained windows at the church, now, too," Emily said.

"What?" Joseph asked.

"You didn't hear about what happened at the funeral? It was horrendous."

"Sorry, Emily—but Joseph," Vaughn said, holding up a hand between them all, "If I remember correctly, you left for Lake Wilburton on Tuesday, returning Thursday morning, correct?"

Joseph nodded. "Yes, and you saw me that morning. I was sick."

Vaughn stroked his chin, nodding. "Sergio was first reported missing last night. Do you have an alibi?"

"I was sick all day," Joseph said, and then stammered, "A-Arturo came over last night. He saw that I was there at home. I helped put ice on his black eye."

"What?" Everyone except Vaughn asked, jaws dropped.

"There was an altercation. We believe the person who attacked Arturo last night had something to do with Sergio's disappearance." Vaughn scratched the back of his head and looked over the group. "If any of you hear anything, let me know. I'm going to check in with Violet over at A Whiskey Bar, see what she may know. I'll be around, let you all fill each other in on yesterday's events."

"Colton, let's get all this done and try to take a break before everything starts tonight," Dana said.

Vaughn turned to leave, while Dana and Colton headed back out to the patio to finish setting up. Emily wiped her eyes a bit more, trailing behind Joseph, who went the opposite direction from Detective Vaughn. Out by his car, Emily filled Joseph in on what had happened at the funeral while he handed her a few copies from inside the Porsche.

"Sergio is missing, just like Stuart Kline was before his body turned up at the funeral." Emily sobbed, delicately wiping her tears with a handkerchief folded over her curved index finger.

"Oh my god, they found his body?" Joseph asked. Arturo hadn't told him that part.

"Yeah, everyone at the church saw it. It's now been roped off as a murder scene. They're dusting the car for prints. The coroner has already collected the body to see if there's any evidence left, although the body had baked in the trunk for a good amount of time. It's all so horrible, Joseph." Emily paused to inhale while her sobs billowed beneath her words.

All so horrible for me, Joseph wanted to reply. "It really is," he said instead.

I have my alibi, Detective Kline's nightmarish words scratched like nails on a chalkboard inside Joseph's head. *Tick. Tock.* It would only be a matter of time. Emily turned and took the copies inside. Joseph paused outside the Porsche. He looked around at Main Street. Was Noah here, watching him, even now? Joseph peeked around, trying to see if there was a plain white boy with a shaved head and a forearm tattoo. There were too many people out and about today. The trees waved around the square as a breeze drifted through, making his search more challenging. He knew that just because he couldn't see him, didn't mean that Noah— *Rabbit*—wasn't out there waiting. He closed the car door and carried the rest of the books inside.

Arturo finished hosing down the lavender and watched himself in the reflection of the glass as he coiled the hose back to the side of the house where it hung. His distorted reflection resembled some horrible sci-fi mutation that pulsed with each breath. He sighed, heading back into Joseph's house. The steel door left unlocked was effortless to move back and forth, and so quiet, too. Past the foyer and down the hall, Arturo searched for his vape.

Walking through Joseph's house, Arturo felt like he was at some wellness retreat, and he knew the layout well. In the bedroom and toward the closet, he found his funeral suit from yesterday, where his vape was tucked inside his jacket pocket. Through the French doors that led to the balcony, Arturo walked out and sat on the couches at the far end situated around the smokeless fire pit. He brushed off the pillows from leaves that had fallen and the twigs that had blown in.

He lay down, bathing in the sounds of the forest. A bird cawed in the distance while only a few clouds lingered overhead in a vast blue sky. Twigs broke in the far distance, and leaves rustled nearby. Arturo continued to smoke, imagining a deer was nearby. They were common in these parts, as well as the occasional bear before they hibernated in the coming weeks.

Arturo's phone vibrated. He checked the screen, Steven Goldstein.

"Hey, Goldstein," Arturo answered.

"Hey, Arturo. How's that eye doing?" Goldstein asked.

"It's still bruised, but the swelling has gone down," Arturo replied, taking another hit of his vape after.

"That's good to hear."

Arturo curled his lip inward, waiting for Goldstein to continue, but there was only silence. He looked around at the surrounding forest, some of it shifting into deep reds with spots of yellow among the greenery.

"So, uh—that kid we were talking about last night was Noah Crane." Goldstein cleared his throat, and Arturo instantly knew who he was talking about. Memories dripped down, revealing only a small, quiet, round-faced boy who wasn't very adventurous. Arturo hadn't seen him since Boy Scouts. He'd assumed he'd moved to a new city after his parents divorced or something. He wouldn't have imagined he'd gone to prison.

"My mother would pick him up for the troop meetings sometimes. Didn't Fisher take the three of us camping once, too?" Arturo asked, analyzing the memories that had puddled together in his mind.

"Yeah, we'd all earned our—uh, canoeing badges? Something water related. I remember Noah forgot swim trunks that day. We always shared a tent together."

"Who?" Arturo asked.

"You and I," Goldstein said in a lighter tone. "Noah and Fisher had their own, 'cause Noah's parents couldn't afford a tent. You know, not every parent could afford to send their kids on every camping trip, Arturo; that happened often," Goldstein stated flatly. "Noah went to prison around the time your mother passed. He's been in prison until recently."

"Recently enough to have murdered Fisher?" Arturo asked, blinking emptily at the trees that swayed in the gentle breeze around him.

"Mmhm," Goldstein said. "According to records, they dropped him off at Baxtor Springs Square from prison. I'm here right now."

"At the prison?"

"Yeah, it's not that bad of a drive, really," Goldstein said.

"Why are you there?"

"I was talking to Noah's last cellmate, Timothy. The guy is doing a life sentence, and they only paired them together 'cause Timothy never took any shit. He was a nice guy, but the moment someone was rude to him, he'd beat the shit out of them. Timothy's a huge guy, very intimidating. They kept each other in line—at least, that's what the guards told me."

"Jesus." Arturo's black eye stung painfully as he tried to focus on what he was learning.

"Timothy was helpful, told me a lot about Noah."

"Like?"

"Noah was always acting up to get more time. Timothy even gave him a tattoo once that added five years to Noah's sentence. He said at that point, Noah already had enough time built up to spend the rest of his life behind bars. He settled down, and all this time later, they let him out for good behavior."

"I saw a tattoo on the attacker last night. I didn't see it well enough, though." Arturo paused, thinking of what Joseph had asked him earlier. "Is it of a rabbit, by chance?"

"Yeah, Timothy said it's a simple drawing. He also said that he used to watch the news with Noah all the time. They were watching the day of the massacre, and Timothy said that this old guy, *Fisher-something* is how he put it, had been on the screen. Timothy said Noah got really heated and walked off. Didn't speak for the rest of the week, and then they let him go. Timothy didn't really understand what he was telling me, but I did."

"He knew Fisher was the cause of the massacre," Arturo said, dumbfounded.

"Now, when we found Fisher's body, the coroner reported that the body had been there for roughly twenty-four hours. Within those twenty-four hours, Noah had been released. There was also a citizen who called in that night reporting that they heard gunfire. I believe this was when Noah killed Fisher."

"Because Fisher had molested Noah."

"Yes, and Noah was the one who attempted to rat on Fisher before going to jail."

"What about Stuart Kline? What about Sergio? You think it's connected?"

"Okay, let's not go roping all crime into one big category now. I'm just focusing on Fisher's murder, trying to help Vaughn. He already has those other two cases on his shoulders and no partner. I'm trying to do my best here, get a promotion maybe."

Arturo laughed, thinking of what he'd told his *tía* just yesterday. *Stop making this into some conspiracy.* "Yeah, totally. Take it step by step."

Goldstein laughed lightly. "Yes. I wanted to say thank you, though. That conversation last night helped me discover this. I think Vaughn will be impressed."

"Where are you going to try looking for Noah?"

"Timothy suggested the Extended Stay over on the east side. I'm going to see if they've seen him."

"Good luck," Arturo offered.

"Thanks."

Arturo hung up and looked at the reflection on his phone. He winced upon seeing his dark-purple eye. He pouted and rolled to his good side, which allowed him to still look out over the trees. A twig snapped, and Arturo shot up, no longer thinking about forest animals moseying their way through.

Why had Joseph asked if his attacker had a rabbit tattoo? He felt himself sink into that same feeling that he'd had last night when he came to Joseph's. He tried to brush it aside and decided to pass the time with what he'd joked about earlier with Joseph.

Reading a book.

Arturo got up and headed to the office, still taking hits of the indica vape. He stepped inside, pushing the door fully open, and looked around the office. He saw the note cards on the wall that plotted out the story of *Rabbit's Revenge* with little, scribbled notes at the bottom. Arturo looked around the room, wondering if that's how Joseph jotted down his thoughts, like some old school detective in a film with a tape recorder documenting a case.

Arturo chuckled and turned to the other side of the room, where all the copies of *Rabbit's Revenge* had sat hours earlier. Now he saw only a single copy on the shelf, lying flat with a large folder beneath it. Arturo imagined it being a private copy in Joseph's collection. He reached for it, and as he pulled, the folder nudged off the shelf with it. Arturo slipped the folder back and looked at the book. The small, fluffy white rabbit was on the cover. He turned, leaving the office, and opened the book. Leafing through some of the pages, he noticed a signature on the title page, much like his own copy. Joseph must've signed this one. Other parts inside were highlighted—small scribbles along the edges.

Arturo felt a little giddy. He assumed this was an unedited manuscript bound for the author to read as they readied him for publication.

At least, that's what he thought.

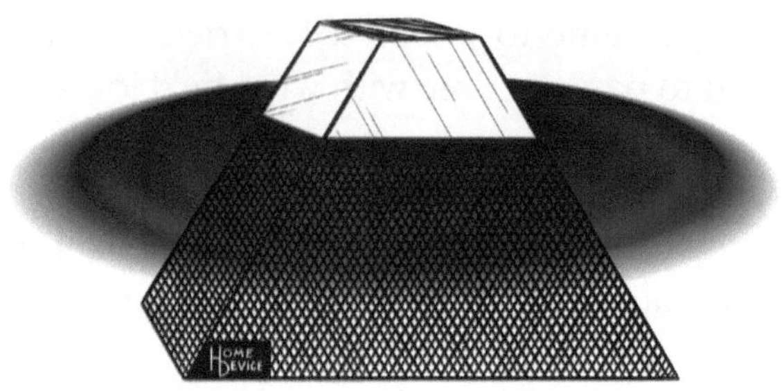

For the rest of the day, Joseph stayed at Baxtor's Books. He wanted people to have eyes on him after Detective Vaughn had come around. He was helpful, didn't throw any sass, and even offered to take the trash out. He wanted them all to see how *normal* he was acting. He had nothing to hide. He didn't even harbor ill will for Colton. He'd done what any helpful good citizen would've done. Joseph didn't even have to lie. Honest to God, he didn't know what had happened to Sergio that night. After Joseph had taken care of him, that is.

Emily walked through the store from the back room, holding a large poster that caught Joseph's attention as he arranged some books on the signing table. The poster read, "Author Reading + Charity Event Tonight (20% off everything during!)." Joseph smiled. The poster was plain enough to imagine Emily using it often for various other authors that would come through Baxtor Springs.

While Emily slipped the sign in the front window and adjusted the lighting, Dana came through with food in a large, covered aluminum tray, steam rising from it. Joseph salivated. It smelled like fresh apple pie. The place was almost ready for the event, and a line of people had already formed outside. Joseph smiled again, catching Emily's eyes as she came over.

"You want a little drink before? To calm the nerves," she asked.

Joseph laughed, hoping his mask was still in place.

"No, not for me. Afraid I'll get too nervous. Cut my finger again," Joseph said, more theatrical than usual.

Emily rolled her eyes and playfully elbowed him, reciting her own version of a quote from Stephen King's *The Shining*. "All work and no play makes Joseph a dull boy." She smiled. Joseph followed her as she walked to the office. She opened the door to a small seating area and desk. Her computer screensaver showed a ball that bounced between two lines—a computer versus computer. Joseph took a seat, and Emily poured herself a small drink in a tiny glass, a port wine that smelled sweet even from across the room. She took a sip and then sat across from him.

"You thinking about the next book at all?"

Joseph laughed and felt his mask slip down. Just for this moment, he'd allow it.

"Yes, I'll have another book out late next year, I imagine."

"Then another author reading night is in our future." She smiled wickedly. A commotion began on the other side of the door, and Emily tossed back the rest of her port. "Sounds like things are starting. Just hang out in here for about fifteen minutes or so. I'll come and get you when we're ready."

She slipped out of the door, and Joseph peeked behind her. The room was filled with people. Some were in line waiting to purchase the book. Others already had books in their hands. The room had a charisma that wafted into the office as the door closed. Joseph felt electrified, just like he did at the last reading. Last time, he'd been nervous about having his face in the spotlight and possibly attracting some *New York Times* reporter who might do an exposé about why his book was selling so *well*. He never expected to figure out who the older man was. He'd never cared to. *Funny*, Joseph thought, how he ended up figuring it all out, anyway.

Behind him, the door opened, and Joseph looked over, expecting Emily; instead, it was Detective Vaughn.

"Evening, Detective," Joseph said standing up quickly.

"Evening, Joseph," Vaughn said, standing near the door. "Looks like Sergio finished a shift Thursday night and then went missing. By your timeline, you couldn't be involved, and Arturo will support that, too, since he was with you. I also saw you later that day, and you did look very sick."

"Okay . . . Why are you telling me this?" Joseph asked, patting for the chair behind him and plopping down.

"Wanted to ask if you had any further information in private; we had quite the audience earlier." Vaughn shifted his weight.

"No, Detective, but thank you."

"Okay then. Thank you for being honest about the relationship you had with Sergio earlier. I want you to know that I don't think I'll have any other questions for you."

Emily entered the office and looked at both of them. Her smile faded along with the noise outside as she shut the door.

"Everything okay?" she asked nervously.

"Yes, just wishing Joseph here good luck tonight is all," Vaughn said, clapping his hands together. "Better go get me a copy of your book. I hear it's terrific."

"Thank you for the support, Detective." Joseph replied, robotically. "Emily, are we ready?"

"We are," she said, the smile back on her face.

Joseph nodded, slipping his phone back in his pocket. Vaughn ducked out first, and then Joseph followed Emily out, hearing gentle applause from the seated crowd to the people standing in the back winding aisles. Joseph looked around the crowd for Noah. Instead, he got a flash of Stuart Kline in the same chair he's sat in last weekend. Just a flashback, and Joseph forced a smile. Emily introduced him as a current number-one bestseller on various lists, and that she was excited to have him here.

More applause from the crowd erupted.

Joseph reread the prologue, a few short pages about how Rabbit—Noah—had murdered Benjamin Fisher. Joseph read with great projection and pronunciation, turning up that theatrical performance once again. No paper cut to stop him mid-sentence.

Applause once more.

Emily closed out with a light joke and directed people to the signing table. Each person approached with the title page already open, and Joseph continued to perform, that spotlight directly on him. He indulged in the small talk. He asked how to spell names correctly. He even jotted down a fun one-liner here and there to make the reader's experience unique.

He smiled, politely thanking each person while handing a signed copy back to them. Joseph turned to look at the new unsigned book before him and felt a dryness catch in his throat. A cell phone was on top of the book, silently playing a video of Joseph putting the plastic bag over Sergio's head and tying the bag as tightly as he could. Joseph watched as a hand dragged the phone away from the book. He drew his gaze up slowly, noticing a thin black line curved on the forearm before him, illustrating the figure of a rabbit. It was a tattoo, beside it the title page read, *Rabbit's Revenge*. Noah stared down at him. Joseph was stoned faced as he looked right back at him. Just two very dangerous men, face-to-face, in a room full of innocent people.

"Evening, Mr. Bailey," Noah said, his voice smooth and low, just like it was in the recording. Sergio was right. He was an average-looking white guy with a muscular build—shaved head and toughness that didn't exactly fit his boyish face.

"Evening, Rabbit." Joseph didn't dare to blink.

"Please, call me by my name."

"Noah." Joseph refused to break eye contact with him, like two dogs sizing each other up.

"Quite a crazy night you had last night, wasn't it?" Noah's plump lips curled into a smile beneath his eyes, which remained deadpan.

Joseph looked down to the book and signed, *To Noah—what an inspiration.*

Noah read this and laughed.

"I think we may just get along," Noah said as his smile widened. Yet his eyes remained lifeless. "Let's take a ride in your car after this," he said, taking the book and slapping it shut.

"See you in twenty," Joseph marveled.

Joseph watched Noah walk out to the patio, where he couldn't see him anymore. A new unsigned book was placed before him, and Joseph smacked on the performance persona that would carry him through the rest of the night, until Emily handed him a drink after the last signing. He gulped it down before saying he was going to head out, still a little iffy from yesterday's nausea. As the door shut behind him, Emily asked if he was going to check on someone, but Joseph didn't hear. He was too focused on Noah, who was leaning against the Porsche vaping that familiar banana-strawberry scent. His held his arms crossed under the streetlight, giving the impression of some heartthrob from another era. Joseph jingled his keys around his finger, and they clattered to a stop in his hand.

"Where to?" Joseph asked as he unlocked the car, slipping inside.

"Home. Your place," Noah replied, following suit and buckling his seat belt.

The motor roared to life as a police car passed by. Joseph watched Noah turn, covering his face with his arm as if he was coughing. Joseph pulled out and shifted gears. The wind picked up between them. Joseph peeked at the rear-view mirror to see the police car make a U-turn. He gulped, but then realized it had taken the parking spot Joseph had left open.

"I've been watching you the past few days," Noah said, looking over to Joseph, settling back in the seat.

"I'm aware," Joseph replied, stone cold. "You've been on my phone. In my house, while I was away, and you've cleaned up two of my messes. One of which, you put me in. I see why now." Joseph took a breath, letting his spine perk up.

"I assumed you'd find out about your phone. That was a given. I cloned it. That video I showed you is in your photos now. Uploaded to the cloud." He laughed. "I've seen everything you've done. Even done some things myself to get a stir out of you." Noah smiled devilishly. "Tell me, when you murdered Detective Kline, did you think he was me?"

Joseph's left eye twitched again, so much that his vision pulsed slightly.

"I did."

"Poor you." Noah laughed. "That must've been frustrating. It was for me, too, trying to figure out how you knew I killed Fisher. Some coding error in the Home Device's software. Did you know? Or even care to find out?"

Joseph sneered. "No, I didn't care to. You may be the Rabbit from the recording that inspired my idea, but coincidence doesn't get you anything. At the end of the day, *Rabbit's Revenge* is simply a dry spy novel." Joseph hadn't taken those cold eyes off the road. That same deadpan expression seemed tattooed on his face. "I don't even fully know what happened in all those recordings. Most of them were duds."

"Those were the nights he molested me. Molested Joshua, too. You're right, though, *Rabbit's Revenge* is a shit spy novel that is only doing well because of Publishing X. It'd be a shame if people found out about those emails between you and the company."

"What is it you want? Money?" Joseph asked.

"I want you to tell the truth—my truth. I know you've already paid for your second book to be a success, why not tell the truth behind the massacre?"

"I write fiction, Noah." Joseph blew past a stop sign that stood over a herd of deer, their black beady eyes staring at them as they passed.

"Even Capote wrote fiction before writing *In Cold Blood*. I read that multiple times in prison. You already live in Baxtor Springs—you can interview people in town, and I can spill everything to you. Everything that happened."

"I already know that Fisher was close with the boy from the massacre. What's your story? It's not just going to come out of thin air."

Noah was taken aback. No one had ever asked him for his side of the story. No one had ever cared to ask. Once he spoke, every little detail he could remember came billowing out.

Arturo couldn't remember the last time he'd sat down and read an entire book in one sitting, but he'd just done it. He was hooked, but not by the writing. Next to one of the first paragraphs in the prologue was a set of highlighted words—*the older man*—and then an arrow that faintly pointed to the name *Fisher*. Arturo was stunned. How often had Joseph said he only wrote fiction whenever Arturo had brought up a strange "coincidental" detail. That question fueled him, and he read an entire—very dull—book about spies. Arturo looked the book over, but he couldn't understand why Fisher's name was written in the prologue.

Arturo began flipping back to the beginning when the book slipped his grip. He was able to catch a flap with the tips of his fingers. He lifted the book back up, and spotted a different signature on the end paper. In thin, slanted black ink, Arturo read the words: *From the Library of Stuart Kline.*

Arturo stood up from the office chair so fast his head spun. His vision grew dark, much like it had when the panic attack had overtaken him. When his vision returned, and his breath steadied, Arturo looked around. He'd never left the office; the chair was touching the backs of his legs even now. His eyes darted to where he'd grabbed the book, and he looked at the folder far differently now.

Arturo dropped the book without a second thought and walked over. He reached up and grabbed the folder. Turning it over, he read the name printed from a label maker: *Benjamin C. Fisher*. Arturo's throat clamped while his mind raced. Why would Joseph have this file? What if Arturo's fingerprints were now on the file? He dropped it, causing the loose papers inside to scatter about. Photos of Fisher's suicide—er, homicide—were now cast about Arturo's feet. His stomach lunged as if he might vomit.

Oh my god, he thought. Arturo was punched in the face with a realization that made his knees cave, and he crumbled to the ground, throwing his hands out for support, but they landed on the photos and slid out. His head slammed into the ground and his black eye screamed in pain.

With his eyes closed, all he could picture was Detective Kline's body stuffed in the trunk, his face not much different than Fisher's had been at the funeral after falling on the floor. Both had been horrifically mutilated. Arturo opened his eyes, refusing to close them again, but he felt trapped as the photos from Fisher's residence surrounded him.

Arturo realized that these photos of the crime scene were exact replicas of what had been printed in the prologue of Joseph's book. He lay there for just a second, noticing that he could smell lavender waft through from the front door, which was now wide open. Arturo realized that the Porsche was almost up the driveway. He scrambled to his feet to look out the window, and he saw that Joseph wasn't alone.

Noah sat beside him, rubbing his shaved head with his hand exposing a small rabbit tattoo on his forearm. Arturo could see it even at a distance. Noah and Joseph knew each other, Arturo realized, but he knew he was discovering this too late. The mouse trap had already snapped: the sweet taste of Joseph's life had lured him in, and now Arturo feared that he wouldn't make it out alive.

"My parents worked a lot, and they weren't always the best at picking me up on time. I was always the last kid, and Fisher would stay with me while waiting for my parents. At first, it was cool. We talked about a lot of things. My parents got closer to him, seeing as he was always there to greet them. He never gave them shit for being late, and soon, Fisher had permission to drop me off at home. It was on his way. We started smoking weed. I didn't think anything of it. I knew it was *wrong* at the time, illegal or whatever. But I trusted Fisher. This went on for about a year, and soon I noticed that there were a few others he'd smoke weed with, too. He wasn't just offering it to everyone. He was selective about the boys."

"How many were there?" Joseph asked.

"Three of us, at the time, before Joshua. But I wasn't around then. The other two, their parents would run late sometimes, and Fisher offered to drop them off since he was already taking me home all the time back then. One of those nights, he told us about a camping trip coming up that weekend. We each had no idea, but he told us to remind our parents. Fisher picked the three of us up and no other scout came. At Lake Wilburton, we smoked weed and swam, and Fisher gave us whatever badge we wanted. The other two slept in a tent together, but I had to share with Fisher. It was horrible. After the trip, he dropped us all off, and I was last. Neither of my parents were home, and he came inside and took advantage of me in my bedroom. He was getting comfortable. When he was through, he presented me with the badges I'd earned that weekend. Told me how proud he was." Noah gave half a smile, his eyebrow raised as if to say *why me,* and he added, "Lucky me."

Joseph turned up the driveway to his house, slowing the car down. Noah felt a lurch in his stomach, and the seatbelt tightened around him. He settled back as his eyes fell on the stars that twinkled in the night sky above them, alongside the moon. The outside air was chilly but not too much. Noah felt relieved to explain what had happened to him. Especially to someone who was going to publish all of this town's wretched complacency. His eyes fell on the house coming into view, and as Joseph parked the car, a comfortable silence fell between them. Joseph hadn't interjected or inserted himself into what Noah was saying. He was listening. How good it felt to be heard.

Joseph tossed the keys in the cup holder, and then he stepped out of the car. Noah trailed behind him as they walked inside, the front door already open. With the smell of lavender and florals in the foyer, Noah enjoyed being back.

"I understand why you murdered him then. You wanted revenge."

"No, Mr. Bailey—I wanted to feel safe out in the world," Noah spoke as they walked past the closed office door. "Just like I know you didn't murder Sergio for revenge. You murdered him for answers."

Noah sat down on the couch and watched Joseph get a bottle of whiskey and two glasses from the kitchen. The house was quiet, and Noah enjoyed the opportunity to be inside again. No longer was he hiding in another room like some dirty secret. He'd been invited in as a guest this time, how things had changed. Joseph returned to the couch with two heavy pours of whiskey.

"I tried to speak up. Told Edmonds about what we were smoking, but he didn't believe me about the weed. Instead, he brought me into his office and sat me down alongside Fisher. He told me that spreading malicious lies about Fisher being a pedophile was a horrible thing. That no other Boy Scout Troop had ever reported Fisher for any wrongdoing. I felt trapped and told the chief about Artie's mom, and they both laughed at me. Told me she'd committed suicide. Then the chief told me Fisher was going to give me a ride home. I ran out and into a convenience store and started trashing the place. Police arrested me for disorderly conduct. I broke the officer's nose who showed up. So more came and took me down. I cussed out my parents when they offered to help pay the bail because I knew they couldn't afford it. I refused to be the reason they'd go hungry. They didn't even show up to my court hearing. It's exactly the way I wanted things to be, so Fisher would never hurt them for what I knew. I didn't want my time in prison to end, so I caused fights and enjoyed spitting on the guards. I eventually racked up enough time that I'd die in there, safe and sound. My *happily ever after,* if you will. I calmed down, thinking I was safe, but then they let me out for good behavior. What a cosmic punch to the face. The first thing I did when I got out was murder Fisher. Especially after the massacre he caused."

Joseph licked his lips. "Artie—Arturo de Leon's mom?"

"Yeah," Noah said casually. "Goldstein was the other boy, but, I guess, nothing ever happened to him. "

"What happened to Arturo's mother?" Joseph inched forward.

"His mother was catching a flight one night to visit her husband in rehab, and Artie's *tía* was going to check in on Artie when she got off from her overnight shift. Fisher told me this, said that we would hang out at Artie's house for a little bit. Then he'd drop me off at home. When we dropped off Artie, we smoked on the back patio. Fisher was getting Artie so high that he began drifting off, falling asleep. I barely had any, and Fisher had me help get Artie into the living room. I knew what was going to happen, and soon they did. And then the front door opened, and Arturo's mother walked in on it all."

Noah shook his head, trying to blink away the memory playing in his mind. He stuttered a few times as he persisted. He felt the urge to pee, not out of necessity but because he felt that same fear he felt that night when he was so young—the tension in the room hot like toxic gas.

"Fisher had screamed at her, asking why she was there. She said her flight had been delayed to the following morning. Things got physical. He threw her into the bathroom and shut the door. When he came out, he said it was time to go. He dropped me off and said if I ever spoke about that night, people would get hurt, and it'd all be because I couldn't keep my mouth shut. I mean, come on," Noah scoffed. "No one was listening to me, anyway. Even when I did speak up, Fisher was there to control everything."

He took the final sip in his glass, and Joseph refilled them both. He set the bottle back on the coffee table beside them and then scooted closer to Noah.

"When's Arturo's aunt, Maria, discovered her body, it was reported as a suicide. Fisher continued to take advantage of me, and I felt like I was going to implode. Why could no one see Fisher for what he was? I told the chief, and all he did was tell me to shut up, to stop rocking the boat with lies."

Noah took a sip, and in that pause, Joseph inched closer once again. He raised his hand and gently touched Noah's shoulder. Even through his shirt, Noah could feel how warm Joseph's touch was. As Joseph massaged, Noah could feel the knots in his shoulder remain tight like a boulder in the middle of a wide river.

"I found you before Detective Kline did," Noah said, looking up at Joseph now. He could feel his face softening under Joseph's gaze. "I'm happy I didn't approach you so abruptly as he did. Then you ran off and didn't take the time to clean anything up. So, I took the liberty of doing it for you. I also learned of the recordings that weekend. I was a little bitter about my murder being published. Fisher remained this incredible member of the community. I wanted to tarnish that, so I did. Sergio was an opportunity to obtain solid dirt on you, my own recording to have. Just in case . . ."

"In case what?" Joseph asked. His hand stopped massaging Noah's shoulder now.

"We've both murdered people, Mr. Bailey."

Joseph took a sip and dropped his gaze. "Yes, and we've helped each other out, too. Where is Sergio's body, by the way? Did you even clean Stuart's car?"

"Of course, I did. They won't find anything in that car. I took Sergio's body deep into the woods. I'm sure nobody will find him for years to come. I parked his car outside of The Whiskey Bar before coming to the book reading tonight. His parents already died in the massacre. I'm sure they'll be quick to chalk it up as a suicide."

"What happened to his face?"

"Hot stainless-steel pan. Nothing like what you did to Detective Kline's face." Noah laughed.

Joseph did, too. "The adrenaline I felt when I killed Kline, the rush…"

They let out a sigh, the type that happens after the brain has been laser-focused for too long. The silence that grew felt comfortable until it didn't. Noah noticed a light down the hall, in the distance. He could also hear someone sniffling. Noah realized they weren't alone. At the end of the hall, near the foyer, a glow from a cellphone. Noah dropped the whiskey glass. It bounced alongside the couch until it shattered on the floor. Joseph leapt up, surprised. Noah pointed down the hallway with tight lips and a death-like stare.

"Someone's been listening to us."

"Goldstein, Noah is at Joseph Bailey's house," Arturo spoke as clearly as he could before hanging up. Tears fell from his eyes. His body was having a visceral reaction to what'd he'd heard. Yet he couldn't partake in that level of emotion—he was too on edge from how they laughed so casually about murdering people.

Footsteps thundered down the hallway toward the office. Arturo quickly deleted the call from his history and swiped to find the audio recording app that came preinstalled on his phone. He figured this could be his only hope to reveal the truth if he didn't survive. Arturo knew his fate if Goldstein didn't reach him in time; he'd heard way, way too much. Before he could find the app, a man appeared in the doorway, and Arturo recognized the figure as the one in Sergio's apartment that night. It was Noah. He'd put that together already after hearing their conversation, but seeing him in the flesh, again, was terrifying.

He charged straight for Arturo, who stumbled, backing away.

Noah tackled him against the wall before Arturo could defend himself, and then Noah slammed him again. Arturo's hearing snapped to a muffled but deafening high-pitch ringing. The back of his head was throbbing. Arturo's legs buckled under the shock, his head fuzzy like a television knocked to a channel filled only with white noise. Noah grabbed him from behind and wrapped his arms around his neck. Arturo attempted to kick back, but it was useless; Noah was dragging him backward, and the grip around his neck was tight. The thin little boy he'd known so many years ago was no longer that by any means.

Arturo struggled for air while his black eye sizzled. He wasn't thinking, merely thrashing instinctually, trying to fight for his life. He slapped at the forearm around his neck and punched back at Noah's head, then kicked the ground with hopes that they'd lose balance and Noah's grip would break. Out in the living room, Arturo saw Joseph just standing there. Then Arturo's frame of vision cast up to the ceiling, and he was slammed down on the ground. He closed his eyes. The pain in the back of his head was so immense, he curled into the fetal position. He was terrified, and that amount of pain left him defenseless. He expected to be getting kicked or punched, but instead, his body was being tapped. Searched. Then his hand was grabbed. Arturo hadn't even realized he'd been clutching his phone the whole time.

He opened his good eye as best he could, his other one completely shut. The pain in the back of his head was blinding. He could see Noah tapping away at the screen, growing more frustrated.

"What's the passcode?"

Arturo sat up, slithering back from the two men standing above him. Joseph stared down with the same dark, angry expression. Arturo hardly even recognized him with that blank, emotionless expression on his face. Where was the man who'd cried to Arturo about his past and who couldn't even get through the night without having some horrific nightmare? Arturo couldn't imagine that other version of Joseph had ever existed. Noah approached and faced the phone toward Arturo. Arturo looked up without understanding that his face, too, was a passcode. He tried to turn away, but Noah grabbed his head, allowing the phone to catch Arturo's better side. Noah let go, throwing Arturo back to the ground before focusing on the phone again, swiping through. The phone now unlocked.

"He hasn't made any phone calls," Noah said, looking to Joseph, who nodded.

"I still heard plenty." Arturo spat out blood and felt a gash in his cheek from his teeth. He licked it and spat again. The smell of blood was intense, but Arturo wasn't afraid of it this time—it only fueled his anger, his desperation to survive.

"Why didn't you ever tell me about my mother?" Arturo asked. Time was ticking, and if things were going south, Arturo was going to be heard. He had questions of his own.

"That aunt of yours took you away," Noah said, shrugging. He chucked Arturo's phone across the room, and it fell face-down, shattering and leaving a trail of diamond dust in its wake.

"No, not immediately. We saw each other a few times after my mother's death," Arturo corrected him. His anger only intensified. "I mean my *mother's murder*. Even the following day, you could've told me."

"I didn't tell you, but I did tell the people in charge, and look how that ended up," Noah said flatly. "You should be thankful I murdered Fisher. He was a horrible man who did horrible things. He deserved what was coming for him."

"What about Kline? Or Sergio?" Arturo asked, looking between both of them.

"Arturo, I—" Joseph tried to speak, but Arturo cut him off.

"Murdered two people." He shook his head and hawked a loogie filled with blood and phlegm that splattered a few feet from him. He never would've imagined spitting in Joseph's pristine house. His nose sizzled with pain that made his eyes continue to tear up.

"You don't understand," Joseph pleaded. But Arturo shook his head with a resounding *no*.

"You murdered two people," Arturo spoke. "And Noah, you murdered Fisher. Fisher murdered my mother. Fisher was the reason behind the massacre. When does the cycle end? What is wrong with you both? There is no justice in this, only more selfish murdering."

"I didn't enjoy killing Sergio," Joseph confessed. "But I had to—he knew too much. I do feel terrible about that."

"You feel terrible? I would, too. Suffocating someone takes too long," Noah interjected, scoffing. His eyes flashed a sense of joy that Arturo noticed. Noah enjoyed every moment of this, relishing the fact that all the secrets were coming out. Arturo could never see Joseph as he once had. He felt violated in every sense, but instead of cowering away, he felt his spine grow tall, and he clenched his fist—he was ready for a fight.

"He only put Sergio here to blackmail you, Joseph," Arturo barked, beginning to feel the adrenaline pumping through his veins, his vision now clear. The pain in the back of his head was there, yes—but the adrenaline overpowered it.

"Mr. Bailey, you understand, though," Noah began, putting his arm on Joseph's shoulder. He looked down at Arturo and spoke in a slow voice. "We need to take care of each other. It's Artie I'm worried about. Honestly, there's nothing wrong with us. Think of this—Artie could go down for murdering Fisher. He has the motive, and he has a life established here. One that he didn't want to give up when Kline came around asking questions." Noah tapped away on Arturo's cracked phone and then turned the screen. Arturo couldn't make it out from where he sat, but he understood the colors on the screen—a message sent through social media. "Now it looks like Arturo sent Rafael the recording of his son being molested. It'll all line right up. Maybe he also hoped that Rafael would murder the chief, so Arturo didn't have to. When the police find his body, we can put Benjamin Fisher's folder with him. I'm telling you, he's deranged, Joseph."

Arturo felt as if he'd been slapped across the face. His cheeks grew hot hearing Noah talk.

"What about Sergio then?" Arturo asked bluntly.

Noah chuckled to himself. Joseph's lips were pursed, as if he was honestly considering what Noah was saying. Arturo felt like he'd been stabbed in the back the moment he was brought out here, but each glance toward Joseph felt like that knife pressed deeper into his skin.

"Chopped up to a missing person case. Even if they find the body, they'll assume suicide. I mean, they did for your mom," he said, glancing at Arturo.

"Sure, my mom—but what about the police coming to find you two right now. They know the day you got out of prison was the day Fisher was murdered. They're piecing it all together. They already know it was you from the start."

Noah scoffed and walked up to Arturo. He kicked Arturo in the face before he could even register that Noah had lifted his foot. Arturo's jaw reeled in a sharp pain. Blood spewed from his lips, and his head rang once more.

"You're bluffing," Noah said, an irreverent tone in his voice that disgusted Arturo. Noah was enjoying every second of this, the power. "Let's get this over with and take care of his body already. We can do it together, Joseph."

"You arrogant fuck," Arturo scolded Noah. He could feel his teeth slick with the taste of his blood.

"What if he's telling the truth?" Joseph asked, his voice small.

"I am." Arturo laughed now, blood dripping down his chin. "You checked the call log, but I deleted it before you got ahold of my phone. I'm not bluffing; I've been buying myself time." Arturo laughed again, and he braced himself now as Noah kicked his stomach.

Arturo grabbed his foot and watched as Noah lost his balance and fell to the ground. Noah locked eyes with Arturo, and with his free leg, began kicking with explosive rage. Arturo's face took blow after blow, but he didn't let go of Noah's foot. Arturo could only handle so much. He'd kept his eyes shut the whole time but now realized that he couldn't open them from the blunt force he was repeatedly taking. His grip loosened despite every effort, and Noah slipped from his grip.

Arturo lifted his eyelids as best he could, and only a slit of vision came through but enough to see Noah standing up, reaching for something in his waist. He pointed a shiny black handgun down at Arturo. He could only lie there, defenseless and wheezing through a nose that must've broken several times over during the kicks. The pain was immense, and for a moment, Arturo wanted it all to just end. The fear, the anger, were too much, his mind froze into nothing but the here and now. Then, he heard a car speeding up the driveway.

The pebbles ricocheted off the metal frame, and headlights shot up over the hill, piercing through the glass. Arturo could barely keep his eyes open, so instead he spread his lips. A wide smile filled with the taste of iron from all the blood in his mouth. From the opposite end of the barrel, Noah snarled like a rabid dog.

"You motherfucker." Noah cocked the gun and flicked off the safety.

He charged toward Arturo, who slunk away from Noah as best he could. Arturo could feel the cold glass from the windows that overlooked the forest behind the house creep up along his neck. He was sweating and hadn't even realized it. All he could see was the ferocious gaze in Noah as he took aim. Arturo winced, trying to raise a hand to defend himself.

Joseph stepped forward and shouted, "No!" as he slapped Noah's arm away. The gun fired, missing Arturo but striking the window, which cracked and shattered into a million pieces into the forest below. Arturo slunk back, the support of the window now gone, and felt his body slip out of the now-empty window frame when he heard more gunfire go off. A bullet hit him square in the shoulder, knocking him back as if he'd just been tackled by a quarterback. In an instant, he vanished over the edge into the darkness below.

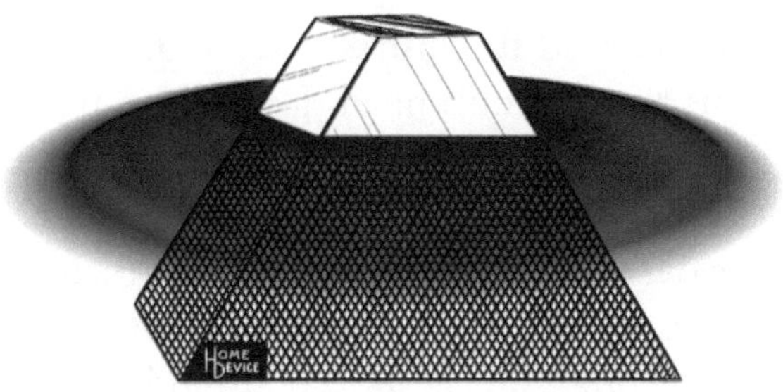

"Stick to the plan now, Mr. Bailey," Noah said, shoving the gun into Joseph's hands. The barrel was hot and stung his fingers, but Joseph was so dazed he hardly noticed. It was all happening so quickly. Noah held an aggressive stare.

"What plan? They already—" Joseph tried to speak, but Noah clapped a hand over his mouth.

"Arturo sent the message to Rafael. That's all we need to cast enough doubt," Noah said. He could hear people shouting outside, and he gave Joseph one final hard look before he turned around and grabbed a thick faux fur blanket off the couch. He tossed it on the smooth floors and slid off the edge, past the glass and into the darkness, where Arturo had just disappeared.

Joseph turned the gun over in his hand. It was heavier than he'd imagined. He looked at the window. A glass shard fell from the left corner and shattered. He scurried away from the glass as he heard voices down the hallway. He stood there, the gun dangling in his hand now, and saw two men—the officer who saw Joseph leave with Noah beside him in the car and Detective Vaughn. Joseph felt stunned—everything was happening so fast with everything on the line.

"Drop the weapon, Joseph," Vaughn commanded him with his own gun drawn, and Joseph followed his order.

He then followed the instructions to get on the ground and place his hands on his head. Joseph was trying to wrap his head around the plan that Noah had instructed him to follow. He let out a deep breath while his hands were brought to his lower back and handcuffed. Vaughn turned him over and lifted him, so he was sitting up. Their guns were still drawn, and the other officer looked around the room.

"Where is Noah—Noah Crane?" Vaughn asked.

"Who?" Joseph's mouth became dry. His arms and wrists ached already from the pressure of the handcuffs. He looked up to see both officers staring down at him.

"Noah Crane," the officer repeated.

"No," Joseph said, his head wobbling. "I don't know who that is. It was all Arturo. He sent the message to—"

"I saw you two leave the event together. Where's Noah?" the officer barked, now stepping forward to hover over Joseph. It felt stupid, but Joseph stuck to the plan. He'd already tried to stop Arturo from being shot out of sheer desperation—and look where that had gotten him. It seemed Joseph was no longer in control of things. Noah was. Joseph felt as if a long con had been played on him.

"I don't know what you're talking about."

"Let's get him inside the cruiser," Vaughn said. The men pulled Joseph up to his feet. They skidded him along the floor to the driveway, past the lavender. Officer Goldstein opened the door of the cruiser, and they tossed him inside and shut the door. The window wasn't fully up; there was a two-inch gap, which was enough for Joseph to hear them speak.

"What are the next steps, Goldstein?" Vaughn asked him.

"Call for backup, possibly emergency services. Sweep the area and begin setting up the perimeter," Goldstein replied without missing a beat.

"Okay. I'll call for backup, then you take the inside. I'll take outside," Vaughn said, already turning and grabbing his cell phone from his pocket; the screen was bright, and soon he pressed it against his ear. Both men had their guns still drawn, headed in opposite directions.

"Wait," Joseph shouted from inside the car.

Both men turned and glared at him.

"Shut it. You had your chance. Now stay put," Vaughn shouted.

Joseph watched them disappear under the silvery glow of moonlight that hung in the sky. Then there was nothing around him. Even the bugs and the forest creatures had grown quiet. The silence was unsettling, and all Joseph could think about was how Arturo disappeared through that window. Joseph hadn't been the one to pull the trigger, but he'd been the one to put Arturo in the situation.

The handcuffs sliced into his wrists painfully. He adjusted his position in the back against the hard plastic seats, but the pain was still sharp. Joseph's mind clogged with thoughts of his reputation going down the drain. Social media would tear him apart. Joseph shuddered. He wasn't meant for prison—he could change his story and start to work with the police if he could get a plea deal, maybe. Or maybe he'd seen too much crime television. He'd never even been inside a police car until this very moment. Let alone an interrogation room. Joseph let his head fall against the side of the window, and he looked at the house under the moonlight with the silent forest around.

It looked like something out of a magazine, how perfect his life had been on the surface.

Noah dragged Arturo's body away the moment he heard the police lead Joseph outside. By the sounds of it, Joseph was sticking to the plan but that didn't matter. The police were already looking for Noah, and it'd only be a matter of time until they dragged him back to that tiny prison cell. All because of Joseph.

Noah looked back at Arturo now, his head slumping from side to side along the uneven ground. Years of leaves falling and collecting, now dead and damp in the night air, rustled underneath them, creating a path in their wake. The night wouldn't get any brighter than this, but in the daytime, someone would see the trail, Noah realized.

Noah felt a tug against his pull and looked back to see that Arturo had turned slightly and grabbed an exposed root in the ground. His strength wasn't much because he couldn't hold on for more than a second. Noah continued to drag him, using both hands around the ankle. The more time that passed, the longer Arturo would have to wake up and possibly regain his strength. Noah moved faster; time was of the essence.

When the forest grew thick enough, he pulled Arturo behind a tree and paused, listening to the silent cold air around them. Resting with his hands on his knees, he looked around the area: broken tree branches, piles of dead flakey leaves, and a large rock. All outlined in the silvery glow from the moonlight above. Noah grabbed for the rock and lifted it over his head. Before he could turn around, though, he felt a kick against his leg that sent him staggering forward with a yelp. Noah dropped the rock, it cracked in two, and he screamed with rage.

He grabbed for the split rock, which now had a fresh jagged edge. Arturo stared up at him with puffy, terrified eyes. Noah dropped down on his frame as Arturo tried to turn and crawl away. With his knees tightly pressing into Arturo's side, he raised the rock, inhaling a deep breath that shot mucus to the back of his mouth. Saliva strands billowed out from his mouth as he screamed through gritted teeth, preparing to bring the rock down.

A gunshot went off, and the rock exploded in Noah's hands. A flashlight trained on both of them, and Noah rolled off Arturo as a second gunshot went off, missing him narrowly.

"Hands up where I can see them!" Detective Vaughn's voice boomed from behind the blinding flashlight. Noah laid there, still trying to think. "I said hands up."

Noah winced. He put his hands up and followed instructions to get on his knees. Vaughn hustled forward, commanding him to lie on the ground. When he walked close enough, Noah threw a handful of dirt and leaves into Vaughn's face, then punched him in the groin when he was blinded by the debris. Vaughn gagged, falling forward, and catching some of the forest bed in his mouth. Noah reacted quickly, bucking the gun from Vaughn's grip.

While Vaughn tried to recover as quickly as he could, Noah gripped the handle and aimed. He fired the gun multiple times. Noah couldn't count how many bullets went off, but each shot hit, producing a mist of Vaughn's blood that dispersed in the air, washing over them. Soon the detective was no better off than his last partner, Detective Kline. Noah scrambled to his feet and walked over. He tapped along the frame and felt the keys to the cruiser. The one Joseph was inside right now, last he'd heard. Noah stood tall, no longer making a noise with the keys in his pocket. Noah looked back to Arturo, who was no longer lying on the ground.

Noah wanted to scream. Somehow, Arturo had regained his strength and took off running. Noah listened and could hear a flurry of leaves in the distance, growing fainter. He thought of the hikers that Fisher had saved. Who would save Arturo now?

"Vaughn!" a voice called not too far from Noah.

He slunk behind a tree, its thick base enough to hide his frame from the flashlight now peeking through the trees. The light grew brighter, and the footsteps close enough that Noah held his breath.

"Fuck! What the fuck happened?" Goldstein shouted, and Noah slowly peeked out. The officer stood over Vaughn's mangled remains with a hand over his mouth. He looked like he was going to be sick, but he swallowed that down. He reached for his shoulder mic and spoke clearly, "Officer down, I repeat, officer down. Requesting back-up and immediate medical services. Situation is urgent, suspect on the loose and armed. Please respond to…" He spoke the address, and dispatch replied, saying that everyone was on their way, but due to the location, it'd take some time.

Goldstein shined the flashlight around the area, and Noah slunk back behind the tree, fearful that Goldstein would come around at any second.

In the distance, a scream erupted that sent chills down Noah's spine. It came from Arturo, as if he'd been attacked by a bear or some other vicious animal. Noah watched as Goldstein took off running toward the scream.

With Goldstein gone, Noah slipped to another tree and then another, moving back toward the house. He prayed that Goldstein would shoot Arturo out of fear after seeing Vaughn.

Arturo felt woozy. The faster he ran, the colder his arm felt as his blood rushed down his skin. He felt sick from the smell of blood, both his own and Vaughn's. He'd watched, terrified, each gunshot an opportunity to move no matter how much noise it made. He'd gotten to his feet and ran, stumbling at first but then finding his footing. Until he'd tripped and slammed into a tree, when he'd screamed so loudly, he could feel his throat begin to splinter from inside out. He could no longer keep his eyes open, and soon the darkness swallowed him.

"*Mi hijo,*" a voice called to him in the darkness.

Arturo could open his eyes, but he couldn't feel the pain anymore. He looked up, seeing the edges of his mother's face in the soft glow of the moonlight. She frowned and pressed down on his shoulder where the gunshot wound was.

"*Stay awake, Mi hijo,*" his mother said, lifting his chin with her index finger. Arturo's head sagged to the side. He felt as if he'd used all his energy to try to escape, only to fail, lost in a treacherous forest that swallowed him whole. His mother wrapped her arms around him, her skin warm and her breath light against him. Arturo stared into her eyes, a magnificent hue of honey-amber. She stared down at him, radiating that love his *tía* had talked about in the photo earlier.

There was so much he wished to tell her, so much he wanted to apologize for. Instead of being able to find the words, all he could do was stare at her. Tears welled with everything he wished to say, and he wept.

"It's all going to be okay, Mi hijo. Stay awake," her voice sang. She faded into the darkness.

Arturo's eyes fluttered. He was trying his best to keep them open but that debilitating pain was returning. As the trees cleared, Arturo saw that it wasn't his mother rocking him from side to side; instead, it was Goldstein. He was trudging through the forest, his breathing heavy as he carried Arturo toward the whirling red-and-blue emergency service lights.

"Where is Vaughn's cruiser?" Goldstein demanded as he set Arturo on a gurney near an ambulance.

Noah floored the cruiser as fast as it could go down the narrow, winding roads of Baxtor Springs. He gripped the wheel tightly whenever he made a turn, bracing himself for it. Joseph flung from side to side helplessly. His initial screams dulled into grunts. A streetlight came into view, the green light clicked yellow and then red. Noah slammed on the brakes, the screeching tires howling in the quiet night, and Joseph's body slammed forward against the black metal grate of the cruiser. Noah saw a zig-zag design indented on the right side of Joseph's face. He plopped back in the backseat, breathing hard.

Noah was breathing hard, too.

He didn't have a plan for what he was going to do, but he refused to return to prison. Timothy, his old cellmate, would probably laugh at him, telling him, *I told you so*. Noah shook his head back and forth, *no, no, no*.

"Victim number one has just left for the hospital. Condition is critical. Victim two, Detective Vaughn, has been pronounced dead at the scene, coroner is five minutes out. Also will be requesting detective assistance from a neighboring county." The dispatcher's voice came through the cruiser's radio. To the side of it was a cell phone. Noah grabbed it and tossed it out the window.

"Another victim added to the list," Joseph said, hunched over and shaking his head.

The light turned green, and Noah sped, taking a hard left turn. The keys in the ignition jingled. Joseph disappeared to one side and then sat up as best he could. Noah watched in the rearview mirror, gripping the wheel tight, enraged.

"If you hadn't lunged at me, Arturo would be dead; you would've just been answering some questions about how he'd done all of this," Noah growled through gritted teeth.

"He's alive?"

"He's the one in critical condition," Noah spat through clenched teeth.

"Is your last name Crane?" Joseph asked.

"Yes, how did you—" Noah stared at Joseph through the rearview mirror.

"They already know your name. You were the first thing the officers asked me about when I surrendered. Arturo wasn't lying about that phone call."

Noah didn't respond.

"You're arrogant," Joseph quoted Fisher. "I guess I am, too." Joseph sniffled, his nose wrinkling. "Arturo was right. How many more need to die so that I can have a pretty house and picture-perfect life? Arturo had a point. It's time. I can't run from what I've done—I'm going to be convicted."

"No—I'm not going back because of you." Noah slammed on the brakes again, so hard that the tires skidded, and the smell of burnt rubber bled through the cracked windows. "I will not be going back to that cell. I don't want to." He then floored it again, tires burning even more rubber, and smoke slipped into the car. Joseph coughed in the back-seat from the fumes.

Noah saw the streetlamps from Main Street come into view. One light was blinding him from the side. He looked out at the driver's side mirror and saw headlights coming up fast. The headlights were flashing.

Noah recognized Joseph's Porsche.

Noah floored the gas, and the cruiser's engine roared forward like a large boat on a lake. It wasn't quick enough. The Porsche came up beside the tail end of the cruiser and slammed into them. The cruiser lost control and skidded to the left. Noah stared out the window into Goldstein's eyes. Neither of them looked away, even as the cruiser spun to the other side of the Porsche, taking a mirror with it.

The cruiser continued to spin, blending everything along Main Street and the park square into one giant blur. The tires screeched, and smoke billowed as the cruiser hit a curb and launched into the air. The cruiser rolled over and over, glass exploding and shattering, and Noah shrieked as the air-bag deployed. He felt as if he'd run directly into a wall, his nose splintered, and he could see it splatter with the pressure from the airbag. He had no control, his limbs flying which-ever way inertia pulled.

The cruiser landed on its roof, skidding and demolish-ing the grass in the public park. It collided with the gazebo, which toppled over without much resistance. Noah heard wood splintering and snapping, combined with people rush-ing from buildings to see what the commotion was. He hung upside down with his seatbelt still intact, a stinging pain com-ing from his nose.

Noah looked over to the passenger side. On the badly dented roof of the car lay Detective Vaughn's gun. He reached for it but couldn't grab it. He unbuckled his seatbelt and collided with the ground hard. He squirmed until he was upright again, fishing for the gun and backing out of the broken window. He looked over to Joseph, who wasn't moving. Blood was running down the side of his face, which looked severely damaged.

Noah panted as he heard footsteps approaching through the grass behind him.

"You okay? You okay?" an elderly voice said.

Noah stood and turned to see Chief Edmonds approaching with a slight sway in his walk, intoxicated. Noah sneered at him. It must've taken the chief a few seconds to recognize Noah standing there, but once he did, he froze dead in his tracks. Noah's arm dangled behind him, the gun out of the chief's vision.

"Noah?" the chief said, his face growing pale.

"Still think I was lying back then, Chief?" Noah asked as he raised the gun. He fired a single shot, hitting the chief directly in the throat. He pawed at the wound, gasping for air, crumbling to his knees. The chief's eyes bulged up at Noah with great shock, as he fell back against the grass and deep gashes that slashed through the park.

Mass hysteria broke out from the people who'd been standing along the sidewalks watching. They ran in every direction, away from where the chief's body lay. Noah watched them all, standing there, trying to catch his breath. Pain from the car accident seeped into his lower back and neck. He wanted to crumble to the floor himself but knew there was still work to be done. All the while, Joseph's argument lingered in Noah's mind. *How many people need to die?* he'd said. Noah snickered, wiping his face.

The responsible ones. And Noah would be both judge and fucking jury.

He whipped around to the sounds of clinking glass and saw Joseph squirming like a snail without a shell on. Noah reached down and grabbed his foot. With all the strength he could muster, he yanked Joseph out of the car. He squealed like an animal at the slaughterhouse, much like Stuart Kline had just a few nights ago. Noah heaved, still clutching the gun. He looked down at Joseph, raising his forearm to wipe his mouth and noticed his rabbit tattoo was covered in his own blood. He locked eyes with Joseph.

He lay there helplessly, staring up at Noah with a trembling lip.

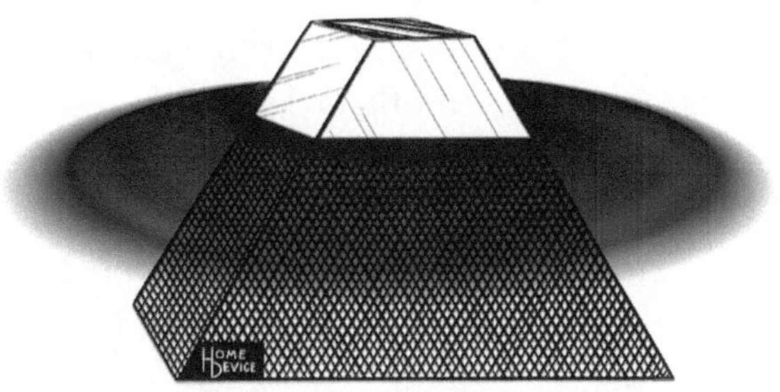

Joseph felt the cold, wet grass against his warm frame. When he spit the blood from his mouth, a few of his teeth went along with it. His mouth seared in unbearable pain. His vision was still blurry, and all he could think about was whether he'd gotten a concussion in the accident. He locked eyes with Noah, who stood over him, heaving like a mad man. Joseph wondered if this was what he'd looked like right before he'd snapped, killing Detective Stuart Kline.

Behind Noah, Joseph could see the lumped remains of whoever had been shot. The crowd behind was scattered for the most part, minus two older women. One of whom had collapsed to the ground, sobbing hysterically while the other tried to get her to move away like everyone else.

Noah reached down and grabbed Joseph by his shirt, pulling him up until he was on his knees. Joseph tilted over, and Noah used the barrel of the gun to lift his chin. He used his other hand to grab Joseph's shirt, keeping him upright.

Joseph looked up, his mouth slightly ajar, the hot barrel of the gun sizzling against his neck.

"Do it then. We both know where we are going to end up," Joseph muttered, watching Noah as he looked away at Main Street. His eyes darted like a feral animal already caught. Noah dropped his grip from Joseph's shirt and stepped back, revealing an officer approaching with his gun aimed. The Porsche behind him hung outside of a building that it'd crashed into. Joseph felt the barrel of the gun stab deeper between the tender muscles in his neck. Noah was standing behind him, Joseph realized, using him as a shield.

"Drop the weapon, Noah," the officer said, widening his stance, gun gripped with both hands.

"Fuck you, Goldstein," Noah spat.

He looked ready to fire. "I said drop it, Noah. You've already given me enough reason to disarm you. If you don't—"

The gun barrel sliced against Joseph's throat as Noah twisted his wrist and fired off two shots. Goldstein fell back. Both shots had hit him square in the chest. The gun powder from the gun brushed against Joseph's face, burning his eyes while the gunshots themselves left him with a deafening ring in his ears. He tried to cover them, but it was too late; his entire body was wincing in pain. He tried to wipe his eyes, too, but all his efforts failed. The handcuffs were still on. Each attempt—every move was another sharp pain in his wrists. The cuffs seemed wet, and Joseph didn't know if it was from the damp grass or if he was bleeding. He felt dizzy.

"I didn't write the novel, okay? I used the ghostwriters. Is that what you wanna know?" Joseph confessed, watching Noah stomp back, towering over him again.

"I read the emails, they never—"

"I deleted my responding emails, I only kept what was pertinent, really,' Joseph swallowed a mix of blood and saliva. He could see that Noah was going to snap at any moment—and he did. All Joseph could do was try to flail his body away, missing another gunshot that grazed his neck. He screamed out as gunfire left a sharp ring in his ears.

Joseph's shoulder screamed out in pain, and he felt Noah's hands dig into it. His fingernails scratched deep as he turned Joseph to face him. Noah pulled so hard that Joseph's torso lifted off the ground. He dangled there help-lessly, watching as Noah raised the gun and jabbed it inside Joseph's mouth. The burning metal barrel of the firearm wiggled past Joseph's lips and bumped painfully against his teeth. Soon the barrel was touching the back of his throat.

"You are no better than that fucking child molester, Joseph. All you do—and have ever done—is take, and take, and take, and ta—"

A gunshot erupted from behind Noah, interrupting his rage-filled rant. Joseph couldn't see where it came from, but he knew Noah had been shot. A puff of misty warm blood washed over Joseph's face; it seeped into his mouth leaving the taste of iron on his tongue.

Noah staggered back, turning to see Officer Goldstein, who had been lying down, clutching at his bullet-proof vest. Noah threw his shoulder, and the gun pointed to Goldstein.

Pop.

One moment, Noah's head was there. The next, it had exploded and rained down on Joseph. The smell and taste of Noah's bits and pieces made Joseph vomit everything he had in his stomach. Noah stayed up for a mere second before falling over Joseph. The gun in Noah's hand fired under his weight as he toppled over Joseph. The pain was growing immense. Joseph stared up at the sky, feeling caught between two worlds. The wet grass and warm sensation filling his chest were physical, but above him, he could see a great many stars. It was a beautiful sight, and soon everything faded to black. In this darkness, there was a peace that Joseph had never felt before. He didn't have to be anyone or worry about his reputation. He didn't even have to try. All he had to do was let go. Which he thought was much easier than the alternative, which would include trials and jails—nothing he ever imagined himself enduring.

He let go all at once, thinking he'd stay in this dark place for eternity.

EPILOGUE

The parking lot for the church, the one across the street, had been completed for some time now. Cars glinted under the cold winter sun, emanating high from a cloudless sky. He spotted a car pulling out up ahead and waited before taking the spot himself. He pulled in slowly, still getting accustomed to the rear wheel electric car he recently purchased. In the passenger seat, two coffees sat, steam rising. Between the cups were two bagged *conchas* he picked up from Mimi this morning.

He parked the car and collected himself. In the rearview mirror, he saw his face still slightly bruised from that night. He sniffled, turning away, and reached for his arm sling. The bullet wound on his shoulder hadn't healed yet, but he could manage driving. Lately, it was the only thing that kept him sane. Long drives and music, with open roads and the cold air against his face reminding him that he was alive—why, he didn't know. But then again, Arturo's therapist was quick to remind him that nobody knows.

With his arm slipped inside the sling, he opened the car door and grabbed for the coffees with his good hand. He stepped out and kicked the door shut. The warm sun dulled the sharp chill in the air. The day was bearable, and snow wasn't in the forecast for another week.

His trunk was packed with two chairs and a large tote filled with blankets and some flowers. When he invited his *tía* here today, she'd enthusiastically said yes. He knew that she would be fifteen minutes early, so Arturo was twenty. He'd also prepared himself knowing his *tía* would chat a lot today, so he'd might as well be comfy during it.

"Arturo?" a familiar voice said behind him.

Arturo turned to see Goldstein standing there. He was wearing a checkered button-up with a matte black coat folded over his arms. On his hip, a detective badge rested beside his holstered gun. He even wore dress shoes. Arturo looked back up, his eyes trailing along his body and then to his half-smile and shy-looking eyes. For the first time ever, Arturo thought Goldstein looked attractive.

"Hey, Goldstein," Arturo said. A peaceful energy between them, and Arturo felt a flutter in his stomach. "What are you doing here?"

"Thought I would pay respects to Detective Vaughn and Kline. Their families are both here today, so I thought it'd be nice to . . ." Goldstein's voice trailed off.

"That's nice of you," Arturo said.

"You?"

"I'm meeting up with my *tía*." Arturo looked to his trunk and then back at Goldstein, realizing he couldn't carry everything himself. "Mind lending a hand?"

Goldstein perked up. "Not at all; happy to help."

Goldstein picked up the chairs and tote bag while Arturo continued to balance the coffees and *conchas*. The day was beautiful, the cemetery full of families gathering to visit loved zones, some drinking out of red solo cups, toasting the departed. Others visiting alone had posted up with books or headphones. People mourned here openly, which still felt strange to Arturo, who'd always kept everything inside.

The street now had painted lines for a crosswalk with a sign reminding people that pedestrians have the right of way and to DRIVE SLOW. Arturo crossed the street with Goldstein next to him. The silence between them felt delicate, and Arturo was reminded of Joseph. He let these thoughts pass without judgement.

In the far back, Arturo saw Sara Edmonds reading a book underneath several blankets and an oversized puffy coat. She reached for a thermos canister at her feet. She looked up, perhaps feeling Arturo's gaze on her. They politely waved to each other, Arturo at a loss for words on what to even tell her. She was the town's newest Rafael, and it was a sad sight. Even after his death, her sunny days were still controlled by her lousy dead husband.

To Arturo's left, a few tables had been set out, and he glanced at a single-window hut on the opposite side. The sign, hand-painted, read, "Dana's Sandwiches," and a sign below read, "always donating 25% to help maintain the land of our loved ones." A few people were sitting, eating their sandwiches with older relatives.

"I haven't seen you since—well, since that night. Did you change your number?" Goldstein spoke up.

"I did, yes," Arturo licked his lips. "Sorry."

"Is it because of Joseph?" Goldstein looked at Arturo with that same look of pity most gave whenever they discussed his mother's suicide—er, homicide.

Arturo cleared his throat. "Yeah, it is. Now he writes me at the bar asking to help him publish his first nonfiction book about the massacre and the man behind it all. I refuse, and he says how it's *our responsibility* to share our side of the story. It's repulsive."

"But you're going to . . ." Goldstein's voice faded, a blank expression on his face.

"Testify? Yes, I will. People can learn of the story in the public transcript for free. I'm not trying to help a murderer make a profit. My therapist has been helping prepare me for the trial, helping me with the anxiety of seeing Joseph again.

They keep telling me I need to talk about what happened. It's just . . . difficult." Arturo blinked.

"I'll be testifying, too. We probably have different dates, but I'm excited to tell them how I used Vaughn's phone to track Noah and Joseph that night in the car. That's how I found them, you know." Goldstein nodded.

"Smart, that would explain the detective badge." Arturo pointed to Goldstein's hip, his holstered gun right beside it.

"Wanna get coffee sometime? Talk about that night?"

"Yes, we can grab coffee sometime. My therapist also reminds me that being social is healthy, too." He cracked a soft smile.

"I haven't even seen you at the bar. Do you still own it?"

"Yes, but I made Violet a partner in the business. I just . . . need more time, and she's great at running the place already," Arturo admitted, feeling both okay and not okay with what he was saying. He used to run the bar with Violet, he used to chat with the chief down at the end, and he used to enjoy being around people. Everything had become so tainted after that night. Now Violet staffed the bar, which was doing well enough, even after the shooting incident at the park square. A few businesses had moved out while others put up signs banning weapons in public spaces.

"Take all the time you need. I'm here for you. I hope you know that," Goldstein said, dropping his gaze to catch Arturo's. He locked eyes and offered a slight smile again. Goldstein's curly brown hair glistened in the sunlight, making him look like a model out of a magazine. Like Joseph. Arturo blinked hard, pushing this thought away.

"You're gonna be okay," Goldstein said, putting his hand on Arturo's undamaged shoulder. His warm grip was soothing. Arturo gave a wry smile, as if he didn't believe him. Although everyone kept telling him this. Somehow, Goldstein's words came off honest enough.

"Arturo, you're here early." His *tía* came up from behind wearing an all-black ensemble. She looked magnificent and the gold necklace around her neck no longer made Arturo recoil.

"Hey there, Maria," Goldstein said, politely waving with the chairs and blankets in his hands.

"*Hola*, Goldstein," she said with a graceful smile. "Are you joining us?"

Arturo stepped forward. He could see a slight sadness in his *tía*'s eyes wash away as he replied. "No, *tía*, he's just helping with the chairs and tote bag."

Goldstein handed them off to her, and Arturo recited his new phone number for the new detective as he entered it into his phone.

"I'll give you a call." He smiled before departing with a slight head bow. Arturo stood there, watching Goldstein walk over to the fallen detectives' families. Maybe coffee with Goldstein would be good. Arturo had to let someone in eventually, didn't he? He looked back to his *tía*, who watched Goldstein, too.

"That's not your boyfriend, is it?"

Arturo turned his neck too fast, a nerve pinching, a remnant of Noah's violence from that night.

"*Tía*, I'm not dating every guy you see me with."

"You both are gay. It's not out of the question."

Arturo looked at his *tía* and then slowly back to Goldstein, who was still walking alone through the crowds.

"Did you just get here?" she asked him, walking forward herself now, too.

"Yes, and let me guess, you got here before I did?"

"Well, I wanted to clean off the hedge, put some fresh flowers. Are those for her?" she asked.

Arturo looked down at the flowers and nodded, a humble smile warming his chest.

"Yes, they are."

"Right here, right here." His *tía* pointed down toward a hedge stone that barely popped up. The stone plaque read Olivia de Leon. The years beneath revealed she only lived to be thirty-seven years old. Only a few years older than Arturo was now. *A Loving Mother* neatly carved below the years. Beside it, a small vase was built into the design, already filled with flowers. Arturo watched his *tía* set the flowers he'd brought on the opposite end, framing his mother's name. They set the blanket out and the chairs, then he handed her the coffee and let her choose between the pink or yellow *concha*. She chose the yellow one, and Arturo set the pink one in his lap.

"Wait," she said, and then from her shirt pocket, she produced a well-rolled joint.

Arturo's eyes lit up, but he raised an eyebrow.

"Let bygones be bygones. I'm not here to be your mother. I never was. I'm your *tía*," she said. She passed him a small lighter and the joint, and he smiled.

Arturo put the filter to his lips and puffed before the other end ignited in bright orange. He took a few puffs and passed the joint to his *tía*. She paused, looking around. Nobody seemed to mind. Then she took a big whiff and blew out the smoke without any reaction. It was as if she'd taken a big shot of tequila without even wincing. That was just his *tía*.

"That is some good shit right there," she said, laughing.

Arturo chuckled, she passed it back, and he let the smoke trail between them, curling in the air like waves along the ocean.

"That night I was shot, I thought I saw her," Arturo shared. His *tía* looked over at him with an expression of compassion, no judgment. "She was telling me to hold on, kept calling me her son. I thought she was carrying me to the ambulance, but it was Goldstein." Arturo took a hit and extended his head back, slowly breathing the smoke out.

"Sounds like a near-death experience," his *tía* remarked. "Other people have reported them. Sometimes the dead come to guide us."

Arturo handed the joint back. His *tía* took another long, heavy drag and blew out.

"It felt so calming to be around her." Arturo took a deep breath and then admitted it aloud. "I'd like to hear about my mother. The one who loved me—the one I didn't get to know."

Tía smiled, handing the joint back to Arturo. She took a long sip from her coffee and a bite of her *concha*. She sat there in silence for a beat, and Arturo could tell she was thinking. A smile grew at the edges of her lips, and soon her dimples resembled Arturo's own. A de Leon family trait, no doubt.

"There is this one Sunday I had with your mother when we were still young. I'm not going to sugarcoat anything for you. She was a real person, after all. We did bad things sometimes—it was thrilling, especially with her by my side. Before she even had you." With the nearly finished joint, she gestured at the church that stood in the distance, the window now repaired with fresh stained glass and a new mural. "Oh boy, one time, we got so stoned right before church—mind you, that was a bigger deal back then—and we could hardly even . . ."

AUTHOR'S NOTE

I'm very thankful for Avalon whose expert eye, guidance, and assistance helped me bring this work to life. Your suggestions and direction were invaluable to the process. Thank you to Mary, Tim, Kevin, Pam, and Patrick for adding the final touches that brought the book to life.

I want to thank my husband, who provided me with emotional support throughout the entire journey. You tirelessly listened to me hash through story concepts, ideas, and made suggestions in conversation that I never knew would turn into some of the most honest reactions in the novel. I love you.

Incredibly thankful to my beta readers—Patrick, Austin, Matty, Sean, Anthony, Jarrett, Jill, Lawren—who gave me feedback on the first draft. You provided me with honest, positive, and encouraging words that really helped push me in the pursuit of making this book a reality.

Special shout out to Luke, who spent many hours during the pandemic listening to my wild thoughts. You are such an incredible person, what a lucky world we have with you in it.

Mom, I love you.

Above all, I want to thank you, the reader, for giving this book a chance. It is an honor and a pleasure to share my work with you.

ABOUT THE AUTHOR

Kyle Zona is a novelist from Los Angeles. He has always been passionate about writing and telling stories, which led him to self-publish his debut novel. Growing up, Kyle was a voracious reader and loved the freedom that the written word could bring. As a member of the LGBTQ+ community, he believes representation is essential.

www.ingramcontent.com/pod-product-compliance
Lightning Source LLC
Chambersburg PA
CBHW020339010826
48970CB00012B/1568